SELF-ESTEEM

SELF-ESTEEM

a novel

Preston David Bailey

Self-Esteem: A Novel

Copyright © 2012 by Preston David Bailey

Self-Esteem: A Novel / Preston David Bailey.

ISBN: 978-0-9859662-1-8

Published in the US by Preston David Bailey

www.self-series.com

info@self-series.com

1. Thriller—Fiction

2. Dark Comedy—Fiction

3. Social Satire—Fiction

4. Mystery—Fiction

5. Self-help—Fiction

for Bill Hicks

The knowledge of yourself will preserve you from vanity.
— Cervantes

Self-knowledge comes from knowing other men.
— Goethe

Here we go round the prickly pear
Prickly pear prickly
Here we go round the prickly pear
At five o'clock in the morning.
— T.S. Eliot

FIRST, AN EXCERPT FROM JAMES CRAWFORD'S UNFINISHED
NOVEL, "TALK IS CHEAPER THAN THE PLAGUE."

He was walking through the garden and it could
have been any garden, but it wasn't. It was a
garden like no other, like

PART I:
Those Who Criticize You

ONE

T HE INCIDENT AT MOTHER GOOSE was the first thing he could remember. That's what he told a crowd of people at a book signing, which is now considered the event that began his most serious descent into psychosis. Drunk on a flask of Scotch he had hidden in his suit jacket, he started by extending the wicked smile of a stand-up comedian about to tell his dirtiest joke, all just to sell *Self-Esteem*.

"Let me tell you about my first memory," he said. "It's my favorite story." It was neither his first memory nor his favorite story, but every time he told it, a new element emerged, a detail regarding how he acted or what he thought. No matter. He was an expert on human behavior — at least *officially* so — and he knew that it is perfectly natural to tell a story the way the story *itself* wants to be told, especially when you're messed up on liquor.

"Stories really have a remarkable authority all their own," he once wrote in *Self-Confidence*. "It's best just to let your stories go. Let them live the way they want to. It will help you live life the way you want to."

As he most often described it, Mother Goose Land was a nursery school on a lonesome two-lane highway north of the small Texas town where he grew up. It was an old wooden house, probably built in the thirties or forties, that otherwise might have been a friendly place if it weren't for that terrifying *Hansel and Gretel* story that his impetuous Uncle Jerry had told him. The dwelling was a cottage, more or less, with a large porch that had a giant gingerbread awning above it. It was at once creepy and hospitable, which is the scariest thing to a child — like a house made of sweets with a witch inside.

Dr. James Crawford was about to tell the Mother Goose story for the last time. He spoke as dramatically as an evangelist, even though he knew his wife Dorothy found it nauseating. "When I was a little boy, my mother worked during the day, so she had to take me to a nursery school

1

called *Mother Goose Land*. And there was a boy there, a boy who always seemed to be there, an older boy. And for whatever reason, he harassed me. I don't think he had it in for me in particular, you see. I just think he knew he could beat me up and get away with it. I was, well, very shy. And that little bastard kicked me, beat me, abused me."

Dorothy rolled her eyes when she heard the word "abused." *No more than you're abusing your body right now*, she thought. Occasionally she would try to point out that we all get picked on as children and it's a terrible part of life and all that, but Jim never listened. He never skipped a beat. She decided not to say anything this time. This was his gig. And besides, it was the nineties in America, and the most evolved people in the world no longer took human suffering lightly, however small.

"He would scratch me. Scream at me. Throw things at me. And it went on without end," Crawford said. "Seemed that way at the time anyhow."

The detail he could remember best was the toy radio: actually just a block of wood painted to look like a radio, with a small springy wire coming out of the top imitating an antenna, a toy that would now seem obsolete, but not completely useless in the right circumstance.

"As he was hitting me, calling me a sissy, I felt I wasn't going to take it any more. I finally got tired of it. Yeah, and this radio was nearby. Nothing but wood, just a blunt object, right. You can't tell me humans don't have animal instincts," he said with a nod.

A few people laughed.

Then Dorothy wagged her head from side to side, mentally lip-synching the sentence that always came next: *For some reason my animal instincts took over.*

"Between punches he asked me how I liked it." Then Crawford would nod, pausing for effect before releasing a verbal stream that rose to the act of liberating violence. "He was beating me. And I saw that toy radio. I saw it lying in the corner and I knew I could use it. And I grabbed it by the antenna and I swung that son of a..." His eyes always became tense, his breath shortened. "I swung that thing as hard as a baseball bat into the side of the little bastard's head."

His small audience became quiet. Crawford sat back and spoke more evenly, his face glowing with contentment. "The boy immediately started crying, screaming in pain. And for me, it felt good. It felt really good."

Dorothy could see the flask peaking through Jim's jacket like a gangster's pistol, casually holstered.

Crawford's tale plunged to a grave whisper. "Then something happened. Soon after, I don't know how long it was, but soon after I came to realize that I didn't feel so good. I thought I was going to throw up or something. And that afternoon when my mother came to pick me up, I was pale and weak. I felt terrible." A dramatic pause, then "I had come down with the mumps, you see."

Crawford described his mother and an older woman at the nursery school talking to each other as he waited in the foyer. From a distance he watched his mother nodding her head while the old woman told the story. The thought of his mother's embarrassment frightened little Jimmy Crawford, but the thought of her anger frightened him even more.

"I was in trouble. I just knew I had done something terrible, something my mother would punish me for. And feeling terrible was just a confirmation of what I already knew. I had been bad, and I was going to be punished severely — not just by my mother but by God himself. It was Him, our Heavenly Father, that I thought was making me sick. Before we even left Mother Goose, God had already started punishing me. It was just a matter of time before my mother would cause me further pain. Then, perhaps, I would die."

Crawford stared at the floor as he described his mother driving him home that evening, his ailing little body doubled over in the backseat. "But she got me to our house and didn't punish me. She never punished me. She never rebuked me, which was even more torture than being confronted. Eventually, I forgot about it. I thought I did. But you know what?" he said raising a finger. "I didn't forget it."

"Years later — far too long a time — my mother told me the woman at the nursery school was glad I had finally stood up for myself, that I had suffered too long at the hands of that aggressive bully. I didn't realize until I got much older that getting sick that day had nothing to do with hitting the boy. God wasn't punishing me at all. I was just sick because I had gotten sick that day. Just a bug going around the nursery school, that's all."

"I thought I knew God's ways for many years, but I was wrong," he concluded. "I was just punishing myself. And all that time my behavior was influenced by those feelings, by that defining moment. The way I thought of myself, the level of inhibition I experienced when confronted by other people — it took me years — and I mean years — to realize that that kid, that little bastard — he had it coming. He really had it coming," he said.

Giving a thumbs-up he added, "At least that's the way I remember it."

His audience applauded.

Crawford picked up the freshly printed hardcover copy of *Self-Esteem* that sat in front of him. A woman rushed forward and started snapping pictures as Dorothy stepped to the side. Crawford didn't mind the flash. He was thinking about how he couldn't wait to get loaded and have sex with his mistress that night.

The glare of the TV screen was bright. That flickering image, that precise sequence, now a regular event in millions of households on weekday mornings, was scary to Crawford, something he turned away from. But there was more to this pattern of lights. It was a collaboration he was involved in. Something he made money from. Something he had created. Something he now dreamed of escaping.

The puppets started dancing.

Those damn animal puppets.

And then the melody, that insidious melody, that clinking and clanking children's song that rose from the silence like a sputtering jalopy begging to be repaired. Then the sing-song singing.

Happy Pappy. Happy Pappy. He's so happy to be our pappy.

Then a close up of the eyes, those dark, empty doll eyes.

"Yessssssiiiiirrrrreeeee!" he screams, his distorted features coming into the frame, a drunk at a party trying to get your attention. "Hello kids!" he says, his head barking out the words in a bizarre staccato. "Welcome to the Happy Pappy Show! You know who I am, don't you?"

All the puppets surround him.

"You're Happy Pappy!" they say, their heads bobbing.

Crawford once had a nightmare that Happy Pappy was actually TV puppet legend Howdy Doody transformed into an ogre by the work of an evil scientist using a malicious concoction created by Crawford himself.

Happy Pappy wasn't just Howdy Doody minus the puppet strings and Buffalo Bob. Yes, Happy was also a cowboy. He wore one of those big, rustic hats. He wore overalls. His yellow-gloved hands were as bright as the midday sun. And yes, he too was happy. But no, it wasn't Howdy Doody Time. Happy Pappy was too strong for that. He had real confidence.

The backdrop was surreal, distorted but difficult to say how or where. It made Crawford think of some remote cartoon land where real people were devoured by their animated creations. A barn with painted knotholes. A fence leading from one side of the frame to the other. White clouds resting in front of a blue-lit backdrop. The entire setting formed from an incomprehensible emptiness — like the crossroads along the yellow brick road.

"And why do they call me Happy Pappy?" he says, his buckteeth wrapping around his corncob pipe like the legs of a spider around its prey.

And the puppets respond, "Because you're soooooo happy!"

Their leader is taken aback. "And why am I so happy?"

"Because you like yourself! That's why!"

"That's right," he says, his stare zeroing in on the camera. "You know kids, you always have to be a friend to yourself *first*." His head then jolts to one side, to a puppy named Sandy. "Why is that?"

"Because that's what makes you feel good!" Sandy says with a toddler's voice.

"That's right, Sandy. And we know a song about that, don't we?"

Happy Pappy nods as the puppets surround him, groupies to a rock star.

And then the song again, complete with a libretto at the bottom of the screen (in case you want to sing along).

Be kind to yourself.

Be fond of yourself.

If you're not a chum you're a bum to yourself.

"Come on!" Happy screams.

Be a friend to yourself.

Without end to yourself.

Remember it's the best thing to do for your health.

"Please," Crawford said, or thought he said. "Turn it off."

She was sitting on the bed, her hair draped over her neck, reminding Crawford of Eve, the Garden of Eden, the fall of Man, Sin with a *capital S.*

"So you're going to be a novelist now, is that it?" she asked with vague disrespect.

Crawford saw Happy Pappy jumping up and down, even though he wasn't looking.

"Going to be Hemingway, are you?"

"I don't like Hemingway. Please. Turn it off."

She laughed softly. "You've always got your self-esteem."

Her laughter became bigger, louder — like an audience. Then there was applause.

"Don't you?" she asked giggling. "Don't you have your *Self-Esteem*?"

"I don't know," Crawford said, taking another drink. "Do I?"

Written across every housewife's afternoon TV screen, *Jan Live* had become an icon of elegance and sophistication. Its beautiful calligraphy, floating above the immaculate studio of greens and oranges, somehow let everyone know that Life *could* provide sanctuary once in a while, that

Life *could* always be better than it really was.

Everyone needed Jan Hershey. The audience of mostly middle-aged women clapped and smiled and cheered as they did everyday at 2pm Eastern Time, 11am Pacific. It was their expressions that revealed the most, revealed their hopes and dreams, as well as the bliss they felt in the presence of their host.

Jan was perfect. Everything about her worked in harmony to form a picture of loveliness and womanhood. Her suit — business-casual — spoke confidence with its effortless design and pastel hue. Her eyes sparkled, her teeth shined, and her hair was more beautiful than silk — a blonde in her late thirties only God could make.

The audience watched attentively, but something was different. She wasn't saying *hello* to the home viewers. She was looking straight at Crawford.

"What is the definition of self-esteem?" she demanded.

Crawford felt like he couldn't speak. "Well," he began slowly, "it's essentially the view we have of ourselves."

Jan nodded. "And you say this is a significant component in our lives? Perhaps the most important in terms of our happiness? Our prosperity?"

Crawford didn't know why, but he felt like he might throw up. "Yes, of course. I..."

Looking icy, Jan leaned toward him. "And where does this Happy Pappy character fit into all of this, Dr. Crawford?"

Almost in unison, the audience started laughing.

"Isn't this the kind of nonsense created by someone with *low* self-esteem?"

"But I..." Crawford couldn't speak.

The audience laughed louder. Some held their sides while others fanned in Jan's direction, delighted by her audacity, encouraging her to go further.

"What's the matter, Doctor?" she said stepping closer, her chin creeping over the top of her microphone. "Cat got your tongue?"

Deafening laughter, Crawford couldn't breathe.

"Just making a buck, aren't you!" she yelled. "You've fooled the poor and the innocent into supporting your drunkenness, your skirt chasing and your hypocrisy. Isn't that it, Doctor?"

Crawford was drowning. "I didn't... I..."

"Answer me, Dr. Crawford!"

Her face was so close she was almost inside his eyes. That's when the studio vanished.

"I..."

"Answer me, fucker!"

A screeching bell sounded.

He breathed. The air came in like a tender breeze through a rickety house and then went out again. And Crawford was back home.

It sounded again.

Dr. James Crawford was to turn fifty-three in two weeks, but this morning he was almost ninety. Reasonably tall and bulky, Crawford had a broad jaw and a high hairline that made him appear more masculine and more confident than he was. Many thought his appearance scholarly, yet almost everyone considered him a tough sort — the type of guy who wore turtleneck sweaters but could still kick your ass.

That is, of course, if he wasn't too drunk. This morning Crawford had a hangover, and it was a bad motherfucker. It would take him a moment, like it always did, to realize where he was and what he had done the night before. But first he needed to know what the hell that noise was. He finally realized it was the telephone next to the bed and reached over and answered it.

"Hello?" Crawford grumbled. He sniffed quietly then waited a moment. "Yes?"

"Dr. Crawford?" The voice was staggering, unfamiliar.

"Yeah. Who is this?"

"How's your self-esteem?" someone asked.

"What?" he said, still only half awake.

"How's your self-esteem?"

Crawford registered. "Who?"

The caller hung up and so did Crawford.

He didn't give it much thought. He was too sick. He was neither awake nor asleep. His mind was swimming in the previous night's booze, somewhere between dreams and consciousness. He put his head on the pillow and closed his eyes. Later, he thought. *Later.*

Then he heard something else. Something faint. It was Frank Sinatra, or someone trying to be Frank.

I've Got You Under My Skin.

I used to love that goddam song, Crawford thought. Then he fell asleep again.

"Jim, it's seven-thirty."

"Okay," he said, instinctively turning on his side.

"Who called?" she asked.

His voice trailed back into sleep. "I don't know."

"Jim? Who was it?"

"Wrong number, I guess."

"You guess?" She waited a moment. "Jim," she said. "Jim," she said louder.

"*What?*"

"How do you feel this morning?" she asked.

Dorothy Crawford was still very attractive at forty-nine. In the last few years she had finally lost much of the weight she had gained after their son Cal was born. But this improvement didn't matter much to Crawford. She could still be an unpleasant sight, especially when his eyes were bloodshot and throbbing. He was fond of her youthful demeanor, her magical adolescence, but he wasn't fond of the morning interview she required each time he awoke from a night of heavy drinking.

Crawford found the sight of her particularly nauseating that morning. It must have been that pink exercise suit, something an eighties porn star would wear.

"How do you feel this morning? Getting out of bed today or not?"

Dorothy had been pretty proud of herself lately. After going through a number of diet and exercise programs over the years, she had finally settled into one she could stick with long enough to see results. For the previous six months, she had been using a program called *Swing and Sweat*, which was where the faint sound of Sinatra had come from. Of course, it wasn't really Sinatra, most likely an unknown lounge singer eking out a living in the exercise market. But from upstairs it was impossible to tell. Crawford only heard the faint sound of tunes he used to love — *used* to love. No longer could he put on a Sinatra album without having the unwanted thought of Dorothy in her pink bodysuit, bent at the knees, reaching in the air and swinging from side to side to the strains of *I Get a Kick Out of You* and *Summer Wind*. Not only had the exercise program tainted one of his favorite artists, truth was he also preferred Dorothy's bigger butt.

"*I said*, how do you feel this morning, *dear*?"

His voice was muffled under the sheets, "I don't know yet."

"I thought we were over this, Jim."

The word "we" meant it was time to roll over and face her.

"Dorothy, please. I've had a lot of anxiety lately." He sat up.

"So have I," she said, standing before him like a field marshal. "And so you had to get drunk last night, is that it?"

"Honey, please."

"Don't *honey* me," she shot back. "What is it that's so damn stressful anyhow?"

Crawford looked straight ahead, straight through his wife.

"I don't know," he mumbled, just before she stormed out, her pink bottom jolting with each step. But he *did* know. For one thing, he had been seeing Jenny again, and the guilt was just starting to set in. Dreams about the Garden of Eden — they always happened sooner or later.

Jenny had done all those things he liked best, all those things he could never ask his wife to do. But Crawford thought of Jenny's skills as a classy menu in a shitty café. The arching of the back, the parting of the lips, the panting of words like "Oh, Jim," "Yes," "Harder," and so on. It was wrong, he knew. Wrong, wrong, wrong — like that one more shot of whiskey that seems like a good idea at the time.

Best of all, though — or worst of all — she didn't object to the drinking. In fact, she joined in.

Oh, yeah, he thought, finally piecing together the evening. That's what happened: after the drinking and the screwing they had a talk, a "discussion" as Jenny liked to call it. Right in the middle of the street she had yelled, "You're not going to treat me like a piece of ass."

But even a public display of anger didn't matter. Her apartment was in a commercial part of downtown Los Angeles and no one was ever around. It was one of those places where the streets always look wet, even when they haven't seen rain in months.

Crawford remembered hearing her yell, "No fucking way," over and over again. *But over what?* He must have told her something she didn't want to hear — like the affair had to stop. Again, he wasn't sure.

Crawford's head ached. He walked into the bathroom without turning on the light and sat on the toilet. He leaned over, his head resting on his forearms.

"Honey?" he heard Dorothy ask. "Are you okay in there?"

He farted.

"Yes, dear. I'm okay."

TWO

C al Crawford was watching the puppets dance, but he wasn't listening. Leaning against the headboard of his queen size bed, his portable audio player beside him, Cal could watch but he wouldn't listen. It was a strange ritual of morning entertainment, something to do while smoking the day's first joint.

The music in his headphones was raucous, the venomous beat taking his head back and forth as he watched Sandy the puppet approach her bouncing mentor. The movement of the characters, out of time with his own, only made the percussion more pronounced and defiant, especially now that Cal was stoned.

Then the advertisement: this made Cal's heartbeat quicken more than the pot — seeing his father with that feigned, toothy smile, with that shit-brown suit on, next to a pile of books and tapes, in front of a goddam purple background, behind a 1-800 telephone number. *What a lie*, he thought. *A very stupid lie*. And how vulgar. And how laughable. And there he is with my name, *my goddam surname*, written on the screen for everyone to see. *Dumbass*.

Dr. James Crawford's Self Series™

Followed by the "claimer," as Cal called it, scrolling up the screen, a psalm giving sanction to a crooked evangelist.

The techniques set forth on the "Happy Pappy Show"
are based on the principles of Dr. James Crawford,
whose Self Series™ *has helped millions improve their lives.*
These principles have been modified to accommodate
the self-esteem needs of a younger audience.

I know what accommodates a younger audience, Cal thought, deeply inhaling another hit.

Calvin Crawford was James and Dorothy's only child, a one-time addition whose imminent arrival had ended the debate as to whether they should get married. Dorothy didn't believe in abortion and Jim didn't believe in pushing her, so when the news came they simply set a date to get hitched and that was that. But Cal's personality turned out to be so unlike either of his parents that it was like a stork had dumped him there to point out that Jim and Dorothy had more in common than they thought.

Long before the venerable Dr. Crawford had struck the seven-figure deal for the *Happy Pappy Show*, Cal was fed up with his father's enterprise. Now it was this puppet shit and the latest installment of the *Self Series*, *Self-Esteem*. Cal felt his father had finally reached the bottom of the capitalist barrel, and for months he cringed at the thought of him.

Cal turned up the music even louder.

Yeah. Rotten Tamales.

Rotten Tamales. Yeah, fucking rocks. What a fucking rock star.

The tune was the title track from his latest album, *Erectum*. A month earlier, Cal and his dad nearly came to blows over a poster Cal put on the wall. It wasn't just an ordinary depiction of Rotten Tamales — a skinny white boy (painted to be even whiter) wearing a monstrous leather bodysuit with shiny spikes coming from every pleat. It was classic Rotten — bending over with what appeared to be a large erect penis ascending up out of his backside under the leather.

"You're not putting that crap on my wall!" Crawford screamed at Cal.

"He's an artist! It's not crap!" Cal yelled back.

Then Dorothy took her usual diplomatic position, telling her husband, "Maybe you don't understand, Dear."

Crawford hated Rotten Tamales since Cal started listening to *Kill Kompletely*, his breakthrough album that sold four million copies. Crawford would sometimes walk by Cal's room and stop in awe of the poisonous sound and depraved lyrics he heard blaring from inside.

Kill, kill, kill. Die, die, die. Fuck, fuck, fuck. Etc.

These kids, Crawford would think. *What can we do?*

In the end, Cal won the battle of the *Erectum* poster because Crawford just didn't give a damn any more. It was pure perseverance on Cal's part, and it was worth the accomplishment. Cal relished the idea that his father would have to tolerate a picture of some skinny punk's leather ass on his wall with what looked like a boner on the wrong side. Every morning he looked at it with such admiration.

"Be kind to yourself, bitch," he said, high as the devil.

• • •

One wall of Crawford's study was covered in the ritual sycophancy of being one of America's foremost self-help writers, "which also means one of the best-selling," he liked to add. The plaques, the pictures, the awards and the newspaper clippings hung neatly in rows behind Crawford's writing desk, which he lovingly called "Old Bessie." The wall he called, not so lovingly, "the Wall of Shame." He didn't like it that way, of course. It was merely a concession following a series of negotiations with Dorothy, which included his proviso that the collection be hidden from most houseguests. One of his first awards was a plaque he received from a small town in Wisconsin proclaiming "Dr. Crawford Day." Accepting the undesired plaque in person was bad enough, he felt. But Dorothy saw it differently.

"We can't just throw it away," she told him.

"Maybe we can't, but I can."

He finally gave in, and the small museum of his accomplishments was hatched. Then it grew, and grew, and grew some more. But he resented all of it. The Wall of Shame certainly didn't serve the purpose his well-intentioned wife thought it would. Dorothy saw such a display as a source of inspiration, something that could give "perspective." But Crawford knew the presence of these things was anything but inspiring — demoralizing, in fact. They haughtily reminded him of what he might have been, mocking what he believed he might someday become. His degrees meant nothing to him. Even his doctorate — the one item he might have wanted on the wall — brought shame. Instead of representing accomplishment, the honorary degree represented fraud — giving him the sense that he would never contribute anything of value, not as a scientist nor as an artist.

But Crawford was typing, his bloodshot eyes staring blankly at the blue screen.

"For you try and you try and you try," *but that's okay. Keep trying!*

"Ah!"

I can't write pessimism, he thought. I can only live it.

I can. I can. Still. Keep going. You're not just a writer. You're a novelist. You're a damn novelist.

Two cups of strong coffee and Crawford's hangover wasn't any better. Since he had not had an all-nighter in a while, this one was particularly bad. Like many struggling boozers, Crawford cradled a morose attachment to self-inflicted soreness, to mind-numbing pain. It was like an old friend he had known for years and couldn't abandon. Although unpleasant, hangovers made him subconsciously aware that the rest of the day could only improve — perhaps the rest of the week, perhaps the rest of his life. He also knew they were one of the few deterrents that might keep him from drinking himself to death.

Crawford noted that this morning his slight paunch hung over his Levis just a little more, pulling his standard white T-shirt a little tighter. But he had to put a stop to that kind of thinking. That was the byproduct of a superficial generation that flipped through celebrity magazines in checkout lines — not what a serious novelist concerns himself with.

Don't end a sentence with a preposition.

William Faulkner never fretted over his belly, Crawford guessed. And why would he? He had bigger fish to fry. Or he had higher mountains to climb. Or he had better shit to do.

Avoid clichés like the plague.

Or something. *Anyway.*

Crawford, once again, was seeing nothing but crap spring from his fingertips — no concept, no originality, just clichés, just nonsense.

Suddenly he felt someone watching him.

Crawford turned to see Cal standing in the doorway staring at him blankly through his frizzled hair. Cal was now dressed for school in what Crawford called his "black death uniform," actually a standard "Goth" look with the essentials of dyed black hair, black shirt, black jeans and black boots. Crawford could avoid the topic of Cal's fashion sense as long as it didn't include black fingernail polish, black lipstick and pale makeup.

"Yes?" Crawford said instinctively.

For the previous year and a half, Cal made Crawford more uncomfortable than anyone since his own father, and consequently, more resentful. But Crawford wasn't about to let Cal know that.

"Good morning, Cal."

"So. Does it have a happy ending?" Cal asked.

"What's that?" Crawford said.

"That," Cal said, pointing to Crawford's computer.

"You mean my current writing project?"

"Uh huh," Cal said. "Your current writing project."

"I don't know yet, son."

"You always say you should just do what you can do. And you're so good at happy endings," Cal said. "Will it have a happy ending or not?"

"I'm sorry, Cal. But I'm busy, and I..."

Cal walked away before Crawford could finish.

Little prick, Crawford thought.

Retrieving the morning newspaper from the driveway was one of Dorothy's morning pleasures because, as she saw it, it was a time for reflecting — reflecting on her lovely Beverly Hills home and the spotless neighborhood where it cozily rested. The lawns were always green and the cars always clean, and seeing this was something else, she thought, that gave her perspective. It reminded her that she and Jim were once poor and aimless, that Jim once had a horrible drinking problem, and during that time Jim was unable to support their family in a manner acceptable to her. But my, my — things had changed. Jim's drinking improved. Relapses became fewer and far between. And he gained focus, as she saw it. He wrote a book. He made money. He wrote another book. He made more money. And the rest, as they say, was history. Retrieving the morning paper was actually a simple pleasure that begat another simple pleasure — thinking about how things were really pretty good.

Heading back into the house, Dorothy scraped her leg on a neatly trimmed shrub near the driveway. "Shit," she said to herself, cursing the small cut.

Things were pretty good. Except for Jim's recent benders, she thought as she inspected her wound.

The drinking was on her mind more and more every day. And then there were those afternoons when Jim disappeared for no reason.

Oh, please. Dorothy knew she was just being uptight about things. She just needed to relax a bit. Oh, you silly nilly, she thought to herself. *Can't you just be happy? You little grouchy ouchy.*

The beat came hard and slow like a brewing storm muffled by distance. Another beat, then louder and louder, and Cal came barreling out of the driveway in his new silver Porsche convertible, looking like James Dean heading for Mulholland Drive. He skidded to a stop in front of his mother, laughing when he heard her shriek.

"My God, Cal. Would you please be careful?"

"I'm fuckin' late, Mom," he said.

Standing straight to look more parental, she said, "Please don't use profanity around me. And turn that music down."

Cal scowled but did as he was told. He was wearing dark sunglasses, gratuitous in the soft morning sunlight.

Dorothy avoided an angry response to Cal by thinking, *Don't lose your temper, it's more important than your keys* — a quote she heard on *Jan Hershey.*

She smiled gently. "Please don't forget we have that thing tonight."

"That thing tonight has fuck all to do with me, doesn't it?" Cal said, his fingers tapping the steering wheel to the beat.

Before Dorothy could answer, her son had hit the accelerator and charged backward into the street with a squeal, reminding her of James

Garner in the *The Rockford Files*. My my, I miss that show, she thought, as Cal sped away.

Dorothy thought that her son needed a good talking to about dangerous driving — an open dialogue to better help him understand the dangers. But, no, that was something Jim needed to do. Jim needed to talk to Cal about a lot of things. Jim needed to share the responsibilities of parenthood, especially issues that related to masculinity, like driving recklessly.

But Jim's recent relapses, she thought again. *I need to talk to Jim about the drinking, I guess, then Jim can talk to Cal about... the driving and uh...*

"I need to put something on this," she said to herself, heading inside to medicate her cut.

The foyer of the Crawford home was a wide-open octagonal space looking onto a semi-spiral staircase on one side. The wood that adorned both the staircase and the trim of the beveled ceiling was a light pine — one that Crawford was never happy with. "Not dark enough," was his opinion. Dorothy had insisted on the color, saying it looked "cheerful" compared to Crawford's more "morose" preference for Scarlet oak. Even though Dorothy chose a fine pine imported from Eastern Europe, Crawford believed the wood gave their home a strange "movie set" quality. What's more, Crawford had never been happy with Dorothy's choice of furniture: mostly a contemporary "California" style with soft maple finishes and upholstery in pastels of green and orange. The entire home, inside and out, was Dorothy's creation. Her rationale for the location, style and color scheme was based on her belief that environment — especially color — was of vital importance when it came to human behavior. The black and Latino ghettos of Los Angeles, she believed, were filled with violence and despair (at least in part) because of the ugly browns and grays that dominated the landscape. Dorothy hadn't actually been to any of these areas, but she had read about them. And she imagined a topography of rundown, spirit-numbing liquor stores, abandoned buildings, fires burning in oil drums and black smoke from sources both legal and illegal littering a starless sky. She actually thought about this inner-city nightmare while creating the new Crawford family home in Beverly Hills, which they had lived in now for three years. It would be the anti-ghetto, filled with beautiful colors that keep away life's "ugly wugglies."

Coming out of the shower, Jim heard the car speed away and knew it was his ingrate of a son. "Little fucker," he said to himself. "I should make him walk to school like I did." This particular morning was too painful for concerns about Cal. He was hung over, mad at himself for the miniscule amount of writing he had done that morning, as well as apprehensive about a few unpleasant things he had in store that day. He was going to put his foot down with Cal, but not this morning.

First things first.

He got out of the shower and dried himself thinking how he'd aged so much since he stopped drinking.

Perhaps now that you've started again, your youth will return.

"I need the disinfectant and a band-aid please," Dorothy said through the cracked bathroom door.

Crawford handed the items to her without asking why.

"You're going to see Lee?" Dorothy asked.

"Yes. I told you that."

Crawford sometimes became irritated by his wife's nosiness, especially concerning business. She had been effective as Jim's manager and publicist during the first stages of his career and, by some accounts, had worked harder than Crawford himself at the creation of the *Self* franchise. Accordingly, many people in the publishing world regarded her public relations expertise as an essential part of Crawford's success. But now that he was successful — after all, he wrote the books — her tone sometimes sounded like a mother asking her son if he had brushed his teeth.

"I have to talk to Lee right away, while I still have the nerve," he continued.

"You mean the nerve you have from drinking alcohol?"

Crawford walked through the door wearing a yellow bathrobe Dorothy had given him as an anniversary gift. "Leave it alone, Dorothy."

"If I can't ask you about that, can I ask you to talk to your son?"

"You can ask."

Crawford took off the robe and threw it on the floor. Dorothy went into the bathroom to medicate her wound. Crawford thumbed through his closet, still annoyed.

"Are you listening to me?" she asked.

He stopped. "I think so. I'm answering you, aren't I?"

"You need to talk to Cal."

Crawford put on a pair of slacks. "Okay," he said with resignation. "About what?"

"You know about what."

He stopped again. "No, Dorothy. I don't know."

"He just seems, I don't know, angry," she said painting the cut with disinfectant.

"Okay, so he's pissed off all the time. Big deal. What kid isn't at his age?"

"Jim, you're not doing your job."

"Oh yeah? And how well are you doing your job?"

Dorothy took a deep breath to keep from losing her temper. "He seems to be particularly mad at you."

"Yeah, what else is new?" he said.

Dorothy came back into the bedroom holding a Q-tip. "It's going to be really embarrassing when the big self-help guru's son is busted for drugs. And who is this new friend of his? We haven't even met this boy. Do you know this Darrin person?"

"Who?" Crawford said, inspecting himself in the mirror. "He's only smoking pot, Dorothy. So what."

Dorothy took one of her standard positions: her husband was choosing not to appreciate the gravity of a situation to avoid dealing with it. Jim countered that most people have periods of loserdom in their lives and that maybe it was even good for people in the long run — a bold statement considering it was not exactly the advice he had given millions of readers. "Perhaps," Dorothy agreed, pointing with the Q-tip, "but your loser period hasn't ended," and that's why, she concluded, they needed to act now — to save their son. With Crawford's splitting headache, this was an especially unwelcome remark.

"Careful, Dorothy," he said gravely.

"You act like you don't care!"

Crawford had no more patience. He didn't need this distraction, not this morning. "I know you want what's best for him. You tell me all the time what's best for him. You talked me into buying him that fifty thousand dollar car. Now *that's* embarrassing." Crawford grabbed his keys and wallet. "Is there fresh coffee downstairs?" he asked.

Dorothy shook her head. "I guess you need it this morning, don't you."

Crawford walked out of the room then poked his head back in. "And by the way, I'm not a guru. I'm a writer."

"Okay, Mr. Writer."

Dorothy stood in the middle of the room shaking her head, unaware her cut was bleeding again.

THREE

Crawford sat at the kitchen table sipping his third cup of black coffee. With his briefcase in the chair beside him and the morning newspaper on the table in front, Crawford felt like a lawyer about to argue for the acquittal of a defendant he knew was guilty. He wanted to think he was prepared for the day ahead of him, but he knew otherwise.

The small TV on the kitchen counter was turned up too loud, but he didn't mind. Something needed to drown out the chatter in his head. When he told Dorothy that he needed to talk to Lee Burns while he still had the nerve, he wasn't exaggerating. For months now he had been despondent about his relationship with Lee — something he chalked up to self-doubt, not a lack of self-esteem. Crawford's association with Lee was atypical for a writer and the businessperson who handled his affairs. Lee was Crawford's agent, his publisher, his attorney, his accountant and his career, guidance and marriage counselor. He was a self-help author's one-stop shop, but more significantly he was a conglomerate that held a monopoly on the business of James Crawford's life. Accordingly, Crawford felt he was in a marriage that could never be dissolved, with a spouse that was increasingly difficult to oppose.

With no time to give himself a pep talk, he simply practiced what he was going to say.

And Lee I just think it's time that we...

Dorothy passed through the hall just outside the kitchen then stopped. She looked surprised he was still there.

"I'm going out," she said.

"Okay," he said, still trying to look like he was reading the newspaper.

Dorothy hated having exchanges with her husband like that. As usual she tried to break the ice as soon as possible.

"You'll be home in time for Phil's banquet, won't you?" she asked, feigning civility.

His eyes didn't leave the paper. "That's what I said."

She approached him slowly with a mother's resignation. "Why are you so grouchy?" she said, running her hand across his broad shoulder. "I think you need to eat more fiber."

He let his guard down a bit. "I'm nervous about doing this damn Hershey show, I guess."

Crawford was now hearing the TV. It was a news program with some kind of discussion.

"You sorry for being mean?"

"Yes, Dorothy, I'm sorry," he said, distracted by the TV.

"No, you're not. You're never sorry."

"Okay. So I'm never sorry," he said, lifting the paper.

Crawford didn't see her look before she walked out. He wouldn't have cared anyway.

He heard his name on the TV.

"In your book where you discuss *Dr. Crawford...*"

It was like being called on Judgment Day.

"Your book doesn't have too many kind words for the popular psychologist Dr. James Crawford, does it?"

"No, not many," the voice said.

There were two talking heads, both men. The younger and better-looking man was the anchor of the program; the other, a gray-haired man in his fifties, was the guest. Below the guest's name was written, "Dr. Thomas Watkins, Psychologist." It was a program on new books, and this Dr. Watkins was commenting on Crawford's.

Oh, shit, Crawford thought.

"And you're steadfast about that?" the anchor said.

Oh, here it comes.

The man leaned forward with a smile that was almost a sneer. "Of course. I just happen to think that a well-known psychologist like James Crawford, who should be thankful that he's got any credibility from the mental health community at all, should not stoop to this, the lowest possible commercialism in our field." Almost sarcastically, he emphasized specific words, making remarks even more wounding. "His *techniques* have not been proven to be *enormously* successful, as some other methods have. And by franchising a children's TV show..."

The anchor interrupted. "But his books and CDs are, however, enormously popular."

"Of course," Watkins said smiling. "That's the bottom line, isn't it?" He paused a moment. "I just don't think children need to be psychoanalyzing themselves at this age in this manner, with the help of some live, animated character. I mean, Dr. Crawford has a new book out. He's got some other products on the market. Isn't that enough?"

"Well, some people would argue that he wants to help a broad range of people."

"Yes," the man laughed. "Or tap a broader market."

Yeah, you got your market. I got mine, Crawford thought as he reached for the TV remote.

"Thank you for joining us, Doctor," the anchor said.

"You're welcome," the man said with a nod.

Think you're saving the world, do you?

The anchor gazed at the camera with the warmth of someone talking to a lover. "This debate may rage on for some time to come. Dr. Crawford has yet to comment on the criticism he has received in endorsing this new program." Turning the ersatz page on his desk, the anchor added, "He is scheduled to appear on the *Jan Live* show this week."

Crawford turned off the TV.

Bullshit, he thought. More bullshit. Bullshit on top of bullshit.

This Thomas Watkins, PhD or not, was right, of course. And Crawford's critics had been growing lately, something that was unthinkable 10 years before.

Maybe I do need more fiber, Crawford thought.

The Coldwater Canyon pass was filled with the run of the mill Bimmers and Benzes of morning traffic — mostly people heading to the Valley to earn money to subsidize status symbols: the cars, the house, the spouse, the lover, the Scottish terrier, the rest of it. Many were in showbiz, either "legit" or pornographic, but Cal looked down on them all with the same contempt. His pot high was still hanging solid as he cranked his 8-speaker Alpine stereo system that could accommodate the brilliance of Rotten Tamales' *Caved in Head*, a motherfucker machinegun rock anthem that screams for the world to change and *change right fucking now!*

The morgue of your morals a shitter, a pisser
Daddy came in the babysitter
And you've damned me to hell, hypocrite shell!
I'm fucking ringing your death bell!

"Fuck, yeah," Cal said, anticipating the "Fuck, yeah" that Rotten cries during the interval. *Tamales got a way with fucking words.*

The music got softer as Rotten whispered his wicked verse:

You think I'm slain
You think I won't fight the battle
But you better fucking watch out, when
(what a scream!)
my caved in head starts to rattle!

The drummer shoots out a crushing beat as Maestro Tamales' howl becomes the ear-splitting shriek of a slaughtered pig.

And you better watch out, fuckerrrrr!

"Yeah, fucker," Cal yelled. God, he loved that line. He wondered who this "fucker" was and why he needed to "watch out." Probably one of these assholes on the pass.

Cal didn't go to Beverly Hills High School, which was the proper one for his residential district. He went to Valdosta Senior High, a crappy public school just on the other side of the Hills in the Valley. It was a decision that Cal was allowed to make himself — or his dad made it seem that way. By the time the Crawfords moved to Beverly Hills, Cal was nearly out of middle school, and his dad wanted him to continue going to a "normal" high school, as he put it, not a "country club high school" filled with spoiled brats.

Crawford had a fit during his first inspection of Beverly Hills High. He thought it was just too upscale, like their house. "Do we want to alienate our child even further?" he asked Dorothy. "He's already being raised in a wealthy household. Do we want to make sure he can't get along with people outside his socio-economic group?"

At first Dorothy was against the decision, but she finally gave in, admitting, "Yes, I guess Beverly Hills High is probably a little snooty-tooty."

Cal got some angst-ridden observations from his dad about fitting in at such a place and so on. "They'll look down on you, Cal. They all come from new money, but you come from really new money."

Cal agreed: it would be Valdosta Senior High.

Crawford wasn't that concerned about Cal thinking he was superior to the rest of the world. Truth was, Crawford just didn't want Cal buying eight-dollar cappuccinos and shopping for clothes on Rodeo Drive. Even the sight of black Goth clothes and Rotten Tamales posters was preferable to that.

Coldwater Canyon Drive was a hissing gauntlet of wealth where Cal felt no more privileged than any other upper-class consumer teen. But after passing Ventura Boulevard then Moorpark then Riverside, the gulf between the haves and have-nots diminished quickly, making Cal feel more *snooty-tooty* than he would have around his would-be classmates in Beverly Hills.

He barreled toward Valdosta through a residential neighborhood at twice the 25-mile-an-hour speed limit and peeked over his dark sunglasses to look at himself in the rearview mirror. Yeah, he looked cool. He knew there would be someone watching. There were always people watching. And yeah, he knew they would say he looked cool in that car and those clothes. He felt them, those unseen spectators, like he could feel the car itself, all fifty Gs of it, surrounding his body, making his high higher, making him invincible.

He whipped down the hill next to the band building — trumpet, clarinet, and trombone players going inside. Then he went through the four-way stop, past the practice field, and into the high school parking lot where he politely slowed down and nodded to the assistant coach standing watch just inside the gate. Coach Lieberman, also a substitute teacher, gave Cal a smirk that spoke mounds of resentment. The way Cal saw it, for a kid to have wheels with a price tag that eclipsed the man's yearly salary, how could he not be resentful? Cal understood Coach Lieberman's pain. Yeah, his car felt good, but part of the bargain was that Cal saw hostility everywhere. It was Cal's cross to bear. Most of Cal's fellow classmates obviously resented his extravagant toy. There were many students from upper-class families at Valdosta High, but few had parents that would dish out that kind of money. A few students had inherited older sports cars from their families. Many drove relatively new Hondas and Toyotas. But none drove around in a brand new 911.

Cal parked and got out of his car, beeping the security system with one motion as he swung his backpack over his shoulder. Then his momentary confidence disappeared as Coach Lieberman came hastily toward him.

"Morning, Crawford," he said in a coach's soldierly clip.

"Morning, Coach."

Coach Lieberman put his hands in the back pockets of his khakis and stuck out his aging abdomen. "Word has it you drive this thing pretty fast sometimes. And that you drive fast with loud music playing," he said, sticking out his bottom lip.

"Is that right?" Cal said, clutching his backpack like a security blanket. "Word has it?"

"That's right," Lieberman said with a commanding nod.

Cal looked at the whistle around the Coach's neck and thought it looked ridiculous.

"I've had people tell me you come down the hill by the band room in your fancy sports car here faster than a bobcat chasing a beaver."

Coach Lieberman waited for a response, even though he hadn't asked a question.

"Do bobcats chase beavers, Coach Lieberman?"

Lieberman stood still and then raised his finger like a cop wielding a gun. "Don't get smart with me boy, you hear?" He put his finger on his hip. "They'll chase anything with two eyes and an asshole, bobcats will. Cattle, pigs, chickens."

"Really?"

"Never mind about that. Just take it easy on the street out there, son."

"Okay, sir."

"I don't care if your old man is a famous guru," he added.

That was below the belt, Cal thought. "He's actually a writer and..."

"Have a good day at school, now," the man said, doing an about face.

Cal walked toward school, his morning high now almost spent.

Son? He called me son? Stupid asshole.

Cal knew Coach Lieberman wasn't so bad, not for a sports guy. After all, inside the school there were scary throngs of determined, hostile jocks everywhere, ready to harass anyone for having something they didn't, especially a brain.

Like every morning, Cal headed toward the front steps of the school entrance filled with fear and loathing. The contrary laughter, the hostile snickering, and the genuine threats were part of walking past the morning jock huddle, where all the guys that proudly wore a letter stood side by side, ready for battle.

"There he is," the first voice shouted. "It's the son of Happy Pappy."

"Did Sandy the puppy pick out your pretty pants for you?"

"I didn't know she liked black so much," another said in a mother's whine.

Cal walked faster, his invisible blinders failing to make him disappear.

"You know, it's okay to be a faggot," one said effeminately.

"Yeah. Just be happy with your crappy fuckin' self."

More laughing. Then, of course, the singing.

"Be kind to yourself. Be fond of yourself. If you're not a chum you're a bum to yourself."

Cal walked faster and faster as he approached the door. By the time he reached the stairs, he was almost running. But the jock flock amplified their voices to accommodate the distance.

"See you later, Gary the Gator!" one said.

They laughed harder, like dim-witted hyenas, and Cal wished he could kill them all and cut them up into little pieces and mail them home to their mothers.

When Cal reached the top of the steps, the bureaucrat in charge of disciplinary action appeared: Vice Principal Gore. Gore was a likable guy for the most part — a tall, affable man with a bald head and a goofy sense of humor. Gore didn't do much to protect the pussies from the bullies, and the pussies didn't like that. But Cal was a different kind of pussy — he understood Gore. The way Cal saw it, the VP was just too smart to get involved in little razzings that happened at school because unpleasant confrontation is just a part of life that happens in all kinds of places. Gore also knew that bullies were a fact of life from preschool to the grave and that pussies had better learn to deal with bullies sooner or later.

"Morning, Cal," Vice Principal Gore said, nodding.

"Good morning, Mr. Gore," Cal said. "How are you?"

"Fine, thanks. You on drugs this morning?" he asked.

"No sir," Cal said.

"Don't lie to me, Crawford," Gore said, looking out over the courtyard. "I know your crowd, and you're all high as damn kites."

"Yes sir," Crawford said. "I mean, no sir. Well, some of the guys are... I wouldn't use the kite analogy, sir."

"Now, now," Gore said, dropping his veneer. "No need to get jumpy. I'm just kiddin' ya, boy."

"I know, sir," Cal said, though he didn't.

"Those football guys down there still giving you a hard time, huh?"

"No sir," he lied again. "Not too bad, sir."

"Well, hang in there, son," he said slapping Cal on the back. "You're almost done. Don't do anything stupid."

Cal knew it was good advice. "I won't, sir."

Mr. Gore casually walked into the school and Cal thought about how he respected the Vice Principal more than his own father and how sad that was.

Cal made his way through the crowded hall to the main bathroom on the first floor, which was so filthy it made washing your hands almost pointless. And yet Cal went there before class, feeling the need to wash something, perhaps the egg off his face. It never worked.

He put his hands under the cold water. *Why, Dad?*

The jocks outside did have a point. It wasn't so much Gore's advice to keep cool or even his own fear of being beaten to death that kept him from responding. The jocks were absolutely right to make jokes about that stupid show. And putting up a fight in defense of Happy Pappy would be even sillier than Happy Pappy himself. *Why that stupid fucking show, Dad? Why?*

Cal splashed his face. You're going to pay a million times for that show, Dad. That's what Darrin says. And Darrin knows everything.

FOUR

reat idea, Lee. You just know everything, don't you?
Crawford was stuck in traffic on Santa Monica Boulevard, struggling to focus on what he needed to say to Lee. He was thinking of Dorothy, of Cal, of Jenny, of Lee, of the new book, of the Jan Hershey show (*Jan Live with Jan Hershey*, that is), of the promotional tour (whatever that might require), and of that damn children's show.

God, now the criticism.

Great idea, Lee, he thought.

This is what will ruin me. This is why I'm an alcoholic, embarrassments like this. I got this disease because I couldn't not get this disease.

Huh?

"Don't rationalize, hypothesize."

And it is a disease, just like they say.

Crawford had always resisted that idea, that alcoholism was a disease, even after several experiences with treatment. He often argued that alcoholism was a "condition," not a "disease." He believed that health care professionals used elevated terminology when discussing alcoholism in order to ease the insecurities of the people who suffered from it, to make it sound more like a natural phenomenon and therefore not the patient's fault. Privately, Crawford knew the terminology of addiction was like that of psychology. Alcoholism, like "neurosis," wasn't as glamorous as a "disease." It was just a common rut people fell into. But several years later, after he got to know the patterns of his own alcoholism (as well as his own neuroses), he realized that terms like "disease" and "relapse" were appropriate for the condition. They represented something as real as pancreatic cancer. And besides, it didn't matter what they called it. Hell, anything could be called a "disease." Normal things. Fear. Depression. Guilt. Being stuck in a sea of cars for that matter. And when you call something a disease, there is always a potential for profit.

"Fuckin' L.A.," he thought out loud.

It should have been a 30-minute drive to Lee's office, but the traffic wasn't moving and Crawford was gritting his teeth. His S-Class Mercedes, with every available accessory from the manufacturer, couldn't do a thing about a traffic jam, though somehow it could give you the impression it could, which caused even more frustration.

The car had been a gift from Lee four months earlier when Crawford finally agreed to *The Happy Pappy Show*.

"That's all you have to do," Lee said enthusiastically.

Crawford thought it was funny — Lee sitting behind his mahogany desk, dressed in one of his spotless Armani suits, fidgeting like a hyperactive child in his luxurious Century City office that could easily have been a plastic surgery clinic for people who don't need it.

"That's it, Jim," he said with a clap and a colossal smile.

Crawford remembered thinking how Lee looked very non-literary, like someone who shouldn't have gone into publishing.

"That's all, huh?" Crawford said solemnly.

Crawford sometimes joked that "Burns Book Publishing" should simply be called "Burns Books." But "publishing," of course, doesn't mean "literary," and Lee had made Crawford a fortune — one reason no one could say the talent of Lee Burns had been wasted on the wrong industry.

"You don't have to do a goddam thing, Jim." He paused. "Well, maybe one little video spot. A couple of little promotionals."

"Video spot?"

Lee was the same age as Crawford but looked much younger. He was a short man, smaller than Crawford, with narrowing shoulders and thinning hair, which some would say made him look older. But Lee's anxious behavior gave him a youthful disposition Crawford didn't have. And to Crawford's constant surprise, Lee was still thought to be a very attractive man, well known for numerous infidelities with beautiful women.

Crawford watched him closely as he sat on the edge of his desk.

"At the end of the program they say this show is based on the *Self Series* by Dr. James Crawford. Blah, blah, blah. A picture. A few numbers on the screen, where to buy our products. Yada, yada, yada. And that's it."

"That's it? And the video spot?"

Lee ignored the question. "All we do is sit back and collect the money." Lee was fidgeting again, shaking his head from side to side, already counting the money they would make.

"I don't like it."

"Why not?" Lee shot back quickly.

"Sounds like bullshit."

"Of course it's bullshit. So what?"

"It could hurt us."

"Hurt us?" Lee laughed uneasily then stood up. "How can it hurt us? Look. We care about children, Jim. That's why we do it. We're doing what we can, not just for sexually frustrated housewives, but for the little bastards they give birth to. See?"

"Uh huh."

Lee reached inside his pocket and produced a single car key, a round black grip surrounding shinny metal. With a sly smile and an assertively cocked head, Lee told Crawford he had a gift for him. To a bystander such a performance might have looked like a sexual proposition. Of course, Crawford knew exactly what was going on. It was carrot time. "Will you do it?" Lee asked softly.

It was moments like this that Crawford knew he couldn't resist Lee. His zeal was impossible to combat, especially since he made everything sound so perfect. It was no wonder Lee got laid so much.

"It's German," Lee said, "like your favorite beers."

Crawford smiled apprehensively. "I know where a Mercedes comes from. And the beer remark isn't appropriate. I don't drink beer." Lee shrugged his shoulders and gave Crawford a sarcastic grin, pushing the key across his desk. Crawford caved in. "I hope I'm not going to regret this."

Lee laughed, triumphantly slapping himself on the thigh and throwing his arms around Jim.

"That's my boy. That's my boy." He picked up the phone on his desk. "I've got to make the call. They want to know right away."

"So what's the name of the show?"

"I don't know. It's a kid's show. It's called *Farmer Bill* or some shit."

"Farmer Bill?" Crawford asked, gripping the key. "Hey, can I give this a little more thought before I commit?"

"Man, you think too much."

Crawford now had a very unusual agenda at Burns Publishing — one that had been on his mind for weeks, one he dreaded initiating. But he would do it with the confidence, *with the confidence of a...*

I can't even think of a decent metaphor, he thought.

Something about that office made him wither with apprehension. It didn't look that different from any other luxury high-rise office. There was just something about it that made Crawford feel three feet tall as soon as he walked in the door.

Intimidation. It was Lee's secret weapon.

"Hi, Kim. How are you?"

"I'm fine, Dr. Crawford. You?" Lee's trophy receptionist said.

"Not too bad."

"Lee here yet?" Crawford said, trying to be inconspicuous as he let his eyes travel from her shoulders to her hips to her legs.

"Yes, he is. Just a moment," she said.

She pressed the button on the intercom. "Mr. Burns, Dr. Crawford's here to see you."

"'Bout fucking time," he said.

"You may go on in, Dr. Crawford," Kim said nodding.

"Thank you." *Tramp*, Crawford thought.

"Dr. Crawford?"

"Yes?"

"Can I tell you something?"

"Certainly," he said, now looking into her eyes.

"I've been reading *Self-Esteem*. And I think it's really helpful."

"Good. Glad to hear it," he said nodding. He started past her.

"Dr. Crawford?"

He stopped again. "Yes."

"I'm always trying to improve myself. My mother always taught me the importance of that."

"Uh huh."

"I read one of your other books. The one called *Self-Confidence*. It helped me so much I read it three times."

"Uh huh."

"So what's the difference?"

"Sorry?"

"What's the difference between self-confidence and self-esteem?"

"Well, let me see. One paid for my master's degree, and the other's going to pay for my retirement."

Kim paused a moment. "Are you going to retire?"

"Excuse me," Crawford said, opening the door to Lee's office.

Crawford walked in as if he were meeting the boss for the first time. The carpet felt especially smooth for some reason. Lee sat behind his large desk, facing the window, looking more like an artist in contemplation than a busy publisher.

"Just a moment," Lee said, looking over the skyline. "I have these moments during the day when I have to just pause and congratulate myself for so much hard work." He laughed to himself. "I'm sitting in the clouds, you know."

"You know what my biggest dream has always been, Lee?"

"Your biggest dream?" Lee swung his chair around abruptly. "You're not here to weasel out of the promotionals are you?"

"No. Not exactly."

Lee took a deep breath and gave one his signature grins. "Sorry. You know what kind of business we're doing with *Self-Esteem*?"

"I think I have an idea," Crawford said calmly, taking a seat in one of the two chairs in front of Lee's desk.

"And that's your response?"

"Did I ever tell you what I've always dreamed of doing, Lee? All my life?"

Lee stood and scratched his chin. "Would you like a drink?"

"Would I like a drink?" The question immediately raised a red flag. Lee was up to something. "Are you offering me a drink of alcohol?"

Lee froze like a child caught shoplifting candy. "Haven't you been drinking? You look like you have. I mean, are you on or off these days?" he said with an affected tone of concern.

"I'm on," Crawford said reluctantly. "I mean, I drank last night."

"I thought so. You know normally I'd say no, but if you're, you know, on. Hell, we all fall down sometimes. It's part of the learning process from the time we're children." Lee went to the wet bar at the opposite end of the room and pulled out two glasses.

"I was saying..." Crawford continued.

"Yeah, yeah. I'm listening," Lee said, pouring the drinks.

"You know how we always talked about the direction of my writing career?"

"Hey you drove here, right? Please just have this one, okay?" Lee gave Crawford his drink, a Scotch and water on the rocks. Naturally, he didn't want to hear about Crawford's "dreams," but he figured it was part of his job. Maybe the drink would shut him up. "Your dream? I think I've heard about that, yeah." He gave Crawford a curious look. "Is everything okay?"

"No, but, you know. Things are tolerable. I'm trying to improve some things."

"You sound like a contestant in a beauty pageant." With a mock southern accent Lee said, "I've always dreamed of raising horses some-day." Lee shook his head. "I'm just kidding you, Jim."

Crawford was a little aggravated but tried not to show it. "I've al-ways wanted to write a novel. That's what I've wanted to..."

"Well then write one," Lee snapped. "What are you telling me for? I've known that since the day we met."

Crawford took a deep breath and said, "No more *Self Series*, Lee."

Lee begged Crawford's pardon. He thought he said no more *Self Series*.

"No more self-help at all."

Without skipping a beat, Lee pointed out that *Self-Esteem* had already sold a half a million copies — in just two weeks.

Crawford said that he was glad to hear it, but it wouldn't affect his decision.

Lee groaned. "I can't believe I have to give you this pep talk every time we are looking at the next project."

"We? Next project?"

"I'm your publisher, for Christ's sake, not your high school football coach."

Crawford pointed out he was a little of both.

"Please, Jim. Don't quit now. Every book you've written since *Self-Confidence* has a guaranteed million-plus sale. It doesn't take a genius to figure it out."

"Figure what out?" Crawford said, lifting his drink.

Lee felt like John Madden or Lou Holtz and it was time to give a pep talk that invoked the supernatural. "Figure out that this is what you were meant to do. This is what *God* created you for. And now you've decided to be a fucking *novelist*?" he said, taking Crawford's drink from him.

Shit, Crawford thought.

Lee sat down on his desk to catch his breath. "What do you want?" he said, putting Crawford's drink to his lips then putting it down.

"That's what I want," Crawford said calmly, "to do what I want."

"Have you lost your mind?"

"Yes, many times."

"You just hate the promotionals, don't you? The Hershey show. Is that the problem?"

"I hate this Happy Pappy bullshit the most. That's got to end."

Lee laughed. "No, no, no. That discussion is over, my friend. Contractually we can't get out of it. And besides, it brings in a ton of revenue for us and for nothing but a signature."

"I don't want it."

Lee gave his best unyielding look. "You signed the papers, Jim."

"Yeah. And I'm sorry I did. But it's made me realize a few things."

"Yeah, yeah, yeah. You've always wanted to be a *real* writer." Lee leaned toward Jim and with rare sincerity said the problem was that Crawford never had the self-esteem to be a real writer. Crawford stood up to leave, but Lee stopped him with a hand on his shoulder. "Just give it a week or two," Lee said. "You should keep writing these books while you can, while people are buying them." He was starting to sound like a sensible parent. "It won't last forever. You can always be a novelist later. That's the bottom line."

"The bottom line? I'm doing the Hershey show and then I'm done. No more self-help promotional book tours. No more prattle groups. That's the bottom line."

Lee was shaking his head. He couldn't believe Crawford's resolve. "Come on. Don't you feel satisfaction from helping people?"

"Shit. Helping what people?"

"Me, for one," Lee said.

He never helps me.

Dorothy was unboxing a new blender she had purchased three weeks before but hadn't opened because she had put it under the kitchen sink and forgotten about it.

Now, why did I buy this? she thought.

"Oh. It's got twenty-four speeds. That's why." Their old blender only had twenty. She unboxed the new one with the conviction of an economist who touts the importance of consumer spending.

And where does he go in the afternoon? Needs some time to think, huh. Yeah, I bet. Dorothy didn't really care about the blender. A saleswoman at the department store had suggested it to her, and out of sympathy more than anything she bought it. She was just using it to get her mind off a promise she had made to herself a long time ago: *If Jim ever starts drinking and cheating again, I'm leaving him. He can do one or the other, and I'll do my best to help him stop. But both — no way. No more.*

With Cal the clock was ticking. She didn't want her son to emulate his father, which she believed would happen eventually. Dorothy took the old blender and placed a sticky note on it reading "charity," and put the new one lovingly in its place. She sat down at the kitchen table and looked at it approvingly, wondering what she could blend. They hadn't used the old one too much, after all. She seemed to recall Cal making a milkshake with it, but then he grew tired of milkshakes.

Dorothy began to cry. She was struck by how sad it was that she had thrown out the first blender she and Jim bought as a couple. And now she felt embarrassed that she didn't even give it to charity. Jim was into margaritas at the time, and like someone who throws out all the ashtrays thinking it will get a loved one to stop smoking, she had scrapped the little five dollar contraption, and now she wanted it back — even though it only had three speeds.

I have thrown so many things away, she thought, wiping away her tears with a tissue. And she had. Since the Crawford family had made self-help millions, she had scrapped just about everything they had as a young, struggling couple. But there was just one thing she hadn't thrown out — her husband.

"And he deserves to be thrown out," she said out loud. "He goddam deserves it." *He blames me for all the bad things and credits me for none of the good.* And since the subject had become a talk show cliché — men and the women they take for granted — it made her feelings all the more difficult to communicate. Not just to her husband, but anyone.

"Yeah, yeah," she imagined Jim would say.

"I know, I know," some of her girlfriends might say.

"You have it so bad," they would all suggest.

She looked at the note that said "United Way" and thought before long she was going to have to donate her husband to charity — like that ghostly blender she now loved so much.

She put her head on the kitchen table and wept harder, wondering if pain really was the foundation of healing.

The traffic had improved, and Crawford was feeling pretty good about the way he handled Lee. What was he so worried about? It was *his* life. He had enough money to last a lifetime. It was a matter of priorities. He had been drinking lately. He had been unfaithful to his wife again. His son was spoiled rotten. He was at least *partially* to blame for those things and therefore he could change them. *Yes, I can do something.* Crawford could be incredibly optimistic after a bad night of drinking — not by deciding to take responsibility but by thinking of taking responsibility.

"Life is one big distraction," he once wrote in *Self-Respect.* "You can distract yourself down or distract yourself up. Go ahead and distract yourself up." Sometimes he thought that made sense.

I must have thought it made sense when I wrote it.

It was one of his more popular aphorisms, and he occasionally tried to think of it when he felt unfocused and preoccupied.

Go ahead and... oh shit.

The mobile phone rang and he picked it up.

"Hello." It was that voice again, the one he thought he dreamt that morning.

"I like your self-esteem," it said.

It was a male voice but... artificial.

"What self-esteem?" Crawford said instinctively, his hostility set off. "Who the hell is this?"

"I'm using your program. And it's already improving my self-esteem."

"How did you get this number? Hello?"

"You once wrote, 'If you want something bad enough, it will come to you almost automatically.' I'll just say it came to me automatically. You told me it would."

"What will come to you, asshole?" Crawford asked.

"Everything," he said quietly. "Everything you have. Everything will come to me. Everything."

Crawford hung up, then threw his car phone at the dash where the bulky thing bounced into the passenger side floor. Right away it rang again and Crawford leaned over, bobbing his head up over the dash to drive, but he couldn't reach it. Unbuckling his seat belt, he managed to grab it and hit the answer button. "Stop calling me!" he yelled, swerving toward the car next to him and back again. "Damn it!"

"I need to see you," a woman's voice said. "Jim?" It was Jenny. He'd almost rather have heard from the asshole caller. "I need to see you," she said again tenderly.

Crawford concentrated on the road. "Didn't anyone ever teach you that it's polite to ask if it's a bad time to call or not?"

"I need to see you," she said.

"Did you hear me?"

"Yes," she said. "I just ignored the question. Those kinds of things don't pertain to a person in love."

"*Pertain,*" Crawford thought rolling his eyes. *Controlling bitch.*

The traffic was starting to slow down again.

"What is it, Jenny? I can't do this. I told you that. I told you..."

"Now, Jim," she interrupted. I want you to come over *right now*."

Jenny had a strange way of making Crawford feel obligated to her. It was something about her voice — sultry, but innocent — that made him lose the resolve he had to end it.

"I can't," he said.

"Just for a little while."

"No."

She hung up.

It was like the booze: he knew he would regret it later. He even tried to talk himself out of it while he was on the way to her place.

No, no, no. Don't do it. Don't do it.

Jenny's apartment and the liquor store — at times they were like the same place, together a perilous safe house that Crawford at once loved and hated. They even went well together. Warmth and confidence and spirit, armor against the forces of uncertainty. Like a womb with a disease. Quiet, smooth, safe, deadly.

There was no use in trying to talk himself out of it for too long. It was there, waiting.

Hmm, don't pertain to a person in love.

I could use that somewhere, Crawford thought.

Just being inside Jenny's apartment could be as gratifying as the forbidden fruit of their lovemaking. It reminded Crawford of his younger days as an undergrad sitting in comfortably messy rooms drinking cheap booze and reading Steinbeck and Faulkner. More bohemian than his college digs, Jenny's place was strewn with an assortment of bric-a-brac she regarded as fine art — paintings from friends and former lovers, black and white photographs she had taken in college, and various figurines she had been collecting since childhood. Crawford jokingly called her place "Harper's Bazaar," a play on her last name.

Crawford stepped into Jenny's apartment still thinking about how he had accomplished something that morning — he had successfully told Lee he wanted a change (or rather, began the process of telling Lee he wanted a change), and for that reason he was feeling a weight off his shoulders. He also knew that since he was on a roll, he might as well cut this cancerous relationship with Jenny out of his life as well.

"Would you like a drink?" she asked nervously. "You're not on the wagon, are you?"

"Not currently," he said. "I'll have one. Sure. Just one."

Jenny gave a slight look of disapproval — not for his drinking, but for his demeanor as he awkwardly sat in a lone chair that divided the kitchen from the living room.

"Sit in the living room," she said.

He moved toward the couch. No, he thought. *You're not going to have power over me that easily. You're not going to treat me like a child.*

As he was told, he walked to the living room and sat on the couch. He nervously moved his hands over his thighs, feeling a sense of dread about how this little get-together could develop once he revealed his new determination to end their affair.

"So why did you act so mad on the phone?" she asked, sitting across from him on a seventies egg chair she'd found at a garage sale.

Uh huh, passive aggression, Crawford thought. *Always when she sits in that damn hippie chair.*

"Jim?" she said, raising her eyebrows.

The couch was a large pillowy beast that made Crawford feel it was about to swallow him whole. "Sorry?" he asked, trying to retrieve one of the pillows from under one buttock, realizing she had made him sit on the couch for tactical reasons.

"You yelled at me on the phone."

"I'm sorry," he mumbled quickly.

"You yelled 'Who the hell is this?' Why'd you say that?"

"I don't know. I just said it."

"You just said it?" she said skeptically.

"I've been getting prank calls." Crawford looked down at his drink. He knew he wouldn't have just one. "Jenny, I got drunk last night in my study."

"You shouldn't do that," she said.

Crawford put the drink to his lips, then stopped. "I know," he said, putting it on the coffee table in front of him. "I know." Jenny had an advantage when he was drinking, he knew. But she always had an advantage. He always drank with her.

"So how's the novel?" Jenny said, as if grasping for something to say.

He looked at the ice cubes in the glass. *We can't do this.*

"We can't do what?"

Did I say that? "We can't do this," he said, mustering just enough courage to look at her directly.

She swirled away from him in the egg chair, cocking her head back dramatically. "I thought we'd been through this, Jim."

"I'm trying to be nice about it."

"You're trying to get rid of me," she said, swirling back.

"Listen to me."

Exterior, night, outside Jenny's apartment. Crawford comes out of the door. He looks tired. He might be drinking again. Jenny follows behind.

"I told you I have to go," Crawford yells at the young woman.

"You always have to go," she yells back.

"I'm just supposed to walk out on everything, right? My son, my wife, everything?"

Jenny looks very determined.

"You're so damn lucky I don't tell everyone what a con man you are!"

Click.

They are facing each other, snarling, prizefighters outside the ring.

"Go ahead and tell them," he says. He looks around nervously. He lowers his voice. "Anyone with any sense already knows!"

Click. What perfection.

"Are you going to call me?" she asks.

He gets in his car.

"Probably not."

He drives away.

"You better!" she screams. "You fucking better!"

My, my. Poor girl. Such low self-esteem.

It had been another shitty day at school and Cal was looking forward to seeing his new friend Darrin Davis. *Or is it Jarvis?* Cal wondered.

Cal brought his Porsche to a screaming halt in front of Tom's Pool Hall and instantly realized it was a bad idea. Not here. It attracted the wrong attention. With the car inches from the curb, Cal lowered his head into the passenger's side to look for his comrade, who wasn't there. Several young men, most of them out of high school — some graduates, but mostly dropouts — stood just outside the double-doors talking and smoking. Tom's wasn't Cal's kind of place. Not that he didn't like its peeling paint and smoky, old-fashioned charm. It was just too tough for a pampered kid who lived in Beverly Hills, especially one with a fifty thousand dollar car.

"My God," one black kid in his teens said, sucking on a cigarette. "This here boy just robbed the damn bank."

"Maybe we should apprehend him," another said, laughing.

Be cool. Look tough. Look ahead. Don't care.

Cal was giving a performance he knew no one was buying. He was a pussy, plain and simple, just like his old man.

The door burst opened, and Cal flinched. It was his friend, appearing as he always did, out of thin air.

"Damn, what you so uptight about, boy?" he said, sticking his head in the car. "You smokin' better shit than me?"

"Just get in," Cal said.

"Hey, why so nervous?"

Darrin got in the car and shut the door without looking the least bit worried about the taunts from the guys on the street. Darrin's slightly more radical Goth look — standard black attire with several earrings and a plain black nostril stud — highlighted Cal's simpler suburban version of the same. His 220-pound body brought the right side of the car down slightly as he put the vinyl case that held his trusty pool cue to his side.

"What up, bitch. Nice car."

"Goddam faggots," someone yelled.

Darrin leaned out the window. "Hey! Go shoot some pool. Go spend your last quarter on a videogame. Fuckin' losers."

Cal stomped on the gas and the tires squealed beneath them. Darrin enjoyed the speed more than Cal did. "Yeah, that's it!"

Cal often thought about Darrin never paying any attention to thugs, or to any of the other people that scared him so much. It was the basis of Cal's respect. Darrin might be a freak, but to Cal he was the coolest guy he'd ever met, period. No one ever bothered Darrin, and Cal knew that it had nothing to do with what he had, what he drove, or anything else. What was important was what Darrin didn't have: fear. And for that he got respect.

"Whew. This sure is a nice car, bitch," Darrin said running his hand across the dash. "How does it make you feel to own a car like this?" It was an oddly sensible question from Darrin. "Has your ego gotten bigger?"

Cal started to feel awkward.

"Has your dick gotten bigger too?"

Cal didn't know what else to do but answer directly, "No."

"Sure? Maybe you should look."

"Maybe I should," Cal said looking straight ahead.

Darrin grinned, then began slowly humming the *Happy Pappy Song*.

"Why are you doing that?" He looked at Darrin, who just stared ahead and continued humming. "Okay, okay," Cal said. "Enough of that shit."

Darrin acted like Cal wasn't even there. "Be kind *hmm hmm hmm* be fond *hmm hmm hmm...*"

"Do you want to walk?" Cal shouted.

Darrin stopped humming. "Damn, man. Relax. I was just about to give you something for your self-esteem. That's all." Darrin reached into his pants pocket and held up a small baggie of white powder.

Cal nodded. "Fuckin' awesome!"

"Oh yes," Darrin said.

FIVE

The tuxedo made Crawford uncomfortable. It always did. The jacket was too big and the trousers were too small, especially in the crotch. As he drove, he questioned why he hadn't bought a new one in almost five years.

Buying clothes is such a hassle, he thought, shifting his penis to a more comfortable position. A new tux never crossed his mind until he had to wear one, probably because he didn't like to go to events where they were mandatory.

"Humans have a tendency to be ill-prepared for things they don't want to endure, hence the importance of deliberate effort," he once wrote in *Self-Confidence*.

Yeah, yeah. What stupid shit.

Dorothy was different. She enjoyed dressing up and going to high-brow events. It's one of life's simple pleasures, as she put it. She felt that her husband's cynicism about such occasions was just the intellectual posturing of a grouchy old man. She concluded he enjoyed protesting about such things — that was one of *his* simple pleasures. So, considering that, there was nothing to worry about. Each of them, in their own way, was going to have a good time.

The California University of Arts and Sciences auditorium parking lot was filled with mid-range luxury cars and formal attire.

A trip to the university campus always included burning contempt for the people Crawford ran into, and an event like this made his disdain break out like a nasty rash. Crawford looked down upon most of the professors as shallow poseurs who didn't respect the sanctity of the institution that employed them. It was bad enough that the student body was filled with slackers trying as hard as they could to do absolutely nothing. They were supposed to be young and stupid. But college professors that taught subjects like philosophy, literature and psychology, they were supposed to uphold a few standards. They were supposed to carry themselves in a certain way. *But this bunch*, they were the types that showed up to a university event and talked about their new cars, their recent vacations and what they had read in some interior design magazine.

But who was Crawford kidding? He was the most embarrassing guest of them all. Doctor Popular, *Doctor TV*. How could he call anyone a fraud?

At least I'm aware of it.

"I don't know what you're fretting over," Dorothy said enthusiastically. "Everyone's going to be happy to see you. This is your alma mater. They love you here."

"Uh huh," Crawford groaned, trying to straighten his awkward tuxedo.

The display above the auditorium read "Dr. Phillip Peters Honorary Banquet." And below that, written in graceful script, "Helmut Vogel Fellowship."

Crawford read the lavish billboard and knew it was time to paint on his meet-and-greet façade and do some bullshitting. Just inside the reception area, Crawford saw them — the men he despised most after himself. He first saw their cocktails — gin martinis — resting lazily in their hands, promising to embellish their mindless chatter. Dr. Jay Berry and Dr. Albert Scott, the kiss ass twins, as Crawford used to call them back in university, two guys who were always together, both with an annoying penchant for brownnosing everyone in a position of power — except for Crawford — while looking down on everyone else. And there they were, same as always, talking big talk, their giant bellies quaking as they laughed at their own stupid jokes.

"I think Phil deserves to be dean of the graduate school more than anyone," Berry said with a sudden affected humility. "He sure worked for it."

Jay Berry, what a bastard, that sorry sackashit that pulled pranks on me, pranks he would never admit to, even after he finished his doctorate. Yeah, of course, there's his yes-man, Albert, still blowing smoke up his own tired old ass and everyone else's.

Berry leaned over to whisper into Scott's ear. "I'm surprised they didn't ask Mr. Self-Esteem over there if he didn't want the position."

Dorothy was distracted by the crowd, smiling and saying hello to people. But Crawford was looking carefully at his two old rivals, wondering what nasty remarks they were making about him.

"Crawford?" Scott said softly to Berry. "He doesn't have time to be dean. He's got a new book and appearances to make. Now he's going after the children's market. A busy man he is."

"Yes, I understand he's putting out an exercise video," Berry added with a snicker.

Crawford was imagining what they were saying. He also knew he couldn't stop their mockery from bothering him, which bothered him even more.

They laughed quietly to themselves, looking up at Crawford, feigning to have just seen him, or he thought so anyway.

"Jim," Berry said. "How the hell are you? Long time, no see."

Crawford decided to go ahead and put on airs. It was more insulting. "Great. Jay. Good to see you. Albert, how are you?"

"Fine, Jim."

Dorothy joined her husband, standing obediently at his side.

"Dorothy, you look as lovely as ever."

"Thank you, Dr. Scott. Congratulations on your new research grant."

He was surprised, or acted like he was. "Thank you so much, Dorothy. But how would you know about that?"

Crawford thought his response was almost paranoid.

"Oh, a little birdie told me," she said.

"Well, thank you, dear."

Berry chimed in, "But we were just talking about your latest success, Jim."

"Congratulations on your new book," Dr. Scott added.

Crawford was clearly uncomfortable. "Thanks, gentlemen. I appreciate it."

Then there was an awkward silence. This was the real insult — saying congratulations and nothing more.

Scott lifted his martini and looked directly at Crawford. "Can I get you folks something?" Berry grinned. "Oh, I forgot," Scott said quickly. "You no longer imbibe."

"No," Crawford said with a forced smile.

Then Scott turned to Dorothy. "Can I get you something?"

"No, thank you. Will you excuse us a moment?" Dorothy said, leading Crawford into the main hall.

"Those jackasses. They don't think I know they talk behind my back? What idiots."

Crawford turned again to give them a hateful look and Dorothy directed him away. "Ignore them, dear. If they talk behind your back they're just jealous of your success, that's all."

"Jealous?" Crawford tried to laugh. "They're downright hateful. They think I'm getting too much attention, too much money. They want fame and fortune more than I do."

"That's jealousy. And why do you care what they think?" Dorothy said, in a motherly voice. "My God, do I have to keep giving you your own advice?"

"No you don't," he said, before taking a breath and calming himself. His discomfort, he theorized, came from conceding that his former doctoral classmates were right, that he was a fraud and a bad joke.

The Crawfords walked in through the main entrance, down the aisle, then up the stairs that lead to the long table that sat at the front of the hall. "Just think of all the things you tell other people," Dorothy said, pointing to their assigned seats. "Follow your own advice. It works."

"Does it?"

Crawford looked down at his name written on a folded card in front of their seats just to the left of the podium. "Dr. James and Dorothy Crawford." Crawford particularly took note of the "Dr." in front of his name. It was ambiguous — a Doctor of Philosophy, a PhD, or a doctor that supposedly heals the sick. Either will do. Take your pick. You just couldn't pick both.

I need a doctor, he thought.

Or a drink.

Crawford frequently thought about his own advice — the same advice that had made him a fortune — but he only believed it while he was making it up, and probably not even then. *Stop negative behavior and face life on its own terms and live a happy life forever and ever. Uh huh.*

But the content hadn't changed much over the years, only the way it was composed. Since the completion of his second book, *Self-Worth*, Crawford began to notice an odd relationship between his writing and his behavior. Increasingly, the writing of these feel-good books made him feel bad, creating a depression that would last for weeks, sometimes months. It was starting to impede the writing process until Crawford ultimately worked out a deal with himself. He had to "postpone" the disparaging thoughts and depression until after the work was completed, bribing himself with the promise of a nice long bender once it was done.

It took writing *Self-Respect* before Crawford became comfortable with this arrangement. Perhaps he just learned to live with it, but it also made the drinking binge that followed much longer and more extreme.

Then he began to believe that the awareness of this pattern was going to drive him mad. Each book was more successful than the last, creating high expectations for the next in the series. And after each book was published, the drinking relapse was markedly worse, making the hole deeper and deeper. So he rationalized the situation, telling himself that his experiences fed his "art." He would dry out and talk to his wife about "calling the muse," even though the drunkenness came after the fact. Eventually he would get sober and write a book about how to get happy and feel good. And after that he would be disgustingly drunk again.

"Any writer who says he writes 12 hours a day is full of shit," he told his editor, Martha Ginsberg, on the phone one night, just after falling off the wagon the day before.

"Not necessarily," she said. "It certainly isn't impossible."

"You know what I mean, Martha."

Martha had edited all four *Self Series* books with such remarkable speed and independence that Crawford often wondered why she didn't write her own self-help books. She almost never called Crawford, even to discuss changes she was making to his manuscript. She just did them. Both Crawford and Lee liked it this way. It was very easy. No politics, no problems, no complaints — just great work.

But Martha was a professional. She didn't like discussing the nuts and bolts of composition, especially with Jim, especially when he was drunk. It was just a job to her, not nearly as fun as working in her garden at home.

And Crawford, being aware of Martha's temperament and skill, couldn't shake the contradictions their relationship presented. *She* was the normal one. *She* was the happy one. *She* was the one who should be telling people how to improve their lives, Crawford knew. But Martha Ginsberg was uninterested in any of that. She was merely a book editor. Her problems were too few to give a damn about the rest of the fucked up world.

"You're so much better than I am," Crawford once told her after she called him to question the context of a phrase, finding him completely inebriated.

"Better off, perhaps," she said, and changed the subject.

That response would stick with Crawford for a long time. Strangely, he only remembered it when he was alone and drunk. Or out in public wishing he was alone and drunk.

Even with intermittent TV appearances over the previous ten years, Crawford could still get nervous when it came to speaking in public, especially at social gatherings, and especially with academics. He kept telling himself that the little ceremony they were having in honor of Peters becoming dean and receiving a fellowship wasn't exactly a *social* gathering and it was barely *academic*.

And what difference did it make?

Crawford kept looking over at Peters, trying to distract himself from the audience in front of him that was now a mass of ghostly silhouettes. Crawford hoped the sight of Peters would help his jitters, but it didn't.

Peters sat quietly on the opposite side of the podium from Dorothy, smiling as Crawford delivered his introduction. W*hat a perfect example of a legitimate scientist in the field of Behavioral Psychology,* Crawford thought. *If there is such a person.* With his neatly trimmed beard and spectacles, Peters almost looked like Freud — without the dog, the cocaine addiction and the ridiculous ambition of explaining the human mind.

"I can't think of anyone who deserves the honor of being dean of the graduate school more than Dr. Phillip Peters."

Mediocre remark.

As the audience applauded, Crawford realized he'd just said what he'd overheard Berry say half an hour before, almost verbatim. But strangely he started to relax a bit.

Nothing's original. Keep going.

"Phil and I have known each other for over seventeen years now, and I know of no one more dedicated to the field of psychology than he is." Crawford hoped that was sufficient. "Ladies and Gentlemen, the new dean of graduate studies in psychology here at our marvelous university, and this year's recipient of the Helmut Vogel Fellowship. Dr. Phillip Peters."

The audience broke into applause, but after a few seconds Crawford didn't hear it. His thoughts about Peters drowned out the noise. His thoughts were a cruel mother pointing to an example of the person he should be. He stood to the side and shook his old friend's hand then saw the audience stand and applaud. He walked over to his assigned seat and waited for the audience to sit down so he could do the same.

Peters awkwardly pushed his mouth toward the microphone and said thank you. Crawford thought of how humble he was in the face of such admiration. No ego, no attempt to impress.

That's why he's the best.

"Thank you so much," Peters said nodding. "The University. The members of our department. Thank you all. It's certainly a pleasure to see an old doctoral comrade of mine who's gone on to bigger and better things," he said smiling at Crawford.

The audience clapped again, but not so loud.

"I guess he had the self-esteem and I didn't."

The room filled with vociferous laughter. Crawford didn't appreciate the remark, even though he knew Peters didn't mean to be cruel. Nevertheless, he now felt more uncomfortable.

And this damn crotch is killing me.

During his brief speech, Peters never mentioned Crawford again. He thanked his colleagues in the department. He thanked the members of the administration for their appointment. He thanked the board at the Vogel Fellowship for believing in his research. He seemed to thank everyone but Crawford.

By the end of the event, Dorothy, seeing that her husband's insecurities had been aggravated by the experience, was especially attentive. "Are you okay, dear? Did something bother you tonight?"

"Can we just go now? I'll feel much better when we're on our way home. Let's just go. Right now."

They both walked to the lobby, with Crawford two steps ahead as Dorothy continued to smile and say hello to others.

"That means tonight, sweetheart," he said under his breath, periodically nodding to the other guests.

"Okay, okay," Dorothy said before grabbing her husband's arm. "Let me just say hello to Joanne Brady over there," she said, tiptoeing away with her just-one-minute finger in the air.

I'll never get her out of here, he thought.

Crawford stood in the foyer with people nodding as they passed. It reminded him just how much he needed his wife. She was the backbone of the family. She'd always been the backbone of the family, keeping them together during the worst trouble, most of it from Crawford's behavior. Then he pulled a rabbit out of a hat. He wrote *Self-Confidence*. But his pot of gold worsened his drinking, his womanizing, and everything else that gave Dorothy grief. After achieving some success, he told himself he had been acquitted of all charges. But he knew he would not have been able to pull it off without her. She suggested writing the book in the first place as a way of helping him through his recovery, and he lashed out at her. He was working on a novel. He was an artist. He couldn't do something so unimaginative if he wanted to. He was wrong.

Crawford watched his wife and thought about how beautiful she was. She looked more beautiful now, actually. Brief moments of their 18-year marriage were flashing before him. What a bastard he'd been, and how impossibly unreasonable. And how wonderfully she'd dealt with it, with caring and diligence. And how had he paid her back for her years of loyalty and sacrifice? By grabbing a bottle at the first moment of fear or guilt, and by having childish affairs to placate his ego-driven longings. Crawford felt stings of guilt all over his body. Then his inner dialogue was interrupted.

"I think people need to be more aware of their own behavior, now more than ever," she said with a slight southern drawl.

"Excuse me?" Crawford asked.

The woman — overweight and middle-aged with an ashen complexion — wore a lime-green dress that looked like it could glow in the dark, too ambitious for a woman her size.

She continued to speak as if Crawford had said nothing. "I think you've helped people do that more than anyone in a long time."

"What's that?" Crawford asked uncomfortably.

She was speaking too loud already. "I *said*," she nodded, "people need to be more aware of their own behavior now more than ever. And I think you've helped people do that."

"Well, thanks very much," he said, trying to turn away.

The praise of an idiot is more insulting than opprobrium from a genius.

"I was amazed in your first book how much you thought about your own behavior. That's commendable. Not many people can look at how they're destroying themselves and the lives of others and be completely honest about it. That's something you can pat yourself on the back for," she said with a wink.

Thanks, bitch, Crawford thought.

"But your subsequent books don't mention any of these personal problems at all. You've changed."

What are you my mother? Go away, idiot.

"And I have a problem I'd like to discuss with you, James."

She used his first name. Crawford wanted to tell this lard ass to go buy a mirror and get to know herself a little better, but he resisted. Boy he could use a drink. "Excuse me," he said, stepping past her.

"But, James. I want you to take a look at my *Self Series* workbook.

Fuck your workbook, he thought walking away.

"But my workbook, James" she said with the whimper of a neglected child.

"That's Dr. Crawford to you, not James," Crawford said bluntly. "Where's my wife?"

Dorothy looked like she was enjoying the conversation with her old friend, and Crawford wasn't going to rush her. He motioned her to the side. "I've got to get out of here," he said in her ear.

"I'm ready when you are," she said.

"No. Take your time. I want you to," Crawford said. "It's turning into a counseling session here. I'll wait for you at the side entrance. Take your time, dear." He kissed her on the cheek. Crawford sneaked out the side door wishing he was drunk enough not to feel self-conscious about it.

. . .

Peters was sitting alone, smoking his pipe and appearing to stare into the ceiling of the light pollution that blocked the night sky. Crawford had so much respect for his old friend that his inclination was to leave him undisturbed, but he desperately wanted to talk.

"I thought you gave up smoking, Phil."

"I did. About a million times," he said smiling. "I know. That's an old joke."

Crawford sat next to Peters on a bench that was nothing more than a concrete slab. Even outside the staff entry, surrounded by crushed soda cans and cigarette butts, Peters still looked the venerable academic.

"It's probably not a good thing for a dean to have such a common addiction," Crawford said. "You need a more unusual one."

"I think you're quoting something I said to you about 10 or 11 years ago, pal," he said, taking another puff off his pipe.

"But alcoholism," Crawford said looking at the ground, "it's a little more exotic than nicotine addiction. Supposed to be, anyway."

As a rule, Peters was skillfully standoffish when it came to emotional matters, particularly outside the formal environment of his office. But speaking to Crawford was different. He had to ask him how things were, not just as a friend but also as a therapist. That's how their relationship had been for years.

"How are you, Jim? Everything all right?"

Crawford answered that he was okay. He was afraid to look at Peters, like he was a child about to confess a transgression to his father. "I'm doing that stupid show next week — you know, to plug my new book."

"Oh, yeah?"

"Yeah, I hate that shit."

"What? Jan Hershey Live? That's one of the top shows on TV. You don't want to do it?"

"I look at what you've accomplished over the last decade and I just feel embarrassed. Four great, serious volumes of research, tons of articles. Now you're head of the department. Me, I went off to become a snake oil salesman."

Crawford gave Peters a small grin as if to say he was kidding, if just a little.

"You didn't mention my teen counseling center," Peters said, pretending to be serious. Then he laughed.

"Oh, yeah. That too," Crawford said, now looking at Peters directly.

"Your books are great, Jim. People love them, and therefore you're really helping them. Most people would say you're a greater success than I am."

Crawford appreciated this compliment, but he could sense a slight indignation in Peters' tone. *But surely not*, he thought. *He's too evolved for such small-mindedness.* "I don't know what people say. I'm getting out of this business, Phil," Crawford said, now showing a modest confidence. "Soon, I'm getting out for good."

Peters blew smoke from his pipe. "I'm not going to try and talk you out of it, if that's what you're looking for."

"No. That's not what I'm looking for."

"You could probably teach advanced psych here if you wanted," Peters said, looking at his watch.

Crawford took this as being an offer of consolation, but didn't want it regardless. "No. I'm going to finally finish my first novel. I never say to people that I'm going to quit and write fiction because that's what I've been writing for years." He smiled. "I'm going to write a novel — then I'll write another. It's what I've always wanted to do. I just never had the courage or something."

Peters raised his eyebrows. "The self-esteem?"

Crawford couldn't help but give Peters a dirty look. "That's the second time tonight."

Peters laughed. "Lighten up, would you? You're wealthy. You have a beautiful family. You're in good health." Peters turned over his pipe, tapping out the ashes with his shoe. "Appreciate life a little. Quit grumbling about some talk show. We all have to do things we don't want to. So what? You think I want to be here tonight?"

Crawford relaxed a bit. "Oh yeah? Appreciate life, huh?"

"Of course," Peters said, standing. "It's the only thing that makes people happy, to appreciate life. We're just spoiled kids. We'll complain about anything. You know that." He paused a moment then grinned like an encouraging uncle. "Don't you?"

Crawford didn't know what to say. "I guess I forgot."

Peters pointed to the sky and told Crawford to look at it. Crawford looked, but could only see the haze of light. "Many of the great philosophers have said that you look up at the stars and you realize what trivial little problems we humans are down here."

"You mean *have*," Crawford said.

"Yeah, sure. Whatever." Either Peters had lost his momentum or he was being rude. "The stars always tell us something, don't they?"

"The problem is," Crawford said, "you can't see the stars here. See?" he said, pointing to the sky.

"Maybe that's it." Peters said, shelving the subject. "By the way, you might not want to teach, but how about being on a board of advisors I'm putting together for the fall semester? Might look good on your résumé."

"What would I have to do?"

"Almost nothing. Give your opinion."

"Oh, I get paid big bucks for that, you know," Crawford said as he looked up at the sky.

"Uh huh," Peters grunted with an almost cynical grin that Crawford didn't notice. "Think about it."

They sat in silence just looking at the sky.

"Sorry, think about what?" Crawford said.

On the way home, Crawford avoided conversation, feeling afraid he might say something to Dorothy he would regret. Thoughts of Jenny were creeping into his mind. His one-word answers to Dorothy's questions were not anger this time but self-loathing. The revived affair had been going on for several weeks, and even though he felt the urge, Crawford could only maintain what little order he had in his life if he put off a confession to Dorothy another day. *One day at a time.*

As they were pulling into the driveway, Dorothy tried to get a complete sentence out of her husband. "So what did you and Phil talk about?"

"Not much. You know Phil, nonchalant as always."

Peters was an anchor that brought back Crawford's respect for psychology's highest goals. Whenever he was around Peters, he realized there was in fact much to learn about human behavior from serious study, and that perhaps this study could improve people's lives. Peters brought to mind Freud, Jung, Skinner, Maslow, Eysenck and Szasz — all of whom still meant something to Crawford. They were the originators, the men with the ideas, the framers of the Constitution of the mind. But Crawford hadn't come up with a unique concept since completing his master's thesis. After that, it was one rehash after another. Even the quotations cited in his books — from Plato to Shakespeare to Dickens to Mark Twain to Bob Dylan — were all straight out of *Bartlett's Quotations*, nearly all of them sprinkled in without much understanding of the original context of the quote, or for that matter, the significance of the quote to his own work. It didn't matter. His followers loved it, and for a short time he felt like an originator himself.

But wait! Crawford had come up with *one* concept since that terrible thesis paper, one that he presented in his first book, *Self-Confidence.* It even caused some discussion — not much, but some — in the halls of psychology. It was his *Child-Adult-Self Theory.*

There had been the *Inner Child Concept* (or ICC), the contemporary version accredited to the likes of John Crenshaw, "America's foremost personality development expert" (as he proclaimed himself). Crenshaw's theory states that the key to discovering "the true self" is to discover the "inner child" of which you must become your own parent.

Become your own parent?

Crenshaw and others like him declared that only by confronting the indignity of one's upbringing could an individual finally purge the cruel and authoritarian system of parenting that damages the child and creates a repressed adult, destroying the "true" self, which never had a chance to exist.

Huh?

Simply put, people need to get in touch with themselves as children — love that child, nurture it — so they can get in touch with their "real self."

Bullshit. Crawford, aware that Crenshaw's inner child spent week after week dominating the *New York Times* non-fiction bestseller list, set his sights on confronting Crenshaw's (and not his own) inner child — and with more than just a toy radio. As a result, Crawford came up with the "adult-as-child" theory, which he later called the "child-adult-self." Dorothy had initially been concerned that there would be a lawsuit if Crawford didn't distinguish his theory clearly from Crenshaw's, but Crawford was way ahead of her. His concept would be different, a lot different. He would follow Crenshaw's theory in maintaining that the adult was carrying around the unhealed wounds of childhood. But his concept would differ by proclaiming that yes, there was still a sick child inside — but *independent* of its adult self. No, that child didn't need to be "healed" with love and affection. The "parent of self" needed to use its own authoritarian measures to control the *child-adult-self* that was trying to take control. *Yeah, that's it.* Crawford had come up with something monumental, he thought — something that would have housewives plopping down $19.95 by the station-wagon load.

"The inner-child is not a part of you. You are an adult. Your child-self exists as it did when you were a child. You grew up. It did not. These two beings — you and your child-self — are not one person in two manifestations. They are actually two separate individuals vying for control of your being."

Crawford's revelation came about while arguing with Dorothy over his drinking — at the time, the worst it had ever been. She had called his drinking "childish," which gave him an idea. It was his *child-self* controlling his *adult-self* therefore creating a *child-adult self* which had an inclination towards drunkenness. *That was it!* His child-self, who admired the self-indulgences of drunk old Uncle Jerry, had the alcohol problem, not his adult-self. Crawford told his wife that his drinking wasn't so much "childish" as it was "child-selfish," a term he later coined as a part of the *child-adult-self vocabulary*.

"This is why I don't have any self-confidence," a shitfaced Crawford told his wife, putting on the eyes of a sick puppy.

Dorothy thought the theory of the *child-adult-self* made sense, and perhaps this was something he could pursue. He needed to pursue something, she thought. And without Crawford's knowledge, she did a mass mailing of query letters to publishers and agents with a book proposal.

"My theory concedes [sic] that self-confidence is a matter of telling the child inside to behave," she wrote in her husband's name.

And later, to Crawford's disbelief, it worked. It certainly worked for a man named Lee Burns.

Crawford would later write, "Discipline your child-self. Do it today! He or she will listen to you."

Crawford wasn't in the mood to discipline his child-self that evening. He was in the mood for drink. After all, Crawford was parking the car in the driveway these days because he was superstitious about it being in the garage next to Cal's.

I even avoid his car, Crawford thought. *Pathetic.*

"Cal better be in bed," Dorothy said.

"He's okay," Crawford reassured her, trying to shun the topic. "Is there any of that coffee fudge ice cream left?" Crawford asked as a diversion.

Crawford walked to the front door just a few steps behind Dorothy, watching her look through her purse for her keys. His abhorrence of Dorothy's butt that morning was forgotten. As often happened after a day spent hung over, Crawford was overcome with a healthy affection for his wife, a physical one bordering on teenage horniness. It was probably best to keep the passion at bay, but a little tenderness couldn't hurt. As they reached the front door, Crawford grabbed Dorothy by the waist and pulled her close.

"Come here, honey," he said tenderly. "You're something else. You know that?"

She was surprised.

He kissed her on the neck then held her close. It felt good to him. And like that warm feeling of security he got from a first drink, he couldn't let go if he wanted to.

"Wow," she said. "I guess you need to talk to Phil more often."

Dorothy didn't know what to think, but she suspected something. Over the years, she had noticed this kind of behavior only when Jim was up to no good. But she indulged him nevertheless.

Perhaps it was only the drinking, she thought. And we can work through that together.

Crawford kissed Dorothy's neck as she held her hand to the side of his face.

"What's that?" she said.

"What?"

Crawford thought she'd found something incriminating, though that would have been impossible.

"That," she said, looking at the ground.

To the left of the front door was a package wrapped in brown paper. It was small, like a paperback novel. Dorothy picked it up, and just then Crawford felt an uneasy stiffness come over him. Could it be from Jenny? Could she be trying to get revenge by telling Dorothy of their affair? *But with a book?* Dorothy could have said "boo" and Crawford would have jumped.

The package had a small note attached, which Dorothy pulled off. It was a three-inch piece of paper, like a small postcard folded in half. Dread ran through Crawford's mind.

The note was handwritten, and Dorothy read it aloud. "Stage One complete. I'm going to follow your program to the very end. Love, Happy Pappy." Dorothy giggled. "Happy Pappy?"

"Let me see that," Crawford said, hiding his relief that it wasn't from Jenny. Crawford's hand shook. Then he realized out loud: "It's probably Jay and Albert." Crawford looked over his shoulder and scanned the street as if they might be watching. "Yep, probably them, a prank from them."

"Berry and Scott? Are you kidding? We saw them tonight."

Crawford huffed as he scanned the lawns across the street.

"Dr. Berry wouldn't do that," she said.

"It's the two of them, Dorothy. All they did in graduate school was pull tricks on me. And they did it together as a team."

Dorothy wasn't in the mood to argue. "Uh huh. We've had this conversation before."

"They just wanted to make sure this evening was ruined for me."

Dorothy noticed that her husband's hands were shaking, as if he were about to strangle the former classmates right there. All she could do was try to calm him down. "Wait a minute. What makes you so sure it's a prank?" she asked. "You don't even know what it is. Look, it's probably nothing." Dorothy ripped open the package and pulled out the contents. *A videotape.* "See? It's nothing."

Crawford grabbed it from her and turned it over. It had no label, no writing, nothing. "A videotape," Crawford said. "Something to aggravate me, no doubt."

"Berry and Scott were at the banquet tonight, Jim."

Crawford ignored her. "It's probably a porn film or something. You know, with the Happy Pappy theme song playing or something like that. That's the kind of thing they would do."

"And what would be so horrible about that?"

"What? What's so horrible? Berry and Scott did this kind of thing all the time when we were in school, Dorothy."

"Did what?"

"Pulled pranks on me."

"Okay. You've told me that before. And?"

"You have no idea. They were elaborate."

"Elaborate?"

"Very elaborate. And they still haunt me, their pranks. There's never any resolution." Crawford was looking at the tape, convinced of his conclusion. "Got to make sure I know my place. That's their job."

"I think you're overreacting, Jim. We don't even know what it is. Look, if it's a porn film then we'll just watch it together. Okay?" she said with a wink.

No, I'll watch this by myself, Crawford thought. He also thought of getting out of those pants that were choking his balls. Crawford wouldn't allow himself to consider a worse scenario: that the package might have been left by a deranged fan who wanted to do very bad things.

SIX

Cal heard a car door slam but didn't pay much attention. He was sitting on the edge of his bed talking to Darrin on the phone, listening to his strange proposition. It had been two hours since his last hit of weed and his high was in recession. Cal hated coming down. It made him feel groggy, like waking up after a night of eating too many sweets. And coming down from that other stuff, Cal was both restless and lethargic. But he just didn't feel like smoking more.

Cal had sensed his new friend might help him overcome his troubles at home and at school, but Darrin was already starting to make Cal a little uneasy. Darrin was a self-proclaimed "idea man," and Cal liked that about him. But Darrin had an idea that made Cal nervous. All Cal could do was keep telling himself that Darrin was the coolest and that this thing was probably okay.

Cal first met Darrin at a dirty, rundown used bookstore deep in the Valley called Zip Dance Used Books & Comics — not that Cal read comics or books or much of anything at all other than magazine articles on Rotten Tamales. Cal's pot connection, Larsen Finn — or "Larney," as he was called — worked part-time at Zip Dance helping its owner, a Cuban smuggler of mostly cigarettes and electronics, load, unload and sometimes deliver contraband, most of it from South America. Larney was a skinny white boy with greasy hair and crooked, auburn-colored teeth who wore the same filthy, hole-ridden Aerosmith T-shirt every day. But despite his unkempt appearance, Larney was very serious about a number of things — especially his illegal activities. For example, it angered Larney when his two-dozen or so pot customers dropped by his "regular job" for a purchase, which he warned them not to do. Larney knew that his little nickel and dime marijuana racket would not sit well with his boss, Oscar Arroyo (or "Fidel," as most people called him), since it could bring just enough heat to put Fidel in the joint. Larney was so afraid of Fidel that he couldn't quit his job to concentrate on his pot business, which started to pick up after he got seed money from working at the store. Unfortunately, that meant more buyers coming by his day job to procure.

"Just fucking page me, dumbass," Larney often said to ridicule a stoner out of the store.

But Larney was different with Cal. Larney admired Cal's fish-out-of-water status, attending a shitty public school in the valley while living in the lap of luxury in the Hills. He thought Cal's dad was the coolest self-help author since Thomas Harris, maybe cooler. And Cal was trustworthy compared with the other dirty little puffers he dealt with. Once Cal, without a hint from Larney, had whipped out a credit card and bought a hundred-dollar vintage comic book on display next to the cash register when Fidel walked in on them discussing a new arrival of some kick-ass smoke called Morning Lights. Fidel didn't suspect a thing. Larney was pleasantly surprised, subsequently making an exception with Cal when it came to store visits.

"So what are you doing here?" Larney asked, turning down the volume on AC/DC singing about how hard it is to be a rock star.

"Eh, fucking batteries are dead," Cal said, holding up his pager. "And I was in the neighborhood. Okay to talk?"

Larney gestured with his eyes to a bulky guy browsing the twenty-five cent paperback section in the rear of the store. "Just wait until this guy leaves, cool?"

But Cal didn't have time to respond.

"'Scuse me," the guy in back said heading for the register. "What's this doing here?" he said, holding up a paperback.

"Sorry?" Larney asked.

"Do you have any idea what this is?" he asked, completely ignoring Cal. "Look," he said, putting the small book on the counter in front of Larney. "Look at that."

"So? What is it?"

"This doesn't deserve to be in the twenty-five cent pile."

Right away, Cal was struck by the guy's dynamism. He'd never seen a boy his age have an opinion about something in a bookstore, especially a book.

"What? You think it's too much? It's only a quarter, man," Larney said.

"No, it's not too much. It's *too little*."

"What?" Larney said, tilting his head. "I don't understand." That's when Cal saw what this stranger was holding: a battered copy of *Lord of the Flies*. "It's about to fall apart, man," Larney said taking the book from the stranger's hands. "It's got coffee stains on it." He opened the book. "It's got writing in it. The back cover is torn off. What's the big deal? It's not worth a dime."

"The big deal?" the guy in black said. "Not worth a dime? It's just a work of genius is all." He paused a moment then his opposition waned. "It's too bad you treat great books like this, reduce them to the sacrament of the twenty-five cent table."

Cal took notice of the word "sacrament."

Larney tactfully tried to shut the guy up. "Look, man. The people who owned that book read it, enjoyed it — enjoyed it until it almost fell apart. It's been appreciated, dude. Now it can be appreciated by someone who can't buy a new copy. Nothing wrong with that. Right?"

"I guess you're right," the stranger said.

"I've read that book," Cal said. "I don't read a lot of books, but I've read that one."

"Good?" the stranger asked, raising his eyelids.

"What?" Cal said, caught off guard.

"Is it good? And if so, what's good about it?"

Cal thought the guy was crazy. "What's good about it? Lot of things."

"Yeah," Darrin said taking a step toward Cal. "Have you really read it?"

"He said he had," Larney chimed in. "What do you want?"

"That's alright," Cal said raising a hand. "I'll answer the question."

The boy crossed his arms then stepped back as if he were a drill sergeant expecting a mutiny.

"It explores themes of civilization. It asks the question 'Is man's natural condition barbarism and cruelty or conformity and society?' And which is better."

"Good," the stranger said slightly rocking on his heels. "Not bad. But what about the theme of the loss of innocence?" he asked academically. "What about the power struggles of society?"

"Look, man, I'm just here to talk to my friend. Okay?" Cal said.

"Sorry." He looked disappointed and plopped down a quarter on the counter. "I just like talking about this stuff. That's all."

The strange young man walked out with his copy of *Lord of the Flies* without looking back, and Larney, checking the store one more time, slid Cal his quarter bag of Laughing Buddha under a copy of *Creem* magazine. "Weird guy, huh?"

"Oh, I don't know — probably just wanted to talk."

Cal thanked Larney and walked out of the store clutching his stash in his left front pocket. The trepidation he felt was fun, exciting — walking on a public street with something that might land him in jail, even if it was only until his mom showed up to bail him out. But the fun was temporary, and Cal wanted to get to his car and away from Zip Dance as quickly as possible. But there was the strange literary critic, a few yards from him, sitting on a bus-stop bench reading Golding's masterpiece.

The sight of this young loner, sitting alone, reading a thing of beauty that could fall to pieces at any moment, made Cal sad. It was sad how he resembled an old man who'd lost his wife years before and no longer had anyone to tell his war stories to, his baseball stories, any stories.

Cal was just about to get in his car and drive away when he decided to do something he'd never done: speak to a loner.

"What's your name?"

He turned around surprised. "Sorry?"

"I said what's your name?"

"I'm Darrin," he said extending his hand. "Darrin."

It was strange, Cal thought. The confidence he had shown in the store was not confidence at all. Maybe it was desperation. Maybe it was fear. Or maybe it was confidence. It was hard to place this guy.

"Need a ride somewhere?" Cal asked.

"You bet," he said without hesitation.

Cal would come to know Darrin as the most fearless guy in the world. Then Cal would better understand how complex fear can be.

"All I got to do is drive there? That's it?"

Darrin assured him that was all.

"I don't know, Darrin."

Darrin gave one good reason after another and Cal responded the same way.

"I don't know, Darrin."

Cal was lying back on his bed rubbing his temples when he noticed his mother standing in the doorway.

Darrin asked another question, but Cal didn't hear him.

"Everything all right?" Dorothy asked.

"Got to go," Cal sighed before hanging up.

"Everything okay, Cal?"

"Fine, Mom." He turned on his side away from her.

"How did your research paper come out?" she asked with motherly enthusiasm.

"Fine."

"Then you got it done?"

"Yes, mother. I got it done." Cal looked over his shoulder and emphatically said goodnight before curling up again.

Dorothy clumsily stepped into the room knowing she was an uninvited guest.

"Are you sure everything is okay?" She knew when Cal wasn't telling the truth.

"*Yes*, mother. *Goodnight.*"

"Okay. Goodnight."

She began to walk out, then thought of the videotape on the front steps.

"Cal?"

"What?" he said, now annoyed.

"Did anyone ring the doorbell this evening?"

"No."

"You didn't hear anyone on the front steps? Or maybe a car door slam?"

Cal didn't know what she was getting at, but like his father, he always assumed the worst. "I've been here by myself all night, just working on my homework. That's all," he said defensively.

"Okay. Okay. You grumpy lumpy."

He looked at her again. "What?"

Dorothy wanted to give Cal a hug goodnight but stopped herself. He wants to be treated like a man, she thought. That's what men do in their most immature moments.

Cal listened to his mother walk down the hall and close the bedroom door. He reached over the side of the bed and touched the bag of marijuana he had tucked between the mattress and the bed frame. If only I was older, he thought to himself, I would be free from them.

Dorothy had learned long ago to accommodate the insecurities of one man. It had taken years but she had done it. Now she was dealing with the insecurities of two — one adolescent in years, the other in temperament. But that's what strong women do, she told herself. Either that or they just give up completely like her mother did. Dorothy Crawford, however, wasn't giving up — not on Jim and definitely not on Cal. She had invested too much time and effort in them and in making their multimillion dollar house a home.

As Dorothy dressed for bed, putting on a reddish-brown nightgown she set aside for romantic occasions, she caught herself questioning what people can do by effort alone, what they can accomplish by their own design. It was her version of wondering if she was doing the right thing. Was there such a thing as "the right thing" after all? She usually stopped herself, recognizing the influence of Jim's never-ending neuroses. This time she didn't.

. . .

Once, after going on a two-week binge following the completion of *Self-Confidence*, Crawford told Dorothy he had finally cracked the greatest mystery of human behavior. He said he had been watching a TV program where a woman blamed all her problems on her parents. They were cruel to her. They mercilessly yelled at her. And as a result she was psychologically ruined for life. She had trouble getting along with others. She had trouble with intimacy. She had trouble holding a job. Her greatest revelation was that her self-destructive temperament was the product of a horrid childhood, and that pissed her off.

Crawford rambled on for half an hour about people blaming their parents for their troubles. "That's one reason most behavioral psychologists are full of shit," he said. "They think every human action is attributable. And if they're right," he said, barely able to stand, "we don't have fucking souls. You realize that? We're just like chemicals responding to each other the only way we can."

His laughter was repulsive, his philosophizing self-important. "We respond to our parents, to the people around us, who responded to *their* parents and the people around them. And on and fucking on and on and on. Since we were amoebas coming out of the fucking swamp, just a bunch of fucking, you know, chemicals," he had said before gulping down the last of his cocktail.

This was Jim's broadside against determinism, Dorothy guessed. So she put him to bed like she always had and hoped he would feel better in the morning.

"Maybe I *do* believe there is no independent will," Crawford had said just before passing out. "I don't have any will. Maybe nobody does. Maybe we're all just reacting. Maybe that's what fucking happens. Maybe that's what's happening now," he said, passing out with his mouth as wide open as a hungry baby bird's.

But Dorothy believed her husband had grown up since then, and hopefully she had as well. Sometimes she brought up issues of "maturity," and Jim responded well — better than the prior tactic of "responsibilities." Dorothy felt you had to stick with the more immediate and trivial matters of existence. Contemplating "independent will" was just insanity.

Dorothy sat in bed reading a romance novel she'd purchased in an airport some time ago but never had the chance to read. During her college years, she would have been embarrassed to read such pulp in front of Jim, but now she didn't care. It was the kind of reading she had enjoyed since her youth. And why shouldn't she read these books if she wanted to? Lately she had become more self-confident, and she was starting to understand what an important factor it played in the everyday health of the two men that made up her family. Not being accommodating was sometimes the best strategy. Perhaps *her* self-esteem was the best thing for Jim and Cal.

I was too easy on Cal, she thought. *And I didn't need to put on this damn nightgown either*. She was getting up to change her nightclothes when Jim walked by their bedroom holding the videotape and a note pad.

"Where are you going?" she asked.

"I'm going to stay up a little bit. I want to go over my notes for the Hershey show."

"So let's see what's on the tape," she said slyly, now glad she hadn't changed.

"It's just a joke, like I said."

"Apparently it wasn't so bad."

"No, not so bad," Crawford admitted.

"Come on. Let's see."

Crawford sat on the edge of the bed as the broadcast snow turned to a speckled image of a makeshift living room at a local TV studio.

"It was Jan Hershey's first job," Crawford said as the opening credits rolled.

Jan Hershey in her late twenties was ten years younger than the new best-selling author she was interviewing, but when she sat next to him he immediately looked 20 years older. Or Crawford thought so.

"Welcome back to the morning show everyone," Jan says.

Crawford noted that the tape was roughly cut to include only his portion of the program. Crawford was all the more convinced it was Berry.

"Today we have the author of the sizzling new bestseller *Self-Confidence*, Dr. James Crawford."

Crawford remembered how he thought it was ridiculous that she used the word "sizzling." It was still ridiculous.

"And it's helping an unprecedented number of people improve their lives."

Yeah sure, Crawford thought. An *unprecedented* number. He looked over at Dorothy, whose smile was all nostalgia.

"Now, you hadn't actually written anything before you wrote *Self-Confidence*, is that right?"

A subtitle appeared under Crawford's bloated face. Crawford thought it was ironic they put his name on the screen right after she'd said it. The subtitle was an ugly green — prehistoric by current standards. But it looked like the latest thing compared with Crawford's blue plaid polyester leisure suit.

"That's right," Crawford answered clumsily. "Well, I had tried writing a novel, but never actually completed anything."

"I see," Jan says.

"Look at that suit," Dorothy said. "And your hair. Oh my God, this is funny."

"Yeah. Real funny."

"When did you decide to write a self-help book?" she asks.

Crawford remembered being more uncomfortable than he looked.

"I don't know. I was in pretty bad shape in a lot of ways. My education had put me in a lot of debt. I didn't have a job at the time. And I didn't have any prospects for one."

Crawford wondered why he was so eager to impart such personal information.

"I'd forgotten all about this," Dorothy said.

"You've also stated you had a problem with alcohol," Jan asks frankly, as if trying to be a real journalist.

"That's right," Crawford says, nodding reluctantly.

Crawford had had only one previous television appearance. He had since forgotten how eager he was to please this bitch.

"And it was worse than that, wasn't it?" Jan nods, her eyebrows rising in unctuous concern.

"Yes it was," Crawford says.

Dorothy was still smiling. "Boy, you look nervous."

Then: "Would you like to share with our viewers?"

That's so fucking typical, Crawford thought.

"Yes." Crawford's head drops like a wounded animal. "I thought I might take my own life. That's how bad things were."

I didn't really think that. Why did I say that?

"You bought a gun. Didn't you?' Jan asks, shaking her head before the audience gasps.

"Yes."

"That's terrible, Doctor."

"I kept the gun in my desk. Which, oddly enough, motivated me to write. I was so scared after that. It was either write or die."

Dorothy turned to her husband. "You never had a gun. Did you?"

"No," Crawford said.

God. It was so popular to be pathetic back then. Shit, still is.

"So you saw how bad off you were, and then you pulled yourself out of that rut."

Crawford is smiling. His optimism (or relative optimism) now breaks free of his memories of self-destruction. "For some reason I realized it was a lack of self-confidence, and I just documented the whole experience for others."

"You don't talk like *that* any more, dear," Dorothy laughed. She put a reassuring hand on Crawford's shoulder, and Crawford almost flinched.

"I shaped it into a program. It was a natural thing for me to write because I was going through it at the time."

Without realizing it, Dorothy's love pat was angering Crawford even more.

You're my wife, not my mother.

"Your life was in disarray, you say... a total mess." Hershey's enthusiasm is growing with Crawford's, their song and dance in harmony. "And in that state of mind you produced a best-selling book?" She looks at the camera and tilts her head. "Maybe *my* life should be a little more in disarray."

"I'm turning it off," Crawford said, grabbing the remote.

"No, wait."

"You know, Jan, people are strange animals. I think the public's awareness of those circumstances has actually helped the book become the success it has. I think it communicates to people that they shouldn't give up."

No wonder I never watched this.

Crawford became more aware of Dorothy rubbing his shoulder and it bothered him. He felt like a boob already, and her comforting hand was insulting. Berry got me again, he thought, *and she doesn't even care.*

"Why would you let this bother you?" she asked sweetly.

I hope it was Berry, he thought. Crawford reached up and brushed Dorothy's hand off his shoulder and jumped from the bed, clicking off the TV.

Yes, it's long past time that I get Berry for all that humiliation he dished out to me over the years. This is a good thing. Paying him back will be a triumph for me.

"Honey?" Dorothy asked, "Are you thinking too much again?"

"If you'll excuse me, I have some notes to look over." Crawford hit the eject button and yanked the tape from the VCR.

"It's really late, Jim" Dorothy said, a skeptical look on her face.

"I won't be long," he said, storming out of the room and slamming the door.

Dorothy knew it was a lie but she was too fed up to do anything about it. *Let him drink himself to death*, she thought as she got up to put on her pajamas.

Crawford threw the notebook on his desk. It didn't contain a single word. Crawford's inclination toward pen and paper was a product of his brief Alcoholics Anonymous days. He didn't take notes during the many meetings he attended. It would have been ridiculous to write down anything said by members during their tearful "sharing." He just scratched little pictures of things, which relieved his nervousness slightly while he was fighting his thirst for drink. Tonight it wasn't helping. His mind was too distracted.

Regret. Accomplishment. Disappointment. Arrogance. Guilt. Embarrassment.

Dorothy. Phil. Lee. Cal. Jenny.

Fucking Happy Pappy.

Booze. It always came back to booze, especially with those sets of stressors.

Crawford put the mysterious videotape in a small VCR that rested under an even smaller TV. He hit the rewind button then stop.

"You've also stated you had a problem with alcohol."

"That's right."

"And it was worse than that, wasn't it?"

Look at that patronizing nod. Bitch. And I even wanted to bang her after that.

Crawford stopped the tape.

He wanted a drink. He always wanted a drink, but it was approaching the hour when it really got tough. The craving time was as reliable as the nightly news, and so was the struggle that followed.

Every night, when he was "on one" (and some nights when he wasn't), a heated debate occurred inside his head, one that needed to be resolved prior to the liquor stores closing at 2am.

It took him back to Texas, to his teens, to the lakes and country roads where he used to spend Saturday afternoons drinking two-dollar twelve packs with the Cherokee boys who were always up for it. It took him to California, to his undergrad years, when he could drink a fifth of rancid bourbon and not be paralyzed by a hangover the next day. It took him to his early twenties, to his first European trip, downing wine with a bunch of Algerians in southern France, or drinking ouzo with a bunch of old fisherman in northern Greece. But the best years to remember — and therefore the worst for his condition — were the ones just before he got married, his graduate school days. Oh, yes, when his closest buddy Cecil occupied a small lake house that could have been in the middle of nowhere but was just an hour's drive from his alma mater. When a variety of alcohol — beer, wine, spirits — was always in great abundance. When young women came out in droves and he could ignore them until he chose not to. When John Coltrane and Shostakovich and Miles Davis and Bartok and Frank Zappa and Stravinsky and the Rolling Stones and (of course) *Dark Side of the Moon* accompanied conversations of philosophy and politics and theater and literature and sex and life and death and (of course) mental illness. And when he could take walks by the lake and enjoy a peace and quiet that, like a good night of lovemaking, was best appreciated in contemplation.

All those wonderful memories made a good argument for surrender. Then...

The rebuttal. Ugly words like *responsibility*, *duty* and *cirrhosis* popped into his mind — vain, ineloquent attempts to keep him sober.

Yes, it's difficult to make ugly words romantic.

Then a more frank attempt. Sentences like *Don't do it*, *This can't go on*, and *You'll pay for it later*, all of which made Crawford thirstier. Those arguments turned desire into rebellion, thirst into defiance, and sobriety into an abrasive Victorian governess who needed to lighten up.

All this internal quarrelling made Crawford realize there was nothing glamorous about being a drunk. It merely *was* — like standing straight or wearing shoes. Sobriety required a kind of religious faith that he couldn't accept. Crawford was an atheist before the God of Sobriety, an unholy deity who demanded unrelenting devotion. But the God of Inebriation, well, he only required the keys to the car. *You shall have no other gods before me.*

I'll save my soul tomorrow, he thought as he put on his shoes.

As he backed out of the driveway, Crawford's eyes were trained on the bedroom window, as they often were when he was going "on a run." If the light came on, it would be like a siren going off during a prison break.

Backing slowly... slowly... there... is... no... light... no light...

He made it. He got away undetected. *This time.*

There was something disheartening about escaping so easily. It triggered more paranoia.

She's going to find out. She's going to be pissed. She's just waiting until I get back so she can smash the bottle and cry a little.

Until the cash hit the counter at the liquor store, he might as well keep arguing with himself. It made the drive less painful.

Don't do it. Don't do it. Turn around. Go home. Go to bed.

Happy Time Liquor was pretty run down, the store that marked the end of Easy Street (relatively speaking) and the beginning of Hard Luck Boulevard. Crawford couldn't go to the "exclusive" deli and wine dealer that served his community. It closed at nine. He wouldn't have gone there anyway. The owner, and often times the patrons, knew who he was and what he supposedly hadn't done in years. The little Indian man at Happy Time was not so well-informed and Crawford wouldn't care if he was.

The place was empty and would have been quiet if not for the TV playing behind the counter.

"Is that all for you?" the Indian man asked with a heavy Hindi accent, putting the requested fifth of Lowlander Pure Malt on the counter.

"Yes."

While the Indian was ringing up the purchase, the sound of the TV behind him grated on Crawford's overburdened nerves.

There were three young black men, all wearing knit caps and dark clothing, pounding their fists into the low-angled camera. The beat was hard and deep. *Boom. Boom. Boom.* The setting was an urban wasteland with burning oil drums barely illuminating surreal, grim structures. The lyrics, from what Crawford could tell, were fuming with violence and hatred of the white power structure and anything else they could think of. *Damn, what the kids listen to these days.*

Here and there we are in the ghet-to
That's me and JB, your worst [bleep]in' foe
I've got a [bleep]in' nine, I got [bleep]in' [bleep]
And I'm 'bout to let go on your [bleep]in' [bleep], [bleeeeeep]

Crawford thought about the sense of power these slum fantasies tried to convey. He thought about the discontentment it contrived to relieve. But why was this Indian listening to it? It was really getting annoying.

"You like that stuff?" Crawford asked.

The Indian, wrapping the sack around the neck of the bottle, was caught off guard. "I don't drink."

Crawford gestured toward the TV. "No. I mean do you like that kind of music? You have it playing pretty loud."

"Sir, it's for the customers."

"Some clientele," he said to himself.

The Indian handed Crawford the sack with his change. "Excuse me. Can I ask you a question?"

"Yes?"

"Why is it that these musicians try to look like criminals or something?"

Crawford looked at the TV again. "I don't know. Maybe it's the criminals who are trying to look like *them*. These guys are artists, you know," he said holding up four fingers as quotation marks.

"Uh huh," the man said. Then he added, "Low self-esteem, perhaps?"

Crawford laughed and the man looked puzzled.

"No. I don't think so," Crawford said.

"I'm glad to hear that. Good night," the man said.

Crawford scanned the street. His mission was to be undercover and unrecognized from home back to home, from study back to study. Sometimes he was afraid that a tabloid photographer might get a picture of him leaving such a place, but then he remembered that he could always say he had a relapse. But he always double-parked his car in the alley next to the store, just in case.

He walked around the corner, and without a sound, a car passed in front of him abruptly, causing him to stumble back to the sidewalk.

"Shit!" he yelled.

He had slipped and fallen into a small puddle of something, cushioned only by the base of his right hand.

"Goddammit!"

He got up and inspected the bottle to make sure it wasn't broken. He looked down the street only to see taillights that didn't identify the car.

"What the fuck," he moaned, picking himself up off the pavement. *Fucking kids*, he thought.

He brushed the dirt from his hands onto the sack then reached in his pocket for his keys.

After tonight, this is it, he thought as he walked to his car. *This is the last time.*

Then there were headlights behind him again. He turned to look. It was the same dark car — a sedan of some kind — traveling fast. Crawford staggered out of the way, back onto the sidewalk, almost falling again. He looked over his shoulder to the driver's side of the car. He meant to give the finger, but the car went by too fast this time, taking the next turn before Crawford even saw the taillights. He couldn't even see the make.

"Goddam asshole," he yelled. "Goddam!"

Goddam Happy Pappy.

Goddam. Happy Pappy. Happy Pappy? The driver was wearing a Happy Pappy mask. That piece of shit was wearing a Happy Pappy mask!

He stopped and took a deep breath. His heart was racing. He looked down the alley, then back again.

That's the only thing I saw, he thought. Just the face, smiling.

No. He stopped himself. Surely his eyes were playing tricks on him.

It was him. I mean, it was a guy wearing... I saw it. No. You didn't see anything. You're imagining things. Do they sell those damn things? They don't sell those things, do they? No. Wait. Surely I'm seeing things. Light plays tricks on you sometimes, especially when you need a drink. It was probably just some other ugly bastard.

Crawford tried to forget about it, putting the bottle safely under his arm.

"I must be losing my mind," he said as he got in the car.

Crawford looked over at his purchase, sitting in the passenger's seat. He started to wonder if maybe his mind wasn't going. Just following his liver's lead. *Would I go crazy and not know it? Shit. Isn't that what madness is? And is this kind of madness caused by alcohol?*

Better just get home.

The bedroom light was still off, and everything looked the same. It was calming. The guilt wasn't going to be too bad.

Crawford went through the side entrance where he grabbed a towel from the laundry room to clean his faintly soiled pants. While rubbing the small wet spot on the back of his leg, he noticed one of Cal's "uniforms" lying in a hamper next to the dryer. Black. All of it. The same color as those rappers on TV, but stylistically worlds apart. Was this his way of trying to get attention? Or trying to wield power? Maybe it was low self-esteem.

Fuck it. Who cares?

Crawford threw the towel into the hamper then looked at the bottle he was cradling. What could he criticize Cal for? He was a teenager. He had an excuse. *Should I talk to him like Dorothy says? And if so, what about?*

Crawford went to the kitchen and got a glass and a small bucket of ice. He walked down to his study thinking about how dark and remote it was, and then sat down at his desk. He thought he could almost stop right there and just go to bed, just stay sober. It seemed that way — so close and so easy, but he just couldn't do it — or wouldn't. In times like this he wasn't sure there was a difference.

He looked at the tape, then at the note.

`I'm going to follow your program to the very end.`
`Love, Happy Pappy.`

Crawford closed the door and poured his first drink.

SEVEN

Mumbling voices.

You know, Jan, people are strange animals. I think... actually helped the book... it communicates to people... give up.

"Huh?"

Crawford remembered playing late Shostakovich string quartets (8, 9, and 10), but he couldn't remember pushing in the videotape. The incoherent voices were a dream, but the sound of the TV snow woke him up.

He looked at the violent sparks of light bursting in front of him. He looked over at the bottle sitting next to the TV — half empty.

No, half full. The glass is always half full.

The bucket now held nothing but water and a few small pieces of ice. He put his hand on his temple. He couldn't tell if he was in pain or not. He was so saturated with alcohol that his mind was more than intoxicated. It was numb.

He stared ahead blankly, watching the tiny lights on the TV screen dance like crazed fireflies. It might have been a few seconds or an hour.

Then he saw Happy Pappy.

The *Happy Pappy Show* was coming on.

Did I see this?

It was the same unbearable song, but something was different.

Crawford leaned toward the screen, his forehead contracting slightly to lift his eyelids.

The image was blurry. *Or is it my eyes?*

There were no dancing puppets and the set didn't look right. It looked like something out of *The Cabinet of Dr. Caligari*. The lines ran in every direction except up and down, and just looking at it made Crawford feel faint.

What the hell is this? Crawford thought, squinting his eyes.

Then the face popped into the frame from the upper right corner, looking down sideways, but with a smile more intense.

"Hello, Dr. Crawford!"

Crawford sat up.

"You've come a long way in just a short while, haven't you?" Happy Pappy says, nodding sarcastically. "Doggone it, that program works!"

Crawford laughed at his confusion. It was so ridiculous.

The set looked mocked up, but the host looked exactly like the one on the show — same plump body, same ridiculous costume, same insidious voice.

Happy Pappy stepped aside, revealing a man tied to a chair. He was wearing a dark suit and had a pillowcase or something draped over his head. Crawford's laugh melted, and he could feel his body shaking.

What the hell? What is that?

He could barely make out the man's mouth, the only part of his face that was exposed.

Whatever was tied around his midsection looked unlike the rest of his clothing. It was like a grotesque form of modern art professing to convey hidden beauty.

"Like you always say! One stage at a time is the best way!" Happy Pappy screeches.

He holds up a copy of *Self-Esteem*, filling the frame beautifully like a professional photograph in *Jan* magazine. He opens the book with the authority of a minister ready to read scripture. "Your introduction to the first stage is so wonderful and true," Happy says, his grin climbing up the side of his face like a vine devouring a derelict house. He holds up a finger to emphasize the point. "Stage one. Silence those that unjustly criticize you."

He moved to the side again and Crawford could see the bound man struggling.

Berry and Scott? Did you...

Happy's face jumps back in, filling the frame even more. "And that's what this sourpuss has been doing! He's been badmouthing you on TV and everything." He moves closer like a monstrous marionette, his face half eclipsed by the shadow of the camera. He speaks softly. "He thinks your show is hooey! Can you believe that, Dr. Crawford? He thinks you're full of *shit*." He shouts, "What the *fuck* does he know?"

"What the fuck?" Crawford barked, his head bobbing toward the screen, his breathing heavy.

Happy Pappy holds up a large kitchen knife, the kind used to slice bread. It shines brightly, casting a hotspot on the lens.

Crawford felt a small vibration course through his body. *This isn't real.*

"He won't be putting down our show any longer!"

Happy Pappy reaches inside the small hole that exposes the man's mouth. Crawford thought he heard the faceless person moan.

"No," he is trying to say. *No.*

"Shut up, sourpuss!"

Crawford saw the tongue. *Yeah, he's definitely holding the guy's tongue.*

Happy Pappy's body leans forward seductively as he lifts the knife slowly, enticingly. In his other hand he pinches the man's tongue with his thumb and forefinger. He looks over his shoulder — to his one-man audience.

"Stage one complete," he says, nodding serenely. "Stage one complete, Doctor! *Silence those that unfairly criticize you.* Thank you for your time."

The screen went to snow.

Does this require a response? Crawford was thinking. He let the tape run.

He picked up the bottle and filled his glass. Then he hit stop on the VCR.

Comedians, he thought. *I get them all.*

Then the text appeared.

The techniques set forth on the "Happy Pappy Show"
are based on the principles of Dr. James Crawford,
whose Self Series™ has helped millions improve their lives.
These principles have been modified to accommodate
the self-esteem issues of a younger audience.

Crawford lifted the glass and took a sip. He took a breath, taking in the bouquet, before downing the rest. It felt good and warm *for the moment.* Looking at the bottle, he knew he would be feeling pain very shortly. *God, that's too much*, he thought. *What am I doing?*

And why did those fuckers send me this tape? I'm not going to respond to this.

He hit the eject button and pulled it out. The small movement made him grab his abdomen. The liquor was turning on him, but it was still doing its job as far as confidence went. He threw the tape in the wastebasket next to his desk.

"Fuck you. Fuck you all."

What if it's a stalker or something?

No. Hell, no.

"*People are going to try to get at you, take away your confidence and purpose. Jealous people. Find a way to avert them. Just find a way.*"

God, my shitty books.
God, I better get some sleep.
"God, I need help."

"Jim."
    Yes.
    "Jim?"
Crawford's eyes opened wide, allowing a current of light in, one that gave life to his vile hangover. He closed his eyes. He was face down on the living room couch, still in his clothes, with a large pillow just under his chin. He turned over on his back and instantly felt a horrific soreness in his neck. He looked at the empty bottle of Lowlander, lying broken on its side on the coffee table, its last lifeblood emptied into the basin of a large candle.
    "Jim," Dorothy said again.
    Crawford opened his eyes to see his wife upside down, standing over him.
    "Are you awake?"
    "I think so."
    "So did you enjoy it?" she hissed.
    "I think so."
    The tone of Dorothy's voice made Crawford cower much more than the pain of withdrawal. It wasn't the anger but the disappointment that made it so difficult to take.
    Dorothy sat in a chair next to the sofa. "Why, Jim?"
    Crawford turned on his side, away from her. "I don't know."
    "How many times have we been through this, Jim?"
    Crawford took a deep breath. "Please, no clichés."
    "Help me to understand. Why does this happen? Have you been upset about something? Is it something that I did? Was the banquet last night so terrible?"
    Crawford rolled on his back again then sat up. "I can't explain it to you. Okay? I just can't. Sometimes I'm overwhelmed by this feeling that I would rather die than not drink. Okay?" He leaned back wearily. "Difficult to understand?"
    "Jim, if that's what's happening, it's killing you. And it will succeed if you don't fight it."
    "I am fighting it."
    She stood up. "No, you're not! You call that fighting. You've gotten drunk three nights in a row now."
    Crawford saw she was trembling.

She was right, of course. She deserved more of an effort. But with the room spinning like it was, Crawford just couldn't confront this now. He needed to do something else first.

Crawford struggled to his feet and headed upstairs without looking back at his wife. He had to go. *Now.* He approached the main bathroom upstairs and passed it hesitantly. "I'll make it," he told himself. Walking faster, he rushed into the master bedroom, barely making it inside before dropping to his knees and spraying the inside of the toilet with orange vomit. The first heave was violent and disgusting. Then a breath, then more. *Yes, the first heave is the hardest*, he thought, before the acetic brew came pouring out again.

"Hard things, once accomplished, are the most gratifying."

Crawford realized he must have gobbled down some kind of snack before he passed out — either Cheesy Cheesos or Taco-Flavored Tortillios, maybe both — something with artificial orange coloring, something only a drunk or a stoned teenager would eat.

He reached over and closed the door and prepared for another surge. This one was a bit disappointing, ending with a small amount of bile sliding down the front of his tongue.

"Are you okay?" Dorothy asked through the door.

"I'm fine. Just give me a minute," he gasped, before retching again.

Crawford was taken aback when Dorothy opened the door. In all their years of marriage, she had never opened the door while he was throwing up. He looked up at her, wiping a small bit of puke from his chin with his forearm.

"You have two choices, Jim. You can be a drunk or you can be a husband and father. But not both."

"Can we talk about this later?" Jim said, almost in his talk show demeanor.

"I thought you said no clichés."

"Never again," he interrupted. "Never. This is it. I promise."

A sudden contraction brought him over the toilet once more.

Dorothy had to raise her voice to accommodate the noise. "I mean it, Jim. I'll leave you."

She turned around and closed the door behind her.

"I believe you," he yelled after her.

Crawford sat down with his back against the wall. The first round of the sickness was over.

"Stage one, complete!"

The evening was coming back.

"Stage one, complete!"

The tape.

"You've come a long way."

He and Dorothy had watched the old Hershey program, but there was the other part.

"Silence those that unfairly criticize you."

He paused a moment.

"He won't be putting down our show any longer!"

Happy Pappy cut a man's tongue out.

No. Hell, no. Crawford thought he was losing his mind. It was like the DTs he'd experienced during his first detoxification years ago — strange nightmares about sex and death and childhood.

And now I'm having nightmares about Happy Pappy?

No. He saw that.

"Shut up, sourpuss!"

Wait, he thought. *The tape. Where is it?*

Crawford thought of his study. He had to look at the tape again. The only way to find out if he wasn't completely nuts: look at the tape.

Crawford washed his face as his heart began to pound. The image became clearer with each heartbeat. He needed to look. He had to. He walked slowly down the stairs to his study, breathing heavier with every step. He opened the door and smelled the alcohol he had spilled on the floor, which almost made him retch again. He picked up the wastebasket next to his desk where he thought he put the tape. The wastebasket was empty.

I imagined it all, he thought. *Thank God.*

But the basket had been full of trash.

He walked up the stairs and called to Dorothy.

"What do you want?" she called back.

Crawford walked into the kitchen where Dorothy was sitting at the table, reading the newspaper with a cup of coffee.

"Did you take the trash out?"

"Don't I always?" she said, without looking up.

"What about the wastebasket in my study."

"It had trash in it, didn't it?"

"Did you see the tape in there?"

"The tape?"

Crawford looked out the window behind her and could see the garbage can by the side of the street was empty. "Son of a bitch," he said.

"What?" Dorothy asked.

"Son of a bitch."

Crawford turned around and saw that Cal was standing in the doorway.

"You want me?" Cal asked.

"No," Crawford said exhaling, "not you."

"Yeah, right," Cal said.

Crawford went back upstairs and took a shower, got dressed, and made himself as presentable as possible despite the pain coursing through his body. This was a habit of Crawford's: the day after a "bad one," he spiffed himself up as if initiating drastic life changes. Occasionally, he would catch himself thinking, *Yeah, I've heard that before.* But then he would replace those thoughts with favorites like "A journey of a 1,000 miles begins with a single step."

Step... Step... *Stage one, complete!*

His mind was everywhere, but it kept returning to the wicked images of the videotape, to what he hoped were just delirious thoughts.

How could I imagine that? I'm not that creative.

Maybe it was like that turkey incident years ago, he thought. During one drunken Thanksgiving, Jim was in charge of cooking the turkey because Dorothy was busy with her mother that morning. He had to get up early, around six, to make sure the damn thing was in the oven. He had been in bed only a couple of hours, having stayed up until four drinking with an old friend. Still drunk, he pulled the bird from the sink where it had been defrosting. The moment he grabbed it, the slippery creature, all twenty-four pounds of it, came alive. It started flapping its wings, gyrating wildly, struggling to get away from him. Crawford screamed. He fell backwards, and landed on the floor with the turkey on top of him. Then he dragged the turkey safely outside and into a garbage can.

He never told Dorothy. He simply bought a cooked turkey at the grocery store and swore he'd never drink again, or at least never to get so *insanely* drunk. This, after all, was back in the *post*-good old days.

Crawford decided there was just one sensible explanation for this Happy Pappy tape: alcohol delirium. That's what it had to be. *No more comments on the subject until further notice.*

As he drank his coffee at the kitchen table, Crawford saw Dorothy in the hall looking at herself in the mirror. She looked wonderful.

"I'm going to make some changes, Dorothy," he mumbled to himself.

"What? Did you say something?" she asked.

"I'm going to make some changes," he spoke louder. "Some real changes."

Dorothy clearly wasn't in the mood. "I see."

"I know you've heard it before."

"Yeah, and I know that you know that I know. So why bother? Just don't say anything, Jim. Nothing."

Dorothy walked past the kitchen without looking at him.

"Honey, I've been having these dreams or something. And I'm going to talk to..."

"Don't say anything, Jim. Nothing," she said going upstairs.

Crawford got dressed. Maybe I'll go talk to Phil, he thought. And when I come back home things will look different. *Just get out of here for a while.*

Crawford stormed into the garage, got into the car and revved the engine to convince himself he was determined to make a change. *Today is the first day of the rest of your life.*

Yeah, yeah. Whatever.

"Take small steps."

God, shut up.

He was backing out of his driveway when suddenly a flowery basket appeared just inside his right field of vision — then some blonde hair. He slammed on the brakes. Little Isabella from down the street passed behind the car on her bicycle. Shaken, Crawford put his hands on the wheel and calmed himself before looking back again. She didn't stop. She just looked at him with an odd, lingering look.

Little kids know, he thought. They always know.

"All you can do is move forward, toward the future."

After he got the car on the street, he felt better. He took a deep breath and picked up his mobile phone. He dialed the one number he knew by memory that was not on his speed dial, and for good reason.

It rang four times. "Hello, this is Jenny. I'm not here right now." She laughs. "Well, I might be here. Just leave a message."

"This is Jim. I was calling to make sure you know it's over. It has to be. I'm sorry. It has to be over, Jen. I want to apologize." He held his breath. "Okay, goodbye." He hung up, throwing the phone in the passenger's seat. Then he gripped the steering wheel hard.

Goddam it. I shouldn't have left that message. Jesus, get it together.

The phone rang and Crawford froze. He knew it was Jenny calling to give a rebuttal, but without thinking he answered it.

"Look..."

"Stage two."

"What?"

"Stage two. Do you know what stage two is, Doctor?"

This wasn't just his imagination.

"Who is this?"

The caller paused a moment, then his voice was even quieter.

"Stage two."

"How did you get this number?"

"Don't you know what stage two is? It's *your* stage."

"My stage? What the hell do you want?"

"Stage two. Eliminate the harmful things that are destroying your life. That's what stage two is."

"What do you want?"

"Stage two comes after stage one. And, as you know, stage one is complete."

"Berry?"

The caller hung up.

The voice was familiar, Crawford thought, even at a whisper.

Crawford's image of Happy Pappy on the videotape was becoming clearer. No, it couldn't be. Perhaps it was guilt or...

Perhaps you're blocking...

No! Crawford tried to stop the self-psychoanalyzing self-talk self-esteem self...

"And what's with this *stage* bullshit," Crawford said, trying to distract himself. *It has to be Berry. Berry's fucking with me, trying to drive me crazy.*

We must lose our sense of self-consciousness.

He felt a pang of thirst. *No. God, no. Don't do that. Don't go down that road. Not yet. Not now. One day at a time.*

It was good he was going to see Peters.

The sight of the campus was comforting to Crawford's bloodshot eyes. Those old buildings, with their traditional architecture and grand aspirations, gave him a boost of optimism.

He parked his car in the visitor lot then crept through the front door of the psychology building hoping not to be noticed. The halls were relatively empty except for two young women walking toward him. The shorter one, a nerdy girl Crawford recognized from somewhere (perhaps a lecture), caught his eye.

Oh no.

"Dr. Crawford?" she said, as if to an old friend. "Oh my God!"

I don't have to talk to her.

"Is that you?" she said, her eyes widening with excitement.

"No, sorry," he said, walking quickly past. Crawford marched down the main hall and was almost breathless when he reached the open door to Dr. Peters' office, so he stopped and listened to the baroque music coming from inside. Peters frequently listened to Bach or Handel in his office, which Crawford found appropriate for other professors but not for

Peters. He just didn't seem like the type that liked music. A young man, probably a student, was just leaving, and the music made the exchange seem like a scene from British television.

"Not at all," Phil said. "Don't worry about it."

"Are you sure?" the young man said.

"Of course I'm sure. Loss of innocence is an admirable subject, even in psychology."

"Thanks so much," the student said, shaking his hand.

Peters looked past the young man and noticed Crawford standing there. "See you next week," he said to the young man, patting him on the back as he left.

Trying to ignore his own unease, Jim walked into Peters' office and closed the door as if it were his own domicile. He sat down and Peters turned off the music.

"Oh, no," Crawford said. "You don't have to do that."

Peters ignored the remark. "So this is a surprise."

Crawford thought that Peters could see right through him. He could see he was on a bender, that he had gotten drunk after the banquet, that he was having another crisis and needed to talk. Crawford tried not to show his shame.

"How are you?" Peters asked.

"Good enough, I guess."

"Have a seat."

Crawford sat down among the volumes of books lining the walls and looked over at the empty boxes piled in one corner. Peters was obviously getting ready to move to his new office upstairs. He always kept the room dark, with the blinds closed and just a few low-watt desk lamps. It didn't seem practical, but it looked more academic, like a library. Crawford was glad it was dark, though; the less Peters could see of him the better.

"Getting ready to move, huh?"

"Yeah. Getting ready."

Crawford took a deep breath. "I miss this place. You did the right thing, Phil."

"Is that why you came here? To tell me I did the right thing?"

"Is this a bad time?" Crawford asked.

"No, not at all. There are no bad times," Peters said as he calmly leaned back in his chair to an unsettling creak. "I'm putting off this move anyhow. I like this office better."

Crawford felt more like a student than a friend. "You did the right thing, Phil."

"What does that mean?" Peters asked.

"You're a professor. You've got respect." Crawford was at a loss.

Peters didn't look like he was in the mood for a sappy discussion. "Is something wrong, Jim?"

Crawford realized he didn't have much to say. Then he thought of something the good professor might help him with. "My son won't talk to me, Phil."

"Why is that?"

"Well," he began awkwardly, "I made the deal for that show and..."

"Happy Pappy?" he said, expressionless.

"Yes," Crawford said, his eyes veering to the empty boxes in the corner. "People are on TV calling me a charlatan."

"What does that have to do with your son?"

"He's right to despise me."

Peters laughed nervously then gained his composure. "Come on, Jim. Don't bullshit me."

"I've started drinking again." Crawford looked at the floor, fumbling his words. "I mean, I haven't stopped. I've... I've stopped then I started again. And I..."

Peters sat quietly then looked at his watch. Crawford wondered if that meant he was trying to say he didn't have time for this.

"I've been boozing it up, Phil."

"I'm sorry to hear that." The tone of his voice definitely suggested he didn't want to hear it.

"I don't know what to say, Phil." He leaned back in his chair and looked at the ceiling. "I'm sorry. I'm just wasting your time."

"What's your rationale?"

"What?" Crawford asked.

"What's your rationale? For drinking, I mean. Is it your son? Because of your son's behavior? His disapproval? What?" Peters looked like he wanted to get to the bottom of this.

"Lots of things, Phil. Dorothy and I haven't been getting along. I got this goddam tape last night. And some asshole has been calling me."

"Someone's been calling you?"

"You know, some prank caller."

"Is that all?" Peters said.

"Last night I had this weird dream about... I think it was a dream. You see, I got this videotape. And last night I thought I saw..."

Peters took a deep breath. "What are you talking about, Jim?" He took off his glasses and set them on his desk.

Crawford felt naked. "I don't know."

"Hey. Jim. Buddy. What are you so up in knots over? Huh? You're rich, successful. You can do anything you want. Don't worry about these things. I mean, who doesn't get down in the dumps on occasion? We live in a society that tells us we're supposed to be happy all the time. That's the problem. We used to talk about this in college, remember? Desire making the lot of Western civilization miserable. You used to say you were going to become a Buddhist, remember?"

Crawford smiled. "I remember."

"You don't think I have problems?"

"No."

Peters let his scholarly hair down and laughed out loud with an air of surrender. "Why are you here, Jim? For advice?"

Crawford felt a little more relaxed. "I guess. You always gave the best advice, Phil."

"That's what I do for a living. We give it different names: therapy, counseling, research." He paused a moment, looking closer at Crawford's disheveled appearance. "But advice is also what you do for a living. Isn't it?"

Crawford saw that Peters was getting irritated, something he hadn't seen in a long time.

"And you make more money at it than I do," Peters said directly.

"And? What does that mean?" Crawford said, as if the remark were unwarranted.

As Peters sat on the edge of his desk and put a comforting hand on Crawford's shoulder, Crawford noticed that Peters had his sleeves rolled up. *His sleeves rolled up? Peters?* Crawford couldn't remember seeing that before. The sleeves made Peters look completely different, like a leisurely posing model in a bourbon or a cigarette ad. Crawford had known him for more than twenty years and this was the most conspicuous difference he'd seen in him in all that time.

Or am I going crazy?

Are you? he thought.

Am I?

"Just use your own best advice, Jim. You know that," Peters said laughing, his teeth looking very white.

"That's what everyone should do, but they don't. I know that."

"Lucky for us. And climb back on that wagon, okay? That's what people do. That's what smart people do."

Perhaps he's mocking me, Crawford thought, while feeling more and more like an idiot. These "needs" he had were embarrassing. *Why talk about your stupid little problems?* A little bit of the resolve he had felt earlier that morning surged again with a breath and a nod, and Crawford stood up to leave.

"I think I know what it is, Phil. This Happy Pappy bullshit — I'm going to have to end it. It has to stop. I'm going to tell my publisher to reverse the licensing deal we signed."

"Can you do that? I mean, contractually?"

Peters was starting to look like himself again, rolled up sleeves or not. Crawford was surprised Peters would say such a thing. He wasn't the type to raise the finer points of contract law. But by doing so he only made Crawford's resolve stronger. "I don't know. But it's going to stop." There was an uncomfortable silence. Crawford wondered what he expected from Peters. "Who am I to tell people how to live, Phil?" he said, with his eyes still at the floor.

Peters looked baffled. "I want you to do me a favor," he said, like he was trying to change the subject.

"Sure, anything."

"I'm looking for seven psychologists to review my research for the fellowship. I'd feel honored to have you on board."

The request made Crawford immediately feel more respectable. "Sure. What do I have to do?"

"Just read what I've written and give an opinion or two. It won't take much time," he said. "Feel free to say no."

"No, no. I'd be happy to."

"I just need to get your signature here," he said, grabbing a document on his desk. "This just lets the money people know I have an outside review panel."

"No problem."

Peters put the document in front of Crawford and gave him a pen, pointing to the line where he needed to sign. As Crawford signed, Peters began rolling down his sleeves. "So how's the novel coming?" he asked.

Cal opened the front door slowly. "Hello? Anybody home?" Both cars were gone, but he wanted to make sure no one was home. His parents weren't ready to meet a guy like Darrin. They just weren't cool enough. Cal knew that Darrin didn't mind being an unwanted guest. Such a cool guy couldn't be bothered with such minutiae.

Cal yanked his head to the side signaling Darrin to come in, and Darrin walked in, body erect, like a foreign dignitary at a state dinner.

"So this is it," he said sticking out his bulbous chin. "Home, huh?" He looked at Cal, who felt anxious and embarrassed.

"Yeah. Home sweet home," Cal said, clearing his throat. "If it were my choice, I wouldn't go for the *Better Homes and Gardens* look, but..."

"It's not your choice," Darrin said. "Like a lot of things."

Cal nodded in agreement but wondered if Darrin wasn't being a little disrespectful. "If my parents come home, you wouldn't mind leaving out the back, would you?"

"No," he said, impassively looking over the polished mahogany coat rack that sat in the foyer. "Good thing I don't have a coat, huh?"

"Why's that?"

Darrin ignored the question. "They don't like you having friends over, is that it?" He said, pausing on a picture of Cal at twelve. "Or is it just me?"

"I don't think they like me having friends at all." Cal led Darrin into the living room. "My mom wanted me to be friends with some guy — her friend's son — but I didn't..." Cal hesitated.

"You didn't what?" Darrin said, clapping his hands as if to accelerate the exchange. "What?"

"I didn't like the guy." Cal laughed nervously. "I don't think he liked me either."

"You can't plan friendships, Cal. It's like trying to plan who you are. You can't do it. You just got to be who you are, who you want to be, who you like being, all that shit. It's very simple."

Cal nodded, not knowing whether Darrin was being earnest or not. This actually happened frequently, and in such situations Cal always assumed Darrin was being serious. "I think you're right. You know a lot of things, Darrin. Real smart things," he said. *That was a stupid thing to say.*

"Thanks. You're pretty smart yourself," he said with a wink.

Sometimes Cal thought it was odd the way Darrin smiled at him. There was a little too much affection in his glance. But Cal tried not to give it much thought. He figured Darrin was just trying to be sympathetic.

They walked through the main hall, then past the living room and kitchen area. Darrin, unlike many of Cal's friends, didn't seem too impressed with the place, and Cal liked that. Darrin just looked at all the family photographs on the wall. And so intensely, Cal thought.

"You gonna call John Wayne a queer?" Darrin said under his breath while staring at a photograph of a seven-year-old Cal in a cowboy outfit.

"What?" Cal said. "Yeah, that was at my grandmother's house. We used to go there in the summertime. You know, before she died."

Darrin looked at Cal as if he'd been rudely interrupted. "I don't give a fuck where it is."

Cal was surprised. "No problem, man."

Darrin laughed loudly, showing his teeth, which he rarely did. "I'm just kidding, bitch. Lighten up."

Cal sat on the floor of his room playing one of his favorite video-games, *Ruthless Road Rage*, where you can shoot people and then run them over while on your way to making a crack delivery. It was good for "getting out your frustrations," as he liked to tell his mother. It was a common expression among teens, a fashionable rationale.

Darrin sat quietly at the small table in the corner cutting up lines of coke.

"You know that chick Diane Grant? I heard she's had three abortions. That's what I heard down at the pool hall. Apparently she's a whore," Darrin said placidly, curling the sides of his mouth like an old woman.

"Really? I don't believe that," Cal said, putting bullets into a Mexican street thug. He then pulled out a tire iron to smash his skull.

Darrin glared at the coke in front of him. "It's true. She's a little whore."

"You shouldn't say that. You don't even know her. I like Diane Grant." Cal smashed the Mexican's head.

"You could fuck her if you wanted. You have a nice set of wheels. That's more than enough. Tie her up," he said. "Stick it in her butt. Do what you want to her."

Cal felt uneasy. "Hey. Come on." Cal said.

"You heard me, dog."

"That's sick."

It wasn't the first time Cal had heard a piece of Darrin's sexual advice.

"I'm only kidding, dude," Darrin said.

Cal escaped back into his game. After beating the Mexican to death, he got in the car and was hauling ass down the street. He just felt like driving. "Isn't it pathetic how people have to prove themselves by what they drive and what they wear?" Cal said, wanting to steer the subject away from tying up Diane Grant.

"Sounds like something daddy would say." Darrin had a sinister grin. "Look." He held up half a soda straw. "Come to daddy."

Cal pressed pause and put down the game controller. He gripped the straw carefully then leaned over the mirror and snorted the line in one smooth motion. He tilted his head back slowly as his nose turned numb and his eyes filled with water. "That's some serious shit," he said, hoping to sound cool.

Darrin took the game controller with a pleased grin. "Damn right."

Darrin wasn't in the mood for a nice little drive. He wanted to kill people. He took out a sawed off shotgun and blew a woman's head off for no reason at all.

"I don't know," Cal said, his heart beating faster and faster.

"What?"

"I don't know about this thing, Darrin. It doesn't feel right."

"What thing?"

"You know, that thing."

"It feels right to me." Darrin didn't avert his eyes. He just kept blasting away. "It feels more than right to me."

"We shouldn't be getting involved with this shit, man."

"You look pretty involved," he said grinning.

The coke had given Cal the confidence to say something he had been thinking for days. "I mean we shouldn't *deal* the shit."

Darrin pressed pause on the game and looked at Cal. "We're not dealing. Look dude, it's only to get some money for the summer. That's all. You want everything you got to come from Mommy and Daddy? It's a couple of car rides. That's it." He looked angrily at Cal. "You already agreed."

The coke hadn't given Cal that much confidence after all. He nodded slowly as he felt his rapid pulse. "Okay, just this once."

Darrin pressed play and went back to his homicidal chores. "Just once and we're set," he said calmly.

Cal watched Darrin play the game. He watched him get out of his car and stab a woman. He hissed, "Die motherfucker. Fucking die." He raised his voice a little louder. "Die." He looked at Cal. "See the expression on her face? That's funny, huh?"

Crawford hurried back to his car thinking about the last thing Peters said to him. He shouldn't fret about things like a dumb TV show. He should stick to the important things like his family and his long-term goals. *Yeah, yeah.* Can we be concerned with what we choose to be concerned with? Or is that all just a bunch of psychobabble bullshit? Can we pick our priorities? Our obsessions? *Or am I just going to do what I'm going to do*, Crawford wondered.

Crawford decided to think about something else — his novel. That was the answer. Yeah, just think about that, he thought. *But what novel? You don't have a novel. Just some notes, that's it.*

Turning on Santa Monica Boulevard, Crawford decided to set goals — timelines, that sort of thing. If he couldn't think about the novel, he'd think about goals for the novel. It was so much easier working on the *Self Series* because that type of writing didn't require anything close to a linear approach. Putting the "program" into stages was arbitrary. It didn't matter when "Silence those that unjustly criticize you" came along, just so long as it came along. Maybe this idiot prank caller knew that too. Maybe that was part of the joke. Maybe fiction didn't require a linear approach either. Maybe life didn't. And maybe the caller knew that too.

Crawford pulled into his driveway, taking note of Cal's car — Cal's very expensive car that Cal didn't pay for. When he was Cal's age, Crawford didn't have a car. This was something he reminded Cal of often, never getting the response he was looking for, not getting a response at all.

Crawford just didn't care to see Cal much any more. He sometimes told himself it was wrong and tried to feel guilty about it, but it never worked. He didn't care to see his son much and that's just how he felt. Of course, Cal didn't want to see him either.

Little fucker. If he's in his room playing videogames and smoking dope, he thought, that's fine with me. Just so he leaves me the hell alone.

Crawford went straight to his study to see if he could hash out a few hundred words of quality fiction before Dorothy got home. His afternoon hangover had turned into a craving for more booze, so the distraction of trying to write was even more important.

To Crawford the difference between writing a novel and a self-help book was stark. The thought of "the novel" as a form had so many possibilities that Crawford found himself panic-stricken just by the idea. And he always thought of the possibilities much more than the final product — hence no novel.

Crawford sat in front of his computer slowly scrolling through the text of his uncompleted work of fiction. Twenty-two thousand words. He'd added exactly ten pages in the last year, and that was the most productive year in five.

The novel was about a number of things, of course, with a number of layers — layers upon layers. It was about a psychologist (or psychiatrist — he hadn't decided) who wanted nothing more than to help ordinary people with their problems, but along the way this led to a troubled patient doing evil things. That's one thing. It was also about a sociopath named "Melville" who liked to kill fish before he decided killing fish wasn't actually an act of power since they don't have "souls." It was about modern man's inability to set aside its individual desires for a larger collective goal that could... uh...

"Am I disturbing you?" his wife said.

"No you aren't," he said before he realized who it was. "Come in."

"Cal left. He went somewhere with that Darrin character." She sat down next to him. "Have you ever seen this guy?"

"Who?"

"Cal's friend, Darrin."

"No, I haven't."

"I haven't either. I don't like it when he doesn't introduce us to his friends."

"He hasn't done it in years, has he?"

"I guess not."

"He's getting older. Give him the choice," Crawford said. "Don't worry."

Dorothy looked uneasy.

"Come here," Crawford said.

She stood and Crawford pulled her onto his lap.

"I want to tell you something." It was always hard for Crawford to make such proclamations sound fresh. "I'm sorry for acting like an idiot. And I want to thank you for putting up with me. I'm going to make it up to you, sweetheart. After the Hershey show and after Cal's graduation, we're going on a good old-fashioned family trip. Okay?"

"Okay." She smiled. "Will you talk to Cal?"

Of course not. "Of course," he said.

Carol Clarkson was Jenny Harper's one and only friend, a woman who had known the details of Jenny's love life for nearly two years. Carol had been an eyewitness to Jenny's brief affair with the infamous Dr. Crawford, and she was standing by, as always, to help her friend bring that romp to a close. Dr. Crawford, as Carol liked to point out, was a man who could be called a lot of things, but never a friend. Carol — she was a *real* friend.

Jenny frequently availed herself of Carol's open offer to call her anytime, day or night. Carol was an unofficial "sponsor" during Jenny's difficult "withdrawal" periods — always there to listen to Jenny's tearful "never again" declarations. But in Crawford's case, "never again" never crossed Jenny's mind. Crawford's celebrity status was more gratifying to her than coitus with a sex-skilled nobody. Carol found Jenny's penchant for married men as irresistible as the tabloids in a checkout line, but hearing intimate details about Crawford was on another level.

There were frequent rumors that Jenny was addicted to married men. She often had men suitors who were unmarried, but they were not interested in her for very long. She herself was bewildered by this. During emotional outbursts she would say, "I mean, are single men just not enough of a challenge or something?"

But Carol never responded to these remarks. Carol never responded because she never "judged," as she saw it. Jenny just needed to get it all out and then they could go have a nice high-calorie consoling meal, which Carol was always up for, despite her need to lose weight.

Carol stopped on the dark street outside Jenny's apartment. It was raining.

"You're not going to make a big deal out of this break up, are you?" Carol asked.

"Big deal? When do I ever make a big deal out of anything?"

Jenny laughed, then Carol laughed with her. This meant Jenny was taking things in stride.

"Just don't let it get you down. That's all."

"I won't. I was acting like a dimwit the whole time. I don't know what I was thinking."

"You can have any man you want. Don't forget that. Just because the asshole wrote some book."

Jenny laughed with minor disapproval. "It wasn't just the *books*," she said. "But thanks for spending time with me."

"No problem."

Jenny hugged Carol, then got out of the car, running inside to escape the downpour. Carol waited until Jenny was safe inside the building, thinking *Oh, my little lost friend.*

Something Carol never admitted to Jenny — partly to save face and partly because Jenny knew it anyway — was that she was jealous of Jenny's troubled history of romance. Carol had frozen pizzas and fat-free cookies, and it had been nearly four dress sizes and a decade since she'd had a lover that didn't run on batteries. And for this disparity, Carol in fact hated Jenny.

When she stepped inside her building, Jenny took note of an unusual odor. The place was dark and something smelled mildewed. She wondered if a pipe had broken or something. It made her feel even lonelier than she was already. The old place felt bohemian, but it wasn't hospitable.

Why is the hall light out?

Standing at the door, Jenny put her bag down and fumbled to get her keys. Her 24-key key ring was too much. She sorted with her thumb and forefinger and found the one she needed. Now she was thinking about changing a number of things. Fewer keys, fewer married men.

She unlocked the door and reached inside the apartment and turned on the light.

The light must have hit him in the face as he stood behind her, with his mask on — the best one with the best fit. He must've stepped slowly toward her, as he felt his smile growing larger. He knows he has to get her to the van alive.

It's within my power, he is thinking.

She is walking to the hall bureau. She is taking off her earrings. She is looking in the mirror, inspecting her face from every angle. She is obviously concerned with her aging looks — concerned with her shelf life as an object of beauty.

He might have tightened his yellow gloves so he could feel the fabric brace across his knuckles. He pulls out the cloth laced with sodium pentothal and steps behind her.

Will she see me?

No, he thinks, *her vanity is too great.*

EIGHT

D orothy decided to make a nice dinner, something she routinely did after she and Jim resolved an issue. It officially meant a problem was over, which also meant there was nothing more to discuss.

She decided to make one of Crawford's old favorites: chicken zucchini lasagna. He complained that the dish was responsible for helping his middle-aged gut protrude over his beltline, but Dorothy rationalized it was a healthier indulgence than single-malt Scotch.

Crawford decided it would look normal to lie on the couch in the den and prepare for the Hershey show by looking over some of his notes, which were essentially a rundown of *Self-Esteem*'s major points along with some mildly entertaining remarks and observations he could use as time wasters.

"Honey, Cal's home," Dorothy yelled from the kitchen.

So what, he thought. *What am I going to do? Run to the door and throw my arms around the little prick? Little bastard drives a fifty-thousand dollar car.*

The thought of the car was becoming more and more annoying. Crawford tried to concentrate on his notes but the "entertainment news" on TV was stealing his attention. There was an up and coming young actor who had just been arrested for beating up his girlfriend in a New Orleans hotel room. Crawford had never seen the guy, who was apparently a big hit on primetime. Crawford looked at the kid's dark, angry eyes. It looked like Bourbon Street or somewhere else in the French Quarter, a place where Crawford had gotten smashed several more times than he could remember.

Crawford looked at his notes.

I guess I'm just going to wing it, he thought.

Then he heard Dorothy raise her voice from the kitchen, as if she'd been trying to muster the courage to do so for a long time. "So where did you go this afternoon?"

Crawford shook his head thinking, *I knew she'd ask me that.* But before he could open his mouth, he heard Cal answer the question.

"I just took Darrin home. Damn. What's the big deal?"

"Have you been crying?" Crawford heard his wife say.

Crawford got up, walked to the kitchen and stood near the doorway.

Dorothy had her hands on her hips as if to show authority. "You could have said something. I made dinner. Why are your eyes so red? Have you been crying or something? Is something wrong?"

Crawford poked his head around the corner and saw Cal with his back to him. He didn't need to see Cal's red eyes to know that he hadn't been crying.

"I'm just tired. What's the big deal?"

"You could be a little more polite, Son," Crawford said. Crawford figured if he wasn't going to make an issue out of Cal being high, his son could at least show him some face.

"Oh, really? Father," Cal said.

"Your mother is worried about you."

"*You're* not worried, though. Are you?"

Crawford looked at Cal's glazed eyes and wondered if he hadn't been blasé about Cal's drug use. "I'm a little worried about you too," he said.

"About me? Maybe you should worry about yourself."

"Cal," Dorothy started. "Don't talk to your father..."

"What father?" Cal said, storming out of the kitchen and up the stairs. Dorothy looked as if she was going to stop him then Crawford shook his head.

"Let him go."

"I just don't know what to do," she said, throwing her oven mitt on the counter.

"Don't do anything. He's a teenager. There's nothing you can do."

"Nothing, huh?" Dorothy said before sinking into a long silence.

She burned the chicken zucchini lasagna.

Crawford just wandered back into the den and sat on the couch. On TV the "entertainment news" show had ended. The local news, which in the last decade had pretty much become entertainment news with a little weather, had begun. The title card behind the newscaster read, "Famous Psychologist Missing." Crawford knew they were talking about Dr. Thomas Watkins, a somewhat well-known psychologist, but one few people recognized from TV.

Crawford stared at the screen wondering what his tongue looked like.

• • •

Jenny couldn't remember where she was or how she got there. She just knew this couldn't be real. She started to struggle. She started to breathe heavily. She realized her hands must be tied or she wouldn't be struggling, but she couldn't feel her hands. She couldn't feel her arms. She wondered if she still had them. *But I'm moving, so I must have them.* She moved again. She tried to speak, but couldn't. She tried to open her mouth but something was covering it. There was a blinding light, then a beeping sound, like a recorder of some kind. There were footsteps — slow, lumbering footsteps. Surely I am dreaming, she thought. Then she saw the reflection of a large knife in front of her face. Then she heard a voice — an expressionless, unfamiliar voice.

"Stage two."

She could feel his breath, not her own, streaming from her nostrils.

"Eliminate the harmful things that are destroying your life."

Then it was the blade again.

"You know all about Dr. Crawford's program," he is saying.

Jenny thought that surely she was dreaming. No, she knew she was dreaming. *That's right.* And that was the end of that. And since she knew she was dreaming it was what they call a "lucid dream." *That's right.* And in lucid dreaming you can create any circumstance you want. She had tried to get Jim to read some material on the subject to see if perhaps he could insert lucid dream manipulation into the *Self Series*, but he acted like an asshole and didn't want to hear it. *Okay, maybe I can talk him into it now. Okay, I don't need to talk him into that. Trip to Acapulco. Trip to Acapulco.*

It's a TV show. There's that Happy Pappy character. It's a biography program. *Is this about Jim? That's not what I want.*

Maybe it was Jim who was dreaming. He had an imagination like that.

Happy Pappy was born to Mr. and Mrs. Pappy of Blissville Road. Happy's mother, Joy Pappy, breastfeeds little Happy with her pink popsicle nipples that Happy delightedly sucks for their fruity nectar. Happy's father, Glee Pappy, watches with pride, staring at the little camper's distinctive nose and cheeks. "He will be Happy when he grows up," he says, "and he will let nothing get him down. And I mean nothing."

Happy starts to walk, petting the fuzzy flora and fauna that litter their serene backdrop. "Do you feel good?" he often asks the natural beauty around him. "Yes we do!" the flowers and trees gaily reply. Everything seems perfect.

But there are problems: Old Man Glee starts to drink too much root beer at night, which makes him blissful at first but later a bit cranky. And Joy, as a result of taking care of her young son, is sometimes too tired at night to humpty hump with Glee, which Glee blames on little Happy. Joy also says she hates the smell of root beer on a man and Glee sometimes gives her a mean spanking for saying bad things to him. Soon there are more than just a couple of problems. Young Happy grows into adolescence hating Glee and starts to dream of killing him and running away with Joy to another backdrop. Glee becomes aware of Happy's resentment and starts to give him nasty slaps while high on root beer.

Since there are no other creatures around besides the Pappies and the furry animals that dance and play, Happy starts to fall in love with his mother Joy. His weenie gets hard at night thinking about her big lollipop boobies so he...

"Christ! I said Acapulco! Acapulco!"

Then the breath of a whisper on her neck: "You aren't dreaming, little lover."

As Dorothy puttered around in the bathroom, Crawford sat in bed looking at the ceiling, his right wrist resting on his forehead, his eyes sagging with fatigue but unable to close. The thirst was killing him, *but it's killing millions of others as well. I'm not alone.* This thought didn't make things any easier for Crawford. He felt no universal link to the millions who shared his disease. As a matter of fact, he despised them.

"Distract yourself into positive thoughts."

That's in *Self-Confidence,* he thought. What bullshit. *But wait. I came up with that when I was inebriated. Is that right? That's right. I came up with the idea long before I wrote it. And yes, I was piss drunk.*

Crawford had come up with almost all his good ideas for the *Self Series* while he was smashed. He drank to rebel. But then he needed to rebel against the rebellion of drinking. And he decided at some point that there was no greater rebellion against drinking than self-help.

Crawford had been in the habit of rebelling against anything he could think of since he was in his mid-teens. Later, he rebelled against himself rebelling.

To Crawford college was about whether you were attracted to the light or to the dark. And at some time or another, Crawford had come to the decision that the dark was more meaningful than the light. The dark was interesting, engaging. The light was easy, ordinary, predictable, obvious — like a 60-watt bulb. Damn it, depressing things were *in* and what wasn't *wasn't*, and that's all there was to it.

But after he married, after his child was born, after "the dark" hadn't paid off like he thought it would, Crawford had a revelation. He would rebel against the dark. He would take that frown and turn it upside down.

He would turn his back on the gloomy doomy poseurs and think about the wise words of Thomas Paine and Benjamin Franklin and Gandhi and Einstein and Eleanor Roosevelt and Helen Keller and Dale Carnegie.

Yes, Carnegie. Dorothy had given Crawford a copy of Carnegie's classic *How to Stop Worrying and Start Living* after Crawford had identified worry as the prime reason for his heavy drinking. "It's all about worry, honey."

"Read this," she said, throwing the book in his lap as he lay on the living room couch, recovering from a bender. "You won't need to drink ever again."

It was that simple.

Yeah, right. Crawford was skeptical of the book for many reasons. He especially liked to make jokes that it was published just prior to Carnegie's death.

Crawford was soon struck, though, by Carnegie's maxim, "Cooperate with the inevitable." That was pure genius. If you looked at it in a certain way, *it could be as depressing as they come,* but it wasn't.

"Cooperate with the inevitable." He said it often to himself as he fought to stay sober. It was inevitable he would stop drinking. In life or in death, he would eventually stop. And with that in mind, Crawford drank less. And soon, Crawford was working on himself like he did as a boy back in the days of his paper route. He put aside Carnegie and started making notes: little lessons to himself on how to live. It worked. It helped him improve. Things changed. He started to write thoughts in notebooks and record them on tape. The ideas he was especially proud of were neatly typed using his old electric typewriter. And they all seemed to flow from one idea: let things happen that are going to happen and move on. It gave Crawford a strong sense of relief to think this way. It gave him... *Self-Confidence.*

Crawford at some point realized that these notes, these typed and scribbled pages, made up the largest body of non-academic writing he had done in his entire life. As Dorothy began to organize them into a manuscript, Crawford realized that the size of the work rivaled that of his doctoral dissertation, which was short by the university's standards.

The strangest thing was that the act of writing had improved Crawford's confidence. Perhaps he *could* write that novel someday. Perhaps he *could* have that confidence (the *self*-confidence, rather). *Self-Confidence* was finally published to mixed reviews and fantastic sales. And the light had won for a while.

Eventually, however, Carnegie's "Cooperate with the inevitable" didn't offer the same comfort it once did. Then it didn't offer any comfort at all. Perhaps it even made Crawford's worries multiply. What was "the inevitable" after all? And how would you cooperate with it?

Okay, Cal is going to experiment with marijuana. That's inevitable. Cooperate with it. Okay, but what if he moves on to harder drugs? Ecstasy, then speed, then cocaine, then crack, then heroin.

Naw, that's not going to happen. That's not the inevitable.

Or is it?

Crawford had thought Dorothy was right, that he hadn't been thinking of his son enough. But what could he do? Every time he thought about Cal it started a conversation in his head that disturbed him. And such a disorder was what made him want to drink. And drinking didn't help the promotional appearance on the Hershey show, writing the novel, working things out with Lee, trying to be happy, and stopping the nuts of the world that think they are Happy Pappy.

And the more Crawford thought about Cal — especially his ability to avoid discipline — the more helpless he felt. Suddenly Cal's last words were eating at Crawford's fragile pride: Maybe you should worry about yourself.

Crawford mimed the words in baby talk. *The little prick.*

Dorothy came out of the bathroom combing her hair. She was wearing that nightgown he loved so much. Crawford started to think how beautiful she looked, but the thought went away.

"Don't worry about him, Dorothy. He'll be just fine. Just let him get through adolescence. That's all. We all went through it."

"He's my son. I'll always worry about him."

She sat on the edge of the bed, and Crawford rolled on his side away from her.

"Worry is just a part of life, okay?" he said.

Silently and blankly, Dorothy mimed Crawford's words.

PART II:
The Harmful Things

NINE

CRAWFORD'S EYES SEEMED TO FORCE THEMSELVES open. He thought he heard a noise but now there was piercing silence. He had fallen asleep without knowing it and now he was awake and alert and oddly so. His sleeping patterns were always a befuddled mess while he was "on one," and this moment was what he theoretically thought of as the *Strange Alertness After Initial Sobriety While Sleeping Past Liquor Store Hours* Syndrome.

It was impossible to know whether he had heard a noise or not, but he could have sworn he did. *Yes, it was a car. A car squealing away.*

So what? he thought.

The digital clock next to his bed read 3:40am. *Thank God, the liquor stores are closed. I made it. I made it without drinking.*

Oh God, he thought, *the liquor stores are closed.*

Crawford carefully got out of bed and went to the window, pulling the curtain slightly aside to take a peak outside and spy the source of that strange noise. The street looked normal and peaceful like it always did.

Just a noise. That's all.

Crawford was just about to close the curtains when he noticed something at the front door — just a corner of something that wasn't blocked by the awning. It looked like it could be another package, just like the first one, sitting in the same place on the front steps.

A package? Another package? Again?

His first inclination was to wake Dorothy, but no, *bad idea. I'll take care of this myself.*

He put on his robe and slippers and quietly stepped into the hallway outside the master bedroom, looking over his shoulder to watch his wife sleep.

"I can't even handle a practical joke, baby," he whispered. "You deserve so much better."

He closed the door slowly then looked down the hall, standing up straight, extending his chest.

I can do better. Yes, I can.

Crawford walked down the dark steps in time with the ticking of the grandfather clock, which sounded curiously loud. He pressed his ear against the door then looked through the peephole.

How ridiculous this is, he thought. *You cowardly piece of shit.*

Crawford opened the door, and the wind felt curiously warm, like the hot breath of a dog but dry as a bone. He stepped onto his front porch and stood in front of two packages at his feet. Both were wrapped like gifts — one the size of a videotape, the other bigger and flatter.

Crawford looked beyond his dark front yard to the silent neighborhood around him to see if he noticed anything unusual — a car, a light, something. But there was nothing. Same old neighborhood, safe and sound. Apparently they had come and gone. *They? He? Her?* There was no way of knowing. *If this is Berry, he's more ambitious than I thought.*

Crawford took the two packages down to his fortress of solitude and sat at his desk, placing them in front of him. He sat back in his chair, hesitant to do anything. He knew the smaller package was probably a videotape. But the other? There was a small envelope on top of the smaller package, and he picked it up and opened it.

"To Dr. Crawford from Happy Pappy. Your program works!" Crawford read aloud.

Fucking clowns. And Dorothy will never believe it. Never.

Just like college days.

There were never any whoopee cushions. There were never any saltshakers with the lids unscrewed, never any super glue in door locks or laxatives in drinks. No itching powder or stink bombs. Nothing that could be defined or recognized as a practical joke. Which alone could drive the average person completely nuts. But that wasn't the worst of it. This subtle approach to harassment had a far subtler cousin: the absence of a finale.

One pestering thing after another never had a prank's logical resolution, never the coda, never the laughs of having embarrassed or humiliated, never the adolescent gloat of having caused frustration or inconvenience, never any explanation of payback, retribution, or revenge, never any indication of whether that revenge was served hot or cold (if, in fact, it was revenge) or even if it existed at all. There was never even a denial, which was not surprising in the absence of an accusation. And there was never an accusation because there was never any solid grounds for one. What Crawford believed his classmates Albert Scott and Jay Berry were doing to him was so brilliant in its variation and irregularity that he could never bring himself to confront them about it. Crawford was certain they were put on earth to drain him of his energy, make his life more difficult, and cause him endless aggravation. But he could never prove it. He could never catch them. He could never make a distinction between their silent assault and the tribulations of everyday life. Truth was, he could not know for sure.

But I do know, yes! That was the slap he always gave himself. "They're fucking with me constantly!" he would tell Dorothy. "I know it, I know it!"

Dorothy was always unconvinced. "How do you know? You've never seen them do these things. You're just paranoid."

"I know I'm paranoid. But I'm still right," he once said after some research data disappeared. "Those guys are trying to break me."

Dorothy's rosy assessment would not be challenged. "Oh, please. You just have bad luck sometimes. We all do. Life is full of these little things."

And "little things" they were. Occasionally they were bigger, but mostly they were just little things. And oddly, the smaller they were, the more annoying: keys lost, phones unplugged, notes and books misplaced, bookmarkers changing locations, clocks changing times, oddly coincidental misinformation, half truths, misunderstandings, and confusion. Bigger things generally meant less trouble. Crawford discovering a flat tire or that an important book was missing was an end in itself. But the small things always came at a bigger cost: distraction, loss of focus, schedules not kept, late work, late bills, people pissed off, more work, and (worst of all) more drinking.

And thus it went on for the entire duration of Crawford's college years with Berry and Scott. Always there. No pattern, no consistency. Never ending. Never resolved. No closure. And Berry and Scott were responsible for all of it. Crawford was sure of it. And it never went away until graduation.

Apparently it never went away at all. *Apparently.*

Crawford put the note down and grabbed the second one from the larger package. Crawford again read aloud. "To Dorothy from Happy Pappy. A little something for your self-esteem."

"Fuck it," he said, tearing open the smaller package. He was right: a videotape. Crawford had resolve. He wasn't drunk this time, and he was going to look at this thing square in the face. He clicked on the small TV next to his desk and shoved the tape in the VCR.

"It's the fucking *Happy Pappy Show*," he said, shaking his head. The video the night before wasn't just the drunken nightmare he had hoped it was.

The insidious theme song plays and the title scrolls across the screen, but it looks different. The puppets are in the background, but they aren't moving. Then the head pops into the screen: Crawford's monster, Happy Pappy.

"Yessssssiiiiirrrrreeeee. Good morning, Dr. Crawford! We're moving right along with your self-esteem!"

Berry and Scott wouldn't go to this kind of trouble.

The ghoulish marionette holds up a new hardback copy of *Self-Esteem* just to the left of his head.

Would they?

"Time for stage two!"

Crawford felt a jolt of adrenaline course through his body. Happy is smiling at the book like a proud father admiring his infant child. He opens the book like a sacred text and begins to read. "The second stage is to eliminate the harmful things that are destroying our lives." He turns to the camera. "That's good advice, Dr. Crawford!" Mr. Pappy moves away from the camera to reveal a woman tied to a chair. She sits flush next to a table, almost like a child in a highchair ready to be force-fed. There is tape around her mouth, and it's stained.

Crawford leaned toward the screen slowly. He could see it was blood. He could also see that the woman was Jenny Harper.

"Oh God," he said.

Happy Pappy slowly tiptoes with exaggerated movements toward Crawford's mistress. Her bound and motionless body is in strange contrast to her tormentor's bouncing, overjoyed face. Then he speaks again, looking at the camera with the book tucked safely under his arm, his head bobbing grotesquely. "We all know that fucking someone besides Mommy is really naughty. It's really bad! That's why a little cocksucking whore like this one needs to be eliminated before she destroys our lives!"

This can't be real. Jenny, is it you?

Happy Pappy holds up the book again. "It's time to read some words of wisdom." He leans in. "That's Dr. Crawford's wisdom, boys and girls," the masked head barks.

He turns behind him and whips the tape off the woman's mouth, making a screech that rivals the woman's awful scream. She gasps for air.

"No," she weeps.

"What?" her captor says, his right hand to his ear.

"Please mister," she gasps, her eyes filling with water.

"My name is Happy Pappy, you little fancy pants." He lets out a great laugh then puts the book in front of her.

"Now you're going to read the word. The word! You're going to read some Crawford," he says.

"Please, please," she whimpers.

"You don't have to say *please*," he says, shaking his head.

She turns away from him, almost as if she is looking over her shoulder. He puts the book just under her chin, then his yellow-gloved hand points down like a plane crashing into the page.

"I said read, you little bitchy witchy."

She cranes her neck, turning away as if this would end the nightmare.

The corncob pipe jutting from the left of Happy's mouth swivels in tandem before he strokes her trembling face.

"Okay. Okay," she gasps. She looks down at the book then back at her tormentor. She looks at the book again, and her mouth shakes as she tries to speak. "People," she says, struggling. "People usually recognize right away," she coughs, "when they've created a relationship with bad things or bad people." She swallows painfully. "But many times we continue these relationships..." She starts to weep. "We continue..." She breaks down sobbing.

Happy Pappy strokes her hair. "Yes. And why is that?" He brings the book to his chest and reads. "Because we're afraid to eliminate them from our lives!" Then he turns to the camera. "Not unless you've got self-esteem," he yells, his head nodding slowly.

He sets the book down on the table next to Jenny's chair then leisurely picks something up — a large kitchen knife.

Crawford felt like he was choking. "It's a hoax," he said, his right hand coursing through his hair. "It's a hoax."

If it's a hoax it's a first-rate job, by golly.

Jenny peers up at Happy.

Crawford saw a look in her eyes that he thought he'd seen before. *This isn't acting. Holy Christ, this is real!*

Happy Pappy stands in front of Jenny, blocking her from view. Then he turns back to the camera.

"Stage two, Doctor!"

He turns back around and slowly brings up his right hand, the knife facing downward.

"No," she cries. "God, No!"

"You don't need God when you've got self-esteem!" he roars. "You *are* God," he giggles, then thrusts the knife into her neck.

He turns to the camera one last time. "Yes, boys and girls," he screams, the mask sprayed with blood. "Stage two complete! Stay tuned for Stage three!"

The screen goes blank.

Crawford couldn't move. He gripped the side of his chair to make sure he wasn't asleep, staring into the broadcast snow, which reached out and engulfed him.

He turned to his left, where his cocktail would have been sitting the night before, but nothing was there. His fingers scraped the surface of his desk as if he could summon Scotch from its smooth surface. He undid the top button of his shirt, feeling a cold sweat around his neck, then sat back in his chair looking at the snow on the TV screen as if it might hold a clue to the source of this madness.

"It's a hoax. It's just a hoax," Crawford said.

It didn't look like a hoax.

Crawford picked up the phone.

I'll call the police. Just call the police.

I'll tell them about the tape. Tapes? Do I tell them about the tape last night? He was about to punch 911, then he paused. *Or I'll tell them I'm being harassed. But then you have to tell them about the tape. Both tapes. Or I'll tell them to check on Jenny Harper. I'll just start with Jenny. I'll see if it's a prank first.* Then he looked at the empty box on his desk. He grabbed it and looked inside. Nothing — just empty. *The other package. The package addressed to Dorothy.* He tore off the anonymous wrapping. It was a picture frame. A cheap frame. He turned it over. *A black and white photograph.* One of Crawford and Jenny outside her apartment. Crawford's face became a furious grimace. Jenny's mouth was open, apparently firing back. Her eyes were filled with despondency and fear. *When was this?* There was a note tucked inside the frame and Crawford opened it. It was typewritten, like on an old typewriter.

```
Dear Mrs. Crawford,
A little something for your self-esteem.
```

"God damn it!" Crawford yelled out loud.

The amount of work a prank like this would take was beyond the level of Berry and Scott. But who was it and what did they want? If it was a hoax then Jenny would have to be in on it, which would be very unlikely.

Or would it? Do I know her? Do I really know her? She was angry, very angry. And what do I do now?

Crawford looked at the phone again. He looked at the numbers 9-1-1.

"They'll think you did it," he said to himself. "They'll think you're cracked." *You'll have to tell them you've been having an affair with the woman in the video. There'll be some big guy who blows smoke in your face and wants to know where you've been the last several days. And you've been drunk the last several days! You saw her when? You can't remember. You had a fight. About what? I was ending the affair. I think I was ending the affair. I need to get sober. My wife is going to leave me.*

And you're the guy who wrote them books that tell people how to live? this hulking brute of a cop asks before he goes out into the hall grinning like a panting dog and calling his drinking buddy who writes for a small-time tabloid.

And what do I do?

Crawford couldn't even trust himself to make a decision, especially not without a drink. *Impulse.* Crawford grabbed the tape and photograph and went upstairs. He couldn't risk waking Dorothy, so he retrieved some clothes that were in the guestroom next to his bedroom — a pair of dark, pleated slacks and a white Oxford shirt that had been retired because of the sweat stains under the arms. He got dressed quietly then grabbed his briefcase from the downstairs hall closet and put the tape and photograph inside.

What am I doing? I need a drink. Without one...

When the previous night's alcohol started to ebb in his system, Crawford would feel like his soul was being taken away from him and he would have none of that now.

"There's comfort in accomplishment," Crawford had written in *Self-Respect*. "It's soothing to be doing. You have won when you are done."

During the last week of his last year in the master's program in clinical psychology, Crawford was tired, having stayed up for five days straight writing and rewriting his thesis. He'd stayed pretty drunk the whole time — sipping from a flask of bourbon as he typed — but was still able to write a pretty decent paper. Back in those days, he had an old manual typewriter that he'd inherited from his Uncle Jerry — a little appliance Crawford favored over a fancy-shmancy electric job. As he put it, "I have a lot in common with this thing. We can both take a shot of whiskey in the gut and still dry out and keep working."

Crawford often said his thesis had taken two years to research and write, but the truth was he had researched many topics on and off for two years — writing countless notes and endlessly reading journals — without having written a single sentence of submittable text. The reasons for his procrastination were many: time spent studying for the comprehensive exam (that was the excuse he gave to others, though he rarely studied), frequent changes in his argument, general laziness, drunkenness, and more drunkenness and laziness. The biggest problem, he knew, was fear.

His final argument was very simple, but it was also a great deal more unusual than those being presented by students (like himself) specializing in therapy and not assessment.

At the time, there were all kinds of new methodologies. Clinical psychology is all about method, and those who want to be pioneers try to forge ahead with a brand new method that will change the discipline, or they suggest revising an old one to make it more effective. If you had guts, you'd come up with a new therapy. Wimps went the interpretation route, or worse, emphasized procedure.

It was highly unusual for anyone to write a master's thesis proclaiming a new therapy. This was something people did for their doctoral dissertations, and rarely ever then. Usually psychologists wrote about new therapies long after their PhDs were completed and then after years (and sometimes decades) of additional research. But for Crawford it was partly a joke and partly a fantasy to be the "father" of a new therapy. Besides booze, what gave Crawford the confidence to take such an intrepid jump was the inspiring attitude of his unorthodox, nonconformist advisor Dr. Tony Watkins. More of a die-hard evolutionist than a psychologist, Watkins hated unoriginality more than anything. The bearded old Southerner, looking a bit like Darwin himself, believed that as man progressed, so too must his approach to therapy. Crawford found it odd that Watkins never came up with his own therapy, just a few undistinguished papers on how to approach theory.

"When are you going to write your manifesto?" Crawford once asked him in class.

"Manifesto? That's for you all to do," he once said. "I'm just a teacher. I studied to be a teacher, so I'm going to teach. If I quit teaching, I'll be an actor and do the great works of Shakespeare on the stage," he joked. "The day I come up with my own therapy is the day I've lost my mind." It was a humble edict for a man who held such high standards for his students.

Despite Watkins' values he was surprisingly flexible. When Crawford requested to change his thesis topic, Watkins gave approval both times without a fuss. His first was called "Clinical Depression and the Benefits of Masturbation Therapy." Crawford had once read an article claiming that frequent masturbation helps prevent prostrate cancer. The theory said the practice purged the gland of carcinogens and, perhaps, made the cells more resistant. Armed with only a gym sock and a Farrah Fawcett poster, Crawford did the clinical trials single-handedly and came to the conclusion that masturbation actually helps depression, which in turn helps the body fight disease. A problem popped up, however, when it came to suggesting the actual therapy. After brief consideration, he realized there was no way he could produce a 25,000-word document on jacking off. He also had trouble finding anyone willing to participate in the research. Watkins loved the idea, but didn't complain when Crawford wanted to change direction.

His second proposal was called "Sanction Therapy," a "pre-therapeutic therapy" that tackled the idea of whether or not a patient needs to give himself permission to heal before he goes through the healing process. Crawford never submitted a formal written proposal to Watkins, who later called his pitch "a pre-proposal." But the idea was enough to keep Watkins hungry for more.

The third proposal turned out to be a charm. Watkins appeared to like the idea more than Crawford, but Crawford knew, at the very least, it was a more research-worthy topic than masturbation. In other words, it would be easier for him to bullshit his way through. The proposal was also vague enough to leave him breathing space on just about every aspect of the paper — structure, style, and (most importantly) content. Crawford was probably more surprised than anyone that he was able to write the 78-page document as fast as he did, especially since he made almost all of it up as he went along.

When he typed the last words on a Friday afternoon, it was time to celebrate. And celebrate he did, until his binge came to an abrupt end on Monday morning when he got an unexpected call from Jay Berry.

The morning air seeped through the crack Crawford had opened on the driver side window. The breeze and the passing scenery were just enough to wake his senses from his day-old hangover.

He grabbed the car phone and punched at the numbers.

The phone was finally picked up and rustled across some unknown surface. "Hello?"

"Lee?"

After a sigh, "Who the hell is this?" He was still half-asleep. "What the hell time is it?"

"I have to see you."

"Jim?"

"I have to see you."

"You want to see me *now*?"

"I have to see you." Crawford raised his voice just a little. "Now."

"Now?"

Crawford was winding through the dark curves of the Valley-side Hills, an exclusive neighborhood notoriously populated by pornographers, rap stars, and B-list actors. Crawford felt his fear momentarily overridden by anger, an emotion that popped up every time he was within five miles of Lee's home. It wasn't that Lee was wealthier than he was or that Lee lived in a bigger and nicer home. It wasn't that Lee lacked worries and personal problems. What angered him was Lee's control over Crawford, including his nagging conviction that Crawford needed to get his shit together so he could make Lee even more money. Of course, Lee always used the word "we."

"If you could increase your output a bit," he once said nonchalantly, "we could be doing much better. Think about it."

Crawford felt his publisher's pressure to exploit the self-help obsessed public was one of his greatest hurdles in improving his own life. Lee, unlike Dorothy, wasn't concerned with Crawford's problems. And as Crawford saw it, he should be. Who the hell was he not to be concerned? Weren't those the things a friend cares about? Then Crawford got in touch with his most rational self. He might just be jealous of Lee. Maybe he just resented Lee's ability to let go of his fears and insecurities and just worry about getting richer. Crawford thought that Lee's outlook might be something to aspire to. *Maybe.*

Probably not, though.

Lee lived in a giant mock art-deco home built in the 1960s that hid behind a tall, slender line of shrubs. The roof was the only part of the structure visible from the road, which lent the property a fashionable secrecy. It wasn't anonymity that Lee loved. It was the prestige of anonymity. If you are trying to stay out of the public eye, chances are you do so for good reason, and to Lee that was very hip.

Crawford stopped his car in front of the large iron gate, which had a gaudy "LB" written in large, baroque lettering. Lee wasn't trying to hide from anyone. Nearly every time Crawford waited for Lee to pick up the intercom, he felt patronized by the letters' gaze.

The front gate opened with a sharp buzz and Crawford drove through. Lee was standing on the front steps in his bathrobe, arms akimbo, revealing, even from a distance, that he was displeased with this unexpected visit.

Crawford slowly pulled the car up to the front of the house and Lee angrily motioned for him to turn off his lights.

"Damn it, Jim," he said approaching the car. "Don't wake my kids up. It's five o'clock in the morning, you know."

Of course he's pissed, Crawford thought. *He doesn't know about the tape yet.*

Crawford got out of the car holding his briefcase close.

Lee put a hand on his hip and thought how this better not be about Crawford's contractual obligations, in particular the Hershey show.

"What the hell is it, Jim? Is this about the Hershey show?"

"No, Lee," Crawford said. "Can we go inside?"

Lee rolled his eyes then shook his head. "What is it now?" he mumbled. "I feel like I'm your fucking psychiatrist."

The interior of Lee's home grated with its exterior. The straight lines and lack of right angles on the outside suggested a minimalism to be found on the inside that wasn't there. The strange hodgepodge of styles started with a foyer of uncouth white light and gold fixtures — a recurring irritant when Crawford was hung over. But this time he wasn't paying much attention to Lee's style crimes. There was a real crime to discuss.

"A tape? What are you talking about?"

"You have a VCR in your office, right?"

"No VCR. Why?"

"The den then?"

"What is it now, Jim?" Lee looked at a modern grandfather clock sitting in the front hall and sighed. "It's five in the morning."

"You have one somewhere? You have a VCR somewhere, right?" Crawford asked with the tape in hand.

Lee laughed to himself then led Crawford into his den. "A tape. A videotape? You got me up at five in the fucking a.m. to show me a videotape? Yeah, I've got one, but I don't even know if it works. I switched to DVD a year ago. Haven't you?"

"It's serious, Lee."

"Serious? What is it? A murder or something?"

"Yes."

"Really?" Lee froze. "Really?"

Crawford took a deep breath. "I think so."

Lee laughed. "What? You killed someone and videotaped it. Is that it?"

"No, Lee."

"Good. 'Cause if you did, you could have waited until later to show me."

"Just sit down."

"The old thing is in the cabinet under the TV," Lee said pointing.

The look on Crawford's face was serious — resolute, almost confident. Lee was therefore a little more respectful. "Okay," he said sitting in front of the TV. "Show me."

Crawford turned on the TV and pushed in the tape. It needed rewinding. "Look. Someone's been calling me at home and on my mobile phone. And then someone sent me a videotape yesterday." Crawford took a deep breath. "It has some guy dressed like Happy Pappy."

Lee smiled as if relieved. "You got a fucked up sense of humor, my friend."

"Shut up, Lee. I got drunk, okay."

The smile disappeared from Lee's face. "So?"

"And I thought I dreamed the whole thing. Then I get another tape. I get this."

"Thought you dreamed what?"

"What's on this tape," Crawford said urgently.

Lee held up his hands. "Okay. Okay. I have no idea what you're saying. Just play the damn tape."

Crawford hit play and Lee leaned forward. Three seconds later the image of Happy Pappy came on the screen.

Yessssssiiiiirrrrreeeee. Good morning, Dr. Crawford! We're moving right along with your self-esteem!

Lee chuckled then looked at Crawford. "You're kidding, right?"

"When do I ever kid, Lee?"

Time for Stage two!

"You aren't trying to tell me something, are you?"

"Shut up, Lee. Just watch."

Without a sound, Lee watched the tape to the end, until the Happy Pappy mask appeared stained with blood.

"Jesus," he muttered. "What?"

Crawford pressed stop on the VCR and removed the tape.

"Someone left this on your door?"

"This evening."

Lee grabbed a cigarette from the end table and lit it. He stood up. "The woman, she's that publicist you worked with a year or so ago, isn't she?"

Crawford sat down in a chair. "Yes," he said mechanically.

"And you've been bangin' her, right?"

"Don't use words like that." Crawford coughed. "I just ended it."

"When?"

"Just yesterday. I think." Crawford nodded, "Or maybe..."

"Whatever. Let's call it recent. How did you do it?"

"I left a message on her machine." Crawford couldn't put the events in sequence. "But before that we had an argument, I think. I was drunk and..."

Lee began pacing over Crawford like a trial lawyer. "Did she know before you left the message you wanted to end it?"

"Yes, but what does that have to do with anything?"

"Then she was angry?"

"Yes, of course, but what does that have to do with anything? I mean, we've got to go to the police, right?"

Lee took a drag of his cigarette and relaxed. Still in thought, he walked over to a red leather chair and sat down, putting his feet up on the small stool that accompanied it. He took a longer drag of his cigarette. "You know, Jim. This might be a fake."

"A fake? You saw what happened. That was no fake!"

Lee put his index finger to his lips. "Be quiet, Jim," he said softly like a governess. Lee let out a cool sigh to try to impede Crawford's growing panic. Lee seemed to be even more relaxed in a crisis than in ordinary life.

"She might be doing this to get back at you," he said looking away, nodding.

"Come on. I know her. She's vindictive, but she wouldn't stoop to something like this."

"How do you know?"

"She's not that creative."

"You don't seem so sure."

"I'm sure. Look at this." Jim pulled the photograph from his brief-case and handed it to Lee.

"What's this?"

"It's a photograph."

"I can see that." Lee looked at it and immediately recognized Jenny. "Oh that one," he said with a smile. Lee sat up. "So? What about it?"

"So?" Crawford touched his brow. "This was with the tape. With a note to my wife."

"What kind of note?"

Crawford handed him the note. "Look."

Jim watched silently as Lee read the note, nodding his head as if it made the situation completely clear.

"Someone's trying to blackmail you." Lee put down his cigarette.

"Blackmail? They haven't asked for anything."

"Not yet. They will. The tape is a fake, Jim." Lee handed Jim the photograph. "Unfortunately, this isn't."

"How do you know the tape's a fake?"

"Why is this picture addressed to your wife?"

Crawford stood up as if sitting were painful. "How the fuck should I know? We've got to go to the police."

"We?"

"Okay," Crawford said turning to leave, "thanks for your help, bud-dy. I'm going to the cops."

Lee stood up. "No, wait. Just sit down a minute." Crawford was breathing heavily now. "Please." Lee put his hand on Jim's shoulder.

"Please, Jim. Jeez, you got me up at 5am. Who else could you call?"

Crawford sat down in Lee's only comfortable chair.

Lee leaned toward Crawford like a doctor addressing his patient. "I want you to go home, Jim. Just go home and wait. Wait and see."

"Wait and see what?"

"Just go home and wait."

Crawford was in awe of Lee's nonchalance. He immediately thought Lee was only thinking of the financial dangers. "I can't believe you."

"Go home, Jim," Lee said slowly.

"Well," Crawford said standing, "good night, Lee." He paused as if waiting for a response. "Okay?"

"You can't go to the police, Jim."

"Why not?"

"This could ruin you."

Crawford looked at Lee with amazement. "Ruin me? I should have known better than to talk to you. You're concerned about business? Is that it? Your precious Happy Pappy franchise? Is that it?"

Crawford turned to leave, but Lee put his hand on Crawford's chest, stopping him like a customs official. "You'll be the prime suspect."

Crawford was silent. This had occurred to him, but only for a moment.

Lee began walking slowly toward Crawford, as if to embellish his point. "The first thing they'll do is ask you if you know the woman. Then you'll have to tell them all about the affair. You'll have to go ahead and tell them about the message on the machine because they'll find it anyway."

Crawford hadn't thought about the message.

"Then you'll be the prime suspect. Then they'll have no choice but to incarcerate you because they don't have anyone else. Then the press will get the story and it'll be a fucking circus. Then Jan Hershey will have a very different show this week. Then your wife will leave you and take everything you've got. And this is all before any evidence has been found. This is before they've found a damn body."

"But what can I do, man?" Crawford said. "What can I do? Nothing?"

"You can do whatever you want, Jim. but what I suggest is that you wait and see. I'll help you figure something out. But you can't go to the police. No way."

Crawford thought Lee might be right.

"Go home, Jim. I'll call you later. You need some rest. You have the Hershey show tomorrow."

Mentioning the show made Crawford feel nauseous. "God, that

show. Lee, I don't know if I can..."

"You can," Lee said.

"Lee, please. Listen to me. Maybe it's possible we could contact the show and tell them..."

"Don't even say it."

TEN

I'll just go home and decide what to do when I get there.

Crawford gave the finger to the "LB" on the gate as he pulled out of the driveway. The dawn was just beginning to make the sky a pale gray, reminding Crawford that time was passing and he needed to make a decision right away. *When I get home. When I get home.* It was almost six o'clock — the time when stores could legally sell booze again.

Crawford felt sweat on his brow despite the chilly air coming through the window crack. The message he had left Jenny played in his head between glances at the digital time on the dashboard.

This is Jim.

5:55

I was calling to make sure you know it's over.

5:55

It has to be. I'm sorry.

5:55

It has to be over, Jen. I want to apologize.

5:56

Maybe it's a fake, he thought. Maybe it's all a fake — like me. Maybe that's the point: maybe someone is trying to tell me I'm a fake.

But I know I'm a fake.

About halfway between Lee's house and his own, Crawford pulled over to the side of the road next to the fashionably small bakery that served only the surrounding neighborhood. Crawford had to decide if he was going home or to Jenny's to...

To do what? Investigate?

But what if she really was abducted?

Oh, she wasn't, he thought.

The message on the machine! It has to be erased!

The street formed a Y that split on either side of the bakery — the

110

northern route taking him home, the southern route to the freeway and to downtown.

Crawford saw a small gray-haired man merrily wobbling toward the front door of the bakery, unlocking it to begin his day. He looked so normal, so serene, but the sight of him made Crawford nervous. He pulled his car up just enough to be outside the man's view.

Go home!

But I've got to see. I've got to see.

Lee's neighborhood made Crawford nervous. It wasn't just the kings and queens of industry perched high in the hills, but the people who served those kings and queens — the little shopkeepers who did things like bake bread. They were looking down on him too. They were hard-working. They had honest professions. Crawford looked at the little man opening his bakery and stopped himself from stomping on the gas to get out of there.

But he can't see you.

What are you going to do? Decide!

But he's not judging you.

What does it matter?

Crawford pulled forward and turned left. It was strange driving down to Jenny's at that hour. He had always gone during the late afternoon when she could get off work early and Dorothy would be busy running errands. Crawford's on-again, off-again relationship with Jenny was regulated by discretion. Jim's customary response to Jenny's inquiries about availability was "When I can get away." He had "popped in" on her half a dozen times in two years. It was nice popping in. It had a magical way of leading to a pleasantly spontaneous sexual encounter: he opens the door, her eyes brighten in surprise and they embrace — like a husband coming home from a business trip two days early. But popping in this time...

She might be dead. She might really be dead.

Hold it. Slow down. She's not dead. You don't know that she's dead. You didn't see any real proof that she's dead.

But if she isn't dead then she's in on this whole charade and she could be there ready to...

Wait, just get there and...

Crawford found himself in front of Jenny's building, parked in the very spot where the photograph addressed to Dorothy was taken. Seeing the building from that angle produced a blaze of shame, a feeling that somehow he could be behind all of this.

"Hold it. Get a hold of yourself. Think." *Think like a detective, not like a goddam psychologist.*

"He was sitting right here."

Or was it she*?*

The clock on his dash now flashed *6:00*. The whoosh of brushes slapping the pavement made Crawford look up: there was a street cleaner coming toward him. He was going to have to move his car.

Crawford envisioned himself taking the picture of him and Jenny.

Taking a picture of yourself? Idiot.

He parked on a side street next to an abandoned car then walked around the corner to the front of Jenny's building. The building now looked like a different place, more isolated, more forlorn. He took out the two-key set he had kept hidden in the glove compartment for the past three months. Crawford never wanted keys to her place, but Jenny had insisted he take them in case she needed him (as she put it) to wait for her inside. He gave in and took the keys, knowing the gesture was only symbolic — Jenny's way of getting her hooks in deeper.

Crawford took out a pair of driving gloves that Dorothy had given him as a gift that he never used. Thanks, Dorothy, he thought. She was right. Someday they would come in handy.

He opened the main door and scanned the entrance nervously. Luckily there wasn't a person in sight, which didn't calm Crawford's nerves at all.

Crawford walked up the three flights of stairs. He had never used the elevator for fear of being in a confined space with a nosey tenant, and he certainly wasn't changing course this morning. Walking up the empty stairwell he observed a number of things he had never noticed before, trivial things. A sticker on the floor. A scratch on the railing. A stain on the wall. Even the smell was more prominent. But obviously it wasn't the building that had changed. It was his senses, more acute for some reason. He needed a drink as soon as possible.

Crawford huffed and puffed up the stairs, and just as he was reaching the fourth floor, he heard soft footsteps. He peered down the corridor where a small, old woman in a tattered green bathrobe was putting a garbage bag in the chute at the opposite end of the hall. Crawford froze. She slowly walked back to her apartment without looking up. But he was sure the old woman had seen him. Perhaps it wouldn't matter. She had seen him before.

Crawford approached Jenny's door and felt like he was making a mistake. Maybe he would incriminate himself.

A door cracked open — the old woman's door — and through the small space Crawford barely saw the back of her gray head. It sounded like the woman was talking to someone, speaking quietly, in a Slavic language. Maybe Russian. Maybe Czech.

Crawford's hands were shaking. He put one gloved hand on Jenny's doorknob and turned it slowly.

God, it's unlocked. Crawford didn't even wonder why. There was no time. Silently he pushed the door open and slipped in, looking behind him at the woman's gray head, still turned away. He walked backward, slowly closing the door behind him. Then the floor creaked beneath him. The woman stopped speaking and turned to look. Crawford got the door closed just as he caught a glimpse of the woman's profile.

She didn't see anything. But he would have to make this quick.

Crawford's breathing became labored and his heart pounded, his senses more acute than in the stairwell. Jenny's perfume, one he never particularly cared for (let alone the amount she used), filled the room like the stench of booze in a shabby dive.

Sunlight was now peaking through the corners of the windows, which were covered by dark Venetian blinds. Jenny liked her apartment dark, even though she was always talking about spending more time outdoors in the sunshine.

Then his senses stirred again.

The clock over the fireplace ticking. A faucet dripping in the bathroom.

"Hello?" he said, leaning forward. "Jen?"

Only the clock ticking. She isn't dead on the floor, he thought. But the bedroom, the bathroom — she could be lying in there.

Crawford jumped as the phone rang next to him.

It rang again. Crawford sat down in a chair next to the phone.

It rang again.

He sat there watching the phone, like a child waiting patiently to receive a punishment he knew he deserved.

It rang again.

Then the machine picked up.

"Hi, this is Jenny."

Her voice sounds so young. Why does it sound different?

"I'm not here," she giggles.

She's so sweet.

Shut up. She's not that sweet, he thought.

"Maybe I'm not here. Just leave a message, okay?"

Wait! The message I left! Is it still on the tape?

Beep.

Crawford leaned over and listened.

There was silence. It was like there was someone on the other end. He couldn't hear anything — no breathing, nothing — but it was like something told him someone was there. Crawford leaned further. Then he felt as if someone were watching him. Crawford heard him breathing. Or *her*? Was that breathing?

Click. Dial tone. No message.

Crawford looked and saw a "1" blinking on the answering machine. But was it his message or the caller's non-message? If so, someone had already listened to his message. Maybe it wasn't even the same tape.

Crawford jammed his finger down on the play button. Nothing but silence. Wait... there was a quiet hum. Breathing, something. *Beep.* The message ended — the silent message he had just heard.

I dialed the right number, damn it!

Crawford flipped open the top of the answering machine, grabbed the tape and put it in his jacket pocket.

But what should I do with it? Destroy it?

I'll decide later, he thought.

Crawford stood up and took a deep breath.

Okay, next. I have to.

He walked down the hall toward Jenny's bedroom. Every other time he'd gone into her bedroom he didn't walk — or he couldn't remember walking. She had her legs wrapped around his waist, kissing his neck devotedly. It was all very symbolic, Crawford knew. He did it because Jenny loved the expression "swept off her feet." He also did it because he liked the brief sensation of power.

He peeked around the corner.

"Hello?"

Nothing. The bed wasn't made, just a scrambled mess of pillows and blankets, like it always was.

"Not making the bed helps me feel young," she once told him.

Was she still young? Crawford sat down on the bed and it felt cold, he thought, so cold.

On her nightstand was a picture of the two of them, the only picture he had thought existed. It was a trip to Acapulco — a short vacation Crawford pulled off by saying he was attending a psychology conference in Detroit. Crawford told Dorothy she would be bored by the desolation of Detroit, and she agreed to let him go alone. It took more creative lies to explain the suntan when he returned.

Crawford picked up the picture and gazed at Jenny's exuberance. Her smile was so genuine. Her bright yellow shirt, covered in palm trees, was so youthful. She really was a wonderful girl.

Was?

Crawford thought of the gruesome image on the tape. *The knife. The screaming.*

God, I hope you're okay.

But if you are okay, you're an evil woman, he thought.

Crawford put the photograph inside his jacket and walked back into the living room, then the kitchen. Yes, the kitchen — or its contents — was the second important reason he'd come to Jenny's apartment.

He opened the cupboard to find the standard assortment of bottles Jenny kept for basic entertaining. Jenny loved to have people over and she loved to drink. So being able to make her guests any cocktail they desired was something she cherished. Brandy, cognac, rum, vodka, tequila, a number of aperitifs — Jenny had it all. But Crawford's poison was single-malt Scotch, and an unopened bottle of Lowlander Pure Malt would do him just fine.

Crawford took a paper sack from under the kitchen sink and put the bottle inside.

Chaser.

Then he reached inside the fridge and pulled out a couple of cold bottles of Budweiser and put them in the bag.

Crawford approached the door and felt vile. He had just rationalized a trip to Jenny's to see if she was there safe (and if she wasn't, to find out why), but he had really been interested in getting something to drink.

He pulled the picture from his jacket. *I'm such a selfish piece of shit.*

He took one last look at the living room and then the kitchen, trying to find one small sign of abduction, or perhaps her involvement with the production of the tape. He couldn't keep his mind off the bottle in his hand longer than a few seconds, but he tried.

Anything?

He turned toward the door and noticed something. *Scratches.* He looked closer. There were four small scratches, about three inches long, along the right side of the doorframe. He tried to remember if he had seen them before. Was this damage old? He ran his gloved fingers along the unusual abrasion. It didn't look old, but it didn't look brand new either.

It doesn't matter, he thought. *What can I do?*

Crawford slipped into the hall and out of the building, just as he had come in. The rustling of the sack under his arm made him nervous, but the contents would take his paranoia away soon enough. Crawford walked down the stairs and out into the early sunlight, pulling his sunglasses from his jacket. As he reached his car he realized that he hadn't locked Jenny's door.

Go back?

But then, that's the way I found it, he thought.

The sack rustled under his arm, and the sound was reassuring. *I deserve to have these friends with me.* After all, he wasn't responsible for all of this chaos. It wasn't his fault.

"Anxiety is sometimes just a product of guilt, which is sometimes very irrational — a product of unfortunate circumstances," he had written in *Self-Worth*.

He put on his sunglasses and got in his car, putting the key in the ignition. He pulled the bottle of Scotch from the paper sack and put it on his lap. There was nothing so pleasurable as popping open a brand new bottle of 12-year-old single-malt Scotch. He turned the bottle top slowly with his thumb and index fingers, leaning over to savor the first draft of bouquet escaping from the bottle. On the console between the two front seats rested Crawford's stainless steel coffee cup. He took off the plastic cover and poured four fingers then put the lid back in place and capped the bottle. He thought what a shame it was to pour such fine Scotch into an ordinary coffee cup, but what the hell.

Crawford took the first swig, letting the flavor saturate his mouth. He could taste the mild influence of the coffee, but actually, it wasn't that bad.

"Be optimistic like your life depended on it," he had written in *Self-Worth*.

Or was that *Self-Respect*?

He took another sip, then another. The coffee taste was kind of a nice change.

See, he thought, most folks are about as happy as they make up their minds to be.

I wrote that in, um...

He felt warm. He turned the key in the ignition.

Oh, that was Lincoln.

Anxiety: gone, for the time being.

Abe had a corncob pipe.

Dorothy was getting into her pink sweat pants and black tank top, talking to herself in teeth-grinding tones that she longed to unleash on Crawford. But her husband was nowhere to be seen. And during Jim's long absences, during these moments of frustrating powerlessness, Dorothy felt she was constantly on the defensive, arguing why she was the kind of person that deserved better, arguing points that no one could hear.

There was almost nothing that could help, almost nothing that could chase the arguing demons away, except a little exercise. Time for *Swing and Sweat*.

"You got rhythm and it's time to swing and sweat!" Johnny Campa, the announcer/singer/coach, said in his tuxedo workout suit.

"Okay," Dorothy said aloud, taking in a deep breath before bending down to touch her toes.

"Okay, our warm-up. Let's slo-o-o-owly touch our toes," he said, bending over. "While remembering that we love ourselves. And we love our bodies too, don't we?"

"Yes," Dorothy whimpered. "We love our bodies."

Jim obviously doesn't love his body, or mine either.

Johnny began with a slow, soft rendition of *When Somebody Loves You.*

Dorothy sang along while doing her deep-knee bends, thinking about her heart and what it had felt, and about those kisses and when they are more than just kisses. She thought about looking and touching and how those things mean so much. She thought about discovering how it is to be a lover. *Or not.*

The song was once a favorite of Jim's when he only knew the Sinatra version. *Swing and Sweat* had put an end to that.

And I guess that's my fault too, she thought.

This had only happened once before: the song becoming difficult to listen to during the second verse — the part about every smile becoming worthwhile, about the caring and sharing, when somebody loves you.

Jim had such confidence when they first met. Sure, it was the liquid kind, but it was still confidence.

He had confidence in my love, until he wrote Self-Confidence.

"Isn't this great? Just take a deep breath now," Johnny Campa said.

And she did.

Dorothy was on the phone with her mother, having called her because she didn't know who else to call. Now she was starting to regret it.

"You can't do this forever," her mother told her.

"Yes, mother, I know," she said.

Dorothy, still in her pink gym clothes, sipped her coffee nervously, keeping her eye on the hall, waiting for Cal to come down.

"What did I tell you when you married him?"

"A lot of things, mother. Maybe I should call you later."

"I don't see how you can..."

Dorothy took the phone away from her face and yelled into the ceiling. "Cal. I need to talk to you." Again she listened to her mother rant.

"Talk to him. Right now. Talk to him. Tell him you're taking a stand."

"I don't know where he is."

"You don't know where he is?"

Just then Dorothy heard Cal's car screech out of the driveway. She looked out the window just in time to see the 911 speeding down the street.

"I have to go, mother. Now my husband *and* my son have disappeared. I'll call you later."

"Listen," her mother said harshly.

"Goodbye." Dorothy said, hanging up the phone.

Dorothy was angry with herself for calling her mother. She often called her when she needed someone to unload upon. The problem was that she never felt comforted after a conversation with her — just the opposite. But she kept calling. Year after year, drinking episode after drinking episode, she would call her mother, give her a synopsis of the current crisis, and then hang up with regret after listening to her mother's unwelcome lecture on her recurring oversights and failures. But Dorothy couldn't help it. She considered it her only addiction. She was wrong.

Dorothy liked to take a bath instead of a shower when she was depressed, and this morning she was ready for a long one. She turned on the water, ready to shut the bathroom door and shut out the world for a while, when the phone rang. She knew who it was.

"Yes," she said sternly. There was a long silence. "Hello." Nothing. "Speak!"

"Dorothy?" the gravelly voice finally said.

"Where the hell are you?"

"I just wanted to talk to Lee about the Hershey show, that's all."

"And you went to talk to him in the middle of the night?"

"Like I used to tell people," Crawford said in a mumble, "when you have the courage to do something..."

"Yeah, yeah. You should go ahead and do it. That's bullshit, Jim. What are you doing?"

"I'm... I can't talk right now."

"You called me to tell me you can't talk? Why can't you talk?"

"Because I can't."

Dorothy could tell he was smashed, but she wasn't going to mention it. She knew, and he knew she knew. "I feel like I'm talking to a child, the same child I've put up with for almost 20 years."

"You are," he said softly. "You are."

"Look. Call a cab right now. Or have Lee bring you home."

He calmly told her that Lee was not there.

"Then call a cab," she shot back.

"I'll be home soon."

"You better be. If you take too long I might not be here when you get back."

"That might be better for both of us, sweetheart." He hung up.

Dorothy's heart pounded with anger. She started to think of all the episodes she'd been through with Jim, trying to get him sober while trying to remain hopeful.

She went back into the bathroom and slipped into the soothing tub. She stared at the tiny bubbles that clung to her pale skin.

Maybe it's time to go, she thought. Maybe it's time.

ELEVEN

Darrin asked Cal to pick him up in front of Tom's Pool Hall around eight o'clock. Cal thought this was a strange request since Tom's didn't open until one in the afternoon. And none of the other businesses on the block were open since most of them were drinking establishments. Cal wondered why Darrin didn't just invite him over to his place. But he never talked about where he lived. The area code of his telephone number, Cal knew, was either near downtown or the south side — most likely not a very good neighborhood. But since Cal didn't want to offend his new friend or make him feel inferior, he picked him up at the pool hall, no questions asked.

Darrin sat on a bench outside the ramshackle building reading the morning newspaper. When Cal brought his car to the curb, Darrin coolly looked up like he was waiting for his limousine. There was something about Darrin's demeanor that triggered both admiration and fear in Cal. Darrin's confident manner spoke of a well-adjusted person, someone free of complexes and insecurities. But occasionally Cal felt Darrin's disposition was a cover for something else — not fear, but anger maybe. And it was brief moments like this that made Cal wonder if Darrin was so together after all.

Darrin got in the car without looking at his driver. He closed the door and nodded for Cal to drive on.

"Good morning," Cal said.

"Morning."

Cal looked ahead attentively. "So what's the story?"

Darrin seemed almost sedated. "Just drive. I'll tell you where to go."

Cal slowly drove down the street, keeping his speed under thirty miles an hour. "You all right?"

Darrin looked at Cal. "Of course I'm all right. You all right?"

"Me? Yeah, I guess. I'm a little nervous about missing school. I'm worried that..."

"You're worried your *mommy* is going to catch you skipping school, huh?"

Cal was baffled by his tone. "What's up with you?"

Darrin started to laugh under his breath. "Just relax man. I'm just fucking with you. That's all."

Cal smiled nervously. He didn't like being fucked with.

"Turn here," Darrin said. "Boy, do I have a surprise for you."

Cal felt a little scared. "I don't know if I like this," Cal said softly.

"Really." Darrin looked at him directly. "Don't you like surprises? I do."

Cal thought about his dad. He wondered why he felt so negative about him.

"Life is a series of surprises for those who really live it." Darrin's words were almost heartfelt. "Parents try to tell their kids they can set their own course in life. Do this, do that, life will be good and safe and predictable. It's all a lie, man. Your father has this racket to make money based on this..."

"Don't talk about my father, okay?"

Darrin furrowed his brow. "It's surprising to hear you say that, friend."

Cal thought about how he should try being a little nicer to his dad. Then he wondered what he was doing with this stranger and what kind of trouble he was getting himself into.

Cal didn't have to worry about getting into trouble with his dad. His dad was busy getting into his own trouble. Just half a mile from Jenny's apartment, east of the garment district and just before the river, sat a seedy bar Crawford had known in his college days — Sharkey's Saloon. The bar's most noteworthy feature was that it complied with the alcohol laws of California exactly to the minute: open at 6am, closed at 2am. Most people might be surprised just how many drunks are ready for a drink at 6am, but they were never surprised at Sharkey's.

The proprietor, a man named Sharkey O'Neil, was an old Army veteran who had served in the Korean War. One drunken evening years ago, Sharkey told Crawford he had lost his soul in the war, and that his alcohol intake was actually just medication to stop the pain of no longer being a complete man. Crawford had never heard of someone drinking to remedy the loss of a soul.

"You lost your *soul* in the war?" Crawford once asked him.

Anyone could see that Sharkey had lost his right arm and his left leg (from the knee down) in Korea, *but his soul?* Crawford could never tell if Sharkey was being serious or just eccentrically droll.

"Yep, parts of me are still over there," Sharkey would say in his thick Brooklyn accent. "My soul's somewhere around the thirty-eighth parallel." He'd take a giant gulp of Irish whiskey and then guffaw wildly. "I ain't going to hell. Lost my soul already. Damn. Hot damn. Soul's in Korea," he'd say slamming another shot. "Life's just filled with irony, ain't it?"

Crawford was never sure if Sharkey was punning or if he truly believed his spirit had died in the Far East. Either way, Crawford found Sharkey's penchant for talking about losing his soul rather than his limbs refreshing.

But Crawford wasn't really interested in seeing the bar again, or old Sharkey O'Neil for that matter. He just needed a place to sit down and have a drink. *Or two. Or four.* As morning traffic was just starting to mill around the downtown area, drinking from a paper sack in the car was probably not a good idea.

Crawford thought he would have trouble finding the place; after all, it had been years. And the last time he'd been there he wasn't exactly in the frame of mind to memorize directions for a trip back two decades later. Crawford started to think it was possible (hell, probable) the place was no longer open. The police couldn't be happy with such a dive. And the way Sharkey drank, it would have taken a miracle and a liver transplant for him to still be alive. Crawford was ready to give up when he looked up and saw the place directly in front of him, its neon sign hanging at a 45-degree angle from the base where it once sat.

"Oh yeah," he thought. "That's what it looks like."

Crawford pulled across the street to park and immediately noticed a man lying face down just in front of the ramshackle front door. He thought it was a man. Crawford got out of his car, and as he walked closer, he could see the person was lying with his (or her) forehead resting on a rubber doormat that graced the entrance. He (or she) had short, dark hair and eye-catching red spots on the back of his (or her) neck. His (or her) clothing was of a western style, popular with both rural men and inner-city lesbians. Crawford crouched down to look at the spots on the neck. They looked like bee stings or something. Perhaps they were liver spots from excessive drinking. Didn't matter. Nothing he could do. So he stepped over him (or her) and thought about how nice it was the bar was open.

Crawford walked in hoping to find the old bird that left his soul in Korea, but no such luck. A brawny man who looked more like a bodyguard than a bartender — too dumb to pour a drink but smart enough to bash someone's head in — sat behind the bar watching TV. There were just two customers in the place, old men, both wearing suits with large lapels (probably from the forties) sitting at a table sharing a pitcher of beer. It was perfect.

I guess when you get older you got to take it easy in the morning.

Crawford bellied up to the bar, getting an unusual look from the barkeep.

"What can I get you?"

"A shot and a beer," Crawford said. "For starters."

"What kind of shot?" the man said with a deliberately unpleasant sneer.

"Irish whiskey."

The man lazily reached for the bottle.

"So where's Sharkey this morning?"

"Sharkey?"

"You know, Sharkey O'Neil. Like the name of the place."

"Oh. There ain't no Sharkey, man. The guy that bought the place just didn't change the name." The man poured Crawford his shot.

"So you don't know what happened to him? Sharkey, I mean."

The man pulled out a pilsner glass, looking annoyed. "No, man. Don't know what happened to Sharkey. Sorry." He gave a sarcastic smile while he filled the glass.

Maybe the old guy was dead, Crawford thought. Then he wondered if Sharkey ever met up with his soul again.

The bartender put the beer in front of Crawford. "Three bucks."

Crawford pulled out a fifty from his wallet and put it on the bar. "Keep 'em coming," he said.

As the bartender took the bill, Crawford noticed something hanging on the wall behind him. It was Sharkey's prosthetic arm, dangling by its strap from a nail. Crawford lifted the shot in a silent toast and downed the warm whiskey in one big swig. "Sharkey," he said under his breath. "I hope you got your soul back."

The bartender settled into his TV show again, a local morning talk show that he watched with limp eyes.

His indifference bothered Crawford for some reason, perhaps because Sharkey was always so attentive. That was how he remembered him.

"You know," Crawford started, "I haven't been in a bar this comfortable in a long time."

The man nodded apathetically.

"Places like this just seem really warm and inviting."

The bartender wasn't going to be coaxed into a conversation. "Would you like to watch TV?"

"Oh, I don't know," Crawford said sipping his beer. "Just not any kids shows."

The bartender put the remote control in front of him. "Of course. Anything you want." The bartender picked up a crate of empty beer bottles and walked away to the back.

Crawford started flipping channels.

There was a cable news program with a helicopter shot of a suburban school. The caption under the image read, "School Shooting."

Crawford flipped the channel and took a sip of beer.

There was a trash-TV talk show with a young black girl, probably in her mid-teens, wearing a glossy, hot pink outfit. It clung tightly to her large breasts and thighs. She danced in a strange side-to-side wobble as the audience taunted her with boos and hisses. Crawford thought she looked like a prostitute who didn't know how pitiful she was.

"Y'all just jealous 'cause I know what I want," she says, standing and turning around, shaking her plump bottom. "I can get what I want 'cause I loves myself. Y'all don't know..."

It's even more pathetic that people start their day watching this shit. He flipped the channel.

There was a black female judge in one of those court-TV shows. A gaunt man with a light complexion and a heavy Midwestern accent was shaking his head. "Thing is, your Honor, I tried to do everything to please her."

Then an unattractive woman, apparently the man's wife, spoke up loudly. "You didn't do squat!" she shrieks. Then quietly addressing the judge, "He didn't do a damn thing for me, your Honor, except make me feel like dirt. My self-esteem was gone the day he walked his skinny butt through the door."

"Then why did you stay with him?" the judge asks.

Crawford flipped the channel.

Ah, yes — the lovely Jan Hershey, so big her talk show had syndicated reruns on cable.

Who would watch reruns of this crap?

"I think the main thing here is that parents need to talk to their children. We always need to keep communication open to help improve their self-"

Crawford turned off the TV, mocking her. "We need to talk to our children."

Crawford took another big gulp off his beer. He looked over his left shoulder and saw the bartender staring at him.

"Need another?"

"What I tell you?" Crawford grunted.

▪ ▪ ▪

Cal had started to get nervous right about the time Darrin told him to get off the freeway just south of downtown. He had never been to this part of town and so knew little about it, but its reputation was notorious. Gangs. Drugs. Violence. Actually, it was more industrial than he thought, with railroad tracks across every intersection and several towering smokestacks bellowing out smoke from God-knows-what.

"This is a gang neighborhood?" Cal asked.

"No, man. The residential neighborhoods are east of here. That's where all the crime is. This is all manufacturing. You can't even get shot down here." Darrin took a deep breath and smiled. "You smell that?"

"What?"

Darrin cracked his window. "You smell that?"

Cal didn't have to breathe in heavily. "It smells like shit."

Darrin laughed. "That's exactly right. Waste disposal. Big industry around here. If you ever bring a girl down here be sure and tell her you didn't fart."

"Why would I bring a girl down here?"

"Waste disposal," Darrin said coolly. Darrin raised his eyebrows slightly then laughed. "You need to relax, man."

"What are we really doing down here?"

"Just keep driving," he said, his eyes straight ahead. "We're almost there."

Cal sensed that Darrin was filled with anticipation, incapable of sitting still as they drove.

"I want to surprise you," Darrin said.

Darrin instructed Cal to turn down a narrow road with a series of abandoned buildings on it. Most of them were brick, probably built fifty or sixty years ago.

Darrin smiled with satisfaction. "We're not in Kansas anymore." Then he recognized their destination. "Right here," he said pointing.

"Here?"

"Yep."

Cal pulled into the parking lot slowly, trying to avoid the rubbish that was strewn all over it. It was mostly broken glass and rusty nails from an assortment of wood pieces that came from no telling what. Cal turned off the engine. The building was like the others on the block except for a strange, faded sign that graced one wall.

"My mom's going to find out I skipped school, Darrin. I think I should leave."

"No she's not. Chill, dude."

"This is it?"

"This is it."

Cal was so frightened he couldn't move. "I don't know, Darrin."

Darrin was genuinely irritated. "You don't know? For a thousand dollars apiece? All we got to do is drive across town. It'll be a breeze. Watch." Darrin opened the car door.

"I thought you said..."

"I said what?" Darrin said, with genuine anger.

"No wait, man."

"Quit being such a fucking pussy," he said.

Cal was shocked by Darrin's anger. "You want me to chill?"

"Stay here then," Darrin said getting out of the car.

Cal was more afraid of staying in the car. He got out and locked the doors with his remote, wondering if his car would still be there when they came back. He walked quickly after Darrin, sidestepping the debris on the ground, with a mixture of apprehension and exhilaration. "Wait," he called. "Darrin, wait."

Darrin turned around and smiled.

"Sure, man. No problem."

With a short kick, Darrin broke open the rusted metal door that served as the building's only entrance.

"You've been here before?" Cal said.

Darrin didn't say anything. He just walked inside, motioning for Cal to follow. "Come on."

Light shone down from small horizontal windows, which lined the top of the twelve-foot brick walls. The place was filthy, a thick soot lining every inch of the place. There were chunks of wood and metal on the floor. One wall was showered with giant burn marks. There was a pile of old sewing machines in a corner.

Darrin walked slowly but with certainty, reviewing the place as if he were a safety inspector hoping to shut it down.

"You know what's weird, Cal?" he said slowly. "This used to be a garment factory where a bunch of Chinese immigrants worked. It was a sweatshop. And the guy that ran the place padlocked all the workers inside so they couldn't take breaks in the alley. One day the place caught fire and burned all the people inside. Thing is, they say you can hear all these people crying at night. Like all their ghosts still live here and they're trying to get out."

"Who says that?" Cal looked down at the floor. A small area looked recently swept; it didn't have the debris that covered the rest of the floor. Then he saw a giant stain — a giant bloodstain. "Darrin, where'd you meet this guy?"

"On the Internet, why?"

Cal followed the narrow stain to a dark area on his right. Cal squinted to see what was there, dark skinny figures huddling in the corner.

A camera? On a tripod? Stage lights?

Then it was dark.

Dorothy got dressed wondering what would be the best way to tell Jim she wanted a divorce. Or did she want a divorce? Should I threaten him first? she thought. Or would a mere verbal threat not be taken seriously? Should she retain a lawyer, even while just considering it, or would that be too much of a declaration? *And have things gotten so bad that I should do that?*

Dorothy knew she had to do something. She knew that when Jim disappeared in the afternoons he wasn't just going to the beach to meditate, as he once told her. Sometimes her anger would rise and fall with no perceptible motivation at all. One minute she would be cussing him out, the next saying she was sorry — all without him actually being there. This had driven her crazy for years. But the pattern had shown an unusual one-sidedness recently: she was starting to condemn more than forgive. And what made it serious — for her marriage in particular — was that it felt good.

"He would be lying in the gutter right now without me," she said turning on the coffee grinder. "Maybe he needs to try the gutter lifestyle for a while. Then he wouldn't take me for granted."

And that's how Dorothy felt — taken for granted. *Think about it.* Who had put so much love into Jim's career? She had. Who had put so much love into staying fit and attractive so her spouse could be proud at social gatherings? She had. Who had put so much love into the beautification of their home? She had. And for what? Money? She didn't care about money — only about nice things. And gosh darn it, Jim wasn't a nice thing these days.

"Yes, perhaps I need to look into obtaining counsel," she said to her reflection in her die cast stainless steel digital control coffeemaker. "And I need to get some better coffee. This coffee isn't even organically grown."

The Beverly Hills Yellow Pages was filled with the Bergs and Steins of divorce law, and she knew any of them would be pleased as punch to represent her — even without knowing that the words "prenuptial agreement" had never been spoken between her and her husband.

"You need someone who will play hardball," one advertisement read. "A true scrapper who knows California law and who is willing to..."

Jeez Louise. Such aggression. Such hostility. I want to be diplomatic.

"We negotiate child support, alimony, and other matters as professionally as possible."

Too straightforward. Too dull. I need someone down to earth.

"High-profile divorce is our specialty. We can handle the press like no other law firm, leaving you free..."

Sounds like they're star struck. I don't want star struck. This should be very low-profile.

"We know when and how to throw mud."

My God. Nasty. I don't want mud involved.

"We understand that you are devastated, and we can help."

Bullshit sympathy. Heads tilted sideways as they're seeing dollar signs. I don't want that.

"We provide references to psychotherapy professionals who specialize in divorce-related depression and psychosis."

This sounds interesting. Divorce therapists. I didn't know. But that might antagonize Jim even more, getting therapy through my divorce attorney. I just don't know.

"Our founding partner is the author of *The Sexy Prenup: the hot way to...*"

Prenup. I don't have a prenup.

Those words rang out like *there's no place like home.* It was liberating how it echoed in her mind: no prenup... nup... nup... nup. *Maybe I can just represent myself in all of this. Yes. Maybe I can just get a book or something and fill out all the papers myself and show them to Jim and tell him I'm serious. That will be enough of a threat. No, not a threat, a stand, yes. A real stand. By myself. And there won't be a big line in the sand that a lawyer would draw. "My client, blah, blah, blah." I can do this myself, like the time I painted the lawn furniture. I really can. I always wanted to go to law school, sort of. But I don't even need law school. There's no prenup after all. I could get as much as I wanted all by myself. Yes. And I would feel even better.*

She stopped herself a moment. *It was meant to be.* Dorothy looked through her purse and pulled out something Jim had given her as a token peace offering a few months ago: a gift card for fifty dollars at a bookstore. Maybe he gave me this card for a reason, she thought. Maybe he was crying for help. Maybe he wants me to buy a book on divorce. Maybe if I threaten to divorce him it will help him find himself, and if he's already aware of this subconsciously...

Dorothy went upstairs to get dressed.

Not a bad idea.

"And I can pick up some organic coffee while I'm out."

■ ■ ■

"Hey buddy."

The amount of time Crawford had been drinking in Sharkey's was unclear, but however long it was he was now about to pass out. He was leaning on the bar with his chin on his forearm, his eyelids slowly moving up and down like the sea at low tide, when the bartender tapped him on the shoulder.

"Hey buddy."

Crawford's eyes snapped open; he looked almost offended he'd been touched.

"What?" he said slowly. "What d'ya want?"

"Hey, don't you think you should head home?"

"Home?" Crawford mumbled. "What the hell is that?"

There was a soft thud — a peculiar thud — and the bartender looked past Crawford out the window. Then another thud. Then another. *Bump, bump, bump, bump.*

"Oh shit," the bartender mumbled.

"Earthquake?" Crawford looked out the window and saw a lime green 1978 Cadillac sedan with heavy detailing — shiny spiked rims, florescent lights, the whole nine yards. It was garish as hell, but more menacing than anything.

"What is it?" Crawford asked.

Three young black men dressed in black hip-hop baggy pants, pullovers, and knit caps got out of the car.

"Fuckin hell, that's what," the barkeep said.

The door creaked open and the three men coolly walked in the bar like they owned the place. One guy wearing dark sunglasses walked ahead of the rest. He surveyed the room then looked at the bartender like they owned him too.

"Rakim. How are you?" the bartender asked with a nervous rub of his forehead.

The man sat down next to Crawford, his two henchmen taking seats to his left. "Just give us a fuckin' round," he said. "You know what we havin'."

Crawford watched the bartender put three short glasses on the bar and fill them with ice like his life depended on it.

Peeking over his dark sunglasses, Rakim looked over his right shoulder and examined Crawford closely. Crawford tried to ignore him.

"Hey, man," the young man said.

Crawford kept looking straight ahead.

"Hey, man," he said again.

"Yeah?" Crawford said without looking.

"Do I know you?"

"I hope not," Crawford said.

While Dorothy sat on the bed getting dressed, she thought about her mother's reaction to Jim after taking him home for Thanksgiving.

"This isn't serious, is it?" her mother asked her during a phone conversation the following week.

"It's pretty serious," she said with obstinate enthusiasm. "Don't you like him?"

Her mother responded gravely, surprisingly so. "I just think he's not the right kind of guy for you, not for the Dorothy I know."

The Dorothy her mother knew couldn't believe her mother's bluntness but nevertheless took it in stride. Her mother was very protective and had never liked any of her previous boyfriends.

Dorothy tried to sound confident, like an adult: "Well maybe now I'm a different person — different in a few ways."

"Okay. Like how?" she asked.

"Mother! Why are you pressing this?"

"Because I love you, that's why. I'm your mother. I'm supposed to give you advice on these things."

"This is advice?" From her second story apartment, Dorothy had her eyes trained on the walkway in front of the building, eagerly keeping an eye out for her handsome new lover.

Her mother didn't know what to think of her romantic excitement nor the stubborn rebellion in her voice. "You sound to me like you know what I'm saying is true," she said.

Dorothy decided to give up — something she did often with her mom. "Mom. I have to go."

"Then you're mad?" her mother asked.

"No. I have to go." Dorothy saw Jim coming up the walk with a bottle of wine under his arm. "Really, Mom..."

"Okay, okay," she conceded.

"We can talk about this later," Dorothy said.

Yes, we'll talk about this later, her mother often thought as she listened to Dorothy's tearful monologues of regrets and misgivings over the years.

Dorothy's mother still lived in San Bernardino County, and Dorothy's best gauge of how her marriage was doing was to count the number of times "Upland, California" appeared on the phone bill. During her worst moments, Dorothy could pick up the phone and resume a conversation she had ended days ago.

"This is it," she said to her mother with no introduction whatsoever. Her mother knew exactly what she meant. "I see," she said contentedly.

"I can't take this any longer."

"Take what? What has he done?"

"I can't talk about it. I'll just say he's not here. I'm going to wait until Cal comes home, and then we're both coming over. I don't know how Cal's going to react, but please handle it, whatever he does."

"And Jim?"

"Out getting drunk, I guess. I don't know where he is."

"Dorothy, should I make dinner for tonight? For you and Cal?"

"No. Just wait. I'll call you later, mother," Dorothy said, looking at her suitcase on the bed. Perhaps there was still a Dorothy her mother didn't know.

"I could make a nice pot roast," her mother said.

The smell was strange, like something he'd smelled a long time ago, perhaps while on a camping trip when he was younger. It was that wet kind of smell, like after it rains, but in an old wooden building or something.

After Cal tried to move, he no longer thought about the smell. There was a sharp pain on his right shoulder, right at his neck. He was lying on his side, resting on his left arm, and when he moved he could tell the floor was wet.

His temple began to throb, then he reached up to touch his forehead. It also was wet.

Is it blood?

He felt like he'd been struck on the head, but he couldn't remember. The room was dark, with just the outline of light coming from what looked like a large door.

He started to remember the day: skipping school, the neighborhood, the smell, the buildings, the warehouse. And he remembered Darrin. And something about some coke, picking it up, running it across town.

"Darrin," he said as if he'd just awoken. Then louder, "Darrin. Darrin! Where are you?" he cried.

Cal tried to move again, this time realizing his feet were bound together. He swung his body from his hips and heard the sound of a chain rattling across the floor. He was chained to something.

"Darrin! Darrin, help! Fuckin' help me, man!"

The door cracked open, throwing a shaft of light on Cal. It opened further and a silhouette appeared at the door.

"Darrin?"

"Cal?" It was a strange, low voice.

"Who the fuck are you?"

The figure was motionless. Then it said... "Be kind to yourself."

That voice: the one he tuned out in the morning with loud music. Cal could now see the person had a large hat on.

Then he saw the large nose, the pipe. *Oh, God what is this?* Cal put his hands beneath him and tried to pull away. "Who the fuck are you! Where the hell is Darrin?"

"Be a friend to yourself, Cal," he said, stepping into the light, his exaggerated features eclipsing the glare. Cal thought he must have been dreaming. "Be a friend to yourself," he said again, turning away. "Little prick."

Entrée Vous Books was Dorothy's favorite bookstore, a locally owned place that stuck out among the run of the mill corporate retail shops in the area. To Dorothy, the experience of being surrounded by millions and millions of words, along with a small but charming coffee shop, had a way of making her feel smarter. She had read *Pride and Prejudice* and *Wuthering Heights*, and had attempted *Anna Karenina* before giving up a respectable third of the way through, but she always found literature too nebulous and demanding, and preferred short non-fiction that was written to make the reader a happier and healthier person. No, she wasn't well versed in the classics, but at Entrée Vous it didn't matter. She loved walking past the James Crawford collection, admiring the beautiful hardcover editions with the free bookmarks that had Jim's face at the top. In fact, even though she never said this to her husband, the *Self Series* books were some of her favorites.

Dorothy was embarrassed knowing she was there this time to browse the legal section — specifically the divorce section — and decided to browse the other sections until she happened upon her objective.

Biography.

What an interesting group of people, those who read historical biography, she thought. Wouldn't dare pick up a tabloid magazine but would want to know the dish on Attila the Hun. That's so cool. I should read one, perhaps a woman from history. Susan B. Anthony maybe. They put her on that dollar and all. Maybe someone even further back. Joan of Arc. Was she a real person, Joan of Arc? And what was the "Arc" part? *Oh phooey.*

Housekeeping.

Decorating.

I just love...

"Can I help you with something?" a young woman asked.

Dorothy immediately noticed that her nametag read 'Dorothy.' She said nervously, "I'm just looking. Thank you."

"Not looking for anything in particular?" Dorothy asked Dorothy. "A graduation gift perhaps?"

Oh, yeah. Graduation is *coming up.* "Not really, no."

Dorothy could obviously sense the hesitation. "There must be something you had in mind?"

"No."

"Are you sure?

Darn it, woman. "Actually I'm here to buy a do-it-yourself divorce book to threaten my husband with. Got any of those?"

Dorothy the clerk's demeanor didn't change; she still grinned like a cat. "We certainly do, ma'am. It's in the legal section, third row on the left. Right next to *Bankruptcy.*"

"Okay, Dorothy. I think I can find it."

"Anything I can do to help, just holler. And be sure and visit our coffee shop."

"Okay," Dorothy said, forcing a smile.

"And what was your name?" the woman asked.

"Dorothy."

"No kidding?" the woman said, grabbing her nametag. "That's my name too."

"No kidding," Dorothy said, before doing an about face.

Everyone's selling something.

She walked past books with pictures of Winston Churchill, Abraham Lincoln, Martin Luther King, *that Chinese guy that was really evil*, Hitler, some other men she didn't know. *For Christ's sake, who would read a book about Hitler? Does that make people think they are smart?*

And why should I care what Dorothy thinks about me buying a book on divorce, Dorothy thought. *Put little may-I-help-you Dorothy in my shoes and see how she would hold up. I am going to browse the divorce section like I came here to do.* And she was determined not to feel bad about it. *It's not like I'm buying a book on Hitler.*

She crossed a long, wide aisle that separated the Literature, Biography, and Arts sections from the Legal, Financial, and Self-Help. The chasm created by the two seemed large — as if those who designed the layout insisted on a degree of segregation.

Also, the covers look so different on this side. The tasteful photography and subtle colors found across the aisle were replaced by bright, gaudy designs and ugly standard fonts. The language was also inelegant by comparison. Words like "How to," "Get the," "Become a" *blah,*

blah, blah. Self-improvement needed a facelift, she thought, before seeing him standing there near the checkout.

His big warm smile. Correct posture, as she had reminded him many times. *And he didn't want a cutout of himself in books stores. He's so funny wunny.* She thought he looked very handsome standing there. There was a woman, an attractive one, *and she's looking him up and down. I bet she's not thinking about the book. I bet she's thinking how she'd like to fling her big boobs in my husband's face. And Jim hasn't been* that *unfaithful. My God, he could have a different bimbo every night. And it's a lot of pressure being a public figure like he is. Of course he's going to want a drink occasionally. After all, one day there will be books about him on the other aisle. With Washington, Lincoln, Jefferson, and that evil Chinese guy.*

Dorothy's eyes stopped in front of a stop sign — simple, bright red, a tacky font — declaring "Stop Now." Dorothy picked up the thin volume and read the title. *How to Halt Divorce in its Tracks. Fourth Edition.*

Hmm, she thought. *Should this be in the legal section?*

She cautiously looked around before opening it to the Table of Contents. Chapter 1: How to Turn Bitter Hatred Back into Love.

Hmm.

Chapter 2: Nip It in the Bud.

Yes, she *would* nip it in the bud. This divorce had to stop and it had to stop now.

Walking past the cutout of her husband, she held her selection close to her breast. Buying the book would be her affirmation of love for that day. She paid in cash before walking past Dorothy, who reminded her to come again.

"Damn. I can't believe I ran into you, man," The young Rakim said, his arm now wrapped around Crawford's shoulder. Crawford was now trying to sip his beer at a slower pace. He knew he'd need to leave soon. Rakim looked smaller and less dangerous with his confident strut tamed by a barstool.

"Dr. James motherfuckin' Crawford," Rakim said proudly. "In my little watering hole." Rakim was smiling with exhilaration and surprise. He looked like he had never smiled so wide in his life. "I can't tell you how you've changed my life." Rakim turned to the bartender. "Another drink for my man here. Anything he wants. And hurry the fuck up!"

He slapped Crawford on the back, his expression changing back to warm hospitality. Crawford tried to smile but was mostly trying to remain upright.

Rakim continued with a flood of compliments. "Hell, I wouldn't have shit if it weren't for you, man. I wouldn't have fuckin' *shit*," he said again. "I wouldn't be a world-class recording artist. Hell, I definitely wouldn't own this bar."

"You own this bar?" Crawford muttered.

He leaned in toward Crawford, who languidly looked down at his beer. "You know what I'm sayin', Doc? Listen to me. I owe this bitch all to *you*, motherfucker," he said.

The bartender put another draft in front of Crawford and poured him another shot.

Rakim kept talking. "Bro, I read *Self-Confidence* fuckin' years ago, when I was just a little kid. That started it all, man. I'm readin' that new one a'yours *Self-Esteem* right now. Self-esteem pretty important, huh?" he said taking a swig of his Manhattan.

Crawford said, "I don't think you have anything to worry about, Mister, Rakim?" Crawford said before downing the shot.

Rakim let out a great laugh. "That's right bro, all thanks to you. Let's celebrate." He raised his glass in a toast and Crawford halfheartedly did the same. Rakim turned to his two buddies next to him. "Raise 'em up, Niggas. Come on." And they promptly did. "Anything you want to say, Maestro?" Rakim said. "We're all motherfuckin' ears."

Crawford coughed. "I think I'm going to be sick."

Rakim laughed out loud. "Naw, man, shit," he said before downing his drink.

Dorothy tried to pretend she had some important things to do that day, but the truth was she only had the common chores of every other day, made just slightly unusual by the fact that her husband was AWOL.

She was already angry with herself for telling her mother that she was leaving Jim. She didn't know if she was leaving him or not, she just said so perhaps to gain some "clarity" or to muster up a bit of nerve to do something else.

Besides the small deli next to it, the drycleaner was the only other business at the bottom of the hill that served their neighborhood exclusively. It was one of those area businesses where people are more sociable simply because they know they're talking to other people from the same income bracket, or the way many of them saw it, from the same side of the tracks.

Dorothy could barely muster up the concentration needed to pay the patiently waiting Chinese man the money she owed him. She was gnashing her teeth at the thought of Jim getting wasted in some bar. "Keep the change," she said after finally pulling a fifty out of her wallet.

Dorothy hated running into other people from the neighborhood, especially the hodgepodge of housewives who wanted to believe that Dorothy was part of their demographic and so had lots in common, lots to talk about and lots of time to do so. Usually she could avoid such chit-chat; other times it was impossible.

"Thank you very much, Miss Crawford," he said, bowing graciously.

"Dorothy Crawford?" said a woman's brassy voice slow and deliberate, from the front of the drycleaner. "Mrs. Dorothy James 'Self-Esteem' Crawford," she rattled off. "Is that you?"

Dorothy knew who it was before she reluctantly turned around. It was Cynthia Norton, also known as Ding. Cynthia considered herself such a natural born hostess that she took her nickname from the sound of a doorbell.

Ding was the wife of a wealthy commodities broker who lived just down the street from the Crawfords. She invited Dorothy and Jim to almost every party she threw because, as she put it, "We have to socialize with our *famous* neighbors too." Dorothy always came up with an excuse not to go, but that never deterred Ding. For her, it was try and try again. Accordingly, she was a big fan of Jim's books, even though, as she once told him with a wink, "I don't really need the advice."

"What on earth are you doing in the drycleaners so early, dear?" Ding asked Dorothy.

Dorothy immediately noticed Ding was wearing a necklace that looked a little flashy for a trip to the drycleaners. It looked a little flashy for a trip to see the Queen of England.

Dorothy forced a smile. "What on earth are *you* doing in the drycleaners, Ding? Don't you have some houseboy that does this kind of thing?"

Ding leaned in, "You know, I had this Korean boy that did all my running around. Tommy Kim. Remember him? And wouldn't you know it — he went and got an engineering degree during his time off, behind my back." She laughed caustically. "Can you believe that? He's building rockets now for the government or some such thing. Got to get another, I guess."

Dorothy had returned to thinking of Jim. "Another what?"

Ding acted irritated by the question. "Another Korean boy. Or some other kind. What's the matter, Dorothy? You're acting kind of strange," she said.

"I'm sorry," Dorothy said, trying to give Ding her full attention. "I'm just really busy right now."

"I know how it is dear. I'm entertaining eighty people in two weeks. I guess you got my invitation?

"Oh sure," Dorothy said, pretending to remember it.

"And I guess you're coming?" she said with an unapproachable grin.

Before Dorothy could answer, Ding noticed a blouse on top of the clothes Dorothy was holding. "This is beautiful. Where did you get this? Is this silk?"

"Mrs. Norton, I've really got to go."

"Mrs. Norton?" she said with a huff.

A mobile phone started ringing, and both women looked to see if it was hers. It was Dorothy's.

"I see," Ding said.

Dorothy answered without checking the number on the phone.

"Hello?"

"How's your self-esteem," the voice hissed.

What the...? "Sorry?"

"How's your self-esteem?"

"Can I help you with something?"

"Maybe. Maybe we could help each other."

"Who is this?"

Ding was giving the man her ticket, trying to act like she was ignoring Dorothy's conversation. "I'm sorry. You're Korean, right?" she said to the man.

"I'm putting on a show," the strange voice said. "And I want you to be in it."

Dorothy hung up the phone and put it in her purse. Ding turned to Dorothy again, eager to resume their conversation.

"Always be sure and call me 'Ding', sweetheart. That's what my friends call me."

The phone rang again. Dorothy didn't want to answer it, but she didn't want to talk to this idiot woman.

"Hello?"

"I thought we might talk in person. I'm out in the parking lot. Take a look out the window."

Dorothy walked to the window to find only three cars in the parking lot. Her Volvo, Ding's bright yellow BMW, and a slightly battered, white Dodge van. It was parked facing away from the businesses, with two back doors that had different colors, both of which were windowless.

"I'm in the van you're looking at. I can see you in my rearview mirror."

"What do you want?"

"I want you to be on my show. *The Happy Pappy Show*."

Dorothy rolled her eyes. "I'm afraid I can't."

"Come on out."

Ding interrupted. "So you're coming to my party?"

Dorothy walked toward the door. "I'll talk to you soon, okay?" adding "Ding," as she walked out.

The van was parked two car lengths away from her car, and Dorothy's first inclination was to go up and give this dummy one upside the head. It didn't even cross Dorothy's mind to call the police, as she never was one to overreact to a prank, which this obviously was. She was trying to think of who would have her mobile phone number and who might make such a call, but she couldn't think of anyone. Actually there were lots of people who had her number, especially women she knew from various social gatherings. Few of them, however, were men. It must be the juvenile son of one of her female friends, she thought. And in that case it's no big whoop.

She decided to approach the van and see. She slowly walked to the driver's side of the van, the side opposite her car.

If something happens to me, the people in the bakery and drycleaner will see anyway, she thought.

She could see the driver's side window. It had been tinted dark but cheaply so, as it was starting to peel off around the edges.

Dorothy stood in front of the window, her dry cleaning now hanging over her shoulder. She waited a moment, then knocked on the window. Nothing. Then the van started up. Dorothy took a step back, and then the window came down.

The first thing she saw was the hat. Then the eyes, exaggerated and comical, surfacing from under the brim of the hat. Then the pipe.

Dorothy fell back a step and caught herself. "Who are you?"

"I'm Happy Pappy," Dorothy heard him say. But the voice sounded sharp and tinny, like it was a small recording device making the sound.

"I'm Happy Pappy." This time she knew it was a recording, the same as the first.

"I'm Happy Pappy," it repeated.

Dorothy walked to her car, trembling as she pulled her keys out of her purse.

"I'm Happy Pappy," she faintly heard again. She looked over her shoulder in disbelief.

What kind of sick tootyhead...

The truck started up. She got in her car and sat down, and through her rearview mirror could see the van pull away.

Now, calm down. It was just some idiot in a mask.

The van was gone. She looked at her mobile phone, which lay in her open purse, and thought about calling the police.

"Hello, nine-one-one."

"I just had a man call me."

"Sorry, Ma'am."

"I had a strange man call me. Then I saw him in a parking lot."

"Who called you?"

"I don't know."

"Well, did he hurt you? Are you injured in any way?"

"No... I..."

"Where are you? At home?"

"No. I'm in my car."

"Is this man there now?"

"No. Well, he left in a van just a few minutes ago."

"Did he threaten you?"

"No... I..."

"Did you write down any information like a license plate?"

"No I didn't. Damn it."

She decided not to call.

Just drive.

Dorothy got on Pico Avenue and headed for the Robertson district. She felt like hanging out in an anonymous part of town for a while. As she drove, it crossed her mind that she might be trying to act too rationally. She thought about Jim's reaction to the videotape and how she told him he was being paranoid. The Crawfords had been fortunate not to have experienced any stalking fans in their six or seven years in the spotlight, but Dorothy started to think there was a first time for everything. Maybe the tape was noteworthy. Maybe the man in the parking lot wasn't just some harmless prankster.

She thought about Jim and about his drinking.

Maybe I need to be a little more open about his concerns, listen to what is troubling him.

He could, after all, be a great husband at times, and he did try to stay sober most of the time — *well, a lot of the time* — *well... some of the time.*

Well, he tried.

She thought about how she hadn't been very attentive to his needs. That maybe he needed to talk about a few things and maybe...

My God, I've been watching Jan Hershey too much.

Dorothy turned on Robertson and a van appeared in her rearview mirror. It looked like *the* van, but she couldn't be sure. In a city this big there had to be hundreds. But was this the one?

She tried to look at the driver, but couldn't see anything because of the glare and the distance. She couldn't make out any window tinting. She couldn't make out anything.

Dorothy took a left, and the van, two car lengths behind, followed. She decided it was a good idea just to pull over and get some coffee. She turned left on a side street and the van went by on her right. She felt relieved right away, like her initial thoughts about Jim's paranoia were true after all. *Someone was just playing a prank. You're thinking too much.* She found a parking space, then put an hour's worth of change in the meter. She was just going to walk around a minute, catch her breath and relax. Then she saw a white van coming toward her. It had to be the same van.

She turned and walked quickly in the opposite direction. *What am I running from? I'm in public, on the street.* She thought perhaps she had caught Jim's paranoia. *I don't know, just by sleeping in the same bed?* Or maybe it was just from being around him, thinking of his behavior all the time. But whatever it was, she felt a strong desire to get away. Anywhere.

She reached Robertson and headed south, a street lined with a number of stylish shops, crowded with people. She felt more comfortable. Then out of the corner of her left eye she saw the white van, moving slowly alongside her.

Dorothy turned toward it, ready to scream, but then she hit something, knocking her to the ground.

She looked up to see only the glare of the sun then someone eclipsing it.

It was Peters with two fingers on his forehead just above his left eye. "My gosh, Dorothy. Are you okay?"

"Phil?"

He reached down to help her up. He had a strange expression on his face, she thought. She'd never seen the respected doctor so surprised. She took his hand, which felt cold, and got to her feet, dusting off her behind and straightening her clothes. She felt relieved to see the face of a friend, but when she began to speak, her relief turned to embarrassment.

"I'm sorry. I wasn't watching where..."

"Dorothy, are you okay?"

"Phil. Yes. I'm fine. I just..."

Peters only had her wellbeing in mind. "You didn't break anything, did you?"

"No. I just fell. I..."

Dorothy looked behind her nervously. "I thought someone was

following me, and I..."

Peters gestured toward a small coffee shop behind them. "I was just about to have an espresso. Why don't you come and join me? Relax for a bit."

It felt unusual, the two of them, probably since they had never been alone together, never without Jim. But Dorothy knew there wasn't anything unusual about it. They were just going to have some coffee.

Dorothy looked at her watch. "Aren't you supposed to be at school?"

"Hey, I'm the dean now. I can do whatever I want."

TWELVE

Crawford finally passed out on the bar after downing four more shots, courtesy of the establishment's grateful proprietor. While Rakim was relieving himself in the bathroom, his sidemen were starting to take an interest in Crawford. One of Rakim's men, a big guy named "J," reached inside Crawford's jacket and pulled out his wallet. Rakim came back just in time to see what was happening.

"Damn, man. What you doin?" Rakim said. "This motherfucker changed my life. And you're stealing from him? Give me that shit, bitch," he said, snatching the wallet from his hand.

Rakim put the wallet lovingly back in Crawford's jacket pocket then turned to his associate. "You're a goddam embarrassment, J. If I want you to, you're going to carry this guy home on your back then suck his dick when you get there. Get me?"

"I sure do," J said.

Rakim turned his attention back to Crawford, whose nose was flat against his forearm. "Dr. Crawford? Yo, Dr. Crawford? You okay, Doc?"

Crawford was out, and Rakim gave J a ruminative look.

"I didn't do anything to him," J said. "I was just interested."

"That's right," said Rakim's other man, B. "He didn't do nothin."

"Yeah, sure. But thanks for reminding me that we can't just leave him here like this. The people that come in this joint will rape, pillage, and burn the motherfucker." Rakim yelled for the bartender to get a glass of water, and he did as he was told. The rapper then pulled a pristine handkerchief out of his jacket pocket, and after dipping it in the water, dabbed Crawford's lifeless face. When Crawford didn't come to, Rakim reached inside Crawford's other jacket pocket and pulled out his mobile phone.

"Dr. Crawford. Dr. Crawford," he said. "Is there a number on this phone we can call to have someone pick you up? Hey, Doc!" he said louder.

Crawford lethargically moved his head from side to side on the bar. "I can explain everything," he mumbled. "I can explain."

Rakim patted Crawford on the shoulders reassuringly. "You don't have to explain shit, bro. You're in my drinking establishment. You my guest, Doc. You jus' take it easy, bro."

Crawford lifted his head, trying to piece together where he was.

"You just passed out there for a while, Dr. Crawford." Rakim's men were standing on either side of him. "You're all right now. You're among friends. I hope you don't mind me saying, but it's kind of early to be downin' shots, bro. But I figured you bein' a writer and all, you got a flip flopped, fucked up schedule like I do. Matter of fact, it's almost my bedtime."

"Oh," Crawford said, reaching for the glass of water on the bar.

"Don't drink that, man. Let me get you a fresh one. Joe, another glass of water for the man. Now!"

"Someone killed my lady friend," Crawford said, staring blankly at the floor.

"Say what?"

"Someone killed my lady friend and videotaped it. Sent me the tape."

The bartender put the glass down and Rakim slid it toward Crawford.

"Here man, take a drink. No offense, bro, but I think you might be imaginin' thangs. You've had a lot to drink."

Crawford took another swig of water, his eyes still trained on the floor. "No, there was a tape someone sent me with a murder on it. A woman I know. A woman I was fucking. That's why they killed her." Crawford looked in front of him, then over to Rakim. "The tape was real. The goddam tape was real."

"What tape?"

"A videotape I got in the mail. I mean... someone left it on my doorstep. I watched it while I was drunk. I've still got it, I think. Somewhere."

"Hey, man. I don't deal with damage control, but I got a few friends that might be able to help you out if you want."

"Help me out? Help me out how?"

"You know, somebody's fuckin wit' you. You know, help out."

Crawford looked up at the barkeep. "Can I have another beer?"

"You sure?" Rakim said with his eyebrows raised like a concerned mother. "Rakim doesn't want you to pass out on him again."

"I'm sure. Another, please. I'm a professional. I know what I'm doing."

"You heard the man," Rakim said, almost tenderly, and the bartender pulled out a pint glass and filled it.

"Like I said, if you need help..."

"No thanks, Rakim. I think I'm just gonna have to deal with this one myself." Crawford looked thoughtful. "We really got no one but ourselves, do we?"

"That's right, man. We don't," Rakim said solemnly. "You wrote that in *Self-Confidence*. Remember?"

"Did I?"

"Man, you need a ride home or anything?"

Crawford pulled out his mobile phone. "No thanks, man. I got it taken care of."

Rakim raised his Manhattan and clinked Crawford's beer glass. "We'll do whatever the doctor says."

Dorothy suggested to Peters that they take a window seat. She ordered an orange cappuccino and Peters said he'd have the same.

"Right away," the waiter said.

"That isn't what you normally drink, is it?" Dorothy asked.

"Yes it is," Peters said.

Dorothy still felt uncomfortable and forced a smile. For some strange reason she felt like she was betraying her husband. "So that was quite a banquet the other night, huh?"

"Yes it was." Peters put his palms together at his chest as if he were pondering every word. "But it was a little too much for me, I'm afraid."

Dorothy nervously looked away from Peters' gaze as she spoke. "Too much? What do you mean?"

"I don't know. Just not my cup of tea."

Dorothy didn't press any further, but looked at Peters intermittently as they sat in silence. The waiter arrived with their order and Dorothy relaxed. Then a moment later she felt as if someone were watching her and she looked out the window again — not just out but also up and down the street.

"Something wrong?" Peters asked, moving his hands back to his chest.

"No," she said, forcing another smile.

It was more than just his accomplishments in research that had gotten Peters to his position; it was his easy-going manner. Genuine or not, it worked for what his profession most often demanded — talking to people. He had a strange way of opening people up even when they didn't want to be. Whether it was his spectacles inflating his already welcoming eyes or his fatherly beard, it all contributed to a disposition that easily opened emotional floodgates.

"What is it, Dorothy?" he asked again, ignoring his cappuccino. She looked at him as if she had to. Peters leaned back in his chair slightly. "You know, Dorothy, sometimes people think it's a big deal to tell me things — you know, simple things, when something is bothering them, or whatever — and that's ridiculous. I'm a human being first and a psychologist second. You and I are sitting in a coffee shop having a cup'a Jo. That's all."

"What do you mean?" she asked.

"What's on your mind, sweetheart?"

Sweetheart? She never thought she'd hear him say that. She gave a slightly embarrassed smile and so did Peters, which also surprised her. "My husband can be a pain in the ass, Phil."

"I know he can. I've known him a long time. Which is not to say that I'm criticizing him. I can be a pain in the ass, too."

"Yeah, but you're not a drunk."

"No, but I've got more than a few vices, believe me." He paused a moment with a reassuring smile, then said, "So it's the drinking?"

"I don't know. I always thought we'd be over this stuff by now."

Peters looked over his glasses. "The drinking? He'll never be over that, Dorothy. That's the nature of the disease. You know that."

"Yes, but..." Dorothy paused as if she were afraid of what she might reveal.

"But what?"

"He's been acting strange."

"Strange?"

The waiter approached again and asked if he could get them something else. Dorothy shook her head, and Peters waved the boy away quickly.

Dorothy was feeling grateful for Peters' company. "Thanks for being concerned about me."

"If I can do anything, just let me know."

There was an awkward pause, then "It's not just Jim, Phil."

"What do you mean?"

"I mean it's not just Jim that's bothering me. We've had some strange things happen lately."

"Strange things? Like what?"

"Well, for one," Dorothy said carefully, "I had this guy call me on my mobile phone a little while ago. I was at the dry cleaners and he was sitting in a van in the parking lot with a Happy Pappy mask on."

Peters snickered, which Dorothy thought odd.

"I'm sorry. A mask?" he asked.

"Yeah, a mask. I thought he was following me when I came in here."

"Did you call the police?"

Dorothy was almost offended by the question. "No, I didn't."

"Why not?"

"Well, I thought they might laugh like you just did."

"I'm sorry," Peters said. It was the only time Dorothy could remember Peters showing anything close to remorse. "It's just your husband is a famous self-help book writer. You're going to get some weirdoes every now and then. I even get them and I'm not famous."

"You're a little famous," Dorothy said exhaling heavily. She really was exhausted.

"Dorothy. Do you want to come to my place this afternoon? Just relax and talk about this?"

She didn't look up. "You know that's an embarrassing question."

"Why? It shouldn't be. I just want to help you."

She looked up at him as her eyes filled with tears. "That's nice of you, Phil. But I can't."

"Why not? I'd like to discuss something with you, Dorothy."

"Something important."

"What, Phil? Tell me."

"At my place, okay?"

They walked onto the sidewalk where the afternoon sun was starting to introduce itself from behind the morning clouds. Dorothy figured it was around two in the afternoon. It looked like she was going to waste her entire day. Of course, her main task was to decide what she was going to do if Jim didn't come home, as well as what she would do if he did.

And what about Cal? He had always been the most important consideration. But the way he had been acting lately, she didn't want to think of him at all. She had weathered the hardest parts of her marriage with a *what's best for the child* attitude, but now that Cal was months away from being legally grown, that defense wasn't standing up.

"I really enjoyed our little chat, Dorothy," Peters said awkwardly.

Dorothy knew this was a polite remark. They hadn't really had a chat at all.

"I appreciate it, Phil. You're a good friend to both of us. You know that?"

Dorothy, still feeling unsettled and vulnerable, put her arm around Peters and gave him a hug — the first she'd ever given him.

"Anything I can do, Dorothy," he said softly.

Dorothy looked up at Peters' tall frame. He looked so respectful and authoritative, so in control. She thought about her husband and how weak he was, how his petty affairs were so demeaning — not just to her but to him as well.

She caught herself holding onto him a moment longer.

"I'd like to show you something, Dorothy. But it has to be at the right moment."

"What?" she asked. Peters was the most remote person she had ever met — though she knew she didn't really know him well.

"I'd like to show you something, something special."

She paused a moment.

"It's something that can help you," he said.

It was noon and Lee Burns had his head cocked back and his eyes closed. He couldn't help it; he was in ecstasy. He had just spent the morning with his second top selling writer, Donovan Heller, who cracked the corporate business/motivational market just three months ago with a top seller called *You Can Sell It ... and Keep It Too*. Lee and Heller had just spent the morning working out the details of his next release entitled *Fortress Around Your Account*, along with an accompanying wall calendar.

Donovan is so easy to deal with, Lee was thinking. So professional. Never humdrum or difficult about anything. Always thinking of money. No silly aspirations to be an artist.

Since the publication of Crawford's last book, Lee had been wondering how long the franchise would hold out. He knew, for example, that the *Happy Pappy Show* was going to be a dagger in the heart of the *Self Series* in the long run. But the way he saw it, it was going to sink pretty soon regardless. He always knew this, even though he never gave a hint to Crawford. Yes, there'll be a time when you can write your little novel, he often thought. Yes, self-help books have to go sometime. Even most diet books don't cross generations like novels do. There's no self-help *Catcher in the Rye*. The next generation looks back, sees that the people who bought those books are still fat and miserable, and they try something else.

Lee's head eased further back as he let his mind drift away from business. Thing was, Kim Cox, Lee's devoted secretary for the past seventeen months, was on her knees performing an act that would allow her to take the rest of the afternoon off with pay.

Surprisingly, the suggestion of such an arrangement had actually come from Cox herself after reading Crawford's formative work *Self-Confidence*.

When we have self-confidence, we not only see opportunity awaiting us, but we create it proactively. For example, have you ever thought about suggesting a mutually-beneficial arrangement with someone like your spouse or your boss, but chose not to for fear of being rejected?

Cox loved the way Crawford put things into perspective.

It could be any arrangement at all. It could be suggesting to your wife that you make dinner one night a week in exchange for having a group of buddies over to watch the big game that weekend. Or...

She thought he was so diplomatic, too. She always imagined what a wonderful home life he must have.

You could ask your boss what you might do in exchange for new benefits or enviable responsibilities.

She also loved that his suggestions allowed you to be creative.

It's all really just a matter of self-confidence.

Lee was breathing intermittently as his eyes lolled. As he leaned back further, he thought of how well all the tie-ins were doing, how effective the promotionals were, he thought of...

The phone was ringing. Lee came back to the present.

"Hello?" he said into the air. "Why isn't someone answering the phone? Oh, yeah. You wanted off early," he said to his lap. "Hold your horses, there. It could be my wife."

Kim looked up at him, insulted. She had been making an effort, putting on a performance that contradicted her mood.

"Hello?"

Cox got off the floor and slapped Lee's chest. "Now I'm going," she said.

"Fine. Go," he said, gesturing with one hand and muting the phone with the other.

She walked out, slamming the door.

This better be good, he thought. "Hello?"

"Lee? Lee Burns," a voice grumbled.

"Yeah. Who is this?"

"It's your star fucking client," the drunken voice said.

A faint "That's right" could be heard in the background.

"Jim? Where the hell are you?"

Lee knew that a taxi was the only way to get to the East L.A. address Crawford had given him. He wasn't about to drive his own car and have it disappear from those streets. In fact, he tried to think of a way of not going at all. But when he thought about giving the task to an office grunt, he realized he had no choice but to deal with it personally. Not only was he going to make sure that Crawford was on the Jan Hershey show the next day, he also was going to make sure that no one with any credibility would be able to report that Dr. Crawford was getting shitfaced in a bar the day before.

The driver looked Mediterranean — dark hair, a swarthy complexion, an unfamiliar accent — but Lee had no idea what the hell the man was.

But if one characteristic redeemed Lee of his ignorance, it was his keen awareness of his unawareness. He knew he was lacking in many subjects, but he could easily accommodate it. He was the type of person that always laughs at erudite jokes, even when he didn't understand the reference. "Just roll with it," was his attitude. So "Oh, that's clever," was his customary response.

Years ago, he even told Crawford of this weakness and suggested he make a story out of it for one of his books. Lee came up with *The Man Who Laughs at Jokes He Doesn't Understand*. Crawford initially agreed and then decided to ditch the idea, thinking it too much a part of human nature. "We all laugh at jokes we don't understand," he argued. "And sometimes we don't laugh at what we want to. It's as old as civilization."

Riding in the back of the cab, Lee was attempting to be civilized. He was trying not to laugh at what he thought funny: the thick black hair on the back of the man's neck that looked like a dyed-black Brillo pad scrubbed to nonexistence. And he was trying to laugh at what wasn't funny: the cab smelling of a combination of cheap perfume, antiseptic and a vile combination of blood, urine, and vomit.

In order to ensure he got to where he needed to go, and equipped with awareness of his ignorance, Lee would try to communicate with this man for the duration of the ride. He also thought it might help him ignore the nauseating smell of the interior of the cab. He leaned forward to look at the man's name on his license, but didn't even try to pronounce it.

"So, uh... sir?" he said sheepishly. "Make trips down here often?"

In broken English, the man said, "Not les hahf to."

"Know anything about this place? It's called Sharkey's."

"Badtha."

"Bath?" Lee asked, thinking the guy could use a bath.

"No. Bahd-tha," he said slowly.

"Bad?"

"Yah. Yah. It's badtha place. Loots av badtha peepahl."

"Peephole?" Lee asked.

"Badtha peepahl. Badtha place."

Lee thought the driver might be using slang by saying *bad* then wondered if *peephole* was slang too. "Sir, I want you to stay outside for me, okay?" Lee said slowly. "You understand?"

The cabbie rocked back and forth. "Yah. Yah," he said.

Lee spoke deliberately. "I want you to stay and wait because I'm coming right out. I'm going right back to my office. Understand?"

"Yah. Yah," the cabbie said again.

Lee could see the man cupping the address in his hand just above the steering wheel.

"Almost there," he said.

Lee leaned back in his seat then leaned up again, remembering not to touch anything.

The cabbie looked closely at Lee in his rearview mirror. "Oolmoost der."

"So you'll stay and wait for me?" Lee asked nervously.

"Yah, Yah. Shoor, shoor," he said. "Here tiz."

As the cab pulled to the curb, Lee knew the place was bad — bad like *bad* — no question. The first thing that crossed Lee's mind was to tell the cabbie just to keep on going past the place, which was surely filled with bad peephole.

Crawford was getting stinko in this dump? Lee thought. This guy is becoming more of a liability than an asset every day.

Becoming? Hell, he's been a fucking liability since you met him.

No, that's not true. What about all those books he's sold? he thought.

No, those books I've sold for him.

And that TV show, what a moneymaker, he thought.

Yeah, but I could get any asshole on the planet to write a book telling about how he was down and out and pathetic and wanted to kill himself and he came back and put his life back together and put his family back together and bought a nice RV and crossed the country in it while he wrote all these big secrets that allowed him to get his shit together and now he's passing them on to you, the consumer, who...

"Here tiz, mistour," the cabbie said.

"You're waiting for me, right?"

"Yah, Yah. Shoor, shoor."

"Wait for me, okay? I'm coming right out, understand?"

The cabbie rolled his eyes like a teenage girl raised in Southern California. "Under-stadt. Yah, Yah. Shoor, shoor. But need fare for dis trip."

Lee got out of the cab and handed the man a fifty. "I'll be right back," Lee said, stepping on the sidewalk then over a man (or woman) passed out in front. That's when Lee heard the cab squeal away.

The cabbie yelled out of the passenger's side window in nearly perfect English, "Got another call, buddy!"

"Asshole!" Lee yelled after him with his middle finger in the air. "Asshole! Understand that!"

The putrid lump of flesh lying face down on the pavement rolled over. "Hey, man. You got any change?"

Lee assumed it was a man. "Fuck off, buddy," he said.

Boom chicka boom chicka boom...

The first thing Lee noticed when he entered the bar was the rhythmic Machiavellian sound. It was like a drum beat made with sticks and stones — primal, harrowing, evil — that and Crawford slouched over the bar with a wide grin on his face, staring straight ahead. J and B, were clinking bottles and playing imaginary bongos on their thighs, accompanying Rakim in his rap version of *The Happy Pappy Song*.

"Yo. Be kind to yo-self," Rakim, with his sneakers squeaking heavily on the bar's sticky floor, did a side-to-side step in front of Crawford and pointed at him. "Be fond of yo-self."

Oh Christ, Lee thought in desperation, before thinking that maybe Crawford could do a self-help rap album.

"If you're not a chum you be a fuckin' bum to yo-self, bitch. Be a friend to yo-self, without end to yo-self."

J and B leaned in, making percussive sounds with their lips.

"Yeah," Rakim nodded, "yeah," then turned to smile at Crawford, who was next to him. "Ah-ite?"

"You bet," Crawford said.

Lee walked over and put his hand on Crawford's shoulder. "Have you lost your fucking mind?"

"Yes," he said. "I think so."

Rakim began to slow down, "Yo Happy, yo Pappy, Yo Happy, Yo..."

"Have you forgotten about the show tomorrow?"

"The children's show?"

"Yeah. It's called *Jan Live with Jan Hershey*. You're coming with me to my house tonight, Jim."

"I'm going to my own home," Crawford said trying, to raise his glass. "I don't need your sorry ass." Crawford took a giant swig of the beer, much of which ran down the front of his shirt. "Sorry, sorry," he mumbled. "I should go."

"No kidding? You don't need me, huh? My sorry ass? I see your friends here are an influence on you," Lee said, glancing toward Rakim.

"I heard that," Rakim shot back. "You dissin' me, motherfucker? The Doc here has been an influence on me. Can't you see that? Who are you?"

"I'm kidding, man. I'm a friend of his. He needs to go home. Can you help me out here?" Lee said with a pained smirk.

Rakim started getting in the groove with J and B, slapping his thighs. "Just a minute. Don't interrupt Rakim JB."

Lee couldn't believe what he was seeing.

The beat got slow and hypnotic. *Bum Pa Ta Bum Pa Ta*. Rakim rapped slowly, "Respect. Self. Chum. Self."

"You're going on that show tomorrow and you're going on sober. You hear me, bitch?" Lee said resolutely.

Crawford laughed. "That's what I'm talking about."

"Now let's get out of here." Lee turned around and got the bartender's attention. "Hard to get a cab around here?"

"What do you think?"

Lee looked at the bartender then past him at Sharkey's prosthetic arm hanging on the wall. "Is that a... arm?"

Rakim brought the Happy Pappy Rap to a close. "Hode it. J, don't turn the beat around like that, bitch. Damn!"

Lee checked his jacket pocket but couldn't find his mobile. "Can I make a call?" he asked the bartender, pointing to a phone on the wall.

"Yo!" Rakim said, walking toward Lee. The percussion by JB stopped.

Lee spoke directly in Crawford's ear, "I'm leaving you, Jim. Come on or I'm going."

Rakim stood right in front of Lee. "Yo! Man, what do you think you're doing?"

The bartender put the phone on the bar, and Lee picked up the receiver.

"I'm calling a cab for this guy," Lee said calmly.

"For Dr. Crawford?"

"That's right."

"And who the hell are you?" Rakim said, JB flanking him.

"I'm his publisher. He's a writer."

"I know who the fuck he is. What the hell do you want with him?"

Lee was starting to think he'd like to get revenge on that asshole cabbie for ditching him. "I'm just here to help him, that's all."

Lee started to dial the operator when Rakim said, "Put my goddam phone down."

"I'm just calling a cab."

"*I said*, put my goddam phone down, bitch!" he yelled even louder.

Lee did as he was told.

Crawford looked up at Lee and smiled. "You know what I like about you, Lee? You always take care of your shit."

"Thanks," he said with a thumbs up.

Rakim was now standing within inches of Lee. "Wait a minute. You a publisher? A literary publisher?"

Lee was surprised he used the word *literary*. "A book publisher. That's right."

"Let me ask you a few questions before you run off. Is that okay? See, I'm a businessman."

"Sure, young man," Lee said awkwardly, falling onto the stool beside Crawford.

Rakim motioned to the bartender. "Another round here."

"No, I don't think..." Lee began.

"What are you havin, Mr. Publisher?" Rakim looked resolute.

Lee immediately gave in. "Scotch whisky, neat. Whatever you got."

"Get it," Rakim said to the bartender. "Five of 'em." Then to Lee, "Hey man, I was thinking about writin' my memoirs. Would you be interested in publishin' em?"

"Sure. Of course. Send us a query. We're always interested in new writers," he said.

The bartender poured the whiskeys.

"Might sell a shitload. Never know. I've already sold 15 million records with my rhymes. Lots of loyal fans."

"Fifteen... Mill?"

"I'm Rakim, the recording artist, man. I'm the big time."

"You're a rapper?"

"The motherfuckin' word," J and B said in unison.

Rakim said, "Ever heard of my best-selling album *Forty Shakers and a Tool*?"

"I think so," Lee nodded. "Interesting."

"Or what about my critically acclaimed masterpiece *Nigga Porridge*? Motherfucker came out three months ago."

Lee was raising his glass to his lips and stopped in his tracks. "Really? I think I have heard of that one. Wow, you're a famous guy."

"Word," Rakim said proudly.

"What's your name... bro?" He had never called anyone "bro" in his life.

"Rakim, JB. This nigga's J and that nigga's B," he said proudly pointing at each of one them.

"But your name is just Rakim?" Then turning to J and B, "Nice to meet you," he said properly.

"No, man. I'm Rakim JB. This here's J and this is B."

"Oh, collectively known as JB" Lee didn't understand how this worked but couldn't think of the right question to clarify. He downed his shot in one big gulp and barreled over, coughing into the back of his right hand as the rotgut whiskey saturated the back of his throat. "Damn," he muttered. "That's some strong shit."

"Thing is," Rakim continued, "I'm a trend setter." "*Forty Shakers*, that album was all about niggas gettin' nasty with they bitches and hoes.

And that shit's fun, yo, raw. But it's on the way out. All these niggas be doin' that. I knew I needed a new direction. That's why I made *Porridge*. It's a concept album."

"Interesting," Lee said.

"Listen to him, Lee," Crawford said, before downing his shot without a wince. Then he opened his eyes wider as if it woke him up a bit. "Ah. Damn good, Lee."

Lee grabbed the phone again then asked the bartender, "Can you recommend a cab company to call that wouldn't mind coming down here."

Before he could answer, Rakim said, "Yo, man. I'll give you a ride. Look at that dope-ass car out there. I got the best ride in town. Where you need to go?"

"Century City."

"Hell, that's no problem." Rakim put his hand on Lee's shoulder and gestured to Crawford. "This man changed my life with the books he's written. Hell, he *saved* my life." Suddenly his voice was upper middle-class Caucasian. "It would be an honor for me to take you two gentlemen anywhere."

"Is that right?" Lee said.

"What do I do about my car?" Crawford said, holding up his keys.

"Your car? It's outside? Why didn't you say something?"

"I... uh..."

"I'll drive," Lee said, snatching the keys.

Rakim looked disappointed, and then was a rapper again. "Look, when we gonna talk about the prospect of you gettin' my motherfuckin' memoirs published? I can deliver his car later."

"No, man. We'll talk another time. Okay?"

Rakim put a business card in Lee's front pocket. "You better call my ass," he said.

"No problem," Lee said. "Come on, champ," he said putting his hand on Crawford's shoulder.

Crawford put his right arm around Lee as a long line of saliva dripped from the side of his mouth. "I've got to get back to my family," Crawford said, wiping his mouth with his left hand. "Right away."

"Why?"

"Because that asshole's coming after me pretty soon. He's coming after Dorothy. He's going to get all of us."

"Who's coming after you?" Rakim said.

"Hell, I don't know." Crawford's eyes widened, revealing solid red lines running from his irises to his eyelids.

"I went to her apartment, Lee."

"Come on, let's go," Lee said, trying to drag him by his shoulder.

"Come back anytime," the bartender said.

"Fuckin' A right come back," Rakim said. "You better come back."

"Let's go, TV star," Lee said, pulling harder.

"Wait," Crawford stopped him, as if to make a proclamation. In fact it was a proclamation. "I have to take a shit."

"Then by all means go, Jim, go," Lee said. "Take a shit."

"Shit, yeah," Rakim added.

Crawford, looking at Rakim for guidance, lifted his finger toward the back and raised his drunken eyes into a question mark.

"That nasty-ass shitter should have been cleaned a long time ago," Rakim said, giving the bartender a dirty look. "I apologize, Doc. But at least the motherfucker works, unlike some things 'round here."

"Believe me, I won't remember it."

Crawford stumbled into the bathroom and stopped a moment at the stall door to look at the various inscriptions and messages strewn all over it. "Rakim's Office" was the first Crawford noticed, along with the various limericks and promises of sexual services found on any low-budget john. There was a desperate violence in the calligraphy that denounced the surroundings. But like a lot of contemporary art — especially movies and novels — it also served as a collaborator to all that it claimed to condemn.

Crawford opened the door reading, "She got a Lopsided tit that looks like Shit" and "Darnell W. sucks big dicks" with a phone number.

So much anger.

Oh that's this guy Rakim, Crawford thought. On the TV in the liquor store. "I'm in the ghet-to," that shit. Well, what d'ya know. The guy really is in the ghetto.

Thank heaven the toilet didn't smell as bad as it looked, as it gave Crawford the power to take a seat rather than kneel down. Crawford locked the stall door then thought he might pass out, or worse, have a seizure. But he knew Lee wouldn't leave him there, nor Rakim for that matter, and they would have no trouble getting through a puny little toilet door like this. So he went ahead and locked it.

Does it matter?

There were no sanitary seat covers and Crawford was too drunk to care, so he faced the door and unzipped his pants. But just as he was about to take a seat, Crawford realized there was a book resting on the tank lid behind him. Even before he turned around it registered immediately: *a Bible.*

Crawford twisted to the side and picked it up, gripping its spine and noting the faded words "Holy Bible" with "PRONOUNCING" beneath.

Crawford took a seat.

The Book's cover was stiff, its black leather having obviously been exposed to the elements for years, making it feel more like cardboard than animal skin.

Crawford situated each cheek comfortably on the toilet seat, and opened the cover. Stencil-created flowers covered the edges of the first page, which served to tell whom the Bible was bestowed upon.

Holy Bible

presented to

_____

by

_____

Blanks. Apparently it had never been presented to anyone. Perhaps it was purchased by someone as a gift to himself. Those are the nicest gifts anyway, Crawford thought.

The poor Bible looked lonely in this horrendous place. But obviously the urinating and defecating drunks had a certain respect for it. There didn't appear to be any graffiti, no stains, no damage of any kind. Perhaps the patrons of *Sharkey's* knew it needed to be there. Perhaps that's why that unknown someone had left it.

The pages still felt silky-thin. *Only Bible pages feel like that.* Crawford brushed them back and forth a few times just to feel the sensation.

Crawford opened it to the title page but was immediately distracted by the color photograph on the facing leaf. It was a painting called SAMSON IN THE TREADMILL, one of those old paintings Crawford had seen going to church as a child in Texas. They were everywhere, these reproductions — on church programs, church announcements, and church calendars. Everyone was handsome, everyone was perfectly built, especially Jesus.

Sampson is leaning into the mill on his left foot. His face is obscured, but his perfect body is emphasized by the brilliant use of Rembrandt-like shadow and a sexy loincloth. There was an inscription underneath.

> *But the Philistines took him, and put out his eyes,*
> *and brought him down to Gaza, and bound him with*
> *fetters of brass: and he did grind in the prison house.*
> *Judges 16:21*

Hmm, Crawford thought. Wonder why they decided to use this particular painting and this particular passage. Crawford was also starting to wonder if he was going to be able to have a bowel movement. He thought of his grandmother, probably because both the Bible and bowel movements (that is, enemas) were strong reminders of her.

He felt that all Christians could be categorized as Old Testament or New Testament — depending on what he called the Hell-Fire-And-Brimstone Factor. Grandma was definitely Old Testament, and accordingly she thought the entire human race was going to hell for eternity and would deserve every excruciating minute of it. Also very Old Testament was her favorite maxim: "All you need is the Bible."

When Crawford was a little boy he had countered with "What about food?"

"You need the Bible before you need food," she'd quickly answer. "All you need is the Bible."

This wasn't a problem until Crawford started writing his first self-help book. The memory of his deceased grandmother began popping up all the time — even while asleep — saying the same thing: "All you need is the Bible." Crawford had thought that he had long since put his Christian upbringing behind him, but he was wrong.

I can't crap. He contracted his stomach muscles and leaned over. *But I need to. Oh please, God.*

Crawford flipped a couple of pages ahead. "All you need is the Bible," he said aloud. *Genesis.* "Maybe it will help."

Can the Bible help us? Can't we just help ourselves? *Maybe that's what the ancients were doing when they wrote the Bible: helping themselves.*

Crawford suddenly thought about how drunk he was and that perhaps he needed real help. *Genesis.* Chapter 3. *Banishment.* Maybe we needed banishment, he thought.

Or did we? Did it help us? *Does it matter?* Help me, he thought.

CHAPTER 3
The First Sin and its Punishment

Now the serpent was more subtle than any beast of the field which the LORD God had made. And he said unto the woman, Yea, hath God said, Ye shall not eat of every tree of the garden?

2   And the woman said unto the serpent, We may eat of the fruit of the trees of the garden:

3   But of the fruit of the tree which is in the

> midst of the garden, God hath said, Ye shall not
> eat of it, neither shall ye touch it, lest ye die.

"Strange decree." It's like your parents telling you not to drink alcohol and smoke cigarettes when you're a teenager. It's the challenge that makes you want to do it. I wonder why God did this. Then there's Job. God testing people and things like that. My Grandmother said never ask why God does something. Huh, I wonder why she said that.

> 4 And the serpent said unto the woman, Ye
> shall not surely die:

The Devil was right about that. They didn't die. But God said they would. Oh, maybe it's that they'll die eventually.

> 5 For God doth know that in the day ye eat
> thereof, then your eyes shall be opened, and ye
> shall be as gods, knowing good and evil.

You can be like God, autonomous like God. This was the first lie ever told.

> 6 And when the woman saw that the tree *was*
> good for food,

They had all the food they wanted, but that wasn't enough. Damn women.

> and that it *was* pleasant to the eyes,

She could still look at it. She just couldn't touch. Gotta have everything.

> and a tree to be desired to make *one* wise,

Like she cared about being wise. Probably just wanted to look like she cared about being wise.

> she took of the fruit thereof, and did eat, and
> gave also unto her husband with her; and he did
> eat.

Now wait, did Adam know it was from the tree? The tree? Maybe he didn't know. Maybe she just said, "Hey, Honey, have some of this with your mutton." Poor sap. Probably didn't even like it. Probably was just being nice. Probably just wanted to get laid. Or maybe she just nagged him until he gave in.

> 7 And the eyes of them both were opened,
> and they knew that they *were* naked; and they
> sewed fig leaves together, and made themselves
> aprons.

God wanted a bunch of naked people who didn't know they were naked, didn't know good and evil? Huh, being naked is evil? Unless you don't know it, I guess. I really need to read this book again.

"All you need is the Bible," Crawford said contracting his stomach again.

> 8   And they heard the voice of the LORD God
> walking in the garden in the cool of the day:

They heard his voice walking in the garden? Oh yeah, they couldn't see him, I guess. Or else they were crazy. Which means the whole human race is crazy. This book actually makes sense. No wonder Freud...

> and Ad'am

"Ad'am?" Oh, it's a "Pronouncing" Bible.

> and Ad'am and his wife hid themselves from
> the presence of the LORD God amongst the trees
> of the garden.
> 9   And the LORD God called unto Ad'am, and
> said unto him, Where art thou?
> 10   And he said, I heard thy voice in the
> garden, and I was afraid, because I was naked;
> and I hid myself.

I guess King James added the "was" emphasis later. "Because I was naked." He still is, really. He's wearing a damn fig leaf. See if that holds up in court.

> 11   And he said, Who told thee that thou wast
> naked?

Come on, that's a loaded question. I guess all God's questions are loaded, now that I think about it.

> Hast thou eaten of the tree, whereof I
> commanded thee that thou shouldest not eat?

He's God. He knows the answer. The question is rhetorical.

> 12   And the man said, The woman whom thou
> gavest to be with me,

That's a strange emphasis, "to be." He sounds bitter already.

> she gave me of the tree, and I did eat.

Boy, he sells her out fast, doesn't he? Eh, she deserves it.

> 13   And the LORD God said unto the woman,
> What is this that thou hast done? And the

woman said, The serpent beguiled me, and I did
eat.

Excuses, excuses. She used the word "beguiled." What a phony. Or maybe it's just a bad translation.

14   And the LORD God said unto the serpent,

The serpent was still around, huh? He was watching the whole thing?

Because thou hast done this, thou *art* cursed
above all cattle, and above every beast of the
field; upon thy belly shalt thou go, and dust
shalt thou eat all the days of thy life:

"Eat dust," snake. Snakes were walking upright before? Creepy.

15   And I will put enmity between thee and
the woman,

"Enmity." So that's where the battle of the sexes comes from. Or he is talking about between the woman and the snake? Maybe Adam's snake.

and between thy seed and her seed;

Ah.

it shall bruise thy head, and thou shalt bruise his
heel.

Uh huh, lots of fighting. It's God-intended, all this fighting.

16   Unto the woman he said, I will greatly
multiply thy sorrow and thy conception; in
sorrow thou shalt bring forth children; and thy
desire *shall be* to thy husband,

"Thy desire shall be *to thy husband." Does that mean her desire was elsewhere before? Or does that mean the husband will be hornier than the woman? I'm confused.*

and he shall rule over thee.

Damn right.

17   And unto Ad'am he said, Because thou
hast hearkened unto the voice of thy wife,

Uh huh, because he listened to his bitchy-ass wife's bad ideas...

and hast eaten of the tree, of which I
commanded thee, saying, Thou shalt not eat of
it: cursed *is* the ground for thy sake; in sorrow

shalt thou eat *of* it all the days of thy life;

18   Thorns also and thistles shall it bring forth
to thee; and thou shalt eat the herb of the field;

"The herb"? Hmm. What herb?

19   In the sweat of thy face shalt thou eat
bread, till thou return unto the ground; for out
of it wast thou taken: for dust thou art, and unto
dust shalt thou return.

*"Dust thou art." God despises us by the Third Chapter. No wonder we
have no self-esteem.*

20   And Ad'am called his wife's name Eve;
because she was the mother of all living.

He's a semanticist. The first.

21   Unto Ad'am also and to his wife did the
Lord God make coats of skins, and clothed
them.

I feel sick.

22   ⁋ And the Lord God said, Behold, the man
is become as one of us,

Us? Us who? Who is he talking to here?

to know good and evil: and now, lest he put
forth his hand, and take also of the tree of life,
and eat, and live for ever:

I don't understand.

23   Therefore the Lord God sent him forth
from the garden of Ad'am, to till the ground
from whence he was taken.

Just do your business so you can get another drink.

24   So he drove out the man; and he placed
at the east of the garden of Ad'am Cher'u-bims,
and a flaming sword which turned every way,
to keep the way of the tree of life.

*"To keep the way of the tree of life"? What does that mean? Wait a
minute.*

Crawford leaned over and farted loudly then felt a sudden rush of
fear as though he'd just committed blasphemy. His grandmother would

have said so, but she wouldn't have explained why. Farting is natural, Crawford assured himself. It's okay, nothing to be ashamed of. Farting and crapping — it was a subject Crawford thought about in his early twenties to help rid himself of social phobias.

People are all a bunch of shitters and pissers and farters, he often thought, especially around unapproachably beautiful women. And it worked for a while, but it soon proved a catch-22. He thought about them shitting, pissing and farting then he no longer desired them.

Crawford expelled more flatus. *Isn't it strange how we all fear the fart? Something everyone has to do on a daily basis. Something God — if there is One — created. Something, ironically, that creates a pleasant release. It's a philosophical question I should bring up sometime — perhaps in a book or at a dinner party. I could be a revolutionary. If I were to write of this private moment in a book, people would call me depraved and dirty-minded. Someone* brave *would do it. Jonathan Swift would do it, and he was a priest. In Lilliput they dealt with some nasty shit, literally — Gulliver's nasty shit. And what about Redd Foxx, he could talk about farting and shitting. No priest, but what a genius he was. Serious writers and thinkers cannot talk about such things. They don't want to be laughed at. Redd* did *want to be laughed at. He was free. What if I only used the word "flatulence"? Or perhaps the more conversational "to break wind"? When my mother used to say "break wind" it always sounded dirtier than "fart." Oh, screw it, who cares?*

As Crawford was evacuating his bowels he thought he might write a book called *A Release Filled with Shame*, with the subtext: *Why God bestowed upon us the shame of...*

Crawford froze a moment then twisted around and put the Bible back where he found it. "You think too much, Crawford. Wipe your ass." *And don't feel ashamed.* He could almost hear his Grandmother say *You're going to hell.*

"If you're not out here in two minutes," Crawford heard Lee yell. "I'm leaving with your car."

Crawford wept.

And that was the last thing he remembered.

THIRTEEN

*C*eiling. It was a ceiling — a plain old white ceiling. That's what it looked like in the dark. Didn't look familiar, but then again most ceilings don't. One reason the Sistine Chapel is such a marvel.

The sound was silence — not the kind Simon and Garfunkel sang about, but bad silence. For Crawford there was nothing worse than waking up from a real bender and hearing it lingering, waiting like a stalker to remind him of the horrible incidents that hadn't been blacked out by alcohol.

Alfred Hitchcock Presents.

He lifted the sheets to find he was in his boxer shorts, not in his usual bedroom dress. The comforter on the bed was unfamiliar to him, so was the room. He threw his legs over the side of the bed and saw a large glass of water on the night table next to a small bottle of aspirin and a bottle of B vitamins. Crawford, dehydrated so badly his upper lip was sticking to the top of his gums, grabbed the glass of water and drank half of it. Next to the aspirin was a small note pad with something scribbled on it. "I called your wife. There's no need to worry. Get some rest. Take a vitamin. You've got a show to do. Regards, Lee."

Regards? Did he dictate that to his damn secretary?

As Crawford's body absorbed the cold water, his limbs chilled. He slid back under the covers noticing a small digital clock beside the lamp on the night table. It read *3:20*. It was dark outside. Three in the morning, not three in the afternoon.

How could I have slept that long? Have I been sleeping that long? Maybe I just got in bed a little while ago. Maybe I was placed here.

He tried to recall the last thing he could remember. Those black kids in the bar, he remembered them rapping. He remembered...

Lee came and got me. I called him. But that had to be twelve hours ago.

Crawford thought of one time he had been on a hardcore binge — right after the publication of *Self-Assurance* — and he slept almost twenty-four hours. Twelve was nothing by comparison. And as his mother used to tell him when he was a kid, "When you sleep for long periods, it means your body needs it, so go ahead."

What Crawford felt like now was crap, and what he needed now was a drink. He could already tell he was in store for some comedown "willies" — the kind that brings the terror of losing one's mind. He felt like there was a strange flow of electricity running from the base of his spine into the core of his brain, overloading it with deadly current. He didn't have a headache in the usual sense, but his entire forehead throbbed with voltage that felt like a cerebral earthquake.

Drink. No. Drink. That's what I need. No, you don't. Don't. Yes, you do. No, I don't. Drink.

It's dangerous if you don't drink. You need to come down slowly, he thought.

Okay, I'll drink.

Crawford went into the bathroom and turned on the light. The bathroom was so immaculate, more so than his own, with every little item (towels, soap, etc.) so carefully placed, he wished he could vomit all over it. He probably would have, but he didn't feel like it just then. Lee's wife was notorious for her interior decorating (even worse than Dorothy), and the guest bathroom was probably a top priority. Crawford lifted the toilet seat and tried to take a piss, but couldn't. He couldn't do anything except think of getting that "comedown" cocktail.

Downstairs, Lee had a fully stocked bar with some of the best Scotch you can buy and a wine collection that would shame a Frenchman. But Crawford knew that if he was going to have a drink, it had better be just one or two. It wouldn't be long before Lee would be waking him up to help him get to the Jan Hershey show, perhaps pointing a gun to his head to accomplish his goal.

Who the hell are you kidding? You've never stopped at one or two, ever.

Crawford washed his face then inspected himself in the mirror. He thought about how terrible he looked, how old. He hadn't thought that in a long time.

We all pay the price of old age; it's just that some of us pay the premium.

When Crawford thought of himself as old it wasn't the age itself that depressed him, it was what he felt like he'd accomplished at his age — or rather what he hadn't accomplished. He'd achieved a failing marriage and a bad liver, and little else. At his most candid, Crawford knew the

Self Series was nothing but a sham, a hack job, nothing close to what he had set out to accomplish when he first wrote *Self-Confidence.*

And besides, Crawford's major consideration hadn't been the book — not for the book's sake. It was his newborn son, Calvin. Without saying a word, baby Cal demanded more, and things had to improve and improve soon.

Cal's birth was the one event in Crawford's life that made it more difficult to drink than to stay sober. Peering down at the little boy's tiny hands and feet, being slapped in the face with the fragility of his infancy and the responsibility that it demanded, made it almost impossible for Crawford to sashay out the backdoor and into a bar. Dorothy's resultant happiness, her deep love of her child along with her renewed love of her husband, gave her a gentle disposition that Crawford couldn't allow his drinking to thwart. It was best, Crawford believed, to at least give the *appearance* of a father trying to improve things for his family. And that's when he decided that he must produce a quality pop psychology book. Whether or not "quality pop" amounted to something of genuine value was of little consequence at the time. Even buying a new baby carriage was not an insignificant purchase for Jim and Dorothy's combined income, and it was time for Jim to roll up his sleeves and earn some good hard cash.

Years later, Crawford remembered very little about writing *Self-Confidence.* Hearing baby Cal crying in his cradle in the next room and Dorothy taking care of him were the most inspiring sounds Crawford could ask for. Better than silence.

You're going to have a good life, my son.

And Dorothy, you're going to be proud of me, sweetheart.

And Crawford pulled it off, truth be known, with little fanfare and little struggle. It took a few years, but he did it.

But those days were long gone. Crawford tried to invoke those same feelings of inspiration while writing fiction, but he just couldn't do it. Perhaps it was because Cal had obviously lost respect for him — or gained disrespect, however you want to look at it.

And did he really want to be a novelist? A real novelist, like the kind he often talked about? He wasn't sure any more. It might just come from some need to assuage his failure as a psychologist — *and* as a father *and* as a husband.

Crawford looked at himself in the mirror then turned away.

"Well, I'll mosey on downstairs and have that little drink after all."

Hell, just a couple. Just beer. I'm too tired for anything else.

Crawford slowly crept out into the hall, which was dark except for a nightlight in a wall socket just outside the guestroom. The two bedrooms across the hall had no light coming from beneath their closed doors, and neither did the room next door, which had a small wooden plate that read "Emily." Apparently the Burns Family — man, woman, and child — was fast asleep.

When Crawford got down the stairs to the living room, the ticking of the grandfather clock was almost deafening, amplifying his paranoia. He felt like a thief in a museum, ready for a security guard to stick a gun in his face the very moment he approached the masterpiece he intended to steal. There was an irony in the emotions Crawford felt about sneaking alcohol. It was dangerous fun, like the kind an adolescent feels with a picture of a naked girl under his mattress. But like that pubescent pleasure, it was rife with shame — the kind that comes from acting impulsively on base instincts. And for Crawford, it was a shame that could only be eradicated with alcohol.

When the bar came into view, it looked beautiful, horrifyingly so. He always admired Lee's taste, but the bar — *the bar itself* — was his Hope Diamond. Lee purchased it from an old Scottish pub in Edinburgh then paid a fortune to have it shipped to the States to be installed and refurbished. A local legend claimed Sir Arthur Conan Doyle, about the time he was getting his medical degree, had scribbled a story or two on the bar's perimeter while guzzling a few warm ales. It didn't matter if it was true. Like all legends, it was a good story. And aside from its West Hollywood Hills location, to Crawford it looked like home sweet home.

How 'bout a beer that's ice fuckin' cold...

There was a guy Crawford knew in college that always used that expression, *"ice fuckin' cold." What was his name?*

He heard something and froze.

Crawford felt cold again and his body started to shake. He was still just wearing his boxer shorts. He originally thought he would enjoy his couple of beers out on the back patio, but now he just wanted to create his own little bar under the warm covers upstairs.

Crawford stopped for a good ten seconds, moving nothing but his eyes from side to side. *Nothing.* He thought of the possibility of paranoia. Of the willies. Of Hoppy Poppy, *or whatever that guy's name is.*

I'm overreacting. Just like the caller, the tapes. Could just be some prankster. But would they do something so elaborate? Yes, Berry and Scott would.

Would they? Really? What about a stalker?

"No."

You're nuts, Crawford. You're really nuts. Just like Mary Epstein used to say.

"But she was only kidding."
Wasn't she?

The Monday after the five-day writing binge that had produced his master's thesis found Crawford soundly passed out on his battered sofa dreaming of the summer he would spend drunk and carefree, confidently knowing he had a new piece of paper that proved to the world he wasn't a complete loser. He didn't have to submit his thesis until Friday, all his finals were taken, and both his oral and written comprehensives were completed. There was nothing to do but sleep until the afternoon then pick up his thesis from Mary Epstein, a fellow classmate who had been proofreading and retyping it for him for the previous two days.

Mary was one of those people that was so nice, that gave so completely without expecting anything in return, that Crawford felt severe guilt just being in her company. Truth was she had a crush on Crawford, and he knew it. But physically she just didn't do it for him. Sadly, she didn't do it for any other men in the Psych department either. She was more than a little plump and wore large sweatshirts that reached to the knees, and skirts that almost covered her ankles. But she had a wonderful intellect and a charming sense of humor, and everyone liked Mary. She was interested in everything, was well-read, and consequently was very engaging.

Regardless of how Crawford felt around Mary, he certainly didn't avoid her when it came to needing help on research projects. She was fast, meticulous, and refused to accept payment apart from a few slices of pizza and a couple of beers. He also trusted her with his work — the prime reason Berry's call came as such a surprise.

"You sleeping? It's almost noon. Are you asleep?"

"I was," Crawford said with a dry cough. "Who the hell is this?"

"It's Berry."

"What do you want, *fairy*?"

"I just read your thesis."

Crawford woke up a little more. "You what? I didn't give you permission to do that."

"Well I did, and I've got some bad news."

Crawford sat up. "What are you talking about? How'd you read my thesis?"

"I was over at Mary's last night and she let me read it."

"Really? I told her..." Crawford stopped. "Okay, what's the title?"

"*Critical Consequences of the...*"

"That bitch."

"Watkins will know where you got this, Jim."

"Where I got it? What are you talking about?"

"Come on, Jim. I know this paper."

"How can you know that paper? I just wrote it last week."

"This paper was just in the *Comprehensive Psych Review* last month. Some Scandinavian guy. Maybe Eastern European, I can't remember."

"What?" Crawford said.

"Come on, man. You plagiarized this."

Crawford laughed. "Don't give me your bullshit, Berry."

"I'm not bullshitting you. I'm doing you a favor, Jim. All your credit hours could be taken away for this. I talked to Watkins about this very article two months ago. I'm just trying to warn you that if he catches you trying to pass off someone else's work as your own, he's going to throw the book at you. You know how he is about unoriginality. But shit, this is *plagiarism*."

"I didn't plagiarize anything!"

"Oh, yeah? You were going to pick this up from Mary today, correct?"

"Yes."

"After you drag your ass over there, meet me at the coffee shop across from the library. I'll bring the journal and we'll compare the two."

"All right, Berry," Crawford said with resilience. "I'll let you waste my time one more time."

"One more time, huh?" Berry said with a titter. "Across from the library, Jim. About four. I'm only trying to help."

"Sure."

Crawford had to go see what the big joke was all about.

I'll probably get to the coffee shop and Scott will be there and they'll finally have a laugh at my expense. Goddam children. After all, there was no way Berry could fabricate a copy of *Comprehensive Psychology Review*.

Just after lunch, Crawford practically snatched his thesis from Mary's hand as she handed it to him.

"Thanks. We'll have that pizza later, okay?"

She looked hurt, and Crawford felt more guilt as he drove away. Berry might have tricked her into showing it to him, he thought. I should have talked to her.

Crawford looked at the pristine-looking document lying in the passenger's seat and pulled over. He thumbed through it with admiration. *I'll apologize to her later.* It was wonderful. It wasn't just that Mary dotted all the i's and crossed all the t's, so to speak; every sentence, it appeared, had been edited to perfection. All the changes she made were listed on a separate document clipped onto the back. *I'll apologize later.*

So Berry and Scott had succeeded in making Crawford worry about something he needn't worry about.

They won't get a response out of me. They think they can bring me down?

Matter of fact, I should have a few before I go see them, Crawford thought. And he did.

Crawford only saw the shape of the bar against the dim light coming from the dining room window behind it. As the thought of a cold draft made Crawford salivate, the sight of the bar made him think of dungeons and torture.

I'm losing it. It has to do with neurotransmitters and enzymes and shit, but I'm losing it. Self-counseling doesn't work. Nothing works.

His fear could only be overridden by drink. He thought about the small refrigerator underneath the bar, and of headless babies.

He reached for a lamp that sat on the end of the bar next to an antique cash register and turned it on. He stepped behind the bar and opened the fridge. There was no light inside and Crawford couldn't see what the stock was, but he knew it didn't matter. He felt like he was putting his arms into a giant carnivorous plant, but he knew he had to do it. He overcame his fear and grabbed four bottles (*you said only two*) and put them on the bar.

Bottle opener, bottle opener.

Crawford opened a small drawer and stuck his hand inside just before noticing the clear bottles of light colored brew were Miller High Life with twist off tops.

Miller High Life? This bastard has an eighty thousand dollar bar that Arthur Conan Doyle used to puke on and he drinks this crap? Crawford again reached in the fridge and pulled out another pair of bottles. More Miller. *Not even a small selection?* Crawford wasn't in the frame of mind to be finicky about his poison. He cupped the six bottles (*you said only four*) and swung the refrigerator door shut with his right foot. When he turned around to go upstairs, he saw what had produced the little noise.

It wasn't a mouse. It was little Emily Burns, Lee's seven-year-old daughter, standing motionless in the hallway leading to the kitchen. Now more like a husband than a museum thief, Crawford attempted to augment his surreptitious act with congeniality. "Emily. Why aren't you asleep, sweetheart?"

"Uncle Jim? What are you doing?"

"I'm spending the night. You know, your daddy and I are..." He almost said they were having a slumber party, but stopped himself. "We're working on something."

Emily had a glass of pink water in her hand. "I'm not supposed to be getting this right now. This is lemonade, the pink kind. You won't tell on me, will you? I'm really thirsty."

Crawford was struck by how calm the child was after being caught by an adult red-handed pilfering lemonade. But he admired her cool disposition, which helped to alleviate his guilt. They were partners in crime. "Oh, I won't tell on *you* if you won't tell on *me*," he said.

"You? What are you doing wrong?" she asked.

"Nothing," he said nervously. Then laughing, "I should be in bed too. Your dad just wants me to get some rest. That's all."

Emily looked down at the bottles Crawford was holding in front of him, and she stepped forward to take a closer look. "What is that?" She put a finger on one of the bottles. "That looks like pee."

There was a long silence. The child had him thrown. "It is pee," he said with a nod.

"It is? It's pee?" She looked surprised.

"It's pee that comes from yeast."

She turned her head sideways. "From what?"

"Yeast urine, that's what it is."

"What?" She looked almost scared now.

"Why don't you drink your lemonade and we'll go upstairs, okay?"

"You're not going to drink that pee, are you?"

"No, dear. No, I'm not," he lied. He couldn't wait to drink the pee.

Crawford let Emily drink her lemonade then he put the glass in the sink. He returned three bottles of pee back to the refrigerator, taking three he could grasp in one hand so he could take Emily's hand with the other. He took her to her room and tucked her in bed as if she were his own child.

"Thanks, Uncle Jim," she said, cuddling her teddy bear. "Now you won't tell on me, will you?"

"No, I won't tell on you."

Crawford slowly backed out of the room and shut the little girl's door. As soon as the door clicked shut, he thought he heard something: singing.

Be koo mumma suff. Be foo mumma suff. If you moo a moo you a boo to yoo suff.

She's singing the Happy Pappy Song. Is she? Surely not, he thought. He put his ear to the door and held his breath. He couldn't hear a thing.

It was like he hadn't heard it but felt it. Something. The willies were not over yet, and Crawford needed to get that medicine in his system.

"March. Two months ago. Take a look." Berry slid the magazine across the table to Crawford.

"What is this shit?" Crawford thumbed through it. Sure enough, it was a real copy of *Comprehensive Psychology Review*.

"Page thirty-three," Berry said.

Crawford turned to page 33, and sure enough, the title was almost the same as Crawford's thesis.

Crawford tried to pronounce the doctor's name, but couldn't. "U-guh-low. U-guh-lao-ski. Fuck it." It didn't matter. Crawford read the first sentence out loud:

"The rise in American rates of acute psychosis as a serious and persistent psychological condition corresponds to the mounting proliferation of certain types of psychiatric and medical treatments used today."

Crawford looked at his own paper. Berry sat back and took a sip of his coffee.

```
The  increase  in  reported  rates  of  acute
psychosis  in  the  United  States  as  a  severe  and
permanent  psychological  condition  corresponds
to  an  increase  in  a  certain  type  of  psychiatric
treatment.
```

Crawford put the two documents side-by-side. Even the footnotes were roughly the same.

```
(Cox  &  Clinton,  1992;  C.J.  Henderson,  1986;
Rosenthal  &  Rosenthal,  1989).
```

Crawford read the concluding paragraph, the one he could most easily recognize, and he couldn't believe it. "I can't believe it."

"Hey, we all borrow a little sometimes," Scott said sheepishly.

"But I didn't borrow anything." Crawford said with certainty.

"Do you read this journal, Jim?" Berry asked like a high school guidance counselor.

"Yeah, sometimes. But I have never read this."

"Are you sure?"

Crawford read more of the document, becoming more and more amazed at what he saw. "Even the headings are the same. The goddam structure is the same."

"Jim. Come on, man."

"Come on, what? I didn't plagiarize this."

Berry raised his eyebrows. "Jim."

"Jim, what? Are you trying to fuck with me?" Crawford turned the journal over. He looked at the binding. He looked at the print. It even had the library's coded stamp on it. No question, it was the real thing.

"I just wanted you to know he's read this research before. That's all. What you do now is up to you."

"Thanks."

Crawford didn't take Berry and Scott out for a drink. The kind of drinking he wanted to do would only be hampered by their leisurely wine tasting. Crawford drove home with his thesis lying next to him in the passenger's seat, but this time it was face down.

Was it just coincidence? Impossible.

He thought about his seventh-grade math teacher, Mrs. Johnson. "You're nuttier than a fruitcake," she used to say. Maybe she's right, he thought.

Obviously, I read the article in a drunken stupor — one of those nights when I couldn't find anyone to drink with me and I just stayed home and read the pile of crap around me. I guess I thought the whole thing was my idea. My brilliant idea.

Wait.

I do have a copy of the article at home. Yes, I think I do. Maybe under the couch. On the toilet, somewhere. Look for it. Try to remember.

My God, did I do that? Have I lost my mind? he thought he remembered asking himself.

It was as if Crawford blinked his eyes and Lee was standing in front of him.

"Wake up, Jim" he said calmly.

Crawford looked at Lee, whose expression was as stern as he'd ever seen it, and rolled over. "Where the fuck am I?"

"You're at my place, you idiot. Now get up."

Crawford looked at Lee again. He was holding a suit of clothes — Crawford's clothes now neatly pressed.

"Same clothes as yesterday," he said. "Different smell." He threw them on the bed at Crawford's feet. "I was going to buy a new set of clothes for you but I figured this was good enough. It's very common. And that's what the people like about you, Jim. You're very common."

Crawford sat up trying to remember where he'd hidden the three empties. "Lee, I can't go on that show today."

"Like hell you can't. Now get dressed."

"I need to call Dorothy."

"I called her. Now get dressed."

"I don't know if I can..."

"Get dressed!" Lee walked to the door and stopped without turning around. "I'll give you half an hour," he said before walking out of the room.

He'll give me *half an hour.*

The clock on the night table read *8:30*, which meant Crawford had only slept about five hours since his clandestine trip to the bar. Crawford's head was spinning, but he didn't feel nearly as bad as he could have. The three bottles of pee were doing their job for now.

Lee had a large pot of coffee made when Crawford came downstairs, looking surprisingly healthy considering the previous day.

Lee was sitting at the breakfast bar reading the Los Angeles Times. "I'm guessing you need about two cups," Lee said, coldly pushing a cup toward Crawford as he sat down.

"Two will probably work," Crawford said, thinking he'd rather have a Bloody Mary.

"Well there's one cup," Lee said, also pushing a buttered English muffin next to the cup. "And eat that, please," he said, looking at his watch.

Crawford looked down at the coffee cup, took a sip, and fidgeted. Lee's demeanor was especially cold, almost like the head of a security detail that was about to ensure a diplomat's safe arrival at the UN General Assembly.

"You're going to be okay, aren't you?" Lee asked, stone-faced. "No surprises on the show today."

"I appreciate you coming to get me, Lee. But perhaps you shouldn't have. Maybe you should have brought the press to document how pathetic I was."

"Maybe so," Lee said, taking a sip of his own coffee. "But I didn't."

"You know, I feel like the rock star that goes around telling young people not to use drugs like he has. I say how bad my life was before I got sober then I tell people how they should live. The rock star never acknowledges how good his life has been as a result of the drugs and the hard living. What were the songs about? What were people so interested in? Nobody likes songs about getting enough fiber and being monogamous. What do you think, Lee? I've still got a couple of hours to have a beer or two. Today, I should just go on that show and be honest. I should..."

"You should be the product you are supposed to be, Jim," Lee said harshly. "You aren't a rock star. That's a different product. Drink your coffee."

Lee looked like he was on the verge of cutting Crawford's tongue out.

"Now go get ready," Lee said. "We leave in half an hour."

Lee drove Crawford to the studio in Crawford's car, and there was complete silence for most of the trip. Crawford was seeing a side of Lee he hadn't seen in all their years together. The innate politician in Lee was finally fading into the cold indifference of a businessman, and Crawford understood why. Lee was fed up.

Crawford's hangover was entering the nervousness and regret stage — an unpleasantness worse than a throbbing head. The thought of going on TV that morning made him want to crawl under a rock. He kept looking at Lee, who had his eyes firmly on the road in front of him. Normally Lee would be driving recklessly, rattling off all the things Crawford should remember to mention. But this time it was conscious maneuvering and dead silence, like Crawford was being taken to his execution.

Lee looked at his watch.

"Lee, I'm sorry."

"Don't be," Lee said. "Isn't that what you said in *Self-Esteem*?"

Crawford felt the willies coming, but tried to ignore them. "I want you to know I appreciate everything you've done."

"I've been paid for everything I've done, Jim."

Crawford felt tension in his torso. "But after this, Lee, I think we're going to have to part ways. I think all this has to end. I'm sorry."

"Don't be sorry. All things must pass, as George sang." Lee looked directly at Crawford, completely ignoring the road. "But that show stays on the air the rest of the season. Understand?"

Crawford understood.

FOURTEEN

"This is David, our makeup artist. He'll take care of you," the assistant said before walking out and closing the door.

The makeup artist was a thin, middle-aged man wearing faded blue jeans and a T-shirt, sitting on a sofa against the opposite wall reading a newspaper. His feet were propped up on a small stool as if to show off his leather-worn biker boots. His hair was a shaggy bowl cut that looked oddly out of fashion. Crawford immediately thought that David could use a little making up himself.

"Sit down," he said, not looking up.

Crawford gestured toward the nearest chair. "Here?"

"Sure. Anywhere," he said, turning a page.

Crawford sat down and looked in the mirror. He was just now noticing how pale and tired he looked. Could be, he thought, those three bottles were finally wearing off.

The makeup artist still didn't look up. He didn't move at all except for his mouth slowly gyrating on a piece of gum. He quietly giggled to himself, presumably at something he read in the paper, then tossed the paper on the couch. Seeming reluctant, he sashayed to Crawford's back and rested his hands on Crawford's shoulders.

"Dr. James Crawford?"

"That's right."

"*Self-Esteem*?"

"Uh huh."

"Happy Pappy?"

"Yeah. And you're the makeup artist, aren't you?"

"*The* makeup artist? I'm the *head* makeup artist. I make *him* up every day." The man gestured toward the ceiling where a number of Happy Pappy masks were looking angrily down several feet above the mirror.

"What's that?"

"You *know* what that is," he said laughing. "We do that kid's show downstairs. You know that kid's show, *don't you?*" he asked with a giggle.

"I guess so." If the man was trying to make him uncomfortable, he was succeeding.

David opened a small makeup kit on the table in front of Crawford, pulling out a brush. "You look like you could use some color."

Crawford couldn't help but keep looking at the masks, which peered down on him like perverted Greek gods deciding his fate.

"Nice guy?" Crawford asked.

"Sorry?"

"Happy Pappy. Nice guy is he?"

"I don't really know him. He never says much. But if you want to know the truth, I hear he's a real asshole."

"You don't say."

"Not-so-Happy Pappy, he's sometimes called."

"That's terrific," Crawford laughed.

"He doesn't think so."

The smell of the makeup wasn't helping the nausea that Crawford felt could explode at any moment. David had given him a standard makeup job — a pancake with a little extra blush to accommodate his paleness — and now he was working on his eyebrows. The movement of the brush was making Crawford even queasier, and he leaned his head back slightly and closed his eyes to avoid an embarrassing upchuck.

"Not too much on the eyebrows, please."

"Hey, who's the expert here?" David asked, arms folded. "I don't tell you how to write your books."

I wish you would, Crawford thought.

David finished Crawford's eyebrows then Crawford excused himself to the bathroom.

"You're welcome, dickhead," David said under his breath as Crawford stumbled out.

Crawford's stomach now felt like he had eaten a bowl of chili spiked with steak knives. He thought of how he dreaded seeing Jan Hershey. She usually came by his dressing room to say hello before the show, so Crawford was going to avoid his dressing room entirely. He steadied himself with one hand, following the railing to the bathroom at the end of the hall. A small bead of sweat was making its way down the right side of his face and it gave him a chill that felt like night sweats.

Crawford reached the bathroom and once inside was pleased to find it empty. His queasiness was getting worse as he went into one of the stalls and shut the door. He got on his knees in front of the toilet and heard the bathroom door open.

"Dr. Crawford," someone said.

"Yes," Crawford said before a silent belch.

"Sir, it's Roger. You've got ten minutes."

"Okay. Be there in a sec." Crawford could barely wait to hear the door close before vomiting into the toilet. He heaved a small amount of clear liquid, inhaled deeply then discharged a small amount of thick, chunky solution.

Crawford supported himself with a hand on each wall of the stall. *I can't do this. Not today.*

"Not feeling well?"

Crawford froze, ignoring the large chunk of vomit hanging from his lip. "Be there in just a second!"

"I know you will."

Like the rush of cold water hitting him from a showerhead, Crawford realized it was the voice of the man who had been calling himself Happy Pappy. He was there, alone with him, just three feet away.

"Who is that?"

"You know who this is. Don't you?" he said with oily elocution.

Crawford, still on his knees, turned around slowly. The small chunk of vomit fell from his lip to his pant leg just above the knee. He looked down and nervously brushed it onto the floor.

"Not feeling well?"

Crawford's first instinct was to rush out of the stall and strangle the son of a bitch, but he felt like he was so weak he couldn't stand. And he wasn't through purging this mysterious orange gunk. Crawford put his eye to the small crevice between the stall door and wall. He looked directly ahead and could see the mirror behind the sinks. Then looking to his left he saw the brim of a hat — an old country hat. It was moving just slightly, and then it was out of view.

"What do you want?" Crawford said softly, feeling like he might faint.

Then something moved in front of the crack — pale skin, round features, one eyeball too large to be human. Crawford could see enough to know that it was Happy Pappy.

Crawford raised his voice. "What the fuck do you want?"

"What do *I* want? How nice of you to ask." He paused a moment to giggle, then said, "I want self-esteem. I want self-confidence. I want what everyone else wants."

Crawford wished he could smash the door open and knock this bastard out but the door opened the other way, and he couldn't...

A knife flashed in front of the crevice, thrusting a sharp light in

Crawford's eye. The nausea vanished, but now Crawford couldn't breathe.

"The last stage, Dr. Crawford," he said, twisting the knife vertically. "The last stage of your program and I'll be finished."

Crawford belched slightly and suddenly could speak. "So you killed Jenny, didn't you? You really killed her."

The voice became breathy, trying to control its laughter. "Bad things must end. That's what you taught me. 'Eliminate the harmful things that are destroying your life.' That's what you wrote on page one fifty-seven." He giggled again. "I'm sorry, on page one fifty-eight."

"And what about this Dr. Watkins?"

"He was a detractor. An enemy. Silence those that unfairly criticize you. That's good advice, Doctor. And it works."

"So who the fuck are you?" Crawford bellowed.

The knife flashed again and Crawford's heart pounded.

"I'm *you*, Doctor. I'm your creation. I'm a part of you." He giggled again. "And you're a part of me."

"What do you want?"

"Stage three, Doctor. You can have what any other person has."

Crawford now was feeling strong enough to speak, as though his anger were curing him. "I just want to help people, to improve their lives."

"I just want everything you have!" he shouted. "Understand? If I can have what any other person has, I want what you have!"

Crawford leaned back slightly, shaking with fear.

"What I have? And what's that?" he said, pounding his fist on the door with each syllable. "What do I have?" he shouted.

Crawford heard the door slam. Without inspecting himself in the mirror, he rushed out of the bathroom and into the crowded hall. It was like a terminal station with people moving everywhere, hurrying to do something somewhere else. And with Crawford's head still floating, he couldn't train his eyes on anyone. Everything was a blur, like he was inside a carnival ride designed to make him sick.

Crawford leaned up against the wall and straightened his sport coat. The first thing he noticed was the small stain left by the scrap of puke that fell from his lip. It was small — about the size of a nickel — but it looked much bigger.

Self-Confidence, page 235. "When we don't feel right on the inside, it makes us imagine an uncomplimentary outside."

Oh, shut the hell up. You've got vomit on your pants, fool!

"Dr. Crawford?"

Crawford looked up to see Roger, a studio page who barely looked 18, more in a rush than the rest of the people.

"This way, Doctor. We're almost on," Roger said, nervously tapping the clipboard he held in his right hand.

"Did you see a man?"

"Excuse me," he said, touching Crawford on the arm to direct him forward.

"Did you see a man come out of the bathroom just before I did?"

Roger looked confused. "No, sir. We really are pressed for time, though."

"A man with a mask?"

"A mask, Doctor?"

Crawford said nothing. He looked over Roger's shoulder, then to the other end of the hall. "I can't do this," Crawford mumbled.

"Sorry?"

Crawford took a deep breath. "I mean, I can't..."

"Sorry?"

"Could I have a glass of water?"

"Of course. This way, Doctor."

Backstage was even more hectic than the hallway outside. People were hauling around lighting and sound equipment. Large, sweaty men were trying to get things in place with little time to go, and most of them couldn't care less who was in their way. Crawford ducked as a man carrying a small set piece barged right by him, almost knocking his head off.

"Damn it," he said standing up.

"Sorry, sir," Roger said. "These guys aren't very careful sometimes. They're union, you know."

Could that *have been the man in the bathroom? Could any of these grunts be that psychopath? The mask now hidden in a toolbox maybe?*

That was ridiculous, Crawford thought. He might as well suspect the guy who plays the part on TV.

Crawford caught a glimpse of Jan waiting in the wings on the other side. For just an instant he thought about how good she looked. She always looked good. *Bitch.* She reminded him of the cheerleaders in high school he hated but still wanted to bonk.

The music started and the audience began to applaud.

Maybe it is *the guy who plays the part.*

"Jan Hershey!" he vaguely heard the announcer say.

"You'll see a green light at the top of the stage left entry. See it?" Roger asked.

"I see it," Crawford said.

Crawford felt a hand on his shoulder and turned around to find Lee, his head tilted back and his eyes squinting vaguely. He looked downright sinister.

"Lee, I saw…"

Lee pulled Crawford close and whispered in his ear, "You fuck this up and I'll kill you." He was frozen solid then he smiled and winked.

You think you know someone for over a decade…

Something brushed against Crawford's hand, something strange, like rubber. He looked down and could see what Lee was holding — a Happy Pappy mask.

"What are you doing with that?"

"Just be yourself, Jim," Lee said with a smile and a slap on the back.

The rumbling behind the studio walls got louder and louder.

"Mr. Crawford," the stage assistant said. "I mean, Dr. Crawford."

Crawford turned to see the stage left light turn yellow. Then, with a voice that oozed enthusiasm…

"Ladies and Gentleman, Dr. James Crawford!"

Crawford walked through the stage left door and imagined he was an accomplished novelist, speaking at a university to a group of literature students. There were young girls leaning back in their seats seductively, twirling pencils in their mouths as they looked at him with a sense of awe and admiration. There were bearded old men and frumpy old women eager to talk to *the master* about his art.

But the horrifically bright studio lights hit Crawford hard. He thought he might vomit, covering his mouth to let out a painful burp.

Fat people are staring at me, unattractive people, save Jan, who looks composed, but there's some sense of worry in her eyes, she knows something isn't right and I don't know how she knows it, but she knows it, so I better smile because they're all looking at me like I'm their savior or something and fuck that, I don't want to be anyone's savior, I'm just trying to save myself, don't they fucking know that? Glass of water, there's a glass of water on that table there, I need it, I need that water, I better smile, oh, I am smiling, I think.

The moment Crawford sat down the applause breached his stream of thinking. Jan elegantly stepped toward center aisle, but it was almost aggressive, like a baseball pitcher eyeing a batter.

Jan loudly said, "Well!" and the audience became silent at once. "Welcome back, Dr. Crawford."

Crawford nodded then cleared his throat, tasting bitter bile on the back of his tongue. He silently mouthed the words "Thank you."

"Good to see you," Jan said.

"Good to see you," he said softly.

It was all Crawford could do to emphasize the last word. From the corner of his eye he could see the water glistening next to him, waiting to help wrestle away some of his pain. But he couldn't reach for it. Not yet.

"We've got a lot to talk about today, don't we?"

"I sure hope not."

There was just a second of uneasiness before the audience laughed and Jan joined them reluctantly.

"Oh now, come on, Doctor. We'll appreciate as much as we can get."

It was like being harassed in high school by one of those bitchy cheerleaders, but this time there was no desire.

"Okay. Sure."

For an instant Crawford leaned forward in his chair with his elbows on the armrests, locking his fingers, *like a real writer, like a real...*

Then he leaned back again, nestling his shoulder blades into the chair. Nothing helped. His nerves were shot. His tongue started to feel dry and sticky, and his throat felt rough. All he could think about was the water next to him.

Jan walked down a few more steps, reminding Crawford of a lion carefully approaching its prey, or like a savvy anchorwoman about to ask a politician some hard questions.

"Tell us about the latest edition to your *Self Series*, that's so very popular."

Crawford said nothing; his mind was a blank. Then taking a deep breath he said, "That would be *Self-Esteem*?"

The audience laughed again and Jan responded to her tongue-tied guest like a true professional. She turned around to the audience and said, "See what humility our wonderful guest has?" She contrived a giggle then looked deep into Crawford's eyes as if to say, *all right, no more bullshit, quack. I got a show to do.* "Yes, Doctor, that would be *Self-Esteem*."

"I see." Crawford looked down at the floor then to the glass of water next to him, which looked like vodka or gin. *No, vodka.* Crawford wanted to be graceful about it but he couldn't. He grabbed the water and threw his head back like he'd been shot in the forehead, drinking half of it down in two seconds. This created another awkward moment even Jan couldn't turn into entertainment.

"Doctor?"

Crawford took a deep breath and almost felt like he could talk now, like he could breathe. "Well... it's uh... It's kind of the same old thing, really."

Jan laughed nervously. The audience members, sensing Jan's unease, had become too uneasy to laugh.

"You're dealing with ideas that are age-old truths. Is that what you mean?"

"I don't know."

The audience stared with wonder. Jan could barely hide her contempt. "Oh come on, Doctor," she retorted. "I think you know about age-old truths. You and I have been talking about these subjects for years. Now tell us the big secret. What are we learning in this book we haven't learned in the others?"

"Well, I guess it can, uh..."

A man with headphones pointed to a camera which then dollied in close, making Crawford feel even more uneasy.

Crawford glanced to his right and could see Lee standing just off-stage. By his expression, he wasn't joking about killing him.

Jan blinked her eyes heavily, like she was ready to lose it. "Doctor?"

"I'm trying to help people improve their lives."

She relaxed a little. "Well, yes. Of course." She turned again to the audience. "And you've helped so many people. Right folks?"

The audience mumbled its distinctly American form of *hear, hear — yes, uh mm, that's right* — but this time Crawford interrupted.

"I just don't..." he started before they quieted down. "I just don't feel too good today. That's all."

Jan completely ignored his remark. "Doctor, tell us about the three-stage program in this book."

Crawford felt that surge of electricity working its way up his spine deep into his cerebellum and into his cerebral cortex. He realized he had to get through this. He had to be a salesman for the next forty-two minutes.

"The three stages?" he said almost energetically. "Well, it's really pretty simple. The first thing you do is get over what people think of you."

Jan looked at the notes in her hand. "You silence those that criticize you."

"Yes," Crawford said. "Of course, you do that too."

Suddenly he thought of the grainy image of Happy Pappy, hovering over the psychologist — taunting him, laughing at him, cutting out his tongue.

Crawford felt perspiration forming on his forehead and on the back of his neck, the kind of tiny drops that shiver the spine.

Ms. Hershey was not waiting for him any longer. "And stage two, Doctor? Stage two?"

He began slowly...

Just a little while longer.

"Well, you get all the bad things out of your life. That seems like good advice!"

Jan looked at her notes again. "Eliminate the harmful things that are destroying your life."

"Yes."

It was Jenny's hair that came to mind this time. She never allowed herself to look unkempt. But that hair, falling around her face like a bowl of soup dumped on her head. That duct tape around her elegant mouth, like a makeshift clamp remedying a piece of broken furniture. Then the stabbing. Then the blood.

"And the third stage, Doctor?"

Crawford was suffocating. What was he doing on a fucking talk show hawking some product when a killer was out there? What was he doing with a hangover when... "You have to realize," he swallowed heavily, "you can have what any other man has."

"Okay. You can have what any other *person* has," Jan said, correcting him.

"Yes."

Stage three...

I asked him what he wanted.

"Stage three, Doctor. You can have what any other person has."

Crawford could see Dorothy the day he married her. He could see Cal the day he was born. Those were the two happiest days of his life. He had been sober both times. He had kept those memories while so many others were washed away with alcohol.

"*I want what you have,*" the mocking villain was saying.

He wants my... He wants my wife.

Crawford imagined Dorothy tied to a chair, Happy Pappy fiddling with a video camera. "Record! Record! I can't find that damn record button, kids!"

He wants my son.

"*Yessssssiiiiirrrrreeeee.*"

Crawford only saw Jan smiling, her torso rotating to the audience. "Doesn't that sound simple, folks? Yes. Doesn't that sound wonderful?"

The audience was no longer human. Crawford only saw pieces — a pink mouth, black hair, green eyes. He was desperately looking for a face to focus on, someone to anchor him back to the real world. But it was just Jan, rippling on an ocean of human flesh.

"And if you haven't checked it out yet, Dr. Crawford's principles have been made into a fantastic children's show called *The Happy Pappy Show.*"

Now Crawford could swear he was hearing an applause track.

"And it's a real treat," Jan continued, the smile on her face getting wider and wider. "We've got to go to a commercial right now. But first, let's show our home viewers what we passed out to our studio audience today. We've got a surprise for you, Doctor!"

A teenage page came up to Jan and handed her something. It looked like a piece of flesh.

"These are going to be available in stores soon." Jan was distracted. "What? Oh. They're already available in stores? Right now? You can go buy these in stores today?" She looked back into the camera. "Ladies and Gentlemen," turning to the audience as if to say get ready. "It's the new Happy Pappy mask!"

Jan and each one of the audience members, and even the crew, lifted a piece of fleshy rubber material from their laps to cover their faces.

Jan smiled tenderly. "Ladies and Gentleman, doesn't that make you feel better?"

The new Happy Pappy mask. Lee, you sick fuck. Oh God!

Crawford was smothering. He couldn't look away; there was no-where to look. People started laughing — all of them. The faces started to bounce, each of them the killer in the bathroom, the killer who had taunted him for the last two and a half days. The sea of pink, dotted with some black masks and some brown, was distorted flesh coming to a boil.

Then the tune started to play, hitting Crawford like a belt in the face. He felt like he had just swallowed a basketball as he put his right palm to his throbbing stomach.

Then everyone started to sing.

"Be kind to yourself. Be fond of yourself. If you're not a chum you're a bum to yourself."

"Come on!" Jan shouted, her microphoned hand flailing with gusto.

"Be a friend to yourself. Without end to yourself. Remember it's the best you can do for your health."

"Please," Crawford said.

"I think he said something."

"Please," he said again, or thought he said, just before he vomited.

FIFTEEN

Cal woke up and wondered if he was dead or alive. Only his sense of touch made him realize he was still bound, still lying in the dark. The blood covering Cal's lip was dry, as he could feel the crusty surface with the bottom of his tongue. The room was now pitch black — if it was a room — and not even a light from under the door gave shape to the void. Something smelled like sulfur or boiled eggs or furniture polish or God knows what. Cal coughed and spat to get the taste out of his mouth.

"Hello?" a helpless voice said. "Cal, is that you?"

"Darrin? Can you hear me? Darrin?"

"I can hear you. I can hear you." There was an echo following Darrin's voice that made him sound far away but close at the same time. He could be in the next room or he could be sitting in a metal cage just a few feet away. He sounded meek and afraid — a complete reversal of his persona. "Are you okay," he said, sounding on the verge of tears.

"I'm okay, I think. But I can't move. I'm tied up," Cal said.

"So am I."

"Can you see anything? I can't see a goddam thing."

"I can't see anything either."

"How long have you been there?"

"I don't know. Maybe an hour. That man moved me here." There was silence for several seconds. "You know, *the man*. You know who I'm talking about?" Darrin asked strangely, like a child.

"What did you get me into?" Cal said.

Darrin didn't make a sound.

"Answer me!" Cal shouted as he rocked from side to side, struggling with what felt like a straightjacket wrapped in duct tape. "Who told you to come here?"

There was only silence.

"Say something!"

"Some guy. Some doctor or something."

Cal couldn't believe how nonchalant Darrin was. *Why did I trust this pool hall loser?* Cal looked deep into the nothingness in front of him and tried to imagine Darrin's face. He wanted to kill him right then. "A doctor? What doctor?"

"I don't know, I really don't." Darrin's tone of voice was now bordering on blasé.

"You don't know? Who was he? Where'd you meet him?"

There was another long pause. And just before Cal could speak, Darrin said he couldn't tell him.

Cal's anger turned to fury. "You can't tell me? You've gotten me tied up in a warehouse by some nutcase and you can't tell me what's going on?"

"I know," he said with a peculiar joviality. "This guy's nuttier than a fruitcake."

"Who is he, Darrin?!"

Cal heard Darrin let out a deep breath, the echo making it sound like gas escaping from a pipe.

"I met this guy through..."

"What guy?

"The guy... your father introduced me to him."

"My father? What kind of bullshit is that? You've never met my father."

"Yes, I have."

"What about the coke? I thought we were scoring some coke."

"The coke... there never was any coke."

"What?" Cal was still now.

"The man that tied you up, he works with your dad," Darrin insisted.

Cal started moving his clenched fists. "Don't bullshit me, you freak! My father doesn't work with anyone. He's a writer."

Darrin's voice was now even calmer. "He works with a lot of people. Think about it."

"Like who?"

"You're here because your father wants you to be here."

"Stop saying that!"

"Cal, I'm sorry."

A light came from the crack under the door that Cal could barely see between his bound legs. He heard the slow creak of the door, but it wasn't the door in front of him. It was the door next to him.

"No more!" Darrin squealed. "Go away! I didn't agree to this!"

There was a soft giggle. "It's time for the show."

It sounded like Darrin was trying to shout, but his mouth was covered. Then it sounded like a struggle of shuffling feet, kicking and bucking. Finally, the door slammed. Cal stretched his face into the vacuum, listening carefully, concentrating for a length of time he couldn't determine.

First there was silence.

And it could have been any garden.

Then the faint sound of the *Happy Pappy Song*.

Then a muffled cry.

Then silence again.

Eight blue-sleeved arms covered Crawford from his shoulder blades to his knees, moving him forward like he was a battering ram aimed at the door of a medieval castle. Crawford could only see their shoes as well as his own, which were now covered in orange vomit.

Cheesy Cheesos again, Crawford thought. I remember now. I ate a bag of Cheesy Cheesos.

Crawford got to his feet and pushed four stagehands away, and then in one not-so-elegant motion, he started running through the backstage like an angry child deserting his own birthday party. A hand firmly grabbed him.

"What the hell was that?" Lee bellowed.

Crawford was breathing heavily, his lips still glossy wet from the bile that came out of his nose and mouth. "That was just me being myself. The real me. I'm a rock star, Lee!"

"My God!"

All of the production people on the show were getting out of Crawford's way, looking relieved to see his departure. They already had one mess to clean up.

"Where are you going?" Lee fumed.

"I'm going home," Crawford said, looking directly into Lee's eyes, "to see my wife and my son, to see my family."

"The loving family man, huh? That always works in a crisis."

Crawford stopped. "Did you call them last night? Did you really call them?"

Lee's anger subsided with a shake of his head, not as an answer but in resignation; he could say nothing.

"I better not see your face again," Crawford said.

Lee gripped the Happy Pappy mask as he turned in the opposite direction. "Oh, you will."

Crawford turned and went straight for the studio exit. Going out the door, Crawford faintly heard Jan say, "Ladies and Gentlemen, we're back."

Crawford asked a leering page where he might use a telephone before he realized he still had his mobile phone in his jacket pocket.

"Fuck it. Leave me alone," he said, waving the kid away. First he tried the regular line at home but got the answering machine.

"Hello? Anyone there? This is Dad and I'm on my way home. Someone call me on my mobile phone when you get this message. Anyone. I'm coming home."

Crawford felt that cold chill again when he hung up the phone.

What did I say? I said 'Dad'?

The chill got worse as he dialed Dorothy's mobile phone and then Cal's. Dorothy's number provided her curt directive — "Not here, leave a message."

"Honey, call me."

Cal's phone just kept on ringing.

They might be pissed off. They might be trying to punish me by not picking up. Please just let them be mad at me. Please let them just be ignoring me.

Crawford went to the commissary and ordered two bottles of water. The room was almost empty except for the dozen or so cooks and waiters preparing for the after-show lunch crowd. A large screen TV in a corner behind the salad bar made Crawford wonder if the commissary staff had just seen his embarrassing performance.

Then it hit him.

Millions of people just saw me vomit on live television.

Didn't they? he wondered.

Who gives a shit if they did? Good. I finally gave them the real me.

But what if they really did see me? he thought.

They might not have. Those camera people are pretty slick. They could have seen it coming and cut to commercial. Or cut to Jan. Or something else.

"Are you sure that's all you want?" the waitress asked, pushing the bottles toward Crawford.

"Better give me three."

The girl turned to grab another bottle, and Crawford drank one of them, with most of it running down his shirt. The girl put another bottle on the counter and said, "That will be twelve ninety, please."

Four dollars for twelve ounces of water? Civilized. Very fucking civilized.

Crawford pulled out his wallet and looked into the girl's eyes. He could almost see a reflection of himself vomiting. He knew she had to have seen it; everyone there had seen it. The whole goddam country had seen it. In no time there would be speculation in the press, in the media, discussions on talk shows and in op-ed pieces about self-help writers who get sick because of the pressure of TV appearances, or because of too much MSG, or too much medication, or too much plastic surgery, or too much booze. It would be everywhere.

Good, Crawford thought. *Maybe I can be a respected novelist after all.*

As Crawford walked down the hall to the elevator then to the garage, every glance from every passerby indicated the news was out and spreading fast. Oddly though, his hangover was much better and his mood wasn't that bad for a guy who had just humiliated himself on national television. He almost felt confident — like he only did when he had a good after dinner buzz and was getting ready to meet some kowtowing fans.

Maybe I can be William Faulkner. Or Hemingway. I could be Hemingway. Hemingway was a hack. But he got respect. He vomited from time to time.

"Bullshit."

He wasn't sure if he was fit to drive, not being drunk enough not to worry about it, but his fear for the safety of his wife and son compensated his semi-sober apprehension. Crawford tore out of the downtown garage after giving his stamped ticket to an attendant who grinned as if he knew something Crawford didn't.

Go ahead and smile, asshole.

My God. Self-Confidence. *That was the first one. I should have learned from the first one.* "Self-Confidence comes from a lack of self-consciousness. The more we're concerned with ourselves, the more we judge ourselves. And consequently, the less faith we have in ourselves and in our abilities."

Didn't I write that once? Or did I imagine I wrote it?

Faith. Better known as ignorance in the secular world. Made him think of that great Bertrand Russell quote: "The trouble with the world is that the stupid are cocksure and the intelligent full of doubt." The intelligent just don't have any faith.

Do you compromise your intelligence when you lose your self-doubt? Is doubt then just another form of selfishness? Oh, who gives a shit? Freud created mass neuroses when he set out to cure it. Novelists are the real doctors of the soul, Crawford thought. Traffic was light, and Crawford imagined all the people deciding to stay at home so they could hear about Crawford vomiting on *Jan Live.*

Self-confidence comes from a lack of self-consciousness.

Focus... focus, he thought.

Simply put, one of the worst things about alcohol is its uncanny ability to be a distraction from the most important things in life, tangible things that exist in the here and now. It allows (or perhaps requires) your mind to wonder aimlessly about crap like self-consciousness when you should be concerned with more important things like being a father and a husband, or deciding what you're going to do about the psychotic criminal that's been harassing you.

Self-Sobriety, could that be a title? he wondered.

Crawford didn't know *what* to do — about anything. Apparently, he could help millions of others but not himself. He just didn't have the self-esteem.

The self-esteem? Please. Just the self.

Crawford was within a few miles of his house when he tried to call again. No answer at home, none with Dorothy, none with Cal.

His hangover was back again, and his need for a drink rattled the chambers of his wits. It might have had something to do with being close to home, but he wasn't certain. He stopped at Happy Time Liquor and got his usual bottle of Scotch. He was glad to find the Indian wasn't there and that rap videos weren't being played on the TV.

Cal yelled into the darkness. He had just had one of those dreams where you watch yourself doing something really terrible but you can't stop it — a peculiar experience, this fear, considering his circumstance.

"Are you ready to proceed?"

His heart was still beating with fear from the dream. Not even the reality of his captivity was scarier.

He takes his father's gun — the one he found while rummaging through his dad's study years ago. He initially thought it was a lighter, but it wasn't. Then he thought it was a small-caliber pistol, but it's a machine gun.

Cal puts it into the back of his Porsche, actually a Rolls-Royce limousine — a black one, very Goth, very deathly. "Where would you like to go?" Rotten Tamales, driver's cap and all, sits behind the wheel, but Cal feels so self-confident he doesn't care.

Let that grunt drive me anywhere. Where's that chronic?

Cal sits in the back seat smoking his funk, and as the limo barrels through the canyon, Rotten is in the back holding a golden bong to the master's lips.

Flying down that hill, the band room and those poor saps that play sax and clarinet, but Cal sees the ones he wants to hurt: those jocks that huddle outside the main entrance. *They deserve nothing less than death.*

The marijuana makes him sharp. But it isn't marijuana at all. It's a cold glass of drencrom; it's Alex de Large at the Korova Milk Bar.

Boy, I'm really in the mood for a prank!

Cal asks "What should I do?"

Rotten tips his hat. "Taketh thy machine gun and cutteth them down!"

"*Are you ready to proceed?*"

"Do it now!"

The guns — two machine guns, large ones — are not guns, but arms, human arms, extensions of the black leather that covers Cal's body, his fingers large barrels of death.

"Hey Mr. Happy Pappy," they all say at the same time.

Killing every one of them will not be a crime.

"Yeah, their lives aren't worth a dime," Rotten says, as he rolls his fingers on the steering wheel. "Hurry the fuck up. Dust unto dust."

"*Are you ready to proceed?*"

Cal gets out of the car and knows this is wrong.

But it's something I heard in a song. Right?

"Yeah, it's a racket like everything else," Rotten says. "So what?"

Rotten's words ring out like a command from the Almighty. *So what?* It doesn't sound like a command, *but oh yeah, I know it is. I know...*

Cal raises the guns in fast motion and sprays them dead, hitting most of them in the head without even aiming.

There's Coach Lieberman and Vice Principal Gore.

They're laughing so hard, they're about to fall on the floor.

But they don't get away, no — not for one second. Cal shoots them both, but *they didn't deserve it.*

"Ya reckon?" Rotten says.

"No, they didn't."

Then the blood flows from the ground to the trees, and Cal feels sad, but a little pleased. Then he wakes and screams in horror at his deed, but someone is asking "Are you ready to proceed?"

Are you?

Crawford was surprised his briefcase was still in the trunk and the tape was inside. He didn't handle property well during drinking episodes, and sometimes he would wake up from a stupor surprised his wedding ring was still on his finger. He put the bottle inside his briefcase knowing that doing so would ensure he wouldn't lose the case.

Getting out of his car, he looked at his wedding ring resting delicately on his shaking hand. Unlocking the front door of his home, he thought that he was capable of selling it for a drink if the circumstances were right. He thought perhaps he should hide it where it could never be found.

Then what would be the point of having it?

"Honey?" he said, poking his head inside. "Cal?" The silence was indifferent.

The late morning light was somber. "Cal? Is anyone here?" Lights were flickering from the living room, and he carried his briefcase with him as if a purse-snatcher might be loose in the house. The TV was on and it was the news — or what they call the news — with Crawford's picture superimposed behind the anchor*monkey* trying to make the story look "official."

"Breaking News" it read at the top. *Crawford Leaves Hershey Show after Signs of Illness.* Crawford grabbed the remote off the coffee table and turned the TV off. He looked at the ceiling. "Anybody? Hello!"

Crawford clutched his briefcase and walked upstairs, thinking about the gun in his desk drawer. He'd been afraid of that gun for years, but now that fear had a whole new dimension. Would he need to use it?

He also thought that someone might be upstairs waiting to slit his throat or to take him somewhere to make a TV show out of slitting his throat. He wondered if it wasn't the DTs driving him crazy. Either scenario might be the case. *Or both.*

Cal's bedroom door was closed, and he put his ear to it. "Cal?"

He turned the knob slowly and walked inside with the reverence a minister shows a sanctuary. Nailed to the door, Rotten Tamales — the foremost *that's-right-I'm-the-Devil* rock star — looked down on Crawford with a Puritan's gaze.

"Erectum?" Crawford asked the poster, as if it would answer. "What the hell is that supposed to mean?" Crawford took a step back to get a wider view. He put his briefcase on the bed. *Good ol' Rotten Tamales. And my parents got pissed off over the Rolling Stones.* Crawford looked at Rotten's menacing expression — lips pulled tight against the teeth, nose slightly raised in a growl. He was almost congenial, like someone he should find charming, or feel sorry for.

Feel sorry for? Shit. Some sick fuck who has milked millions out of middle-class parents via their stupid, insecure teenage sons? Hell, even worse has taken hard-earned money from destitute single mothers working as waitresses and maids who thought they had to give their kids a little of what the upper-class brats had.

He imagined Rotten Tamales whispering, "But that's what *you do too*, fucker."

"Fuck you," he said.

Fuck tolerance, Crawford thought. Dorothy had told him he didn't understand and she was right. With a calm self-confidence, he tore the *Erectum* poster off the wall and ripped and shredded it, savoring every second before leaving it in tiny pieces on the floor. Crawford looked at himself in the mirror and just for an instant wasn't disgusted.

"No, Dorothy. I don't understand."

Crawford looked around the room as if he'd never been there before. What else is in my house? *My* house, Crawford thought. He began searching Cal's room, starting with the closets then the dresser drawers. The bottom of the closet was filled with tennis shoes piled one on top of the other, none of which he'd seen Cal wear. The dresser was stuffed haphazardly, all its drawers hanging open to various degrees. Crawford pulled out pants, shirts, and shorts, tossing them on the floor.

Black. Black. Everything is black. When Cal was a little boy, his Granny Lou used to call him Sunshine. *I guess he showed her.*

Crawford didn't know what he was doing; he was just doing something, *whatever* — whatever *he* wanted. He had a right; it was *his* house. He was the father; Cal was the son. Crawford clenched his teeth thinking of all the "instruction" he had digested over the years on human behavior, especially on dealing with children. But he couldn't explain this need to trash Cal's room. He had read every major book on child psychology until Cal had gotten to be twelve or thirteen and then he realized it was all bullshit.

Crawford had respected pop psychology and had kept the faith, despite being a backslider in his everyday life. But now it was looming over him like a mob boss who had done him many a favor.

He was in the training business. And once you go in, you never get out.

Training. That's it. That's what it is. Like people are animals. Like dogs that need their faces rubbed in their own shit. People as empty receptacles that need to be shaped properly. That's the rationale. Shaped properly in order to function properly.

"Bullshit!" he yelled.

Crawford reached under Cal's mattress — a hiding place so obvious he hadn't thought of it — and found a pipe, a lighter, and a small bag of marijuana. Crawford had assumed Cal would keep his pornography there like most teenage boys, hiding the really incriminating things elsewhere. Crawford reached deeper into the mattress and found nothing. He wondered if his son had any pornography at all. He hoped so. Looking at the *Erectum* poster torn to pieces at his feet, it would be especially troubling if he didn't.

There was a small pinch of grass in the pipe that had been smoked perhaps once. Crawford put it to his lips and lit it, taking a big hit that felt unexpectedly harsh. After exhaling he gasped for air then coughed violently — his face turning red, saliva filling his nasal passages. He leaned forward, coughing into his cupped hands, then finally stopped, catching his breath. Right away he had that tingly feeling that he hadn't felt since his undergrad days. When he first started smoking, he enjoyed the intense high of smoking after a few drinks. But a year later he found it made him nervous and antisocial. It got to be more like dropping acid than smoking a little harmless pot, so he changed the protocol to smoking only after a good eight or nine drinks. This didn't cause nervousness, but it sure could turn a decent drunk into an unpleasant one — triggering inebriation that brought blackouts, vomiting, and other embarrassing behavior. He finally quit smoking marijuana altogether. Crawford decided that drinking was better, rationalizing he'd graduated to a more mature, Hemingway-style recreation. He was "drinking appropriately" for his age, he thought. But no, actually he wasn't. He was drinking like a frat boy at a keg party.

Surrounded by Cal's dark wardrobe, Crawford took a deep breath then lay flat on Cal's bed, his head next to his briefcase. He didn't know why he smoked the pot; he just did.

Isn't that *the excuse of a child? "I don't know why. I just did... because I could."*

It was an excuse he still used with Dorothy from time to time.

Maybe we all just need to grow up.

Crawford looked at the ceiling and thought of all the ceilings he had seen over the years under the influence.

All those ceilings. Even the Sistine Chapel. I should have been sober for the Sistine Chapel.

He thought of that time waking up in Berry's apartment to unusual patterns on the ceiling that looked like a scaffold made of light. It was beautiful. Turned out to be reflections from a shopping cart filled with empty beer bottles a few feet from the bed. He would later learn he had stolen it from a large liquor store the night before.

"But how did I get it home?" he asked them.

"You pushed it home, twenty-some blocks," Berry told him.

"We just pointed you in a straight line," Scott had said.

"And you made me do it?" Crawford asked.

"Made you? Hell, no. You insisted," Scott said.

Berry and Scott had made jokes about that shopping cart for years, telling Crawford it was a prophecy that his books would be sold in supermarkets.

How do I know I stole that damn shopping cart? Crawford thought.

Those assholes might have lied to me.

He opened his briefcase and pulled out the bottle. He broke the seal, took a deep breath, and then tipped it toward the afternoon sun. It went down his throat smooth and felt warm and cozy in his gut. He looked at the videotape lying in the case. It was cold and distant. It was scheming against him.

Crawford walked down the hall and peeked into his and Dorothy's bedroom as if to find his lovely wife waiting for him in bed.

"Honey?" he said, just in case.

There had always been a maternal element in Crawford's relationship with his wife, especially when he was intoxicated. But now he didn't feel the attendant dread of her authority, even with marijuana in his bloodstream. The naughty schoolboy who had been caught smoking cigarettes in the bathroom felt secure knowing there was someone to answer to.

But where...?

Then he saw the note next to the bed.

> Dear Jim,
>   If you are reading this note, I'm assuming that you have made it home OK. I hope you'll do me the favor of calling my mother and telling her what your situation is. At least tell her you're all right. I will be there soon (at Mother's) if I'm not when you call. I need to be away from you for a while. I think Cal does as well. Please don't fight me on this. I know you have a problem, and maybe it's "our" problem, but I can only accommodate so much.
>
>   Dorothy

There was no "Love," before her name.

Crawford walked down to his study and sat at his desk. He felt like a stranger in his own home. It was stillness, pure silence — the kind a writer dreams of but often wouldn't know what to do with if he had it. Looking at the *Wall of Shame* — especially that ridiculous picture of him accepting the *James Crawford Day* plaque — he thought of how a house does not make a home — nor a drafty old study, even for a writer — not without the ones you love. He had often used the excuse that the burden of raising a family, of being married and being the primary income earner, was the real reason he needed to drink, "to relax" from all those pressures. Of course, relaxing wasn't really the objective. The objective was to get shitfaced. And the only reason people get shitfaced is that they're trying to get away from something. Crawford thought about how he had been trying to get away from this place forever. *This wonderful, warm home.* Apparently, leaning on the bar at a shithole dive felt better, more secure. It was easier, no paternal pressures involved.

Cowardice.

"It's not complicated," he had written in *Self-Assurance*, "until it's duplicated."

What? Cowardice?

He didn't want to call Dorothy's mother. He didn't even have to see his mother-in-law in the flesh to feel so small. He pulled the phone in front of him and put his hand on the receiver. It rang and Crawford froze. It rang again.

"Hello?" he said eagerly.

"Like you've said before, Doctor..."

Oh no. Crawford's heart started pounding.

"You can have anything any other man has." The voice sounded like it was put through a filter.

"Who the hell is this?" Crawford said faintly.

"You know who this is. And you know who *this* is."

Then *her voice*, sincere and unaffected, like he'd always known it: "Jim. Do what he says."

He felt a jolt of helplessness that made his shoulders, his arms, and his hands feel like they had turned to stone. The calmness of his wife's voice made it worse.

"Baby, are you okay? Honey? Are you..."

"I've tapped into your phone lines. All of them. And I'm watching you. You call the police, even from a public phone, they both die. I'll be calling you soon. So don't leave. Watch the show again. It's so much fun."

"Both? Both what? Listen, you son of a bitch!"

"Dad? Are you there?" Crawford heard Cal say before the phone went dead.

PART III:
What Any Other Person Has

SIXTEEN

THE FIRST TIME CRAWFORD CONSIDERED the posibility that he could have brain damage from drinking was when he came home after talking to Berry and Scott and found that copy of *Comprehensive Psychology Review* in the bathroom under a pile of *Rolling Stone* and *Penthouse* magazines. There it was, an article that so closely resembled his argument that Crawford knew if he submitted his thesis it would be the academic equivalent of showing up to a murder scene with a bloody knife in his hand. There were even sections of the text underlined.

Jesus, I can't remember doing that at all, he thought.

Crawford sat back against the toilet and took a drink from his Coors Light tallboy. He had no idea what he would do now. There was no way he could turn in the thesis he had.

God, and I finally thought I did something of value. Something I was proud of.

You haven't done anything at all, he thought, throwing the journal across the room. Crawford did the only thing he could think of besides getting more drunk — he called Dorothy, who promptly came over and listened quietly as Crawford's anguish came pouring out between sips of beer. "Why do you drink so much?" she asked quietly after hearing a salvo of what-do-I-do's.

"I guess I could finish one of the other ones," Crawford said, ignoring the question and referring to one of his previous proposals.

"You didn't answer my question."

"What?" Crawford said, taking another drink.

"Why do you drink so much?" she said louder.

"I don't know." He paused a moment. "Lack of self-confidence. Lack of self-worth, self-respect, self-esteem, maybe."

"Okay, so what do you need to do now?" Dorothy was always so practical when it came to weighing up a problem, even back then.

"I don't know." Crawford finished his beer then crumpled the can and threw it in a wastebasket. "I can get an extension on my thesis. Maybe a couple of months, I don't know."

"No, what do you need to do first?" she said gesturing to the wastebasket.

"Oh, get another beer?" Crawford was so tanked he looked like a little boy, vulnerable and afraid.

"No!" she said walking over to him and putting her arm around his shoulders. "Right now. What do you need to do right now?"

"I don't know," he said, putting his hands over his face. "I don't know."

"Why not stop drinking? How's that for a start? It seems to me that all these problems come from drinking, right?" Dorothy had an alcoholic brother and knew all about the question-response approach to getting a drunk to admit his problem.

"Well, not all my problems. Amnesia seems to be a problem."

"And where do you think that comes from?"

She reminded Crawford of his mother when he was eleven during a spitball incident at school. But before he allowed himself to be insulted by her cross-examination, he realized that she was just about all he had at that moment.

"Okay, I'll stop drinking for a while. But what do I do about my thesis?"

"Write another," she said like a strict mother.

"Oh, I should just sit down and crank out a master's thesis in the next couple of weeks, huh?"

"Yes."

Crawford admired her resolve, but then again, she didn't have to write it. And on what topic, did she propose? It had taken him a year to come up with the one he had.

"Why did you say you drink?" she asked with the coldness of a statistician. "You gave me a reason you drink so much a minute ago."

"Say what?" Crawford honestly couldn't remember what he had just said.

"You said you lacked self-confidence, self-esteem."

"Yeah," he shrugged.

"Why don't you write something about that?"

"I haven't done any research," he snapped.

She assured him he'd done plenty of research. Crawford rolled his eyes.

Handing in a paper to Dr. Watkins on self-confidence or self-esteem could be a blunder bigger than handing in a plagiarized paper. Crawford eventually went back to his panacean masturbation theory, using a made-up patient who beat his depression autoerotically. Mary Epstein was unavailable (or unwilling, Crawford thought) to do the copyediting, so Dorothy helped as much as she could, mostly just locating spelling and punctuation errors.

Watkins was clearly not happy with the result, later writing in his evaluation, "You have always shown a strong potential for independent and original concepts. In academic terms, your problem is that you rarely follow it up with a resolute focus. That's just my opinion. But my opinion is important right now."

Watkins' words were wounding, but Crawford got his degree nonetheless. He had mixed feelings that summer about the whole experience — it felt good to get it over with, but the finale was not as gratifying as he had hoped. He spent much of the summer wondering what he would do next. He also drank. But the conversation he had with Dorothy about his drinking and his thesis always stuck in his mind — even on the day they got married.

Self-confidence, self-worth, self-respect. *Self-esteem.*
Why don't you write something about that?

Crawford pulled the videotape from his briefcase and set it on his desk. He just sat across from it, staring without expression. The tape seemed so innocuous, like a plastic box of nothing. He felt like he couldn't bear to watch it again, but he knew he had to. It was all he had.

He hit rewind and let the tape lumber back to the beginning. He'd almost convinced himself the whole thing was a hoax, but if so, now his entire family was involved. He looked at his hands, stretching them like a pianist player preparing for a performance. In all the years he had been taking substances for pleasure, the most reliable litmus test of his mental state was his hands. For some reason, it made him think of reality, *the here and now*, and his inability to grasp it, if in fact there was such a thing. The world modern man had built around himself — with his TVs and video machines and videogames and digital music and alcohol and drugs and psychology and self-help — it all worked to take him away from what was right in front of him, the real world. And what confirmed this most was the look and feel of his own hands.

He hit play.

The sound screeched out like a car transmission going out.

"Yessssssiiiiirrrrreeeee. Good morning, Dr. Crawford! We're moving right along. How is your self-esteem?"

He's holding up the book to the side of his face. He's imitating someone. Have I done that?

"Time for stage two!"

He's opening the book. There's a bookmark.

"The second stage is to eliminate the harmful things that are destroying our lives. That's good advice, Dr. Crawford!"

Crawford felt a lump in his throat the size of a golf ball. He hit the forward button and the image sped ahead like time-lapse photography. *The woman tied to the chair.* Crawford looked at the bottle waiting patiently on the floor next to his briefcase. *Happy Pappy bouncing next to her. Talking. The book under his arm.* He put the bottle on the desk. *Ripping the tape from her mouth.* He unscrewed the lid and placed it carefully on the desk. *Jenny screaming. Her eyes. Those eyes.* He lifted the bottle to his mouth, his eyes concentrated on the screen. *The monster laughing. Pointing his yellow glove at the book.* He took a drink and put the bottle down, holding the alcohol in his mouth before finding the courage to gulp it down. *That fucking book!* Crawford swallowed and hit play.

"Okay. Okay. Focus. Focus."

Jenny could barely breathe.

"People usually recognize right away when they've created a relationship with bad things or bad people."

She's gasping for air. Is she acting?

"But many times we continue these relationships..."

She's crying. I never saw her cry like that. Not like that.

He hit forward, then play.

Stroking her hair.

"Yes. And why is that?"

He's going to read from the book.

"Because we're afraid to eliminate them from our lives."

To the camera.

"Not unless you've got self-esteem!"

Crawford hit stop and the screen went blue. He looked at his hands again. What could his hands tell him? What could this damn video tell him? He picked up the bottle and brought it to his lips. The forceful odor harassed his quivering nose. He put the bottle down.

Crawford had mindfulness, as the Buddhists say. He was in the moment. He was real. He was a part of everything that's real — everything he'd shut out with alcohol.

Crawford hit the play button then hit rewind, watching the pictures flash by in reverse. It was almost funny, watching this psycho dance backward.

Distraction is never real.

He punched play.

"We all know that fucking someone besides mommy is really naughty. It's really bad!"

Crawford hit the slow-motion button. The image advanced one frame at a time like a grotesque slow-motion replay of a football game.

The face fills the frame, slowly moving from side to side.

Crawford hit play again.

"That's why a little cocksucking whore like this one needs..."

Crawford hit pause.

Wait. A small white spot just above the mask.

He hit reverse, then again in slow-motion:

blip, blip, blip

Pause.

The image was a frozen face, blurred by an upswing, like the mask was melting in a shower of acid. There was an area behind the mask that had a strange pattern, the only thing that made the set different from the real show. Crawford leaned forward.

What is it behind the white spot?

It was a wall — a brick wall. And something was written on it that was faded and old.

Crawford again felt the golf ball in his throat and swallowed hard. He looked down at his hands, but he wasn't sure if they were shaking or not. He thought maybe his whole body was shaking.

He moved closer to the screen and his mind tore ahead like a horse running itself dead. *A wall with a faded word written on it, definitely a faded word maybe an image but part of a word and it was paint, like it was painted on the side of a building in the old days, like large murals for Coca-Cola or Shell Oil.*

He put his face almost to the screen, squinting at the grainy image.

It looks like an S.

Crawford opened his desk drawer and pulled out a legal pad that had scribbling all over it. He tore off the marked up page, threw it in the trash then looked at the image on the screen again.

It's an S.

He picked up a pencil and drew a line at the top of the page, curving it slowly down, while looking at the screen. It was an *S* with a smiley face, a smiley face on the bottom — just two small dots above the bottom of the *S*, like a smile.

What is that? I've seen that.

He wasn't sure if it looked familiar or if he just thought it looked familiar. He looked at his hands, but his hands couldn't tell him anything.

He tore off the top page and held his sketch to the screen.

What the fuck is it? I've seen it.

Crawford hit the stop button on the VCR and turned off the TV, then he glanced at the bottle, looking at it carefully. He picked up the phone on his desk. *You have to call someone*, he thought. *Call 9-1-1. But what will you say? A clown from a TV show has abducted your family?*

They'll suspect you, Lee had said.

And the crazy fucker said that he'd tapped into our phone lines. He said not to even use a pay phone. I guess my mobile phone is no good either?

"Come on, that's bullshit."

What if it's not?

Crawford slammed the phone down on the receiver.

"Son of a bitch!"

He put his fingers to his temple as if he were searching for a button on his head to tell him what to do.

Rely on the successful solutions you have used in the past.

"I'll talk to Peters. I'll talk to Peters." That's what Crawford had done more than once, especially when he was on a terrible drinking binge and couldn't get off, especially when he had some terrible circumstance to deal with. It was always embarrassing, but Peters was the only person that could help.

He'll know what to do. He'll know what to do. Crawford put his briefcase on the desk and put the tape inside. He folded the little piece of yellow paper with the S-shape and threw it in there too. Then the bottle. Lowlander was difficult to let go right now. I'll have that mindfulness later, Crawford thought.

Then the phone rang again.

Crawford put his hands over his ears then looked at the telephone, thinking he would never be able to answer a phone again. But as the phone rang, then rang again, then rang again, he was a coward crouching in a hole.

He grabbed the phone, imitating a gesture he'd seen in a Lee Marvin movie. "What do you want!"

"Whoa, now. Just whoa there big guy," a gruff voice with a Southern accent said. "That's no way to talk to ya best buddy."

For a second Crawford thought that all this Happy Pappy business had been a dream or a joke, but missing a punch line.

"Who the hell is this?" Crawford said under his breath.

"Who the hell is this? I'm offended, ya sorry sack-a-shit. This is ya old college buddy, Melvin."

"Melvin. Melvin Sprawn?"

"Who the hell else you know named Melvin, ya sorry son of a bitch."

Crawford caught his breath. "Just you, Melvin. I guess."

"Ya guess?" Melvin said with glee. "Ha! Ya sorry sack-a-shit!" His voice was still a few decibels too loud, just like in college. "What say we knock back a few cold ones tonight, just like in college?"

"Look..."

"Ya sorry som'bitch."

Crawford felt a sense of relief hearing Melvin's voice. And as much as he needed to tell this guy that his plate was currently full, he couldn't help but sound welcoming. "Melvin. It's not a good time, man," he said softly.

"Not a good time? Hell, you can't tell *me* it's not a good time, ya sorry sack-a-shit!"

There was that same belly laugh. "Yes I can."

"No, you can't."

"Yes, I can."

"*No*, you can't. Look out ya window, ya sorry bastard."

"What?"

"Look out ya window."

"What window?"

"Your front window."

"I can't talk now," Crawford said, hanging up the phone.

Crawford rose from his desk, putting his briefcase securely between the file cabinet and the wall.

Melvin Sprawn. Surely he's not here. Look out the window? What the hell?

It had been almost seven years since Crawford had seen Melvin, and he didn't remember too much about that occasion except that he found him even more irritating than in college. He had almost completely put the memory of the old boy from Arkansas out of his mind, but after hearing his voice, every little idiotic idiosyncrasy came roaring back.

Too damn loud. Too many stupid drawn out stories. Too much juvenile talk about sex.

Crawford met this big, hairy, college freshman named Melvin during the first week of his freshman year in college while they were next-door neighbors at the Hopkins dormitory. With a round mug and the ungainly jowls of a hog, Melvin was a hulking good old boy from a little town in Arkansas who had nothing in common with Crawford except his love of drinking and a penchant for using hangovers to justify the avoidance of academic responsibilities. Crawford first got acquainted with Melvin after knocking on his door to complain about some blaring country music (George Jones, he seemed to recall). It wasn't that Crawford was trying to study; quite the contrary. It was just that the music was competing with his music (Led Zeppelin, he seemed to recall).

Crawford had seen him from a distance once before, in the dormitory's common room, and assumed he might have a confrontation on his hands if he ever stepped on Melvin's toes. Asking him to turn his music down would definitely fall into that category and a confrontation might have ensued, but Crawford never asked. He thought he would, but once Melvin opened the door, Crawford, like the timid 18-year-old he was, didn't say anything about the music. As a matter of fact, he didn't say much at all.

"Yeah," Melvin said with a scowl that stretched across his broad face, his giant body covered in flannel and denim filling the doorway.

"Uh, what's going on?" Crawford said meekly.

"Nothin," Melvin said with a nod. "Can I help you, Sir?"

"Oh, I'm just... I live next door and I thought I'd..."

"Just coming to introduce ya'self?" Melvin said straight-faced. "Well come the hell on in. I like sociable folk," he said, as he gave Crawford a painful slap on the shoulders.

Melvin guided Crawford into the small room, which was identical to his own except for the Southern memorabilia covering the walls: a Lynard Skynard poster, an old Civil War combat photograph, and a Confederate flag.

George Jones (or whoever it was) was lamenting the loss of a woman by getting smashed in a bar, as he would do all semester long.

"So the name's Melvin, Melvin Sprawn. Studyin' business," he said, sitting down and handing Crawford a beer from a 12-pack box on the floor. "Have a seat." The first thing Crawford noticed about Melvin was his very direct form of communication — perhaps *efficient* would be a better way of saying it. Not only did he not speak in complete sentences, he didn't speak in complete words. "Y'self?"

Crawford immediately began imitating Melvin's disjointed style of communication. "Jim Crawford. Undecided."

"Undecided about what?" he asked.

"You know, my major."

"Oh yeah," Melvin said with an embarrassed laugh. "Y'don't have t' decide, y'know. I didn't decide myself. My daddy decided for me. I got to get all educated so I can run his business one of these days, you know, when he gets old and wants to jus' fish and stuff. That's why I'm studying business. Chances are you won't ever decide. Someone or something will decide for you."

Crawford thought that was a surprisingly intelligent remark. "So what kind of business?"

"Bourbon. The kind we make in Arkansas." Melvin leaned over the side of the bed and grabbed a bottle that he held directly in front of Crawford's face — Old Arkansan.

"Old Ark... an..."

"Ahr-kan-zun," Melvin said deliberately, accentuating his Southern drawl. "Dad's jus' gettin' started. Tough business, whiskey. But we gon' do it. Like a shot?"

"You bet," Crawford said with contrived enthusiasm. He gulped down the noxious liquid and coughed violently, which Melvin enjoyed.

"Yeah. Get it, man. Get after it!"

Crawford and Melvin drank many bottles of Old Arkansan together during their first year, and Crawford would later speculate that the gestation of his drinking problem was born from this dreadful brew, distilled by a company destined for bankruptcy. But it wasn't just the drink that was awful; the conversation wasn't that great either, to say the least.

"So what d'ya bench?" was a standard get-to-know-you question, one that Crawford knew only an idiot would ask.

But like most humans wanting to please, Crawford gave him an answer. "Bench? Oh...," Crawford said, before making something up. He'd never actually "benched" in his entire life. He met his high school physical education requirement with tennis and cross-country track, and no benching was involved.

Melvin was one of those people that tried to show interest in other people — what they liked and what they didn't — which was one quality Crawford appreciated. But there was one conversational topic (and later he would discover others) that Melvin was comfortable with that Crawford was not. And that topic was sexuality, and in particular, masturbation.

"Do you like to jack off to magazines?" Melvin asked out of the blue. Strange for their first encounter, Crawford thought. "Or are you a shower man, like to just use your 'magination?"

With several shots of Old Arkansan in him, Crawford let down his guard a bit and responded. "You're saying you jack off?"

"Never have," Melvin shot back. "Too many farm animals in Arkansas," he said before guffawing loudly. "Hell, yeah. Of course I jack off. And you do too, you sorry som'bitch," he said giving Crawford another slap. "Now you a magazine man or you just think about your ninth-grade teacher or som' shit."

"I, uh... I would rather not say," Crawford answered nervously.

"Fine. Fine and dandy. You don't use your handy, 'specially when it's sandy."

That would have been a tolerable stopping point, but Melvin had a way of forcing a conversation into dismal territory. "You know what I like?" he said. "I'm a magazine man. But I like a big damn pussy is what I like, one s'big I can't even produce in my own 'magination. I get mags with the beefy beaver," he said with a wink and a nod before taking a hefty drink of beer. "Know what I mean?"

Crawford's face dropped and his stomach began to churn. Melvin's brand of openness wasn't his kind of conversation. "You know, I'd like to be a writer," Crawford said unexpectedly.

"Say what?" Melvin said.

"You asked what I was studying. I'd like to write a novel someday and..."

"Hey, man," Melvin interrupted. "I'm talking about pussy. I guess you aren't a magazine man. Like to make up your own stuff, huh?"

Melvin continued to describe in graphic detail just what excited him sexually. Crawford hoped that he could get this conversation behind him and never have to hear about large vaginas again. But unfortunately Melvin persisted the whole school year, talking about things like brawny vulvas, large furry anuses, and efficient masturbation techniques. It always made Crawford uncomfortable, always. But instead of telling Melvin Sprawn to shut the hell up — or better yet, just leaving the room — Crawford listened to Melvin talk about every facet of his sexual proclivities all year long. And as time went on, Melvin loved Crawford more and more for allowing this indulgence, while Crawford grew to hate Melvin. It was Crawford's first experience of paying for the pleasures of drinking by compromising his character. Free Old Arkansan came at a price — and a high one.

Crawford walked nervously through the kitchen, then into the living room where he peeked out the window. There was no one there — only a large convertible Chrysler LeBaron parked in the street, and *Melvin wouldn't drive a LeBaron or a convertible.* He was more of a truck man.

Crawford walked to the front door and looked out the peephole — nothing but the afternoon sun saturating the neighborhood with its brutal hue. Crawford slowly cracked the door and again saw nothing. He relaxed a bit.

That asshole. Why did he call me? Why now?

"What the hell you doin', ya som'bitch!" Melvin yelled, springing from behind the door. "Hey, ya famous sack-a-shit!" he said thunderously, slapping Crawford on his shoulder blade with his enormous right hand.

The first thing Crawford saw, even before looking at Melvin's face, was the case of beer he held under his left arm. Crawford rubbed his shoulder and looked at Melvin's face, which was just inches away from his own. His appearance hadn't changed much — he was older and heavier, which was to be expected — but the funny thing was he looked... well, dumber.

"Melvin, this is surprising."

Perhaps it was his used-salesman clothing, which was even more unflattering than his redneck attire in college. He wore a lime-green polyester jacket with large flaps on the pockets, and a not-so-complementary pair of brown pants. He looked like a human-sized mishmash of slime and shit.

"Well, invite my ass in!" he said, grinning like a politician.

Without a gesture from Crawford, Melvin walked right in as if they'd planned a get-together for months. "Nice-ass place," he said nodding.

"Melvin, I'm glad to see you, but..."

"I'm glad to see your ass, too," he said, still appraising Crawford's house. "Oh hell, I'm sorry," he said, ripping into the box of beer. "Still cold," he said, handing Crawford a can. "Still ice fuckin' cold!"

It was like Crawford had never left college: free cold beer, but with an annoying asshole.

Well, maybe just one, he thought. Especially if it's *ice fuckin' cold*.

He took a drink, and like Melvin's voice, at first it was comforting.

"Bought this from one of them camel jocks down th'street. They's the one that told me where you live."

"Great. Glad they could help you," Crawford mumbled.

"Huh?" Melvin said even louder. "Where's the pisser, amigo? I'm sloshin' like a whore on Sunday morning."

"On the left," Crawford said, pointing.

"Put this in the fridge for me, would ya?" he said, shoving the box into Crawford's torso.

You gotta tell this asshole to go away now. There's no time for politeness in this situation. Do it!

"You know, I got married!" Melvin hollered from the bathroom, the door wide open. "Yeah, I know what you're thinking: *again*," he said laughing. "But this one is the last. Till death do me part, I tell you."

Crawford didn't know he was married before and didn't care. He put the case in the refrigerator and grabbed three cans from the box. You were just going to have one, he thought, taking them into the living room.

Crawford heard the toilet flush and Melvin walked in still buttoning up his fly. "Yeah, I found one of them bitches that might jus' put up with my ass."

"I'm glad to hear that, Melvin," Crawford said politely. "But..."

"But I'll tell you all about that later. Guess what I got?" he said with an anticipatory smile on his face.

Oh, no.

"That's right," he said, reaching into his polyester jacket. "I got something that's hard to find these days. But I thought of you, Crawford. I thought of you first." He slowly pulled a 750-milliliter bottle from inside his coat, its label old and frayed. "This here'll do somethin' for ya self-esteem," he said proudly, holding up a bottle of Old Arkansan. "Get me a goddam shot glass, boy. Get me two goddam shot glasses, now!" he grinned.

Old Arkansan certainly was difficult to find, especially since the distillery had gone out of business almost ten years prior, and for good reason. Crawford couldn't help but laugh to himself. *Melvin had proudly brought some of his own vintage 'kansan.*

"I'm a Scotch man these days, Melvin," Crawford said, already thinking of excuses to get the Lowlander Pure Malt.

Melvin cocked his head and looked out of the corner of his eye. "Don't tell me you haven't longed for a little 'kansan over the years. Now, come on."

Just the thought of it made Crawford's stomach turn. Instinctively, he tossed back his beer, which was awful but still better than the thought of that paint.

"I'll get the shot glasses," Melvin said, stomping into the kitchen.

Crawford drank the rest of his beer and sat down, putting the empty on the coffee table.

"Where the hell are they?"

"I don't have any shot glasses," Crawford yelled back.

Melvin came back with two small juice glasses with Mickey Mouse on the front — glasses Crawford assumed had long been thrown away.

"This'll do," he said, putting them side-by-side on the coffee table.

"I don't..."

"Oh, yeah you do," Melvin said, sitting opposite Crawford and lighting a cigarette. "Got this bottle from an old man in my hometown. Been savin' a case for years. He told me it was *for special*. Can you believe that shit? How he could keep from drinking it I'll never know."

Melvin put his cigarette on the edge of Crawford's empty beer can and poured three fingers of Old Arkansan in each glass.

"What are you doing here, Melvin?" Crawford asked.

"Just passing through is all," he said humbly. "I didn't come at a bad time, did I?"

"Well, I..."

"Let's celebrate m'new marriage, ol' friend," he said, handing Crawford a glass. Crawford took it, looking carefully at the color. It was almost the same color as Melvin's polyester pants and about as inviting.

"Gosh, I don't know, Melvin."

"Come on. Just a shot or two and I'll be out of your hair."

Crawford took a deep breath then put the glass just under his bottom lip. The caustic bouquet made his watering eyes blink.

Melvin smiled, "Just like eatin' pussy. So bad, but so good."

The smell brought back faint memories of college, not in any specific way, like a particular place or circumstance, but in a strange collective way, like remembering how it felt to be in your mother's arms before you were capable of memory. Crawford was ready to say a few Hail Marys first, *but oh fuck it,* he thought and downed the shot.

"Get that Arkansan in ya," Melvin said, using the company's rarely used slogan.

Crawford put the glass back on the table, and to his surprise, it wasn't that bad. The aftertaste was decent and as a matter of fact, *that went down pretty damn smooth.* "Hey," he said nodding. "Not bad."

"No, sir," Melvin added, just before downing his own. "To you. And to self-esteem." Crawford didn't know what Melvin meant by "self-esteem." Did he mean to *our* self-esteem or to the book *Self-Esteem*? He knew it didn't matter.

Melvin started to talk. And talk.

And talk.

And with the drink, Crawford wasn't sure how long.

It was just like the old days: Melvin talking and Crawford drinking so he could stand it. He talked about the end of his "daddy's" Old Arkansan company. He talked about being in Asia — living in the Philippines, Korea, Taiwan, Singapore, and Thailand — working as a consultant for various alcohol distilleries, mostly helping with issues like waste disposal.

"You see, the problem in most of these countries is that they distill their hooch with formaldehydes. No kiddin'."

An hour went by. Then another. Melvin was still talking. Crawford was still drinking. The sun had gone down. The dark outside reminded Crawford, even in his listlessly intoxicated state, that he was again fleeing responsibility for the sake of warm escape. Melvin had talked about all those "manly" things that men often talk about: work, work, and more work, but had not yet mentioned his new wife. Crawford asked about her, trying to avert attention from his own.

"Her name's Frida. That's her English name. I can't pronounce her Thai name. And oh, she's really something. She waits on me hand and foot. It's like she was put on this planet to make this Arkansas cracker happy."

Poor thing, Crawford thought, taking another sip of Old Arkansan. *She's just getting out of poverty the best she can. And Melvin is the best she can do. Poor thing.*

"And you remember how I like big pussies?"

Crawford felt his stomach turn.

"Well," he continued, leaning back with a contented smile on his face, "she got one, and lemme tell ya, that som'bitch is huuuuuuge."

Crawford felt his stomach turn again, this time deeper, more painfully. All they needed now was George Jones and they would be back in Melvin's tiny dorm room, getting peckered for no reason at all. *And who was this poor Thai woman? And where...* "You just get back from Asia today?" Crawford asked.

"I did, yeah," he said. We got a hotel room and came d'rectly here."

That's why Melvin hadn't mentioned the Hershey show.

"So this woman — your wife — she's at the hotel?"

"No, she's out in the car."

"What?" Crawford asked, slightly sobered by the remark.

"Hell, I told her that she wouldn't be interested in what a couple'a old bar farts like us'd have to say. So I told her just to wait in the car."

It's May, Crawford thought, and a hot one at that.

"You mean you've been here..." Crawford glanced at his watch with blurred vision. *Screw it.* "You've been here all this time and she's been waiting out in the car for you? The whole time?"

"I told you she wants to make this Arkansas cracker happy. Bet *your* wife wouldn't wait in the car."

Crawford felt a rush of anger. He was asking himself the same question he'd asked himself a million times in college: *What are you doing drinking with this stupid hick?* But he couldn't believe what Melvin was telling him, so he pressed it further. "So you got this woman waiting out in a hot car while you get drunk with an old college buddy and talk about her vagina? Is that it?" Crawford said, raising his voice to Melvin like he never had before.

"Careful," Melvin said in that *I'm still a redneck and I can still kick your ass* voice. "Don't be gettin' persnickety."

"You're a piece'a shit. You know that?"

"What?" Melvin said, putting his beer down. "What did you say, you bastard?"

"I *said* you're a piece of shit. Know *that*?"

Melvin's demeanor changed and he stood slowly, his brown and green polyester rising like a giant oak growing in time-lapse. "I'll talk about my wife's vagina all I want, hear?"

Crawford, not being able to sit beneath Melvin, stood to meet his eyes. Suddenly he felt something he hadn't felt in years: courage.

"I never liked you Melvin. It's not that I only realized that just now. I just realized that you need to know so I don't have to see your stupid face again. You just always had booze and were someone to drink with. That's all. That's why I hung out with you in college."

Melvin took a step back looking like a dejected child.

Crawford continued nevertheless. "After two semesters of you, I was so sick, so *sick*, of hearing you talk about jacking off and about big pussies and hairy assholes that I wanted to fucking puke when I heard your fucking name!"

Melvin gave an embarrassed laugh. "Uh... this is just a joke, right?"

"No, I'm not fucking joking, you big lug!"

Any benevolence on Melvin's face now turned to sour indignation, but Crawford couldn't stop. "Get the fuck out of my house. And take that poor girl out there in the car," he said pointing toward the street, "back where you found..."

Crawford didn't get out the last word before Melvin's giant right fist came rolling across his jaw. He fell back a step and put his hand to his face.

This is my house. This is my house. And nobody in my house is going to...

"You know what?" Melvin said. "Them books you wrote..."

Melvin's left came crashing into Crawford's right eye and Crawford fell to the floor, pain shooting from his temple into the rest of his skull. He looked up but could only see a green and brown blur.

"Them *Self* books you wrote... them's bullshit," Melvin said. "I was sent here by the Lord to tell you that."

"Sorry, but I never liked you," Crawford gasped. "I should have just told you that," he said, raising his hand to shield the next blow. It was the last thing Crawford said before the scuffed bottom of Melvin's size-12 boot brought the next oblivion.

SEVENTEEN

"*Dust, Mud, and Blood*" *by James Crawford. A short dream. Less than 500 words. The kind of dream people don't have these days, but should. They're a dying art form — short dreams — and if they were good enough for the previous generation, by God, they're good enough for us.*

Dust, mud, and blood — that's all he could remember when he awoke. It was Saturday; he knew that for some reason. He was walking down a long corridor in an industrial building. It looked like an old factory of some kind, but he wasn't exactly sure what for, he just knew it was like a factory. There were no people there to confirm the function of the facility, just very industrial looking *things* lying around — not machines, not products, just *things* — manufactured things or maybe things that manufactured things, but not machines, not products. As he looked down at the floor in front of him, he could see dust — dust as if something covered in dust had been dragged, leaving behind a sandy trail about the width of a human body. He kept walking; he didn't want to, but he kept walking. Why did he walk? He needed to. He saw more manufactured things or things that manufactured things — perhaps they were both. Now that he thought about it, he wasn't sure. All of a sudden he could see shapes forming among the manufactured things or things that manufactured. They looked like smiles

    or laughter

        or frowns

            or sobbing.

Then below there was mud — black, sticky mud that must have been sprayed out of the bowels of the earth — a lifeless gunk, food for worms, death itself. Then the manufactured things or things that manufactured seem to notice him. *Had they noticed him before?* They seemed to be laughing or sobbing at him. He walked faster

faster
> faster
>> faster.

They were still there — same as before. Then looking down: there was blood — the blood of *being*, the blood of *life*, spilled on the floor like a million pigs slaughtered for a Roman orgy. The blood did not look like it came from something dragged; it looked as if he was standing on the very spot of the carnage —

looking,
> laughing,
>> sobbing.

Then the manufactured things or things that manufactured looked at him, tilting their bases to the side with childlike curiosity. Then the manufactured things or things that manufactured looked at him with sympathy. Understanding. They pulled back their bases in judgment, then in fury. Then his life — his very soul — became one of the manufactured things or things that manufactured. His very being had disappeared evermore, evermore, leaving nothing but blood spilled on the floor.

Like pigs.

Then the manufactured things or things that manufactured rang with the sound of a thousand bells — not beautiful bells, but ghostly bells; disgusting bells; appalling, mechanical, industrial-sounding bells; bells made from the used parts of obsolete machines. *Ring, ring.*

The first thing Crawford thought was that he had gotten drunk and caused a car accident and now he had to face a family of six in a crumpled station wagon, a family that he'd just murdered.

Ring, ring.

Dust, mud, blood.

Crawford turned sideways to see a pile of crumpled beer cans and cigarette butts on the floor next to the coffee table he was lying under. The phone was ringing, but Crawford had no intention of moving. He wasn't sure how much of his pain was caused by the pounding Melvin had given him and how much was caused by the Old Arkansan. Could be the 'kansan was still working as an analgesic.

Ring, ring.

There was the phone again. What time was it? The sharp morning light coming through the transparent inner curtains suggested it was around 6 or 7am, too early for anyone to call, except for family members or the psychopaths holding them hostage.

Crawford struggled to hoist himself up by putting his left hand on the coffee table and shifting his weight toward it. About the time his face was parallel to the table, his hand slipped and he fell with his right shoulder on a stray beer can.

"Goddammit!" he yelled, howling with pain.

With his nose against the floor, Crawford could smell a strong combination of Old Arkansan, cigarette butts, and cheap beer.

Great. I'll hear about this later.

"Or will I?"

I never did get Dorothy at her mother's. Wait. I didn't try. He said don't call the cops. He didn't say don't call her mother. Maybe she's at her mother's. Maybe I'm losing it. Oh God, please let me be losing my mind.

There was a mumbled sound coming from the family room adjoining the living room. At first Crawford thought that Melvin had decided to stay and perhaps he'd find him in the living room chatting with his new wife with the large vagina.

Crawford got to his feet and limped toward the family room. He looked around the corner, fearful he might run into a redneck fist. The noise was just the TV — a morning talk show with some young pop star as the guest.

On the coffee table sat a fresh bottle of Old Arkansan with a note taped to the table in front of it. Melvin had apparently written the note with a marker he must have found in the kitchen. The sight of his writing immediately elicited sympathy since it looked like the writing of a child — and not a smart one.

Jimmy,

You sorry son of a Bitch. I hope you don't mind me and my old lady using your toilet. (She had to pee reel bad and I did too) I just want to say that I apologize for what hapend. I shouldnt of kicked you like that. I'm not sorry I punched your sorry ass, Im just sorry I kicked you. I figered it was best to let you just lay there and get over it. (I got sick about it) I hope you feel better now. I was also reel mad. And besides, I Did NOT kick you that hard. But the way I think, we can still be Freinds you and me. I never tell you I read those books you wrote (2 of them) and I think they were reel good. I felt BAD like I needed to read them I guess. As a peace oFering, I decided to leave you my last bottle of Old Arkansan, just to say let the bigones be bigones. It's one of the last one's on earth. I hope you enjoy it. By the way, when I said the Lord sent me as a messanger, I wasant kidding, but I guess I failed.

Your freind since college, MELVIN
PS: Call me next time your ass is in Arkansas

How did this asshole ever get out of college?

Crawford crumpled up the note and looked at the bottle. I should stop right now, he thought, but he always thought that. He looked at the morning show playing in front of him. There was a stage out on a New York street. A young woman in her early-twenties with a tightly curled hairstyle wearing a lime-green tank top and skin-tight jeans nodded attentively as the flattering female host asked her about her current project.

Crawford removed the lid from the bottle.

"So, Kristine," the well-designed host said.

Appearing at the bottom of the screen was "Kristine releases new album of all new songs."

"You have said your new song *Whatever* is a love song to yourself. Can you tell us more about this? What exactly is a love song to yourself?"

Kristine beamed with confidence, extending a mile-wide smile that revealed perfect white teeth. "In the last few years I've just aspired to adore all the different things about myself. I've just gotten to where I love my bright and witty side, but I also love my not-so-smart side," she said. "I like them all, my profound side, my sexy side, my creative side. But I like my dummy side too," she said.

"Oh, you don't have a dummy side," the host said, giving the young star a sunny slap on the arm.

"Yes I do. A little. But I love all of my complex and far-reaching sides. Yes, I accept them all."

Crawford could feel the side of his face begin to throb. He brought the bottle to his lips.

The young star continued talking, turning toward the crowd of mostly college-age women as if she'd been asked another question. "And in loving myself I've just become more at ease because I'm not so stressed about how complex I am. And I encourage others to do the same," she said. The audience clapped as the camera panned by their eager faces, many of them nodding at her insight. "And it's helped the relationship I'm in now. My partner just loves me unconditionally."

"Oh that's wonderful," the host said with a clap. "Yes, let's talk about your love life."

The pop star's smile widened even more. "We've been embarking upon a really blessed journey."

Crawford put the bottle down and grabbed the remote, pointing it at the TV.

"And to an extent that I've never really felt before, I feel really blessed and humbled by this bond I have with Tyler."

It's not working. Off. Off. Off.

"That's wonderful, Kristine," the host said, looking into the camera.

"Of course she's talking about Tyler Taylor, the sexy new star of TV's *Dashing Dropouts*, which can be seen Tuesday nights at eight on this network."

Crawford's head pounded even harder as he waved the remote from side to side, pressing the off switch as if the device were a giant bug he was trying to squeeze to death.

Off. Off.

"Fuck!" Crawford looked at the pop queen's neck as he squeezed the little gadget.

"You know, I don't really like to talk about myself very much, but if it helps others, that's what I'm really interested in."

"Fuck!" Finally the screen went dead, and Crawford picked up the bottle again; and this time he drank.

"At least my kid's not into *that* shit," he said, lifting his drink in a toast to the black screen. *God, where is that poor kid?*

Crawford took two more swigs of Old Arkansan so he could make the trip upstairs for a shower. It was a rationalization, but at least it was for something semi-productive. Without Dorothy, the rotgut booze was all he had. *Not such a productive rationalization.*

But *Dorothy. And Cal.*

What Crawford had been avoiding was an urgent, blaring reality.

He staggered past the living room, looking at the mess he and Melvin had made. It looked just like a night in Melvin's dorm room, minus the Lynard Skynard poster.

How could I sit there and drink with that asshole? How could I do that now? Do nothing. It's your wife and son, you sorry som'bitch! But this nut said he tapped into the phone lines. Then what can *I do?*

Maybe this was a rationalization too, he thought, putting his hands over his troubled face.

You call the police, they both die.

Crawford staggered onto the stairs and began dragging himself up by the rail.

I'll be calling you soon.

That's what he said — that he'd call. When will this asshole call? And then what will he say? What? Are you going to second-guess what this crackpot will do? You don't even know who...

Crawford thought about the ringing phone that woke him up.

That was him.

Crawford fumbled down the stairs and charged into the kitchen. The quick movement caused a sharp pain in his stomach. Crawford bent over with his right forearm around his midsection, pounding his other hand on the kitchen counter.

"Goddam it," he said. "*Goddam it*!"

He looked at the caller ID. There was a number there. *A number!* "Four-four-three-seven, six, two..." *Who the hell?* It was Dorothy's mother. It was *Dorothy's mom*'s number.

Crawford had never been so happy to see she had called. *Dorothy did make it to her mother's.*

Wait, but what about Dorothy's voice when Happy Pappy called?

Maybe she's still there and the phone call was just some fake bullshit this guy created. He said he'd tapped into the phone lines. Maybe he taped Dorothy's voice.

But she said, 'Do as he says'. That wasn't taped.

Crawford picked up the phone and punched the numbers. He had never learned how to use Call-Return and wasn't going to learn now.

The phone rang.

What if her mother answers and Dorothy's not there? She'll want to know where Dorothy and Cal are and why I'm calling. She'll be worried. Then she could do no telling what. And if Dorothy and Cal were missing, she'd be the first one to tell the police that I probably killed them in a drunken fury and hid them somewhere. She'd tell the cops to throw me in prison and I'd be there before I had a chance to find out who's behind all of this and that would probably lead to...

The ringing seemed to speed up.

What do I do? Tell her I'm looking for Dorothy, that Dorothy said she was going there for a few days. But surely she'd know that. Surely Dorothy called her. And if Dorothy didn't show up, her mother would call to see where she was.

But she did call, he thought. What if Dorothy didn't tell her she was coming?

Or maybe she did and her mother's been trying to call all night and I was knocked out loaded on the living room floor and didn't hear it. Maybe it was Dorothy calling to check up on me and everything is okay. But she wouldn't call; she's too mad right now.

Crawford hung up.

Crawford's inner monologue slowly turned to his mother's voice.

'*You can't do anything like this with your face swollen and these smelly clothes you've had on since you threw up on television. You should just...*'

Take a shower. That's always been a good place to start. Get into some new clothes and then decide.

The fiasco of the show was creeping back as well. *But who cares!*

"Just shed that old skin!"

Crawford's consciousness screamed from the vault of the *Self-Confidence* book-on-tape.

"Oh, shut up!" he yelled uncontrollably, rushing up the stairs as if to run away from his own thoughts.

The bathroom just off the main hall looked as it always did, except the toilet seat was up and there was a ring of what appeared to be brown vomit around the toilet bowl. Crawford thought when Melvin wrote "I was sick," he was saying that he was sickened by his violent behavior. Apparently not. Crawford didn't mind the ring of puke so much — he had, after all, left many a puke stain on many a toilet bowl. It was the upright seat that made Crawford mad.

"Goddam hick," he said, slamming the seat down.

Crawford looked at himself in the mirror for the first time since the Hershey show. The part of his head that Melvin had stomped didn't look nearly as bad as he thought it would. There was just a little bruising around the edge of his right eye.

Maybe it was the Thai woman, he thought he heard Dorothy say. *And maybe it's not a part of their culture to return the seat to the downward position.*

Crawford rushed into his bedroom, stripping off his clothes as fast as he could.

"I'll go see Peters. I'll tell him the whole story." *Just shed that old skin!* "He'll know what to do. Maybe I'll see Peters, then I'll call Lee, then Lee can call my lawyer. And we'll figure out a game plan." *Yes, I'll figure out something!*

'*People always need a game plan for everything they do! Do you think plays in football are just thought up on the spot? No, the football planner, commonly known as a "coach," always has...*'

Crawford moaned when the frigid water from the shower hit his aching naked body. He would have waited for the shower to warm up, but he was in a hurry to get back to that bottle — the Lowlander Pure Malt, not the Arkansan — and besides he felt like he needed a shock to his system. He was starting to hear sound bites from his books and his mother talking and damn it, something needed to be done fast.

He dried himself off in a hurry and slid into a fresh pair of slacks and a shirt. Both were a little dressier than usual, but they needed to be.

Tie? No tie? *No tie.*

Crawford inspected himself in the mirror and saw his slightly swollen eye was less swollen than before. The cold water had worked. And to his surprise, he actually liked the little injury. It almost made him look handsome.

Handsome is as handsome does. Or perhaps it gave him "character." *Your affection for an injury could be a further sign of self-hatred.*

"Wait a minute. I never wrote that line," he said into the mirror. "Did I?"

It was time to have that drink or two before going over to Peters' office.

Crawford grabbed Melvin's peace-making note and bottle of Old Arkansan off the family room coffee table and headed down to his study. He took his briefcase from the space next to his file cabinet and placed Melvin's gift in its place. He put his briefcase on his desk and opened it, pulling out the Lowlander Pure Malt and taking quick a nip. But it didn't taste the same.

What's with this? he thought. It tasted like maple syrup mixed with Drano. He smelled the rim of the bottle then took another sip. Again it tasted terrible, like some cheap liqueur made in Mexico from eucalyptus trees.

Crawford put the lid on the bottle and carefully placed it on the desk then grabbed the Old Arkansan. He pulled a trusty shot glass from inside his desk drawer and filled it with the precious liquid.

Bouquet good, he thought, swirling the glass.

That thar is some good color, good texture.

He promptly downed the shot, which was even more pleasing than before.

He poured himself another shot, drank it, then another, raising it to eye-level.

Okay. 'Kansan it is.

Crawford opened his desk drawer — that drawer he seldom opened — and reached inside. There it was. Surprisingly cool and smooth, like the surface of that Porsche the first time he saw it in the showroom. He put his hand tightly around the grip, allowing his finger to rest gently on the trigger. He brought it out from its resting place then let his left index finger slowly crawl the length of the barrel. He couldn't stop thinking about how cool and smooth it felt. It was more than a weapon. It was a work of art. And now it was a friend. That story he had told many times, written about many times, about how he was so depressed that he bought a gun. That was all bullshit. He hadn't bought that gun at all. He had inherited it from his Uncle Jerry.

EIGHTEEN

As Crawford walked through the front door, he tightened his buttocks and ground his teeth and clutched his briefcase close to his body. Stepping off the front steps, he felt the bottle roll from the back end of the briefcase to the front, as if it wanted comfort from him. He eyed his car then reached for his keys with shaking hands. The thought of the bottle inside steadied his nerves, if just a little.

Crawford got in the car and carefully put his briefcase on the passenger's side seat. Immediately in front of him he saw a boy bicycling down the street delivering newspapers. The boy had a serious look on his face, like he was concentrating completely on his job, putting all of his focus into every toss of every paper. Crawford looked at the boy's expression. He was way too committed, Crawford thought. He even thought about telling the boy to relax — to not put so much of himself into something so trivial as a job.

Then, for some strange reason, Crawford remembered a documentary he saw on TV years and years ago.

It was black and white footage: Adolf Hitler riding in a motorcade through the streets of Berlin, his body erect, his wave confident and rigid — serious in a way that was both comical and appallingly childish.

Crawford started up the car and stared at the boy.

Crawford had been a paperboy, just like so many other boys. He had been just 13 years old when Elmer Dodson, a friend of little Jimmy Crawford's famous Uncle Jerry (Gerald Crawford), had gotten him a job delivering papers for the *Daily Press*, a small-town rag with a circulation of less than seventeen hundred. Jimmy was enormously excited about his new job, which would bring a whopping twenty-two dollars a week to an otherwise allowance-less early teen. On that monumental first morning of gainful employment, Crawford's mother had awoken him to document the occasion with a Kodak snapshot she would later hang on the wall next to her own high school diploma.

"Now do a good job, Jimmy. Remember, Uncle Jerry is counting on you."

Uncle Jerry is counting on you. That was a big responsibility.

Uncle Jerry (actually Crawford's great uncle) was a retired Army Colonel responsible for writing a column called "Prior Prattle-Tattle" — a bi-weekly diatribe on all-things-wrong in the little community of Prior, Texas. Jerry chose to have his work published anonymously as "Nitpicky Nick" because he didn't want his good name "to add credibility to his ideas." He wanted them to stand on their own. Some of the issues he addressed were carhops not giving enough ketchup packets at the local drive-in hamburger joint and women wearing "too much makeup on the eyes and not enough on the lips."

Jerry was famous not just to little Jimmy, but to much of the Prior community — a famous writer whom everyone knew even though he used a pen name.

Nitpicky Nick was a Crawford, a military man who had fought and killed in Korea. But more importantly he was a modern Mark Twain who deserved a nationally-syndicated column but probably couldn't get one because, as many of his close friends would say, he was "too honest." But in Prior, Uncle Jerry was famous.

"Damn, Colonel," Jimmy once heard someone say to his uncle at a grocery store. "I never thought about that make-up thing. Women had ought to read that one and take note. I'm buyin' some lipstick for my old lady right now. And gosh darn it, she's gonna wear it," the local man said with an affected laugh. "And that damn mascara, well that's going in the trash."

Uncle Jerry would smile and nod, closing his eyes with satisfaction after planting another seed of much-needed insight into a community starving for wisdom.

Uncle Jerry was the first writer Crawford had ever known, and accordingly young Jimmy formed his first impression of what a writer is from his uncle's unusual example. Writers were not just men, Jimmy thought, but tough men who killed people and spoke their minds.

"Ever heard of Ernie Hemingway?" Uncle Jerry once asked Crawford, speaking of the novelist as if he were a close friend. "He used to kill big game in Africa and wrestle large Negroes when he wasn't writing. That's the kind of man *he* was," he once said without explanation.

"Why did he kill big game? Why wrestle Negroes, Uncle Jerry?" Crawford asked.

Uncle Jerry's response was equally arcane. "Because he had to."

Crawford had thought that killing a lion was perhaps a favorite pastime for writers, but he was pretty sure Uncle Jerry had never killed one, though he might have wrestled a Negro.

Every morning, young Crawford would get up at dawn and ride his bicycle to the *Daily Press* and receive his parcel. After he neatly tucked the papers in his side bag, Crawford would feverishly pedal towards the eight square blocks that made up his route. And every morning Crawford threw every *Daily Press* with the gravity of a professional pitcher struggling to wrap up the ninth inning. But on Tuesdays and Fridays, when Uncle Jerry's *Prattle-Tattle* appeared on the second page, it was the World Series of paper delivery. Every paper had to be *at least* on the walkway, if possible on the front steps. No driveways, and certainly no yards. The wisdom Uncle Jerry was bestowing could not be hindered by a clumsy delivery, so young Crawford imagined he was a pitcher in the World Series or even Paul Revere peddling like a revolution depended on it. That was until one very unusual *Prattle-Tattle* hit the walkways.

It was just after his morning route. Jimmy's mother was in the kitchen peeling potatoes for a casserole she was making for a church gathering that evening. The *Daily Press* lay open on the kitchen table. As usual the words *Nitpicky Nick* jumped off the page — as did the words "Was Hitler Wrong about Everything? Nick Thinks Not."

Mother Crawford was peeling quickly, nervously watching the backyard as if an intruder might appear on that ordinary Tuesday morning.

"How was your route, dear?"

"Same. I only had to get off my bike once and throw again."

"That's good, dear," she said.

Young Jim read the first line in the body of the essay: "Even a broken clock is right twice a day. Am I right?"

"This is today's?" Crawford asked.

"Yes," his mother said mechanically before letting out a hefty moan. "I don't know why Jerry thinks he has to say *everything* on his mind. I thought that business about the death penalty for reefer smokers and homosexuals was bad enough."

"What's a homosexual?"

"Oh, never mind," she said, returning to her potatoes. "Shouldn't you be getting ready for school?"

Young Crawford scanned the page.

"Hitler was trying to protect German culture from those who were assertively trying to change it, most notably Jews and Gypsies. Can we blame him for..."

"Mom, what's a Jew?" young Crawford asked.

"Jesus was a Jew," his mother snapped back. "Why don't you get ready for school?" Crawford couldn't understand his mother's irritation.

And Uncle Jerry wouldn't either. Jerry certainly couldn't understand why Ed was so mad. Apparently Ed Proctor, the editor of the *Daily Press*, had gotten so cozy with Uncle Jerry that he had stopped asking to review each article before it went to print. Only the proofreader would see it, and she was an elderly deaf woman who couldn't speak a word. Uncle Jerry's article "Was Hitler Wrong about Everything?" would end *Prattle-Tattle* forever, and with the help of Ed Proctor, it died with a whimper.

As well-liked in the community as Uncle Jerry was, as open as they were to criticisms of "non-Christians" and "non-native-born Americans," a sympathetic take on Hitler went too far.

It was strange to Jimmy how Uncle Jerry's personality changed after the incident. As one lady at church had put it, he seemed to have lost his confidence. He no longer walked into a room with the command of a decorated colonel. The man who had once told Crawford "You can get people to believe anything as long as you act like you believe it" didn't seem to believe in himself any more.

Jimmy Crawford's job as a paperboy officially ended two weeks later when Uncle Jerry decided to go out to his utility shed in the backyard of his home early on a Sunday morning and put a Ruger Mark II 22 (*American made since 1949*) in his mouth and pull the trigger. At the funeral, one of Uncle Jerry's drinking buddies told Crawford that Jerry had died "just like Ernest Hemingway — with his boots on." The fact that they were blood-stained boots from his own gun didn't seem to matter. "He went the way he wanted," the man said.

"I guess so," young Crawford replied.

Crawford wouldn't discover until a few years later, when he read a Hemingway biography, that the man at Uncle Jerry's funeral was probably referring to Hemingway's suicide. Crawford had always assumed that Hemingway had been killed by a lion while loading his gun or something. Maybe he had been wrestled to death by a large Negro. But the young Crawford thought that he understood Hemingway's decision to end his life, and after reading the infamous drinking stories, particularly those in Cuba, Crawford's burgeoning picture of what a "writer" really is was finally complete — tough men who drink hard and live hard and kill animals until they finally kill themselves. End of story.

A great paradox was that Crawford never learned to appreciate Hemingway's writing. Much of it seemed lackluster and pointless — with intermittent commercials about what was right and good. But what Crawford did learn to love was the idea of Hemingway, the idea of the guy who created and destroyed with a cocktail in his hand, then won a Nobel Prize less than a decade before ending his life. Poor Uncle Jerry wanted to be Hemingway, but he only got one part right.

And how silly, Crawford now thought. The idea of Hemingway — the idea of trying to be Hemingway. It's as silly as Hitler riding in a motorcade and trying to be... well... Hitler. And oddly some people thought Hitler was right, even if it was just about "a few things."

Yes, we worship the famous. We worship the prominent. We worship them because we know the world can't be filled with winners; mostly it has to be filled with losers — people who shine shoes and deliver papers. It's just the way it is. We worship the famous (from the world-famous to just the locally-famous) simply because they are famous — famous and therefore beyond our small, little lives. We read about them. We think about them. We defer to them even when we know they are just human beings, even when we know they are wrong, all because they have the will to appear to be right, to be "with it," to be "on it," whatever. Most of them are idiots like the rest of us, and they probably know that more than anyone. The only difference is that they're too damn stupid to admit it. Or too smart — whatever the case may be.

Uncle Jerry was just too stupid.

Crawford put his foot down on the accelerator and rolled down his window.

"Hey!" Crawford yelled at the paperboy. "Hey you!" he said, pulling the car to the curb next to him.

The boy stopped his bike and stared at Crawford. "What do you want, mister?"

Crawford put the car in park. "You know that job you have isn't so important."

The boy looked taken aback. "Sorry?"

"Throwing those papers is not such a big deal, you know. It's just a job. It doesn't mean a thing."

The boy looked at the ground, then reached inside his side bag and pulled out a paper.

"Besides," Crawford continued, "it's all bullshit in those papers."

Carefully he took the rubber band off a paper before unfolding it. "Mister?" the paperboy said with trepidation. "Is this you?"

The boy held up the front page. There was a picture of Crawford in mid-hurl.

Self-Help Writer Loses It on Hershey.

Crawford unlatched his briefcase and pulled out the bottle of Scotch. With his thumb and forefinger he unscrewed the lid and carefully placed in on the dash. He brought the bottle neatly to his lips, then, after taking a deep breath, poured himself a mouthful.

The boy took a step back from the car.

After putting the bottle down, Crawford exhaled as if coming out of unfathomably deep water — eyes wide open, mouth protruding, dribbling Old Arkansan.

Crawford turned to the kid, with watering eyes, still trying to catch his breath. "Yeah, kid. That's me." Crawford put the lid back on the bottle and put the bottle in the briefcase. He put the car in gear. "Just don't take your job too seriously, okay kid?"

"Sure, no problem," the boy said.

Only a mind diseased by alcohol would stop to give advice to a paperboy while his wife and son are being held prisoner by a psycho who thinks he's the host of a children's show.

Crawford was worried about what he would say to Peters, especially considering Peters' inclination to downplay panic. But Crawford was panicking for good reason, and how to communicate that was a real problem.

Crawford reached Santa Monica Boulevard, the boundary that symbolized his departure from the cocoon of Beverly Hills, and opened the bottle again, pouring a liberal amount into his stainless steel coffee cup.

Normally, Crawford would have taken North Beverly Drive to Cannon to West Sunset to get to the University, but he decided to take an alternate route. At first he rationalized that driving south would reduce the chance of being pulled over by the cops. But he needed to give himself extra time to think about what he would say to Peters. He decided to drive south on South Beverly Glen until he got to Wilshire, then head north just before the 405.

That part of Wilshire Boulevard always reminded Crawford of his drinking days in college — those *glorious* drinking days of long ago, the undergrad days, days unregulated by worry or guilt or the responsibilities that caused them. Wilshire had a little joint called the Backwoods Bar that was a popular hangout among psychology undergrads at the time. It created feelings of nostalgia for Crawford simply because it was the first time he gave a reading of his own material. Crawford composed a humorous piece based on *Maslow's Hierarchy of Needs* that he shared with his lowly undergrads at the Backwoods, and it was an inspiring success — something that would give him a source of encouragement for years to come.

In the middle of "H.H." (what the psychology crowd called happy hour), with two-dollar pitchers of beer scattered on a long wooden table,

Crawford, already drunk with beer in hand, stood in front of his class-mates like an Irish captain addressing a boardroom of ragtag sailors in-side the belly of a ship.

"If I could have your attention," he opened, clearing his throat for effect. "I would like to read to you a new paper I'm going to publish in the *Hogwash Journal of Clinical Psychology*.

Many laughed and cheered, some raised their glasses.

"I'm published in that fucker," Dax Davis, a research student, yelled.

"Yeah, me too. So what?" someone else added.

"Please let me begin," Crawford said, holding up the scribble-ridden notebook paper. "I would like to present James Crawford's *Inverted* Hi-erarchy of Needs... *for Drunks*."

The eleven psychology majors responded merrily, no doubt satu-rated with the "mandatory reading" phase of their psychology degrees.

"As you know, my long-time associate, Abraham Maslow, estab-lished a theory that human needs are hierarchical and can be divided into five categories. This, of course, was a radical departure from the two shining examples of establishment genius: Sigmund Freud and B.F. Skinner."

A few booed.

One yelled, "Better known as Sigmund *Fraud* and *Bullshit Fucking* Skinner."

"Now, now. Behave yourselves," Crawford continued. "Let's start by reviewing Maslow's groundbreaking work."

"Let's not," the very nonacademic Cecil Jameson said.

"Firstly, we have physiological needs. This category is probably the best example of Maslow's genius, pointing out that we need food, water, and shelter."

"And beer!" someone yelled.

"Hold on; I'll get to that momentarily. Then second, as Maslow points out, we need safety: the need to be free from physical danger."

"Lions and tigers and bears," one guy yelled before everyone in unison shouted, "Oh my!"

"Category three is the social need, our need to be accepted, to be loved..."

"To get laid!" yelled Albert McLaughlin, known for his active sex life.

"What about a hug from your mother? That's what he was talk-ing about," Crawford said straight-faced to McLaughlin before taking a drink. "Then we have," he said flipping a page, "ego needs, esteem needs. To be appreciated. To have status. To have responsibilities and achieve things."

"Heave things! Leave things!" another guy yelled, sitting down with a fresh pitcher.

"Fuck that noise. I'm on a roll here," Crawford said, taking another drink. "Then, of course, Maslow's last hierarchy of need: Self-Actualization — the need to achieve one's growth." Then speaking with a schoolmaster's elocution, "to *the fullest potential*."

Surprisingly, there were no comedic jeers from this statement. Crawford felt a little uneasy but continued.

"Now I submit that for drunks there's a different hierarchy, a hierarchy that goes backward. Inverted, if you will. Now let's take a look," Crawford said, again flipping a page. "Self-actualization. Drunks first start drinking for reasons of personal growth. You're a teenager. You're tired of video games and feeling up your friend's sister — it's time to get fucked up. Right?"

"Yeah," the group yelled.

"And why?"

"Because it's there?" someone yelled.

"No. Because that's what *adults* do, correct? It's time to reach your fullest potential as a teen and finally become an adult. It's the only goal you have as a teenager, right? And how do you become an adult? You drink. Boom, mission accomplished. You're drunk; you're there. Next we have ego and esteem needs. It turns out that you meet women, or perhaps men, depending on your preference, and you feel a little less confident than you did sticking your finger in the pimple-faced girl down the block. The drinker needs an ego boost! So what does he do?" Crawford furrowed his brow and gave a sinister look. "He drinks more. And more and more. Next you feel like Burt fucking Reynolds. Correct? You're suave and debonair. There you go, category two."

"Albert's reached that one," Cecil yelled.

"No argument from me, Jameson," McLaughlin said.

"Then category three comes along: social needs. Hey, you're a seasoned drinker now. You don't need to get drunk to feel comfortable around others — not all the time. You've already established a group of friends based on your lifestyle, and that group of friends dictates things like social gatherings, like..."

"Like happy hour at Backwoods!"

"That's right." Crawford said pointing. "Drinking becomes a social requirement — not just an ego need but a social need. "

"I don't need this shit," someone said.

"Let me finish," Crawford said, referencing the manuscript. "And fourthly, we have security and safety. After a few years of social drinking, it's true that you no longer feel secure unless you have a drink in your hand. Right?"

"I know I don't," said Taffy Christian, a timid guy from New Orleans.

"This is not something that you need for social gatherings or to create courage among hot chicks; you need it like a warm coat in winter time. You need it like the roof over your head and the lock on your door. You need it just to know it's there because it makes you feel safe. Correct?"

"Amen, brother."

"And last but not least — the last category of *James Crawford's Hierarchy for Drunks* — the physiological need."

There were a few accusatory "oohs" after that one.

"It's a physiological need, all right."

"That's right, brethren. Don't pretend like you don't know what I mean. This is what I like to call *the hair of the dog* need."

That one got a few laughs.

"It's no longer a self-actualization need — your drinking has been actualized. It's no longer an ego need — you don't even have an ego left to nourish. It's not a social need — everyone is sick of your drunk ass. It's not a security need — you're securely shitfaced all the time. You need a drink," he said pointing to the group, "because," he paused, "you really need one! You need it like the air you breathe and the food you used to eat. You need it because it is now *required*."

A strange silence fell on the room as the group contemplated what Crawford just said. He looked up from his tattered notebook and gave a solemn nod, and slowly the group began to clap.

"You're going to be huge," one guy said. "You're going to change the fucking world, amigo!"

"I know," Crawford said, taking a drink.

Out of the corner of his eye, Crawford saw the strange *S-shape* he had seen in the video. He realized that this was probably some kind of alcoholic dementia, which raised the question: how was he going to convince Peters that he wasn't just out of his mind on booze? How would he convince him that all of this shit was really happening, that Dorothy and Cal were abducted, and that he needed help? — and not the kind that comes with a straightjacket.

But wait, *I've got the tape. I can show him the tape.*

But what will I say? Watch this tape?

And what will he think about...

Don't anticipate the response of others. Trying to know what others will do is like trying to predict the weather in Oklahoma. It can't be done.

"Hmm," Crawford moaned. "Hmmmm," he moaned again like a mantra, trying to silence the *Self Series* advice that was now sounding like the audio version of the *Self Series which is offered for a limited time at a special low price to those who have purchased the book and...*

"Just keep on truckin'," Crawford told himself.

Just as he had departed the respectable world at Santa Monica Boulevard, the entrance to his old alma mater signaled a return, and Crawford downed the last bit of Scotch in his cup, nodding to the security guard as he passed through the front gate with his mouth still full of Old Arkansan.

Crawford pulled his car into the guest parking lot adjacent to the faculty lot. Since Peters didn't drive a car to work, there was no use in looking for his classic Mercedes. He did see Berry's tastelessly new BMW and Scott's gaudy SUV, but no sign of Peters' rarely driven car. The way his luck was going, he would immediately run into Berry and Scott, and Peters would be out of the country. But still, he had to try.

Donning sunglasses that caused slight discomfort against his bruised eyebrow, Crawford decided to slip into the psychology building through a utility entrance he had learned about back in his undergrad years. There was no need to sneak in, other than the problem of walking past the students gathered in front of the building.

It would almost be like high school when I was harassed by all the football players, he thought, *except worse.*

Crawford approached the back door, but just as he reached for the doorknob, someone spoke.

"Hey there."

Crawford froze.

"What the hell do you think you're doing?" said a middle-aged black man standing to the side.

Even the janitor's uniform conveyed authority, and Crawford was at a loss for words. "I'm, uh..."

"You, *uh*, what?" the man mocked, scrutinizing Crawford's sunglasses.

"I'm here to see a friend," Crawford said, peeking over the sunglasses. "Sorry if I..."

The janitor looked Crawford up and down, obviously noting his expensive clothing, and then slowly changed his demeanor. The man realized that Crawford wasn't just another college kid sneaking around where he shouldn't.

"Who are you, man?"

"I'm here to see a friend," Crawford repeated, moving back a step toward a bucket and a mop.

"Careful," the janitor said pointing. "Behind you."

Crawford looked down and saw there was a stain on his pant leg where he had brushed against the bucket.

"Shit," Crawford said. "Look at that."

"Oh, sorry about that, sir," the janitor said, moving toward the bucket. "Let me move that out' your way." About two feet away from Crawford, the man reached over to move the bucket then stopped, looking up at Crawford. "You drunk?" he asked.

Crawford paused with embarrassment and considered how quickly people can identify someone who has been drinking.

But then he thought of his wife and son *and why is it that I give a shit what this stupid caretaker is saying to me?*

"Yeah, I'm drunk," he said with irritation. "Anything else?"

"No, sir," the man capitulated. "Dr. Crawford, sir," he added. "Who was it you were here to see, sir?" he said with an exaggerated smile.

"Dr. Phillip Peters, head of the department," he said, stepping toward the door.

"Right this way, sir."

The man led Crawford through the door and up the steps leading to Peters' office.

"I can find it myself. Thanks," he said, dismissing the man coldly. The man just stood and smiled as Crawford walked away rapidly past the hallway that led to Berry and Scott's offices and down the hall leading to Peters'. He rubbed his brow with his knuckles to avoid being recognized by the passing students and it seemed to work.

Not surprisingly, Peters' office was calm and quiet, which made Crawford's nerves beg to explode. Peters' young office assistant was reading a novel that looked epic against her pink tie-dyed tank top. There was a box of cookies sitting on the desk next to her, with a single cookie lying on a napkin with a bite taken. Crawford had met this girl a few times before and didn't like her. He especially didn't want to see her in his current condition.

He tried to smile as he approached, and she looked up with her routine authoritative look.

"Yes, Dr. Crawfords?" she said, putting down her novel. "Can I help you?"

She always called him Dr. Crawfords with an *s* for some reason, even though it was practically a household name. Crawford looked down at the dog-eared copy of *Atlas Shrugged*.

"Dr. Peters? Is he here? It's important."

"Not here," she said abruptly.

"What?"

"Not. Here."

Bitch. "Know when he'll be back? It's important."

"Nope," she said shaking her head. Then she reached for the half-eaten cookie.

Crawford gazed down at the girl's woven bracelets, then at her pale skin, then the sweat stains under her arms, then her mouth gobbling up the cookie. He felt sick.

"Where is he?" Crawford said, coughing into his fist. "I need to know."

"He's moving to his new office today. He's the dean now, you know."

"I know he's the dean," Crawford snapped. "Is that where he is, at his new office?"

"No. He's still packing things here," she said, returning to her book.

"Okay, well where is he?" Crawford said curtly.

With an agitated smile she said, "Actually, I don't know. He's been gone all afternoon."

"I'll wait for him inside," Crawford said, stumbling past her. His briefcase bumped her desk and the bottle inside made its presence known.

"Doctor. I think maybe..." she said, standing.

Crawford swiftly walked into Peters' office and grabbed the door to close it. "I'll wait inside."

The girl put her hand to the door with a concerned expression on her face. "Are you okay, Doctor?"

"I'm fine."

"I saw what happened yesterday on the Jan Hershey show, and I just want to say..."

Crawford slammed the door shut then leaned against it. He took a deep breath and then another. The room was dark and quiet and felt comforting. He put his briefcase on Peters' desk and opened it. He took a drink from the bottle and its warmness agreed with him. He returned the bottle to its hiding place then looked upon the assortment of boxes and books that now surrounded him — Peters' personal library. There was a pile of *Contemporary Psychology* magazines covering a stack of boxes neatly labeled "RESEARCH," while another box had "DISPERSE" hastily hand-written on the side.

The disperse box was inexplicable to Crawford, especially since Peters never parted with any of his books — not ever, not a single one. It hadn't been but a few months before that Crawford had come across a copy of George Combe's *Elements of Phrenology* in Peters' office and realized it was the same one Peters had bought at a conference they'd attended years before. Another time Crawford had borrowed a copy of

How We Think by John Dewey and didn't return it. While Peters was over at Crawford's for a dinner party a year later, he politely asked if the Dewey volume was still helping with his current writing project. Crawford apologized, and Peters gladly collected. Peters never left a book behind, never.

Maybe "disperse" meant something else. It appeared to be the only box not taped shut, so Crawford figured he might as well take a look inside. There was a book sitting on top of the first flap that looked old, but not ancient — obviously one of Peters' psychology books that he had forgotten to pack until the last minute. Crawford opened it to the first page.

```
    Psychology in a Culture of Vanity
         by Dr. Alexander Ugelowski
```

Ugelowski? Who is that? I've heard that name. Crawford stuck his thumb halfway through the book and began to read.

```
The modern man of the twentieth century can-
not surrender himself to principles of love
and self-sacrifice, even for the future good
of his family or community, for he lives in a
"psychological" age where principles of "al-
truism" — outside its therapeutic significance
as an emotional resource — are oppressive and
even offensive to the more sophisticated sci-
entific mind.
```

God, what the fuck is this?

```
Beset with depression, apprehension, insignif-
icance, and a confusing despondency, the mod-
ern man, having long evolved beyond religious
conviction, still hopes to find a contemporary
counterpart to faith's redemptive peace of
mind. As a result, the last enduring holy man
has to be a "scientist" by classification — a
role in modern times only the "therapist" has
license to assume.
```

When Crawford read the word "therapist" it looked like "the rapist." He batted his eyes to thwart the hallucination then thumbed ahead. He inserted his finger at random and began reading again.

```
Modern psychological therapy teaches the pa-
tient, sometimes by association, that he is
```

```
eternally disconnected from the great stream
of mankind and that this isolation has for-
ever existed; it is only now he has evolved
into an awareness of it. Trained to disconnect
with the great mystery of his own being, the
patient's view becomes solipsistic, trampling
the notion of an existence outside an individ-
ualism of here and now. The modern therapist
then rationalizes that the patient's psycho-
logical liberation can only come from aggres-
sively defeating what were once considered
natural inhibitions and by immediately grati-
fying every impulse, regardless of the long-
term consequences. The therapist then teaches
the patient that the key to all his problems
is a lack of mental aplomb and emotional self-
assurance. In short, it's all just a matter of
self-esteem.
```

"Self-esteem" was underlined. The only word on the page underlined, the only mark in the book he had seen. Crawford thumbed ahead
to see if he could find other marks in the book but found nothing. He kept
turning pages. Turning, turning, turning. Nothing. Then...

```
As psychological therapy concentrates its ef-
forts on the vague concept of "self-esteem"
```

Again, "self-esteem" was underlined, and again, Crawford thumbed
ahead.

```
self-esteem
```

Underlined in two places. He thumbed ahead.

```
as "self-esteem" rather than "self-respect"
becomes the gauge by which the therapist com-
municates a sense of
```

Underlined once. He thumbed back.

```
self-esteem
```

Again, neatly underlined. Crawford ran his fingers along the fore-edge
of the book. Again and again, it looked like Peters had underlined them all.
Perhaps it was someone else.
Crawford turned again to the title page and found the book was published the same year his first book was published.

What a coincidence.

Crawford looked at the door, wondering if he should question the secretary about the book. But the words he had read were now drawing his attention.

Ugelowski, where have I heard that name?

Then it came to him. The strange imbalance between an alcoholic's neurotransmitters and synapses — which can sometimes produce the memory of an insignificant incident years ago while blocking the memory of one's own name — now produced a small bio of Alexander Ugelowski.

```
Dr. Alexander Ugelowski: a Polish scientist
who advocated that popular psychology, if un-
stopped, would trigger the end of modern civi-
lization and consequently the world.
```

Hmmm.

That's right. He thought it would drive us all crazy. Then he lost his mind and killed himself. I think.

Or was that just Uncle Jerry?

The brief tranquility he had found in Peters' office now turned to dread. Crawford slowly opened the remaining two flaps on the box, and what he found calmed him like a shot of booze.

Garbage.

Garbage! It was just a box of garbage.

Crawford snickered for show, even though no one else was there to see it. That's why Peters' had the book in here; it's just garbage — empty boxes and empty wrappers. And shitty little books. It's just garbage.

Crawford took out his trusty bottle. "I've been overreacting my whole life," he said, taking a small sip. "Maybe I don't have a drinking problem," he said.

Didn't someone abduct your wife and son?

Are you overreacting to that? he thought.

He put the bottle down and looked into the box again. He slowly stuck his hand in and picked up one of the empty wrappers.

"Duct tape," he said, fingering the wrapper. *Hmmm.*

He threw it back in the box and picked up more debris.

"Kitchen Knives. Set of Three."

He fumbled through the box again, this time a little faster.

"Videotape," he muttered to himself, his hand involuntarily reaching for the bottle. "Unopened, blank."

Videotape?

Crawford took a fierce swig then slammed the bottle on the desk.

No.

Shit, what are you thinking, Crawford?

"No way."

Crawford stood back from the box and saw something round. Something *red*. It looked like a red moon eclipsed by white plastic. There was something very familiar about that one inch of curved red. Crawford's heart was now racing, fed by a stream of adrenaline pouring down the back of his spine, through his guts, into his groin.

Knock, knock! Who's there?

Before Crawford could register the pounding on the door, he instinctively turned to face the light, finding Peters' secretary clutching her copy of *Atlas Shrugged* with an odd expression on her face, like she was also frightened by his frenzied thought.

"Dr. Crawfords," she said nervously.

"What?"

"Have you ever read any Ayn Rand?"

"Huh?" he said.

"I said..."

Crawford looked back into the box and, seizing upon a fleeting moment of courage, grabbed the red object and hid it in his hand in one swift movement.

It was a red *rubber nose* that looked like it had been torn from a mask — torn frantically, as in an act of violence.

My God.

"Ever read any Ayn Rand?" she said.

"Never heard of him," Crawford mumbled, shaking his head with bewilderment. He slowly turned to the girl. "Bitch," he whispered.

"What?"

"I mean..."

"Well, fine!" she bellowed.

"No, not you!" he said, raising his hand to catch her before she walked out. "Wait. I need to talk to you."

His urgency got her attention. "You need to talk to *me*?"

"Tell me something. What is all this stuff? The box here," Crawford said.

"It's Dr. Peters' stuff."

"What stuff?"

"You know, just his stuff."

"What's this box for? It says 'disperse' on it."

She glanced at the box. "No, it says 'dispense', Dr. Crawfords."

Crawford took another step toward her, and in tandem she backed away.

"What are these things?"

Crawford sensed the girl could tell he was drunk.

"I don't know," she said defensively. "Just leave me alone, okay."

"Leave you alone?"

"Is everything okay, Dr. Crawfords?"

"By the way, it's *Crawford*. With no *s*," he said.

"Sorry," she said.

"Where is Peters?"

The flimsy confidence the girl had shown behind her desk was now gone. "Where is he?" Crawford yelled.

"He hasn't been here. He hasn't been here in two days," she said, almost starting to cry.

"Why not?"

"I don't know," she confessed. "He told me not to tell anyone. He just said he'd be gone. That's all he said."

"Have you noticed anything, I don't know, *odd* about the doctor recently?"

"Odd? Like odd how?"

"Oh, fuck it. Never mind." Crawford put the rubber nose in one of his pants pockets then placed the bottle of Scotch carefully back in the briefcase. The small yellow piece of paper with the scribbled S-shape sat in one corner as if frightened by its creator. Crawford grabbed it and unfolded it. He looked at it again, then held it up to...

"What's your name?" he asked.

"Winter."

"Winter? Like the season?"

"No, with a *y* instead of an *i*. But pronounced the same."

"Okay, Wynter. Have you ever seen this shape before?" Crawford held up the paper. "It's a symbol or something, right?"

Wynter looked scared. "I don't know what that is," she said slowly, averting her eyes to the floor.

"You're not looking at it. Look! Have you seen it?" he said, holding it closer.

"What is it?" she said warily, taking a step back.

"I don't know. It's an *S* with a smiley face at the bottom. Have you seen that before?"

"It kind of looks like the Sammy's Cookie logo. But it's not written neat enough."

"Not neat enough?" Crawford said, looking at it. "What do you mean?"

"It's sloppy. It kind of looks like the Sammy's Cookie logo, but..."

"Yeah, yeah," he interrupted. "What's Sammy's Cookies?"

She raised her hand revealing a half-eaten cookie. "This is a

Sammy's cookie."

Crawford put the note and the copy of *Psychology in a Culture of Vanity* in his briefcase and closed it. "What do you know about these Sammy's cookies?"

"They're really good, especially with milk. Wanna try?" she said, again holding up the cookie.

"That box on your desk, are those Sammy's cookies?"

"Yes."

Crawford brushed past her into the reception area. He put his suitcase on her desk and flipped over the box top.

Sammy's Cookies, We keep you smiling! And sure enough, just above the bottom of the *S* were two small dots that formed a smile at the bottom.

"That's it."

"That's what?" Wynter said, looking over Crawford's shoulder.

Crawford turned around and grabbed Wynter by the shoulders. "Where are these cookies made?"

"I don't know," she said pulling back. "Take your hands off me."

"Where are they made?"

"I don't know! I just eat the cookies. I don't work for the company or anything."

Crawford turned around and turned the cookie box over, dumping the contents onto the floor next to the desk.

"Hey! I was supposed to share those with the other girls."

"Shut up," Crawford said. "This is a matter of life and death. This thing have Internet access?" he asked, pointing to the computer on the girl's desk.

"Yes," Wynter said.

"Sit," he said, grabbing the chair and shoving it under her round bottom. "I want to know where these cookies are made, why they're made. I don't know, anything you can find out about them. And I need it in a hurry."

Wynter looked at Crawford as if he were demented. She tried to remain calm. "I know where you can buy some if you really want..."

"Please hurry!"

The girl did as she was told, pulling up a list from a search engine. "'Buy Sammy's Cookies in Bulk,' will that help?"

"No, I don't want to buy any. Where are they made?"

"Let's see," she said, her fingers typing swiftly. "Corporate Headquarters in Louisville, Kentucky."

"Where are they made?"

Wynter typed franticly. "Doesn't say."

"Well, keep trying."

As the girl continued to type, Crawford backed against the wall behind him. What would he do now? He was in the office of the dean of psychology demanding cookie information. Surely, this was going to land him in jail or in the nut house or both. There was nothing left to do but go to the police and risk the consequences. If they weren't going to suspect him of foul play before, they surely would now. And what would the psycho do if he found out Crawford had gone to the police? Would he slaughter Dorothy and Cal like pigs? *Don't think such things.* Like he killed Jenny. *No!* Did he kill Jenny in the first place? Crawford looked at his trembling hand then at the briefcase on the desk.

I'll go to the police. But I'll get good and drunk first.

"The company was founded here. They used to be made right here in southern California."

"Huh?" Crawford said, back in the moment. "What did you say?"

"Sammy's Cookies started right here in southern California, in Gardena."

"Gardena?"

Wynter read the information like a sixth-grader reading a class report, trying her best to impress the teacher. "Sammy's Cookies was established in 1927 in Gardena, California, and prospered there for 22 years until the factory on West Rosecrans and Paxton Avenue was damaged by an electrical fire that..."

"Rosecrans and Paxton. Can you make me a map to that location?"

"I know where Rosecrans is. You just take the 405 south..."

"Make me a map please. Please hurry."

Wynter clicked away and soon pages were coming out of the printer next to Wynter's desk. It felt like a turning point; it felt like hope. And the first thing Crawford thought was that it called for a drink. He eyed his briefcase once more, thinking that Gardena could be a lengthy trip, depending on the traffic.

Wynter held up the two printed pages.

"Thank you," he said, grabbing the pages. He clutched his briefcase and started for the door without looking back.

"Dr. Crawford," Wynter said.

"Yes?" he said turning to her.

"Are you gonna tell me what this is all about?"

"No. I don't know what it's all about."

"Isn't that just the way life is sometimes?" she said, nodding. Crawford could swear he heard Jan Hershey once say exactly the same thing. Crawford turned around and walked out.

As soon as the door closed, Wynter picked up the phone.

NINETEEN

D r. Crawford's Self-Esteem Quiz™ — *Version 3.2*

Please note that the results of this male-only Self-Esteem Quiz, while intended to be analytical, are not entirely scientific.

The Quiz consequently does not precisely determine your level of self-esteem. To verify your level of self-esteem with the greatest degree of accuracy, you should seek an evaluation from a qualified *Self Series™* therapist in conjunction with further study of Dr. Crawford's *Self Series™* books and recordings.

Please respond to the following statements as honestly as possible.

1. I contemplate what other people think of me, even while alone.

    - ☐ Constantly   [5]
    - ☐ Frequently   [4]
    - ☐ Occasionally   [3]
    - ☐ Rarely   [2]
    - ☐ Never   [1]

2. I feel uneasy with the choices I make.

    - ☐ Constantly   [5]
    - ☐ Frequently   [4]
    - ☐ Occasionally   [3]
    - ☐ Rarely   [2]
    - ☐ Never   [1]

3. I consider my friends and work associates to be better than I am in every way, especially in appearance, intelligence, decency, dependability, honesty, and talent.

- ☐ Constantly [5]
- ☐ Frequently [4]
- ☐ Occasionally [3]
- ☐ Rarely [2]
- ☐ Never [1]

4. I seem to hate everything I do.

- ☐ Constantly [5]
- ☐ Frequently [4]
- ☐ Occasionally [3]
- ☐ Rarely [2]
- ☐ Never [1]

5. I feel like I could snap at any moment and do something really, really bad.

- ☐ Constantly [5]
- ☐ Frequently [4]
- ☐ Occasionally [3]
- ☐ Rarely [2]
- ☐ Never [1]

6. My sexual fantasies suggest an underlying resentment and hostility toward myself and others.

- ☐ Constantly [5]
- ☐ Frequently [4]
- ☐ Occasionally [3]
- ☐ Rarely [2]
- ☐ Never [1]

7. I can't stand people.

- ☐ Constantly [5]
- ☐ Frequently [4]
- ☐ Help Me [3]
- ☐ Rarely [2]
- ☐ Never [1]

8. I can't stand myself.

    ❒   Constantly   [5]
    ❒   Frequently   [4]
    ❒   I'm Tired   [3]
    ❒   Rarely   [2]
    ❒   Never   [1]

9. I say "Fuck it."

    ❒   Constantly   [5]
    ❒   Frequently   [4]
    ❒   And Alone   [3]
    ❒   Rarely   [2]
    ❒   Never   [1]

10. I say "Fuck it all!"

    ❒   Constantly   [5]
    ❒   Frequently   [4]
    ❒   Lord, Please   [3]
    ❒   Rarely   [2]
    ❒   Never   [1]

Evaluation

A score of 10 through 25: [Self-esteem too high] You're probably an annoying asshole who either likes yourself too much or likes life too much or both. Do us all a favor and bring it down a notch or two.

A score of 26 through 40: [Self-esteem too... who the hell knows?] You're one of those lackluster people that can't make up your mind about anything, so you answer "occasionally" to everything. Why don't you "occasionally" get a fucking life?

A score of 41 through 50: [Self-esteem too low... Just kidding.] You're a normal human being; get over it. The only decent people in the world are the ones who feel like living pieces of shit most of the time. Congratulations!

• • •

Crawford hurried to his car. The burden of constantly evaluating his behavior was a self-inflicted wound that wouldn't stop bleeding.

"Fuck it," he mumbled under his heavy breath. *Fuck it all.*

The 120-degree heat of the interior came pouring out in one large wave, hitting him in the face. He climbed in and started the car, putting the windows down slightly, waiting for the air conditioner to make it tolerable. The heat was agonizing, but his mind drifted elsewhere. Each time a new bead of sweat made its way down his forehead, his thoughts went from one of his self-help tenets to the next. This was the same problem he had while trying to write prose: he couldn't get it out of his head.

Are you getting enough sleep?

Well, try apologizing to your wife.

If you imagine you are successful, say I'm okay!

They work!

"Fuck it."

Crawford reached into his pocket with trembling hands and grabbed the red nose, putting his finger along the jagged edge. The irregularity of what could have been a tear almost felt good — something uneven, unplanned; something simple and spontaneous, like real life. He put the piece of rubber over his nose, pressing the sticky surface hard to his clammy beak.

Real life.

The car was starting to feel tolerable and Crawford put up the windows.

"A cookie factory," he said to himself. "An abandoned cookie factory?"

I hate cookies.

As Crawford reached to put the car in gear, standing just across the parking lot not a hundred yards away were Dr. Berry and Dr. Scott.

Collectively known as B.S.

They were standing close to each other next to Scott's monstrous SUV, looking like children at a playground trading secrets. Crawford looked at their curled up noses, their smirking grins, Scott's confident, shrugging shoulders. Y*es, they're probably behind all of this. Probably payback for my success.* Crawford slipped the car into gear and thought he might just run both of them over. *Yeah, maybe that will remedy this whole situation,* he thought. *I'll tell the police the whole story. Blame it on them. I'll say I was crazed with anger and couldn't help myself. They were harassing me.*

Indulge yourself on occasion!

"Shut the fuck up!" he shouted.

The two men turned their heads as if on cue, staring straight at

Crawford as if they'd heard him yell. *But they couldn't have.* Berry put his flattened fingers to his forehead to block the sun.

"That's just like them. Acting like they've been distracted from something important. Yeah, some really important bullshit. Fuckers!"

As impulsively as slamming a shot of whiskey, Crawford stomped on the gas and the car screeched in reverse, snapping his head into the steering wheel as if the back of his neck had been abruptly slapped. Then just as abruptly, his head slammed back against the headrest.

"Son of a bitch." The red rubber nose was stuck to the steering wheel. Crawford quickly put the rubber nose back on then looked behind him to discover he had backed up into the side of a parked car. A black car. A black BMW with a new temporary tag in the window. Berry's new BMW.

Crawford pounded the gearshift into drive and slowly pulled the car forward, which came with sounds of broken plastic crunching and metal bending. Crawford stopped and looked. He had put a large dent on the driver's side, from the back door to the rear bumper.

Crawford looked straight ahead and could see that Berry was curling up his prickly nose with disbelief. Scott had stopped shrugging and was now shaking his head. Berry appeared to take an acquiescent deep breath, and the two men started toward the collision.

They both looked taken aback, *but are they?*

Crawford admired himself in the mirror, straightening the rubber nose on his face. After putting the car back in reverse, he put the window down on the driver's side and stuck his head out.

"Crawford?" Berry said. "What are you doing? What the hell is on your..."

"Hello, gentlemen," he called out with a smile. "Didn't think I'd run into you." Crawford put his head back inside and stomped on the gas again, this time ramming into the previously undamaged front quarter.

Berry put his hands to his face as his approach was halted by his shock.

"Are you out of your fucking mind?" Berry yelled.

The red rubber nose slipped a bit and Crawford straightened it a second time. Crawford leaned over and opened the glove compartment. He pulled out his old friend, Uncle Jerry's Ruger. It didn't feel cold any longer. He moved the gun gently to the cleft between the seat and his right thigh. His grip tightened.

Don't do it.
Do what?
I don't know. Kill anyone.
You're not going to kill anyone.

"You're going to pay for that, Crawford!" Berry screamed.

Crawford froze, giving Berry a blank stare. The stare was not deliberate; it just conveyed his feelings.

Let your feelings loose!

I am *letting my feelings loose.*

I have no feelings.

In the absence of fear, I have no feelings.

"What the fuck is on your nose?" Scott was now standing a few
steps behind Berry.

"Yeah. What the hell is that?" Berry demanded.

Again, without calculation, Crawford swung the gun up and out the
window, putting it within inches of Berry's pointy snout.

"You know what the fuck it is. It's a rubber nose. A clown nose!
Okay!" Crawford's hand was shaking, as was Berry's entire body.

"Okay, Jim. Jeez." Berry took a step back, his hands now in the air.
He could barely speak. "Sure, a clown nose. Of course."

"Put your goddam hands down!"

Almost tumbling into the pavement behind him, Scott turned around
and began running toward the psychology building.

"Scott!" Crawford turned the barrel of the gun skyward and fired a
shot. The sound echoed everywhere.

Scott stopped and with his back still facing Crawford, put his hands
up.

"Put your goddam hands *down*, goddam it!" Crawford looked again
at Berry who was now slowly putting his hands to his waist. Crawford
brought the gun back into the car and sat it on his lap. He stared at it
without expression. "Jay?"

Berry could hardly move, even his lips. "Yes, Jim."

"I didn't know it was loaded."

He took a deep breath. "Just relax, Jim."

Crawford looked in Scott's direction. He was still frozen. "Hey, Albert?" he said raising his voice.

"Yeah, Jim." Scott's face was now covered in tears, his hands on
his head.

"I didn't know it was loaded. Please put your hands down."

"Okay, Jim. Can I go now?" His hands didn't move.

Berry took a deep breath and nodded like a prudent old father. "Jim,
why don't you take off the nose and give me the gun?"

"Huh?" Crawford looked past Berry; he looked past Scott, into the
void of bright colors that separated everything from everything. Crawford felt *something* — something *very strong* — something *besides fear*
or *drunkenness*. He felt a *natural* drunkenness, a courage even stronger

than the liquid kind. It was like that moment he had finally reached for the toy radio and clocked the bully all those years ago. It was a moment to seize. It was self-esteem, real self-esteem.

"Why don't you take off the nose, Jim?" Berry said like a psychologist calming an irate patient.

Crawford slowly lifted the gun toward Berry. "Why don't I take the nose off? Because I don't want to take the nose off." Crawford opened the door and got out of the car quickly. He could see Scott starting to blubber.

"Hey, take it easy, buddy," Berry said, again putting his hands up as if he were being robbed.

"Put your goddam hands down and get in the car!"

"What?"

"You too, Albert!" Crawford said, pointing the gun over Berry's shoulder.

"Jay's causing all these problems," Dr. Scott whimpered, pointing at his colleague.

Berry clinched his teeth. "You're such a goddam pussy," he said.

"Shut up! Both of you! Get in the car. In the backseat."

"Really, Jim..." Berry said.

"Now, Albert. In the car."

Crawford reached behind him and opened the back door without turning his back. "Get in, Jay. Albert, you too!"

Dr. Berry took a deep breath and ducked into the backseat.

Dr. Scott started to walk slowly toward the car. "I think this might be something between you and Jay, Jim."

"Please. Call me *Doctor* Crawford," he said, straightening the rubber nose.

Scott started to snivel some more. "Are you going to kill us?"

"I haven't written that part yet."

Berry said, "What the hell does that mean?" sticking his head out of the open door.

Crawford put his free hand on Berry's forehead and shoved him back in. He motioned Scott with the Ruger. "Come on. Hurry up."

"Okay, okay." Scott's reddened eyes were now shedding tears. "Whatever Jay did, I had nothing to do with it."

"Sure," Crawford said, shoving him into the car next to Berry.

Crawford slammed the door then climbed into the driver's seat. "Not a move. I'm warning you," he said into the rearview mirror.

"Where are you taking us?" Berry said.

"You don't know? I think maybe you do."

Berry's pointy nose curled again. "What the hell is this all about,

Crawford? You fuck up my car, now you're taking us by gunpoint some-place? Have you lost your goddam mind?"

Scott put his hand on Berry's knee, "You asked that already. Maybe you should take it easy, Jay."

Crawford put the car into drive. "Shut up! The both of you." Then, with a sly cackle, he put the car back into reverse. "To answer your question, Dr. Berry, yes, I once lost my mind. But now I've found it."

Crawford stomped the gas and slammed the car once more into Berry's BMW.

Crawford laughed. "Sorry Jay, it just feels so good." He looked ahead and saw that there was a small crowd of students staring at him. Three girls and two boys. Had they seen the entire incident? Had they seen him coerce the men into the car with a gun? Would they call the cops? The students started laughing. *Why the hell are they laughing?* Crawford started waving the pistol around. He made crazy faces, widening his eyes and mouth. They laughed even more. "Goddam kids these days. They don't take anything seriously, do they?" he said driving out of the parking lot and through the campus gates.

"You know, I agree with that," Scott said.

I am an interesting person. People are interested in what I have to say.
My inner-voice speaks fondly of myself.
I love my inner-child and my inner-child loves me.
I approve of my inner-adult, and my inner-adult approves of me.
I like being mischievous and playful.
That's what I'm doing right now, being playful.

"I like being mischievous and playful. Oh yes, I do."

"What?" Berry asked.

I have a lot to give the world.
Miracles occur in my life on a daily basis.
I deserve the best.

"I deserve the best."

"What the hell are you mumbling about, Crawford?"

TWENTY

Crawford and his hostages were now close to the 405. The kidnapper gripped the steering wheel determined not to let anything keep him from getting to his destination. Then his mobile phone rang. He put the Ruger between his legs and pulled the phone out of his pants pocket and looked at the number. It was Lee. So this is it, he thought. Good. The kiss-off. Goodbye. *Finally.*

"Yeah?"

"I just want to say one word," Lee said.

It couldn't be fuck off. That's two words.

"What?"

"Cookbook. That is one word, isn't it?"

"What?"

Crawford was now zigzagging through traffic on West Sunset. His two passengers watched the road wide-eyed and silent.

"Cookbook. You know, a recipe book. *Recipe book*? Is that the term they use nowadays, recipe book? I know that's two words. Anyway..."

"What the hell are you talking about, Lee?"

"You just vomited on national television, right?"

"I need to ask you something, Lee."

"Just listen. Jan did this, and it worked. She got fat. She got thin. She started giving dietary advice after she stopped... what do they call it? Yo-yo dieting?"

"I want you to do something, Lee."

"You're not listening to me, Jim. Listen. You vomited on TV because of a poor diet. That's our out and that's our in. Get it? Only the guy who mopped up the vomit knew it was booze and he won't say anything. And if he does we can sue the pants off him, whatever it takes."

"What are you talking about?"

"*The Self Series Cookbook*. I just thought of it. We develop it in the

249

next few months. We get it out in the Fall. Kim's already working on a press release to tell people why you were sick. Look, it's another easy way to get sympathy points, translating into cash. All you have to do..."

"I want you to meet me somewhere right away, understand?"

"But..."

"Shut the fuck up about the goddam cookbook! Listen. You're going to meet me..."

"Meet you? I can't, I'm..."

"If you don't I'm going to kill you, understand?" Crawford could only hear the sound of his own breath.

"I have a meeting," Lee began.

"What? With Kim? Is your secretary taking longhand?"

"Hey now..."

"Get a pen and paper and write down this address. If you aren't there in half an hour, I'm going to tell your wife about Kim's extra duties *then* I'm going to kill you."

"Kill someone?" Scott whimpered from the backseat. "Are you serious?"

"Don't I look serious?" Crawford said, peering into the rearview mirror as he straightened the rubber nose.

"You're threatening me?" Lee groaned. "I've been bullshitting you about Kim. She only gives foot massages."

"Is that right?" Crawford said.

"Hey, what the hell are you doing, Jim?"

"I've got two hostages and I'm on my way to South Central. You're going to be there too. You got a pen? You ready?"

"I..."

"Write down this address. Ready?" he yelled.

"But..."

"I'm serious. Are you ready?"

"Yes, Jim."

"West Rosecrans and Paxton Avenue in Gardena. It's an old cookie factory. Was an old cookie factory. Take the 405 south. No wait, take the Hollywood to the... shit... I don't know. Figure it out! You better be there, Lee."

"Is that where you're taking us?" Berry chimed in. "To a cookie factory?"

"Shut up."

"Who was that?" Lee said.

"I just told you. Be there or pre-pare. Got it?"

"I'll come, okay? I got it," he said. "Just consider the cookbook on your drive so you can give me an answer within..."

Crawford hung up and put the phone back in his pocket. He picked up the gun and gripped the handle.

You'll get an answer all right. We'll all get an answer.

"Sit down and shut up."

There is this old man standing in front of me. He has old-man clothes on and old-man shoes, and they are neat — the way old men wear their old-man clothes. He must have known that he would have to wear these clothes someday, if he were lucky enough to be old someday. "Lord willing," was always his postscript to everything, just like his father. "Lord willing," they both said.

I can't sit up straight or lie down. I feel uncomfortable.

"You think you're unique?" he asks me. "You think you're special?"

"What do you mean," I say. "Of course I'm unique. Aren't we all?"

"I'm dying," he says with a sigh. "I'm dying of cirrhosis," and raises a determined thumbs-up to convey his disgust.

He seems to be ignoring me now. He sits in a swing — like one of those old porch swings Victorian homes in the South have. Surprisingly, his old-man clothes don't look as tidy as they did a moment ago. His face starts to turn from white to gray.

"Many men have killed themselves with drink. That's not unique. You killed me. That's unique."

"I killed you?" I say. "What are you talking about?" I try to sound respectful.

"You killed me with your selfishness."

"I've never killed anyone."

He leans toward me. "You thought your insecurities and fears were like a disease that must be eliminated. You thought they must be removed as if by surgery. That's how you killed me. Your surgery killed me."

His face looks more and more familiar now. He looks like a lot of men in my family — Dad, Grandpa. And a lot of women too, really. The large forehead. The square jaw. Grandma Crawford had a square jaw.

"Are you saying I shouldn't struggle against fear?" I say.

"Of course I'm not saying that. That's one of the things that makes us human. We must have fear as creatures of survival. Fear is necessary. It's a friend to the human race, especially our kind of fear. It's what makes us human. Personal fear in particular." He coughs. "You told yourself it wasn't."

"No I didn't."

"You did. You also told yourself to feel good no matter what you did. You told yourself not to be afraid of what others think. You drank to feel comfortable with yourself. What hogwash. You told yourself to be inconsiderate of others. That's what you said to yourself. What a doctrine of selfishness you've been spreading."

His skin is turning grayer and grayer as his face becomes more familiar, more like my own.

"You don't love life!" he snaps at me before coughing a solid stream of blood that runs down his chin onto his old-man shirt.

I get upset. I start to shake. "Why would I not love life?" I ask sincerely.

"Because you don't love the struggles that are such an important part of life. You don't love the beautiful struggle of life. Therefore you don't love life itself," he says.

The blood on his chin dries and falls in a solid chunk to the floor; a blood bubble separates from his nose and flies away. I'm watching the bubble drift into the air as I look at him. Now he looks likes me. More like I think I look, I guess. *It's me, as an old man, as I imagine him to be.*

"Didn't you wonder what I would think?" he says.

"I didn't," I say.

"I'm the only person you have to answer to."

"How can I do that?"

You already have.

That was inside me for a long time. I had that dream many times. For years I had that dream.

"You were going to write your first novel on dreams, weren't you?" Scott says.

"Please pull over," Berry whimpers. "At least take off that rubber nose!"

Crawford, with his eyes securely on the congestion of the 405, turns the gun back on Berry.

"You read a shitload of Freud, right?"

Berry lowers his eyes then rubs his temples with both hands and shakes his head.

"Answer him," Scott, like a good cop, chimes in.

"Shut up, Albert." Berry's nose curls again. "I was going to write my first novel on dreams, yes."

Crawford puts the gun back in his lap. "And?"

"And I *didn't* reference Freud so much, no."

"You're lying. You did read Frued. I remember that you did. You quoted the fucker every five seconds in college. Remember?"

"Yes, in my undergrad days."

"No, in your grad school days, yes? Answer me, you soulless bitch!"

"That's right," Scott says almost enthusiastically. "Remember? You always talked about Freud."

"Shut up, Albert," Berry says.

"What would Freud say about my dream, Jay?"

"I don't know. I don't know!"

"You told me once, remember?"

"I can't remember."

"Try!" Crawford said, swerving past a long line of cars.

"Holy shit," Berry bellows. "Could you slow down?"

"We have to get to the cookie factory, now. You know that! Answer my question!"

"The old man — is he sitting down?"

"Yes, he is. You know that."

"On what? A porch swing?"

"Yes, I think so."

"And you?"

"I'm sitting in a chair."

"So," Berry says, sitting back, "you're being lifted off the floor. He's being hung from the ceiling. You're on the ground; he's hanging from the sky. You're on a pedestal; he's not."

"So what are you saying, Jay?" Crawford caressed the barrel of the Ruger. "Are you saying you don't know what Freud would say?"

"I don't know. I don't know! Some Freudian shit, I guess."

"How would you like this gun in your mouth? How's that for some Freudian shit?"

"Fuck!" Crawford slammed on the brakes, stopping just short of a collision with a stalled truck. He swerved into the next lane and realized he'd been drifting away — one dream state to the next.

My dreams have to die. My dreams have to be dead.

"What was I saying?"

"You haven't said a goddam thing!" Berry growled.

"Please drive carefully, Jim," Scott added.

Crawford could now see they were near the airport — the three right lanes oozing traffic like ants marching toward a sticky plate. He got on the left side and hit the gas. The traffic was easing up.

"We're going to Gardena, boys. You know that?"

"How the hell would we know that?" Berry said.

"You know where?"

"Of course not," he said.

"You two know all about what has been happening to me, don't you?"

"You're making a big mistake, Jim," Scott said.

"Let's see." Crawford opened his briefcase. There was the Old Arkansan, lying sideways like a satisfied lover. He let the pistol rest against his thigh so he could grab the bottle. "I've got an idea, guys. Why don't we have a little drink?"

"I'm fine thanks," Scott said quickly.

"I think you've had enough already," Berry said.

"You're right. But you haven't." Crawford picked up the bottle then held it up from the bottom with a cupped hand, like he was presenting fine wine in a French restaurant. "Ever had any Old Arkansan?" he asked with an eager announcer's voice as he swerved to miss a slow car.

"Of course fucking not," Berry said. "And be careful."

"Well it's about time," Crawford said, tossing the bottle back to Berry.

"*Old Arkansan?*" Berry read. "I'm not drinking this shit."

Crawford grabbed the gun from next to his thigh and held it up. "Oh yes you are. You think I'm the only one loaded here?"

Berry's eyes widened with astonishment. "Jesus, get some help."

"I'm offering you some help. Take off the cap and drink." He paused a moment, then shaking the gun, "Now!"

Berry looked at the bottle again then took the cap off.

Crawford looked at his red nose in the mirror and turned on the radio. "Maybe this will help? Drink! Drink, you mother..."

A psychedelic Hammond B3.

"Oh, this is good. Like a church."

Duh duh da duh de duh da da da. It was *In-A-Gadda-Da-Vida.*
Who was that? In the Garden of Eden.

"Iron Butterfly," Scott said, as if he heard Crawford's thoughts.

"Oh my God, listen," Crawford said, turning it up. "Drink, Berry!" he yelled.

Berry put the bottle to his lips and raised it slowly, taking a laborious sip. He brought the bottle down and some of the liquid slid down his chin.

Crawford laughed loudly. "Okay, Scott, your turn. Take a big one. Don't be a pussy."

Berry handed the bottle over to Scott, who was less reluctant. He tipped the bottle, taking a drink without a cough or grimace.

"That's right, my boy. All right, Berry, again. And really drink this time. One step at a time!"

Duh duh da duh de duh da da da.

Berry snatched the bottle acrimoniously. "Whatever you say, Doctor!" he mocked before tipping the bottle high this time.

"That's right. That's right."

Berry brought the bottle down coughing, wiping his mouth.

"Nothing you ever drink will taste the same again," Crawford said. "Oh that's us," he said, turning onto the 105.

"Great," Berry said, passing the bottle to Scott. "Great."

"I don't think it's that bad," Scott said, taking another drink before passing it back to Berry.

"I'll have another," Crawford said, reaching the end of the offramp.

"Really, Jim," Berry said.

"Give it to me!"

Berry handed the bottle to Crawford and he took a giant swig.

Duh duh da duh de duh da da da.

"Anybody know the story of this tune?" he asked, passing the bottle back to Berry.

"The story of this tune?" Scott said. Berry tipped the bottle almost as if he wanted to. "Iron Butterfly. Bunch a drugged-out hippies, right?"

"Yeah, who cares," Berry said.

"The guy that wrote this tune was so fucked up he couldn't sing the lyrics — *In the Garden of Eden.* That's what he was trying to sing." Crawford laughed. "In the Garden of Eden." But he was so wasted it came out, "In-A-Gadda-Da-Vida" and they just kept it. Isn't that hilarious?

"Fascinating," Berry said, doing another laborious shot.

"Actually, that's probably a myth," Scott said.

"It doesn't matter if it's true or not. It's ironic, isn't it?" Crawford asked. "I mean, the forbidden fruit. Doing things that promise knowledge. Doing things you shouldn't."

Berry sat back slowly. "That shitty booze is the forbidden fruit," he said with slightly slurred speech. "I don't need any philosophizing to go with it."

"*Duh duh da duh de duh da da da,*" Crawford sang. "We're guilty, gentlemen. Guilty of everything."

Scott handed Berry the bottle again. "I'm sorry," Berry said before taking another sluggish gulp, "but my self-esteem is much higher than that."

Crawford took the turn off the 105 and suddenly there was nothing but black and brown people everywhere.

Crawford passed a street of patchy vacant lots with grass grown around chain-link fences, around what were once building foundations, past undergrowth devouring former sidewalks and parking lots. Most likely these were relics of the Rodney King riots, burnt-out buildings not worth rebuilding.

Duh duh da duh de duh da da da.

"Many neighborhoods in South Central were once pleasant middle-class suburbs," Berry said, "places free from crime and drugs, places where you could raise a family and retire. But the last 30 years or so haven't been kind to Gardena."

"That's right, Berry." Scott said. "It's no longer the garden spot it once promised to be. Overcome by urban growth that swallowed up the vegetable and fruit farms that once fed the local economy, and surrounded by freeways that polluted its once clean air, Gardena is no longer a suburb but an 'inner-city' or a 'ghetto,' as it is sometimes disparagingly called."

"The fuck you guys talkin' about?" Crawford mumbled. "Goddam overeducated shitheads."

Crawford pulled to a stop at a four-way. "Give me the bottle, Scott." Crawford took the bottle and held it up. And saw that there were just a few fingers left. "Not bad, boys. You should thank me. It's the very last of the Old Arkansan."

"Thanks," Scott said meekly.

Crawford tipped the bottle and drained the remainder in two ample gulps.

"Goddam, Jim," Berry said, now slurring under the influence. "Take it easy."

"Take it easy? We're taking it easy." Just then Crawford's rubber nose fell onto the floor. He looked out the passenger-side window and saw an old white woman walking down the street pushing a small metal cart. The cart was filled with several plastic bags, probably groceries or medicine. She wore a dress so thin that it looked like a hospital gown. The pronounced wrinkles on the woman's arms and legs only gave the threadlike garment added transparency, making her appear even more exposed to the harsh city streets around her, more vulnerable to the black and Latino youths that indifferently watched her inch by.

That old woman must be one of those people that once knew a very different street than the one she's walking down now. She probably saw the cafés and small businesses she had known for years close down. She probably saw friends leave and die. And perhaps now she felt left behind — an old woman, waiting for her time to come, waiting for her final exodus from the garden that once was.

She didn't grow up in an age of self-esteem, Crawford thought. She didn't sit around with her parents or friends or husband or children talking about what her "emotional needs" were.

Her hair was combed neatly to one side, showing that she still cared about her appearance.

She probably hadn't thought much about her "self image" over the years. She probably hadn't thought of her "inner-self" and how it affected her "outer-self."

How much do I really care about Dorothy and Cal? Or even poor Jen. She didn't deserve any of this. Dorothy and Cal deserve better. Maybe that's what the old man is saying in my dream. I have to answer to myself for what I did to others. Which includes what I did to myself.

Fade out.

"We just heard Iron Butterfly's classic hymn, *In-A-Gadda-Da-Vi-da*. Now we've got more classic rock from Rod Stewart, Steppenwolf, and..."

Crawford turned off the radio. The traffic light turned green, and Crawford didn't move.

"You guys want to tell me what's waiting for me at the cookie factory?" Crawford was staring straight ahead. A car honked from behind.

"Do we want to tell you?" Berry said slowly. "Do *we* want to tell *you*? Why the hell don't you tell us?"

"What's going on here, Jay?" Scott asked.

Berry couldn't believe it. "What did you say?"

"What... what... what is going on?"

"You're asking me, shithead?"

"I..."

The door handle sounded like a gun being cocked when Scott bolted out into the street, leaving the car door open in traffic.

"Come back here, pussy!" Crawford yelled. Crawford grabbed the gun as Berry moved toward the open door and stuck it in his face. "No, you don't!" Cars were honking as they went around Crawford's motionless car. "Shut the door."

Berry did as he was told then put his hands in the air.

"Put your hands down or I'll fucking kill you!" Crawford looked in the direction where Scott had run. "You sure don't move very fast, do you?"

"What do you mean?"

Crawford stepped on the gas, racing through the two-lane city traffic at forty miles an hour, then fifty. "Tell me!"

"Tell you what?" Berry whined.

"Tell me what's going on! I haven't forgotten about the shopping cart. The shopping cart, remember the shopping cart?"

"What the hell are you talking about?" Berry pleaded.

Crawford looked up and saw West Rosecrans Avenue and turned right.

"We're going to be there in just a few minutes, Berry. I suggest you tell me now what I'm going to find there."

"I don't know anything. I told you."

Crawford stepped on the gas harder. "I'm going to find out."

Berry leaned toward Crawford, who didn't respond to his movement. "I want to help you, Jim."

"You want to help me? Tell me what has been going on the last few days. This is one of your pranks, isn't it?"

"A prank? Are you kidding?"

"Is it?"

Berry leaned back and lowered his quivering voice to a murmur. "Jim, I don't know what has happened to you in the last few days, but I want to help. I think something terrible has happened to you."

"You know it has." Crawford slowly reduced the speed of the car.

"I didn't know, Jim. I didn't know. Please pull the car over and let me drive. Please. You're just experiencing something. Perhaps alcohol delirium. Perhaps just a breakdown. That's all. Everything is okay. You just need to see a doctor right now. You're sick, Jim." Berry took a deep breath. "I have to tell you something. Your wife told my wife a couple of weeks ago that you had started drinking again. The drinking has gotten worse since then, hasn't it?"

"You must have a *Ph* fucking *D*."

"You're sick, Jim. You just need some help, that's all. It's okay. Albert and I will not hold this against you. We're professionals."

"I'm sick," Crawford said thoughtfully, slowing down and pulling over to the curb. "I'm just sick," he said. "That's all it is."

He felt Berry place his hand on his right shoulder. "Jim. Please let me help you," Berry said, moving his hand slowly toward the gun. Crawford looked ahead and could see the cookie factory, the faded *S* barely discernible on a crumbling brick wall. He clenched the gun taut, tightening his finger on the trigger.

"Maybe. Maybe not. We'll find out, won't we?"

Berry looked at the building transfixed, his eyes wandering to the empty building next door. "Oh, that place."

"What?"

"That building next door — it used to be a dress factory."

"Yeah?"

"A number of Chinese laborers were trapped in a fire there years ago."

A paper sack blew across the hood of Crawford's car, and suddenly he felt as if he was in the last scene of a movie, maybe a funeral scene.

Probably a death scene.

"What happened," Crawford said mechanically.

"All the people died," Berry said.

"And the community mourned the loss of the cookie factory." Crawford said, watching the sack blow down the street. "Right?"

"Right."

TWENTY-ONE

Crawford drove the car slowly toward the back of the cookie factory, dodging as best he could the wealth of wood, glass, and metal debris that littered the parking lot. A makeshift basketball net fashioned from the bottle of an old water cooler adorned a chain-link fence on one side of the building. Besides that, there were no signs of life — no cars, no lights, nothing. But there seemed to be a path through the debris to the rusty back door as if someone had kicked the junk aside as he walked in.

That could be just my imagination, Crawford thought after turning off the engine. *But then again, everything could.*

"I tell you, Jim, that Old Arkansan really hit me for a loop," Berry said.

"That's nice," Crawford said pointing the gun at him. "I'll give you one last chance to tell me what this is all about," he said, pointing the gun. "What's in there?"

"I can't tell you." Berry said, calmer than Crawford had ever seen him.

"You can't tell me or you won't tell me?"

"I can't tell you. You'll just have to go inside and see."

Crawford couldn't assess the expression on Berry's face. It was neither informed nor uninformed; apprehensive nor assertive. Wait. A voice. He heard voices, not just one voice. Sounded like Leonard Cohen trying to sing *In a Gadda-Da-Vida.*

"Oh, my God. Voices."

In the Garden of Eden, baby. In the Garden of Eden.

Crawford froze, thinking he'd finally lost his mind. *No, really.* "Shut up!"

"I didn't say anything, Jim," Berry said.

Crawford's voice quivered. "It's just an earworm, that's all. You're not hearing voices."

"What the hell are you talking about?" Berry said.

Leonard Cohen stopped singing.

"Never mind." Maybe Crawford was crazy, but before he'd let anyone take him away to the booby hatch, he was going to see what was in that building. "You go first and I'll follow."

Berry was still calm. "Okay, Jim. You're the boss."

Berry got out of the car slowly, straightening his sport coat and calmly combing his hair with his fingers. Crawford motioned him forward then followed close behind with the pistol pointed at his back.

"I like being mischievous and playful."

"Good, Jim."

Berry walked ahead gracefully, sidestepping the broken glass with each move. Crawford followed, cringing at the sound of small fragments of glass crunching under his feet. He thought about going to the dentist, about having a drill in his mouth, about making mad associations, about losing his mind.

How could his wife and child be in such a place? Was his mistress in there with them? Perhaps dead? Perhaps all of them dead? How could they all be terrorized by a character from a kid's TV show? *Where am I now, emotionally?*

He looked at Berry's profile against the chaos of shapes that surrounded him. An old, decrepit building of browns and reds and oranges. Sharp metal jutting up and down amongst tattered paper and faded plastic. Like an inkblot test where Crawford was to project his anxieties and desires onto an ambiguous image. But it wasn't entirely ambiguous.

Anxiety? Desire? The study of psychology has driven me crazy. No, wait. Just psychology in general, that's made me crazy. Or maybe just self-help.

"I think you should go in first," Berry said, stopping in front of the door.

"You do, huh?"

Crawford raised his gun. "Open it."

Berry looked over his shoulder at Crawford and smiled. "What if it's locked?"

"Turn the doorknob."

Berry gently put his fingers on the knob and turned it slowly. "Well, aren't we the lucky ones today."

"Open it."

"Ready?" Berry said, raising his voice with an irony Crawford couldn't place.

"Open it."

"Yes sir-ee!" Berry said.

Crawford looked at Berry as he turned and slowly opened the door. There was nothing but a black hole in front of him, but Berry's demeanor had changed — it was oddly buoyant.

Berry stepped to the right of Crawford and put his hand on Crawford's shoulder. "Here we are."

The afternoon sun produced a small shaft of light that formed a point just five feet from the door, like a sign directing them to go forward. Crawford looked at Berry then looked into the space. He hadn't expected this: nothing, nobody, not even light.

"What the hell is this?" Crawford said, searching the emptiness as if his eyes would adjust and he would be able to see everything. "Where..." Crawford looked next to him and Berry was gone.

"Berry?" Crawford said, raising his gun. "Where the fuck are you, Berry?"

"You shouldn't use such naughty words, Dr. Crawford." That voice, the one he'd heard that first waking morning — insidious and certain — filled the space from every direction. "People only use those words because they have a condition, a terrible condition. Low self-esteem."

"Low self-esteem? I'll show you self-esteem, son of a bitch," Crawford said, cocking the gun with one swift motion. "Want to see my self-esteem?" he yelled, raising the gun.

Crawford was a moment away from shooting into the abyss when a spotlight appeared in front of him. It was 20 yards away, but Crawford could still see that it shone down upon an old TV in front of an easy chair, the kind they used to make in the sixties. It reminded Crawford of where Uncle Jerry had spent his last days smoking and drinking and complaining about the world. There was even a small table and a lamp — also very Uncle Jerry. Before Crawford could fully make out everything in front of him, he was diverted by the broadcast snow that popped up on the TV screen. It was like someone had just plugged in the old contraption.

"This game again, huh?" Crawford said while slowly walking toward the light. "Answer me!" As Crawford got closer to the makeshift living room, he could see the TV was supporting an ancient VCR as big as a suitcase.

Crawford stood behind the chair and tried to think of what his Uncle Jerry would do in this situation.

He'd probably sit down and blow his brains out.

Not a bad idea, Crawford thought.

Crawford looked closer at the VCR and could see an index card folded in half resting just over the control board. In a child's handwriting, "PUSH

HERE" was written with an arrow pointing to the play button, the U adorned with two eyes forming a smiley face.

Shit.

Crawford pressed play and sat down, feeling more like his Uncle Jerry than himself. "Happy?" he yelled into the air.

The voice replied, "Yes, Doctor. I'm here."

Crawford gripped the gun as if it were the remote control to the VCR.

"No. I mean *are you happy now*?"

"I'm Happy Pappy," the voice said.

Just wait, fucker.

The snow disappeared, replaced by a close up of Happy Pappy leaning into the camera. Crawford moved back slightly, resisting the urge to shoot the screen. "Thank you for coming. We have some special guests today," he says with his head bouncing to the side. "It's a special occasion. Stage three." Crawford expected the opening song. Apparently Stage Three is beyond that.

Crawford could barely make out Cal and Dorothy strapped to two chairs a few feet apart — each with a spotlight on them — each with their hands behind them and duct tape covering their mouths. There was no backdrop, no puppets.

Crawford took a deep breath as if to prepare himself for what he thought he was about to see. He had one comforting thought: someone was going to die when the screening was over.

"Here we have our two guests," Happy says, coming back into the frame. "They were really pretty good to you, weren't they?" The artifice of the child entertainer was nearly gone. Happy was now a resolute master of ceremonies. "They really didn't deserve…" he said, before looking down, as if to a cue card, "…an absent husband and father. The drinking, the whore fucking. They didn't deserve that, did they?" he asks, leaning into the camera.

"What do you want?" Crawford mumbled as if the TV could hear him.

Mr. Pappy took one step to his right revealing a colossal axe that was standing on its head behind him, the largest Crawford had ever seen. It was childishly simple, not only in size but in design, something a comic strip gladiator might use. Crawford could see a tear fall down Dorothy's cheek. Cal looked dreadfully expressionless.

Then the jingle. That itchy little tune. That clinking and clanking children's song with the sing-song singing.

Be kind to yourself.
Be fond of yourself.

If you're not a chum you're a bum to yourself.
Be a friend to yourself.
Without end to yourself.
Remember it's the best you can do for your health.

"Please," Crawford said, or thought he said. *Stop.*

"Come on!" Happy screamed while doing a teasing dance with the large blade. "I like being playful." Happy walked between the chairs that held his captives. His Happy Pappy attire was perfect — the hat, the pipe, the face — but somehow he still looked different than before.

Standing just behind Dorothy and Cal, he slid the axe, handle-first, across their chests.

"Okay! What do you want?" Crawford screamed. "What is it?"

"I want what you have," Happy said, his right shoulder now pointing toward the camera, the head of the axe pointing away behind him and the rest of his upper body looking as if it were ready to pull the weapon across their throats. "That's stage three. You can have what anyone else has, right?"

"No, that's not right!"

"Especially if they don't deserve what they have."

"I..."

"Anything else to say?"

"Please don't!" Crawford pleaded.

Happy Pappy whipped sideways in an action that suggested he had just swung the axe through their exposed necks. For a split second blood squirted on the camera lens before the screen went back to snow.

"God, no!" Crawford screamed. "Please, no!" he yelled into the air before raising his gun with an unyielding pose. "I'm going to kill you, motherfucker! I'm going to kill you! You hear me!"

This was it. This was the bottom. This was weeping and gnashing of teeth. This was...

Wait, he thought wiping the tears away.

"Hold on."

Wait.

"Wait a minute."

It's fake. It's all fake.

"What are you saying?" Crawford asked himself.

You've been trying to tell yourself all along this has been a sham. You haven't been following your own advice. Trust yourself.

"But Dorothy, Cal. Jenny?"

It's fake.

Crawford took a deep breath and listened to the silence. "Excuse me," he said into the air. "This bullshit is not real. You didn't kill anyone.

Why don't you come on out and let's talk?" He waited a moment. "Mr. Pappy?"

"Look down at the floor," an unfamiliar voice said.

Crawford looked down and saw a red stain that stretched to the parameter of where the light stopped. He moved his right foot and *gosh, this floor is so sticky.*

"Oh, God. No!" he screamed. "How could you do this? No, please!" This cry was more heartfelt than the first. It had been years since Crawford had realized how much he loved his wife and son. Now he wasn't concerned with the self-important guilt of the past. This was immediate. This was here.

Crawford raised the gun and put it in his mouth. Blowing his brains out was going to feel good. And it was all going to finally come out the way it wanted to with that magical life all its own. His mind was free from his body. *Little boy used to hit me insecurity caused drinking momma was angry tried to be something anything couldn't be Hemingway Conrad Faulkner couldn't be husband father Uranus the Pope for all the bad things I've done thoughts of self-help too strong no help wanted to be everything rich famous wanted needed loved admired Sinatra Elvis Gandhi Jesus Washington New York London Rome Italian French Chinese Farsi BA MA PhD too macho too gay run away stay play don't delay* "Fuck it! Should have done this a long time ago."

I pulled the trigger and blew my brains out, and boy did it feel good. My head snapped back gracefully. My cerebellum and parts of my brain stem seeped out of the hole at the top of my skull, perhaps with a dash of occipital lobe, but it still looked cool. And it felt really good too. Told ya! *I'm glad I blew my brains out. Everybody cried. Everyone was devastated. Why didn't I think of this before?* he asked himself.

"Things take time," he said. "Didn't your mother tell you that?"

Wait, wait, wait. It's all simulated. The floor is as sticky as... a cookie factory. And Cal. Cal didn't look afraid. And Berry acted like he knew what was happening here. And the gun didn't go off. And I didn't blow my brains out.

Trust yourself! You're one of the best friends you have!

Crawford took the gun from his mouth. "Hello?" he said softly. "Hello?"

"Hello," a voice answered back. A new voice, a different voice, not amplified. "Dr. Crawford."

"Who? Who are you? What is this?"

"It's something we had to do."

"We?"

"As scientists," an old man said, pushing himself into the light on his wheelchair. He looked haggard, but still had the same Darwinian face he had twenty years before.

"Dr. Watkins?" Crawford let the gun slip to the floor.

"Good day to you," the old man said with a nod and a smile. The suit and the haircut were the same.

"You're behind all of this?"

"No, James, I'm in front. At the beginning." The old man looked down at his lap where a yellowed, dog-eared document rested between his trembling hands. The expression on his face was warm, genial. "Remember your first thesis?"

Crawford stared at the old man's nose, mouth, and eyes, which now looked more like Happy Pappy than Charles Darwin.

"Do you remember?" he asked again.

"My thesis? Not really."

"You wrote a thesis you had to abandon because you'd been told it was plagiarism. Remember?"

Crawford wasn't sure any sound was coming out of his mouth as he spoke. "What?"

"When you were in college, you used to know a young fellow who lived in the dormitory who listened to self-help tapes all the time. A time when the first self-help tapes were becoming popular. Do you remember?"

"Oh, yes. Libby? Dibby?"

"Gibby. Gilbert Sebastian."

Watkins lifted the document with respect, as the mad Happy had done with *Self-Esteem*. "He was your inspiration, wasn't he?"

"Yes, I suppose he was."

"You didn't authenticate his name in the manuscript, but we found out who he was."

"We?"

"He used to listen to tapes that promised to help him stop procrastinating. Do you remember now?"

"Yes, I do." Crawford said, now feeling sound coming from his mouth.

"You would go by his room and he would sit there all day listening to things like 'Do it now. Do it now.' Whatever 'it' was, he didn't do it. He became addicted to these tapes, putting off the rest of his life to listen to them over and over again."

"But someone else wrote that thesis. I was just drunk. I copied it from some Polish guy. Ugo... Ugel..."

"Ugelowski. Alexander Ugelowski."

"Yes. Yes. How did you know?" Crawford said.

"Because I am Alexander Ugelowski," the old man said.

Crawford couldn't put it all together, perhaps because he didn't want to. "You are..."

"I'm a lot of people and a lot things you know nothing about, James. But please, continue to call me Dr. Watkins."

"You're insane."

The old man scratched his chin then raised his eyes and continued. "The poor chap that couldn't stop procrastinating needed to be scared out of his wits, you concluded. He needed to be terrified back into living."

"I wrote that?"

"Your thesis was entitled *Terror Inducement Therapy*. And it's brilliant. Just brilliant."

"But we've changed the title," another voice said. "The acronym is unfortunate." A figure stepped into the light looking more like a military attaché than his former self.

"Phil?"

Peters walked into the light and stood next to Watkins with his hand resting respectfully on the old man's shoulder. "You are so much more brilliant than you know, Jim. *Terror Inducement Therapy* is a milestone. We just needed to change the name. We call it *Fear Incentive Therapy*. We feel 'Incentive' is much more elegant than 'Inducement.' And the acronym, like I said, is an improvement. 'Fit' is very positive. The other is a bit too," he paused, "oedipal."

"I think I like the first one better," Crawford said.

Watkins continued. "We realized that you were really on to something, but it was something that couldn't be applied under ordinary circumstances. So Berry and Scott meticulously copied the article, changing a few things, and had it professionally printed to convince you that you had read it before. They even planted that copy in your bathroom. Since you bought the whole thing, it just confirmed that you were right. And that you needed help. We also couldn't have tested it on anyone but you, Jim."

"I'm going to kill you, Doctor," Crawford said expressionless.

"And if so, it would be worth it," he said with a thumbs up. "The first implementation of F.I.T. saved my granddaughter. It's a good thing, a wonderful thing."

"What are you talking about?"

"She had gotten into trouble, my granddaughter." He stammered a moment. "She had met this fellow, a Puerto Rican, I think, or, uh, a Puerto Rican-American. I don't know. Some pimp of some kind," he said. "She got into drugs and, well, other things that were worse." The old man's face grew heavy. "She had fallen into prostitution through an addiction to one of the newest and strongest forms of methamphet-amine. I tried a lot of things to get her rehabilitated, but nothing worked. I remembered your remarkable thesis, that people must be scared out of their destruction. Then I made a plan. I called my grandnephew to do a job for me — a performance rather. He would become one of my grand-daughter's clientele and try to kill her, but fail. And just as she believed she was escaping, I would be there to take her in and emphasize the er-rors of her ways, offer her hope of change." Watkins face grew lighter. "And it worked. I want you to meet my grandnephew, also named An-thony Watkins. The Third, actually."

The image of the Happy Pappy mask emerged from the shadows. His yellow-gloved hand pulled the mask down. It was a young man with an unfamiliar face.

"Hello, Doctor," he said, stroking the mask in front of him. "My name is Darrin. I'm Cal's friend."

"You're Darrin?"

"Yes, sir," he said coming closer. "That's my stage name. I really don't know much about psychology. I'm just interested in acting. You know, the real stuff."

"The real stuff?" Crawford said, thinking the boy looked like an old man.

"The real stuff, yeah, making it real," he said. "I thought I was going crazy for a while, but I realized I was just pushing the envelope."

"Pushing the envelope?" Crawford said.

"I'm not sure what it means, but that's what great artists do. And I'm also a photographer and filmmaker."

The young man's earnestness almost distracted Crawford from his rage.

"Dr. Watkins liked my performance with his granddaughter, and it worked." He let out a sigh of accomplishment. "She had never met me and didn't know we were related. She thought I was really trying to kill her. Isn't that funny?"

"You... you three," Crawford pointed, "are out of your minds."

The old man raised a finger. "Do you feel better, Jim?"

"Where are my wife and son?"

"Answer me first," Watkins demanded. "Don't you feel better?"

"Feel better?"

"Haven't you realized a few things?" Peters asked. "Don't you feel relieved? Ready to start anew?"

"That's my business."

"Hey," Peters said with a smirk. "You signed up for this."

"I signed up for this? What the hell does that mean?"

Peters pulled a paper out of his jacket pocket. "In my office. Remember? You signed," he said extending the document.

Some fucking board of review.

"What do you think I've been spending that Vogel Grant money on?" he said with a smirk.

"This whole thing is insane." Crawford leaned over and picked up the gun from off the floor. He slowly sat back then pointed the gun at the heart of the old man in front of him, who coolly rolled back his chair a few inches. "But maybe I can do something about this."

"There's nothing but blanks in that gun, Jim," Berry said, stepping aside, revealing Scott standing behind him. "Might as well put it down."

"I see. You guys are in on this as well. Up to your old tricks?"

"New tricks, Jim," Berry said.

"We've always liked you Jim," Scott said. "We were concerned."

"Uh huh. Where's my son?"

"Jim, put the gun down," Watkins said.

"When I was a little boy," Crawford began, "there was this kid that used to bully me. He hit me all the time and I was too young to know what to do. Eventually, I ended up hitting him over the head with a toy radio. Just a block of wood, really, but it did the trick. Knocked the little fucker out. I got sick that day and thought that God had punished me for my aggression. I was wrong, of course. But what I realize now is I wouldn't have retaliated in the first place if I hadn't been ill. I hit the kid *because* I didn't feel good because I had the flu or something else. Being sick made me do it. I was lucky to be sick that day. I was lucky because it helped me get rid of that bully."

Scott took out a pen and notebook from his jacket pocket and started to take notes.

Watkins sat up. "Please continue, Jim. We're very interested in your mental illness."

Crawford's small audience stood silent, and he continued with a stare that seemed to heal his blunted, drunken eyes. "You all don't believe in anything, do you? And that's why you have lost your souls."

Watkins coughed. "I think we've accomplished something here today."

Crawford forced a smile. "Yes, so do I. Now give me my family."

All five men nodded.

Crawford heard a loud drip, falling steady. The sound of a single clap. Then another drop, another clap. Then clapping. Clapping by a few people. Clapping by several people. Clapping produced by an applause machine.

"We are so proud of you," a familiar voice said.

Floodlights slowly illuminated the back walls and Crawford could see what he thought he had imagined a moment before: an audience surrounding them of what looked like one hundred or so life-sized cardboard cutouts. They sat there silently, like icons on public signs — black, faceless, characterless shapes.

Stepping into the light, she looked more beautiful than ever, like the day they met. Better than that, the day they married.

"You're proud of me?" Crawford said.

"We knew something could bring you back to us," Dorothy said with a Jan-Hershey tilt of the head, nodding with admiration.

"But why?"

"Because we love you that much, sweetheart," she said.

"But... I don't understand."

"Honey, you don't have to."

"We love you, Dad," Cal said appearing next to her. "That's all you have to understand."

Crawford was astonished at his son's manner. He never looked so mature. The former Happy Pappy looked on in admiration.

"Dad, you acted like a complete asshole. So did you!" he said to his former friend, before turning back to his dad. "But I've realized many things in the last 24 hours. The most important thing is that you're an asshole, but you don't mean it."

Crawford nodded, as did his wife.

Cal put his hands in his pockets, pacing at a ninety degree angle to his father, and Crawford could swear he was thirty years old. "You're just weak. That's all. And I don't mean that in a bad way. And you don't make other people as unhappy as you think. You're not, uh..." Cal put his hand on his chin then looked at Dorothy. "What's that word we talked about, Mom?"

"Malefic, dear."

"Oh, yeah. Malefic. You're not mal-lific. And you're not malicious either, Dad. As a matter of fact, I just learned that drunkenness is a disease. I was like, 'Whoa, wait a minute, that shit is a disease?' And it is. It's like fuckin' cancer or something."

"Don't swear, dear," his mother said.

Cal nodded to her. "And, like, because of, you know, like, society, we think of it as this terrible sin to be fucked up. Sorry, Mom. To be like high on something. And drugs are the same way. And we, like, we put people in jail because we treat their disease as a criminal act. I mean, that's fucked up."

Crawford was moved by Cal's words and spoke before his wife could again curb her son's profanity. "It is, son. It is fucked up. But can we talk about this later?"

"Sure, Dad. Whenever. I'll be here for you, bro," he said slapping his old man on the shoulder.

"And Jenny?" Crawford asked Watkins, ashamed to look in Dorothy's direction. "Is she here?" Crawford asked, looking fragmented again.

"She was going to stick around..." Watkins started.

"And I didn't have a problem with that, Jim," Dorothy interrupted. "Truly, Jim. I didn't."

Watkins looked disappointed. "But Jenny felt it was probably a bad idea to stay. For an emotionally bankrupt nymphomaniac, she really has a heart."

"She does?" Crawford asked.

"Of course." Watkins replied. "That's probably why she said she needed a drink after all this."

"Do *you* need a drink, dear?" his wife asked him gently.

He looked up at her. "No, dear, I don't." Crawford wasn't thinking of drinking. He was wondering where that scumbag Lee was.

Watkins smiled warmly, rolling his wheelchair forward. "There's been lots of healing here today, Jim, worthy of several journals and several fellowships. And I just want to say..."

"I want to be happy!" Darrin screamed like a child who had his toy taken away. "I want to be happy!"

Darrin was wearing that mask again.

"I want to be happy!" he yelled again, his voice muffled by the mask. "I want to be Happy Pappy!" he screamed, and disappeared into the darkness.

Crawford blinked and the masked man reappeared, clutching the axe from the video. Crawford stumbled to his feet and stepped behind the chair holding the gun tight.

"What in God's name are you doing, Anthony?" Watkins said, swiveling around in his chair.

"I'm Happy Pappy!"

"No, by God, you're not. You're Anthony Watkins the..."

It was so quick the old man didn't even get the sentence out. The newly born Happy Pappy had, with one elegant swipe, severed his granduncle's head.

"Dude! What the fuck!" Cal screamed. Watkins' head wobbled toward him like a football.

"Yesssssiiiiirrrrreeeee!"

Scott and Dorothy screamed loudly, but Scott the loudest.

"Christ, help us!" Scott screamed.

"Can I have an award now?" Anthony asked as blood gushed from the top of his granduncle's torso.

"Jim, this is not part of the program," Peters said. "I assure you it's not."

"No shit," Crawford said, lifting the gun toward the chest of the fiendish clown. "I changed my mind. I think I need a drink."

Scott started whimpering a moment and said, "Jim! There's only blanks in that gun. Berry switched them."

"Yesssssiiiiirrrrreeeee!" Happy said, cocking his axe. Crawford's head was next.

"No, they're real," he said, unloading three rounds into Happy's chest.

The axe dropped first, followed by the masked man's limp body. Crawford stood up and stared at the dying body, and no one said a word.

Berry knelt beside Anthony and dragged the mask up from his chin to his forehead.

The young man was handsome, Crawford thought.

"I..." Happy labored. "I..."

"Slowly," Berry said. "Take your time."

"Everybody loves actors. I wanted to be one. That's all."

"We know," Berry said. "That's why we all act."

"I'm not mad at you," Cal said to the friend he never really knew.

"Thanks," Darrin said.

He was dead.

"I think I'd like that drink now," Crawford said.

And that's the last thing I remember.

TWENTY-TWO

*N*othing. No elegant script graced the screen as the image appeared; no eager applause was heard crackling with enthusiasm. It was nothing but Jan, unplugged, stripped down to her compassionate bare essentials, just herself in a chair and a microphone, radiating more empathy than ever. Our lovely host cleared her throat and tilted her head, as she sometimes did when she was about to be thoughtful, and thoughtful she often was.

"Ladies and Gentlemen, life can be..." She paused a moment, putting a finger to her upper lip then looking down at it like a monk in prayer. "Life can be... difficult. It can be..." She took the hand down to her lap and looked up, shaking her head slightly. "Unpredictable."

As her last word rang out, the camera widened to reveal Crawford quietly sitting next to her in khaki slacks and an oxford shirt, looking healthy and vibrant, looking detoxified, free from liquor and junk sex, with a demeanor that spoke of his truest, most genuine self.

"But you know," Jan continued. "You can dodge those, um, uh," she grasped. "Dodge balls," she said smiling as if she'd just found the perfect word, "that life throws your way."

"Well put," Crawford said.

"Just a minute, Doctor," Jan said without pause. "We're having a very different show today, folks. We're going to trace the journey of one man, a man that we all know and love. Dr. James Zechariah Crawford. We're going to look at his incredible journey; his incredible rise, fall, and rise. It's a story, not unlike many of our own," she said grinning. "And, of course, it's a very American story."

"It is, indeed," Crawford said calmly, before taking a deep breath. "Only in America," he said with an awkward laugh.

"Tell me something, doctor," Jan began. "What's it like to be delusional? What's it like to be so out of your mind on alcohol that you imagined all the things about your family and friends that you tell us about in your new book, *Cheaper Than the Plague*?"

"What is it like? Well, um, that's why I wrote the book, Jan. To describe it," Crawford said, to a few soft giggles. "That's what it's like. In the book. The story. That's what it's like."

"Oh I see," Jan nodded. "I haven't actually read the book."

"That book's da bomb, yo," The camera widened to reveal Rakim, in a fancy red blazer and gold medallion, sitting next to Crawford. The audience applauded. "And I'm so glad he included me in it," Rakim said straightening his matching top hat. "He thought he just imagined me, but he didn't. I'm real, yo."

Jan smiled. "You are real. You're a bit of a stereotype, but you're real. No offense," she giggled. "Thank you for coming to share, Rakim. Ladies and gentlemen, Rakim." The invisible audience applauded again. "Oh by the way," Jan said raising her eyebrows, "congratulations on your new album *Porridge*. Five stars, that's wonderful."

"I know it's wonderful," he said. "Jus' like you, Jan," he said, with a wink and a nod.

"And Phil," Jan said.

"Yes, Jan," Peters said, as the spotlight widened to include Peters sitting next to Rakim.

"Ladies and gentlemen, that's Dr. Phil Peters, Dr. Crawford's mentor. Or should I say tormentor?"

The ghost audience laughed.

"Tormentor? What do you mean by that?" Peters said. "I'm not a tormentor."

"No, but we are," Berry and Scott said in unison, seated closely together just to Peters' left. "We've been tormenting this guy for years," Scott said. "And this last one was a doozey, let me tell you."

Jan smiled. "My, my, it was. Boy, do we have a cast of characters for your tribute today, Doctor. Because these are the real professionals in your life that have affected you most. You know what a professional is, don't you doctor? I mean these are real professionals."

At that moment, Crawford wondered about that first psychologist he had seen on TV criticizing him.

"These men saved your life. Would you like to share with us what you learned?"

"I do," Crawford said. "Thinking about what we should do to make us more confident, make us like ourselves more — that's all a bunch of bullshit. That only makes us miserable because it ignores the lives of others. No one should work on their self-esteem. They should only work on self-respect, which has to be earned from others. And the writers like me, the talk show hosts and the pop stars that promise the world to us are nothing but parasites. They turn us into greedy, wretched souls by claiming to provide something that is impossible — perfection. It's life, after all. The things we want like love and respect can only be acquired through hard work and suffering. And even then it will be incomplete. That's just life. We have a society where everyone wants to be loved so much they can be assholes to everyone else. We live in the most vulgar society the world has ever seen. And it's all because we want more than is possible. We still want the forbidden fruit."

"Damn, nigga," Rakim said. "Straight."

"We have created a monster. We start by asking people if they are happy. Then we ask them if everything is okay. We're wonderful people, we let them know. We care. And if they say no, everything is fine, we ask again — just to make sure. Eventually, they start to question their happiness. They start to think that they are not whatever it is that they need to be and, not only that, that it is someone else's fault. They become selfish. They want to have what the people on TV have. They drink, they betray the ones they love, even their children. And why? Because only they matter.

"I can't help anyone. People need humility to help others, which is something I don't have. I was too busy working on my fucking self-esteem."

Crawford looked at the floor and sighed before looking directly into Watkins' eyes. "Now, if that isn't a sick mind, I don't know what is."

It all happened, the whole nightmare.

Crawford could see Lee offstage preparing to make his appearance.

But I wasn't the victim.

Lee gave a thumbs up.

"Doctor? Are you with us?"

In a curious way, Crawford never felt better. He didn't feel physically well, but he felt glad, something he couldn't remember feeling in a long time. He was glad because the party was finally over — that long, difficult celebration that had started in high school and dragged on into his middle-age. And he realized that it wasn't so ironic that it didn't end with a bang.

There really isn't anything like a near-death experience to bring clarity and a better appreciation for life, he thought as they removed the I.V. After all, it is very easy to kill yourself slowly, but when the time comes — the real thing, the moment of truth — your instinct will take over and try to rescue you, whether you deserve it or not. Crawford had been rescued, and he knew he didn't deserve it.

The applause was now in the form of rain. It was strange — the rain, particularly in Los Angeles. The song says that it never rains in Southern California. But as a matter of fact, sometimes it does.

The straps, his wife informed him, had finally been removed just a few hours before, and a wonderful doctor named Watkins expected he could probably eat some soft food by that afternoon. She also told Jim to apologize for peculiar remarks to the nice orderly named Rakim and to the hospital administrator, Ms. Clarkman. Berry and Scott were waiting in the lobby feeling guilty, Dorothy told Crawford, and Lee was with them, explaining why it was unfair to assume *The Happy Pappy Show* had pushed his star client to near madness. He had a better idea now, he told them — *The Dr. Jim Show* — and by God it was going to be a huge hit. They politely agreed.

Crawford was released from the hospital two weeks later, and a week after that *The Happy Pappy Show* was canceled because of poor ratings, primarily the result of protests from an anti-tobacco group that disapproved of Happy's pipe.

INT. COFFEE SHOP - ONE MONTH LATER - AFTERNOON

Crawford sits next to a window sipping an espresso. The scene outside is pleasant, a nor-mal suburban afternoon.

CAMERA PANS BACK to reveal LEE, his publisher, sitting next to him.

                    LEE
          So you're going to Alaska?
          Why Alaska?

                    CRAWFORD
          I don't know. No reason re-
          ally. Perhaps because it's
          so remote. I need seclusion
          right now.

                    LEE
          And Cal doesn't want to go?

                    CRAWFORD
          No.

Cal enters from LEFT, dressed in a WHITE COFFEE SHOP UNIFORM, with a cappuccino for Lee.

> LEE
> Not in for Alaska, huh?

> CAL
> I can't. I've got this job.
> And I've got a car payment
> now.

> LEE
> Well, if you ever want to
> write books...

> CRAWFORD
> Shut up, Lee.

They both LAUGH. Cal smiles then walks away.

There's a TV SET just above the coffee shop
workstation with a cable news show on. ON THE
TV: There's a typical ANCHORMAN and ANCHORWOMAN
team. Crawford and Lee watch. The TITLE CARD behind the Anchorman is a BOOK COVER.

> ANCHORMAN
> (on TV)
> And in other news, Dr.
> James Crawford, the well-
> known self-help writer, has
> a new book out. But it's
> not what you might expect.
> It's a novel. Burns Pub-
> lishing released "The Re-
> covery Channel" this week,
> a thriller about a de-
> ranged psychologist, of all
> things. When asked why he
> had never written a novel
> before, Crawford jokingly
> replied, "I never had the
> self-esteem."
> (pause, smiling)
> And that's the news for
> this hour.

The Anchorman smiles and looks to the Anchorwoman.

> ANCHORWOMAN
> Maybe he was serious, Dr.
> Crawford. Maybe he didn't
> have the self-esteem.

```
                    ANCHORMAN
          Maybe so. How's your self-
          esteem?

                    ANCHORWOMAN
          My self-esteem is fine,
          thanks.
```

```
Crawford and Lee look at each other and grin be-
fore clinking their coffee cups.
```

```
CUT TO:
```

Crawford had finally become at ease with his study, and not just because the "Wall of Shame" was gone, not just because he was a published novelist with decent sales, however mixed the reviews, not because the latest offering, Cheaper than the Plague, was almost finished. He was comfortable because he knew his wife was a floor above him making breakfast and his son was a floor above her preparing for college. And he was comfortable because he was awake enough to appreciate it all. He didn't need those pills any longer.

"Just show up. It will make you feel good about yourself." That was something he hadn't written in any book. He was just talking to himself.

Crawford looked at the American Heritage Dictionary lying open on his desk, and one word caught his attention.

```
pom•pous /ˈpämpəs/ Characterized by excessive
self-esteem.
```

Crawford picked up a pencil and underlined "self-esteem" then erased it. He put the pencil down.

These days he was writing in the morning — fiction, non-fiction, anything. It didn't matter. He was writing a lot, as regular as the ticking clock on the wall. And this morning was no different. Something about being surrounded by cushiony white walls made it easy. The title came without difficulty, as did the copy.

```
             Trips to the Liquor Store
                      By
                James Crawford
```

```
There are countless things that an
alcoholic forgets from one year to the
next, from one day to the next, even from
```

one hour to the next. There are many
friends and lovers he once knew — many
of whom he drank with — that quickly
drowned in recollection in the sea of his
alcohol-drenched brain. He also forgets
the lost jobs, the lost money, and the
lost time. But one thing the alcoholic
never forgets — or rather, remembers
better than anything else — are the liquor
stores he used to patronize and the all-
familiar paths that led him down to those
grimy places of drink. When I was in high
school, it was a wretched convenience
store where a guy named Kevin (a friend
of my sister's boyfriend) gladly sold me
four-dollar cases of generic beer just to
make jokes about how I would also need to
buy toilet paper. When I was a college
student of 20 — using a fake ID card that
read "MEDICAL IDENTIFICATION" — it was a
convenience store across an empty field
from my shabby, two-bedroom apartment
that I shared with a frequently absent
roommate. In those days I didn't even have
a car, but I didn't care. A six pack of
the nastiest, cheapest brew and a pack of
generic cigarettes were just three dollars
and a five-minute walk away. When I lived
in Nevada, it was the Liquor King, a mega
store for the supply-conscious alcoholic,
complete with membership cards and
shopping carts. In the West Village of New
York, it was a small deli owned by Middle
Easterners who cheerfully sold me 40-ounce
bottles of malt liquor for a buck and a
half. In Los Angeles (my adult home for
the longest period) there were many: Happy
Time Liquor, Mayflower Market, and "Rock
and Roll" Ralph's, just to name a few.
It's painful now to think of the things
I could have done, the people I could
have called on, and the places I could

have traveled to when I ventured on those
many thousands of solitary trips to the
liquor store. It's painful now to think
of the price I paid to make my miserable
life okay, to get through one more night,
to convince myself I was still there and
still alive. It's painful to think of the
damage I did to myself when I returned
from my daily trips, eager to wash all the
bad stuff away. But more than anything,
it's heartbreaking to think of how much I
succeeded in destroying so many memories
— apart from those of the avenues that got
me there.

Crawford closed the dictionary and gently put his fingers back to where the keyboard would be.

But none of it really happened that way. No, it didn't.

That's just the way the story wanted to be told.

Yes, it is.

"It is?" Crawford says. "Who said that?"

The clock on the wall stops ticking.

Listen to me.

"Who's there?"

I am that I am.

"I am what?"

I am not happy with you, James. There will be no Eden for you.

"Who are you?"

I'm your heavenly father.

"You are..." Crawford gasps. "God?"

You have worshiped the unclean one. You even called him your father.

"No, hey, you misunderstand. That Pappy guy was no father. He was just..."

I commanded that you shalt have no other Gods before me!

"Before you?"

I have filled you with terror so that you would know that I am the Lord!

Crawford gasps once again.

The devil showed you all of the splendor that evil can bring. You are now a follower of the devil.

"I am weary from crying for help. My throat is dried, which is why I feel like a drink. I can't see anything clearly, My Lord." Crawford paused. *You are My Lord, aren't you?* He leans forward. "Lord?"

Crawford listens. *Lord, are you there?*

Silence, except for the clock on the wall.

I wasn't behind this Happy Pappy business. Was I Lord? Was I just... "Was I?"

"Yesssssiiiiirrrrreeeee!"

"Dr. Watkins, the patient just cried out."

"I'm coming."

The End